The wind blew my hair into my face. If only it could blow away the aura of mystery and gloom that lingered in the old house.

In the sunlight the railing had the sparkle of fresh white paint. I leaned my hand on it. Without warning, with hardly a sound, the whole front section gave way, toppling downward and breaking apart as it hit the ground.

My palm was suspended in midair, and my heart was spinning like a planet wrenched out of orbit. For a heart-stopping instant, I imagined myself falling forward. In a frantic struggle to regain my equilibrium, I grabbed the side railing. Miraculously it held. Trembling in every part of my body, I held fast to the posts and moved my body away from the edge as my mind tried to register the grim reality.

Someone had tampered with the railing after I'd moved into the house, hoping that eventually I would lean on it and fall, but his possible motive eluded me. No enemy is more dangerous than the one who is unknown.

# THE CAMEO CLUE

### A KATHERINE KALE
### MYSTERY

# DOROTHY BODOIN

TORONTO • NEW YORK • LONDON
AMSTERDAM • PARIS • SYDNEY • HAMBURG
STOCKHOLM • ATHENS • TOKYO • MILAN
MADRID • WARSAW • BUDAPEST • AUCKLAND

To my brother, Dr. Nicholas Bodoin,
and my sister-in-law, Karen Bodoin.

**THE CAMEO CLUE**

A Worldwide Mystery/February 2006

First published by Hilliard & Harris.

ISBN 0-373-26555-7

**Printed in U.S.A.**

## Acknowledgments

The author wishes to acknowledge the help of her friend, Patricia Barbara Smith, who read the first draft of *The Cameo Clue* and offered valuable suggestions.

# ONE

THE DEAD CROW LAY IN the yard of an elegant old Tudor, a splotch of jet black on a bed of fallen maple leaves.

As I looked away from the unappetizing sight, a scrawny brown and white collie emerged from the thin woods behind the house. She stopped to sniff curiously at the bird, pressing her nose to its limp chest.

"Leave it!" I said. "Shoo!"

The dog looked up from her revolting find and stared at me, ears at high alert. Then apparently spying something more interesting across the street, she ran past me, zigzagging into the path of a fast-moving white convertible

The angry blast of a horn broke the afternoon silence, drowning out the squealing of tires. Without stopping to think, I dashed after her, while the driver, a red-haired man in a royal blue sweater, braked and veered onto the curb, brushing the collie's fur with his fender. She scampered safely back to the sidewalk with an indignant yelp. The man glowered at me and shouted, "Keep your dog on a leash or I'll run it over, lady!"

Before I could protest that the collie didn't belong to me, he straightened the car and accelerated in a cloud of blue smoke, leaving the stench of hot rubber lingering in the air. The dog lay down on the leaves, panting and wagging her tail slowly. I unclenched my fists and felt my heartbeat slow to a normal rate. I might have been hurt or even killed attempting to snatch her out of danger. We were both lucky.

In spite of the happy outcome of the episode, I bristled. The red-haired man didn't have to be so rude. Where was that small town friendliness the realtor had told me to expect?

"You could have been dead like that crow, girl," I said, glancing at the black splotch. "Go on home."

With the excitement over and tragedy averted, except for the crow, I walked on. This was the day of Maple Creek's annual Apple Fair and no time for ominous death symbols. I refused to think of the dead crow, the dog's narrow escape, and the surly driver as omens shadowing my new life. Today was a celebration of the harvest and patriotism.

Most of the stately old houses in my view were flying America's colors, while smaller flags fluttered in window boxes and clay planters, replacing summer flowers. They were color in motion, red and white stripes and blue star-sprinkled squares waving in the warm October wind. I stood at the corner of Walnut and Cherrywood admiring their beauty while I waited to cross the intersection.

I didn't imagine that anyone, even the apple growers, objected to the theme of the Apple Fair. A person could either drown in the tide of national fervor that had gripped the country or ride along with it. Like the rest of the town, I chose to ride. After a four-year stint teaching English on overseas army bases, I was back in the United States, glad to be home, and vulnerable to patriotic displays of any kind.

At the same time, I was also slightly uneasy. Being on the faculty of a rural school would be a new experience for me, almost like starting my career all over again. Still, I felt that I'd made the right choice. After all, I couldn't stay in Europe indefinitely, and I'd discovered that good teaching positions in Michigan had grown scarce in my absence. I'd been lucky to find the opening in Capac.

The Apple Fair was a welcome distraction from my lingering doubts. I couldn't possibly stay indoors unpacking endless boxes while the strains of "America the Beautiful" drifted in through the windows. I had weeks to finish settling in. The Fair was a one-day event, and I wanted to meet as many of my new neighbors as possible. So I'd changed into a red rayon dress, slipped my wallet and house key into my pocket, and set out for Main Street.

I crossed the intersection and found that I was no longer walking alone. The collie followed me now, occasionally nudging my hand as if to say, "We're together." She wasn't wearing a collar.

When we reached Main Street, the dog melted into the crowd in pursuit of new company and fresh scents, and I followed the music to the heart of the Fair. In the center of town at least three hundred people milled around, munching on apples in various forms and shopping for country crafts. Grouped in front of the Blue Lion Inn, the high school band played "Yankee Doodle," giving the affair the sound of a patriotic rally.

As I scanned the crowd looking for a friendly face, I noticed the tall, lean policeman who stood under a traffic light directing vehicles onto a side street. With his grim expression, he appeared to be anything but friendly. In his dark uniform, he was unusually handsome, though, and well worth a second look—or even a third.

He raised his muscular arm and turned his head slightly to wave a red Taurus to the left. His face was as lean as his body, chiseled in sharp attractive angles, and his smooth dark brown hair gleamed in the afternoon sunlight. One strand fell forward on his forehead from a center part, brushing the top of his eyebrow.

The officer reminded me of a larger-than-life figure, perhaps a mythological hero misplaced in time, but he was only a traffic cop in a small Michigan town who looked bored with his present assignment. At the end of the day, he'd probably go home to an ordinary life and microwave a frozen dinner.

As I would be doing myself.

Aware that I had come to a standstill on the corner for no legitimate reason, I strolled past the officer and turned my attention to the collection of stands set up around the municipal park to promote the apple orchards and Maple Creek Cider Mill, the town's major industries.

Along with the traditional cider and doughnuts, venders offered a variety of apple pastries and pies. Swags decorated with dried apple slices shared space with candles, prints, and bushels filled to the top with McIntoshes, Jonathans, and Red Romes. Everywhere I turned, I saw the colors of the flag swirling through handmade pillar candles, winding their way around grapevine wreaths, and decorating harvest dolls.

Bedecked in autumn finery, Maple Creek was as charming as any small European city. I would be happy here. I'd keep telling myself that until it was true.

For almost an hour I wandered through the Fair, trying to decide which of the many wreaths would look best on my front door and whether I should take home a whole pie or cider and doughnuts. Finally I came to a hot dog stand set up next to a lawn decoration display of scarecrows and witches. Here I saw the stray collie again, sitting and watching franks turn on the grill. She must be hungry, and now that I thought about it, so was I, but not for a hot dog.

For me, the most tempting of the Fair's offerings were the glossy caramel apples. Like the flags, they were everywhere. Pie, doughnuts or caramel apples? I couldn't decide. In the end, I settled on a cup of cider and a doughnut. Whatever else I wanted, I could buy later when I was ready to leave.

As I glanced around, looking for a place to sit down, I noticed a pair of black iron benches in the densely shaded yard of the house across from the park entrance. Of all the vintage dwellings in the town, this lavender Victorian with the purple trim was the prettiest. Strictly speaking, it wasn't a private residence but a business, Sky and MacKay Title, according to the sign under the porch light. It didn't look as if the company was open today. Surely the owners wouldn't mind if I borrowed their yard for the few minutes it would take me to eat my doughnut.

Someone else had the same idea. A brawny man with a neatly

trimmed black beard sat on one of the benches tossing pieces of a foot long hot dog high into the air for a large black dog to catch.

I crossed the lawn, crushing down the crisp red maple leaves that layered the ground, and sank onto the other bench. Giving the man a quick smile, I set my doughnut in my lap and took a sip of cider—a long sip. It was the best drink I'd ever had.

Holding a chunk of bun in mid-air, the man turned to me and said, "There's a good crowd here today. Not like last year. Warm weather always helps."

His hands were darkly tanned, and he wore a large silver ring with black stones and diamonds that glittered in the sun. His camel vest, forest green shirt, and high riding boots suggested 'Country.' Here was the friendly face I'd been searching for.

"It's a perfect day for a festival," I said. "You never know what the weather is going to be like in October."

He threw the last tidbit for the dog and wiped a speck of mustard off his fingers. "They're predicting a rain-snow mix for later in the week."

"I hope not. That's a gorgeous dog. Is he a German shepherd?"

The dog sat at his master's feet, a bundle of energy waiting for the next activity. His owner slapped him lightly on the rib cage and said, "You're close. Tac is a Belgian Shepherd. He's the best dog I ever had, but nobody ever called him gorgeous before." Pointing to the lavender house, he added, "My name's Garth MacKay. As in Sky and MacKay Title."

"Oh—" I was on his property, then, sitting on his bench without asking if he minded. "I'm Katherine Kale."

Before I could apologize for intruding, he said, "I don't think I've seen you around town before. Did you come in from downstate for the Fair?"

"No, I'm a local now,' I said. "I bought the blue Victorian on Walnut." I was about to add that I'd only lived in Maple Creek since last night when he smiled broadly.

"I know that house. You sure turned it into a showplace.

It's been rundown for years. Sometimes I thought about buying it myself and fixing it up, but you beat me to it."

Garth was confusing me with the previous owners. They were the ones who had renovated and repainted the Victorian. Then for some reason, they had promptly listed the property and moved. That same day I'd driven through Maple Creek on my way to visit my new school and seen the picturesque blue house with the "For Sale" sign in the yard. I liked the town, loved the house, and lost no time in making an offer for it. I'd never met the sellers.

I frowned uneasily at the memory of that afternoon. Usually I didn't make hasty decisions. Why had I responded so quickly and completely to the blue Victorian? Because it was beautiful and reasonably close to Capac High School, where I'd just signed a contract, and relatively inexpensive for a historic house in the present market?

All good reasons, but I couldn't explain the instant attraction and my impulsive purchase. A relatively inexpensive selling price was still a major financial commitment for a single teacher. I could easily have bought a one-story bungalow.

What did it matter? Even if I didn't know why the blue Victorian had called to me so strongly, it was mine.

"The realtor told me that the people who owned the house before me did that," I said. "All I have to do is furnish the rooms and do some landscaping. They didn't get around to working in the yard. I've been wondering why they sold the house—if anything was wrong with it."

Garth paused and looked down at Tac. "Now that I think about it, I met the last owners once. They planned to sell that place all along. That's how they make their living, buying rundown properties and fixing them up. I heard they bought a rare octagonal mansion for their next project."

"That's what the realtor said, but I thought she was protesting too much. I wonder why they left the landscaping undone. Curb appeal is so important when you're trying to sell a house."

Garth gave Tac a few rough pats on his head. "They were in a hurry to move on, I guess."

"Still it's strange," I said.

He paused and looked up, his hand now on Tac's strong neck. "Speaking of strange, I remember they thought there was something unusual about the house."

I sensed that, like the realtor, Garth knew more about the blue Victorian than he was saying. "Unusual in what way?"

"Something uncomfortable about it, I think they said. Maybe the floor plan."

That didn't sound right. The rooms flowed smoothly into one another, making the layout one of the house's most appealing features. "I don't think so."

"That's all I know, Katherine." Garth smiled again. His eyes were a blend of blue and green. The darkness of his tan emphasized their light color. I supposed that he spent a fair amount of time outside when he wasn't working at his title business, whatever that was.

"You'll like Maple Creek," he said. "Maybe I can help you out with something sometime."

"Maybe. Thank you. Do you live in this house?"

"No, not here…"

He broke off, his face brightening at the sight of the slender young girl who had just turned onto the walk. She was plainly dressed in blue jeans and an oversized white shirt, and she wore her honey blonde hair in a long thick braid. The black shepherd trotted over to meet her, his eyes fixed on the hot dog in her hand. He licked his chops in a manner that would alarm anyone who was unfamiliar with canines.

"Hi, Garth. I brought you something to eat and a ginger ale," she said.

"Thanks, honey. I'm hungry. Tac, Sit!"

The dog obeyed instantly, and the girl joined Garth on the bench, leaning back against the wrought iron scrollwork.

I broke my doughnut in two and ate it slowly. It was fresh and crunchy, good enough, but the cider was spectacular. As

I drained the cup, I listened to the conversation that was taking place on the neighboring bench.

"Where are you working now?" Garth asked.

"Still at the yard sale. It's dead over there. Everybody's staying close to the Fair, and Miss Valentine keeps leaving me alone. She says she has to find somebody. Why don't you come visit me?"

"I might do that."

"All we sold all morning was a box of buttons."

"Miss Valentine is asking too much for that old stuff," Garth said. "If she isn't around, you'd better get back there before someone steals something."

"That'll never happen. Who would want it?" But the girl got up and gave Tac a casual pat on the head. "As soon as she gets back or Judy shows up, I'm leaving. I'll be at the Cider Mill stand the rest of the day."

"I'll come by there then. Save me a caramel apple," Garth said.

As she walked back to the sidewalk, Garth unwrapped the hot dog and ate it enthusiastically as if he was indeed hungry. But then why had he fed the foot long to the shepherd instead of eating it himself? Maybe he was one of those people who took care of their animals' needs before their own.

Between bites he said, "That's my little sister, Taryn. She's helping out at the Bell House today."

"Where they're having a yard sale?" I asked.

"Yes. Half a block down." He pointed east. "The Bell House is the oldest residence in town. Miss Valentine wants to restore it and turn it into a museum. She pestered everyone to contribute something for the sale. I gave her an old rocking chair."

I got up, brushed crumbs from my dress, and stuffed the napkin into the empty paper cup. "I think I'll check it out. I have a whole house to furnish."

He chuckled. "You'd spend less money in Grand Rapids, but Miss Valentine did get some nice furniture together, if you like antiques. She has a lot of fancy glass, too, the kind that breaks if you look at it"

"I'll be careful," I said.

"Have fun at the Fair, Katherine. I'll see you around."

I left Garth sitting on the bench with the black dog lying placidly at his feet and headed east. The winds were picking up, making it feel cooler. I was glad my dress had long sleeves. Leaves swirled around in the air, trying to find a landing place. They blew against my ankles and flew across the street ahead of me as if they were alive.

I hoped that Garth was wrong about the change in weather, but I knew that these brief golden days of autumn were always short-lived. I vowed to make the most of them. When winter weather came, I wanted to be settled in my new house and acquainted with the town and the people who lived here. Meeting Garth MacKay and looking for furniture at the yard sale were two steps in the right direction.

THE BELL HOUSE WAS a white frame structure with clean, classic lines and gingerbread-trimmed gables. Its only decoration, an American flag, swayed gently in the wind.

Mahogany and maple furniture, mostly chests and tables, was arranged in the front yard in rows, giving customers ample room to navigate between them. On the lawn, a green wicker table set with pink dishes gave the impression that the mistress of the house would appear at any moment bearing an invitation for lunch or afternoon tea. Lamps, crystal candleholders, and china covered every visible surface, often displayed on crocheted doilies or scarves.

The woman who presided over this elegant yard sale sat in a gold Queen Anne chair on the lawn reading a book. Her blue shirtwaist dress and rows of pearls were reminiscent of the fifties, while the straw hat with its long blue ribbon dated from an earlier era. Light brown hair streaked with gray framed her face, and the soft pink color of her nail polish matched her bracelet.

She rose to greet me, saying in a soft voice, "Welcome to the Bell House. I'm Cora Valentine. Please help yourself to a glass of cider as you look around. It's from our local mill. The sandwiches will be ready in a few minutes."

The cider, already poured, gleamed in tumblers that encircled a punch bowl set on a shining maple sideboard.

"Everything out here is for sale," she said. "We have vintage clothing and jewelry inside and old storybooks, the kind your great-grandmother used to read. I'm especially proud of our antique hat collection." She twirled the long blue ribbon on her hat. "The one I'm wearing belonged to my own grandmother. Let me know if you see anything you like. Chances are I can tell you a little bit about its history. Please keep in mind that all profits are going into a fund to restore and maintain this wonderful old house."

Probably Miss Valentine gave a variation of this speech to everyone who came to the yard sale, but the warmth in her voice and her obvious love for her project made her words seem like a personal welcome.

She returned to her reading, and I surveyed the outside area. I decided to look at furniture first because once I began to wander among vintage clothing and jewelry, I would get lost in time.

At present, I was the only customer. Garth's sister was nowhere in sight. She must have returned to find the sale in capable hands and hurried back to the Fair, taking an alternate route. Another blonde girl, wearing a short flapper's skirt, came out of the house with a tray of sandwiches and began to add them to the sideboard.

As I moved past her en route to an arrangement of side tables, I saw an exquisite parlor lamp on top of a tall lingerie chest. Like a glowing jewel, it seemed to beckon to me. The ruby and white cabbage roses on the creamy milk glass globes evoked the graciousness of another era. I could already see the lamp shining in the bay window of my living room. Here was the one object I had to have. Once I owned this treasure,

I would have pure mellow light for all the dark winter evenings to come.

Reverently I touched the sun-warmed surface of the globes, looking for a price tag. With the instinct of a skilled antique dealer, Miss Valentine appeared quickly at my side.

"Now there's a rare find," she said. "The owner inherited that lamp from her Great-Great Aunt Elsbeth and had it converted from oil to electricity. It works too. If you'd like, we can test it in the house."

"It's so beautiful," I said.

"And a real bargain for only seven hundred dollars."

I had a hard time removing my hand from the globe. "Well, that's a little—pricey."

"But you'll be buying a genuine piece of history, not a reproduction from a catalog."

The temptation was great, almost too much to resist. I had my credit card with me, but I also had a mortgage payment to make and furniture to buy. I wouldn't get a paycheck until I had worked for two weeks. That translated into the beginning of December. But if I didn't buy the lamp, I knew that I wouldn't be able to forget about it.

"Don't wait too long," Miss Valentine said. "Someone else is sure to snatch it up. I'm expecting a crowd after lunch."

Garth's comment about Miss Valentine pricing the sale items too high came back to me. In spite of her optimism, I didn't think eager customers would overrun the yard sale soon, all of them descending on this one antique lamp.

She said, "If you really want it, I could come down on the price a little. Say six hundred and fifty dollars?"

"That's better, but I'll have to think about it."

"Certainly, but not too long. My motto has always been, 'When you see something you want, take it before somebody else does.'"

I was amused at the thought of this gracious, soft-spoken lady going through life grabbing whatever she desired. Was she talking about things or people? And had she ever lost something because she hesitated, as I was doing now?

It didn't matter. If ever I'd had an irrelevant thought, it was that one. "I may be back for it," I said and returned to looking at furniture.

As it turned out, I didn't make a single purchase, although I seriously considered the lingerie chest and a glass-topped maple coffee table with an elaborate scrolled design carved into the wood. Finally I decided that the scratches on the table went beyond the fashionable distressed look. And I didn't need the chest yet, although the whimsical wildflowers painted on the drawers were almost as tempting as the lamp.

I left the Bell House knowing that I was going to return. I'd walk back to the Fair, look around a little longer, and maybe have an early dinner at the Blue Lion. While I was doing this, I'd weigh the pros and cons of making the extravagant purchase. Then I'd return to the Bell House and hope nobody else had bought my lamp. It was a simple and sensible plan. I never expected anything to interfere with it.

# TWO

THE GRAPEVINE WREATH was lightweight but awkward to carry. I'd looped it over my arm the way I would a bulky purse, and its long red ribbon trailed down to my hemline. I also carried a witch lawn ornament pierced through with a wooden stake and a red, white, and blue pillar candle. Now, tired of shopping and in need of a snack, I made my way through the park to the Cider Mill stand.

A familiar figure in a blue dress and straw hat stood at the end of the line. Around her shoulders she had draped a long ivory shawl. Its delicate paisley motif and scalloped, fringed border gave her a charming old-fashioned look.

I took my place behind her. "Hello again, Miss Valentine. Is the yard sale over already?"

She turned around quickly. From her startled expression, I guessed that she'd been expecting someone else.

"Oh, no. We'll be open till five-thirty. I'm just taking a little break. I was sitting on the porch drinking cider, and suddenly I started thinking about caramel apples."

I wasn't too late then, but my instinct told me to make a decision quickly or risk losing what I really wanted. "I'm going to buy the lamp."

"I knew you would. Elsbeth's wedding present should go to someone who appreciates the true value of an antique, and you'll be owning a part of Maple Creek's history."

"My new house is part of the town's past too," I said. "They'll go well together."

"Which house would that be?" she asked.

"It's a blue Queen Anne Victorian on Walnut."

Miss Valentine rosy lips widened in a full smile. "My goodness! I know that house. Years ago, I used to live in it."

I couldn't believe my good luck to have met a former owner. "When was this?" I asked.

"Oh, way back in the seventies." Her voice took on the special tone of barely suppressed excitement I'd noticed when she'd talked about the lamp. "Your house has a story attached to it too. Just like one of my antiques."

"What kind of story?" I asked.

The line moved perceptibly, and we each took a few steps forward.

"How would it be if I tell you about it back at the yard sale? We'll have more time then."

"Well, all right." My curiosity was clamoring to be satisfied, but sometimes in life one has to wait. "I think I'll go back for the lamp now." I glanced down at my other purchases. Would I be able to carry any more? "Or maybe I should go home and come back with my car."

"Whichever is best for you, but if you want to take the lamp now, I could give you a shopping bag for the wreath and candle. Or I could hold it for you until tomorrow. "That witch is a darling." She touched the lawn ornament's green hair lightly. "It feels like straw."

"She's going to decorate my front yard. I'll be able to manage better with a shopping bag," I said.

During this brief exchange, Miss Valentine had moved to the head of the line. Peering over her shoulder, I saw gallons of cider and trays filled with doughnuts of every kind, but no caramel apples.

Taryn was working at the stand. She had brushed out her braid and applied glossy plum colored lipstick. "Hi, Miss Valentine. You've come for a caramel apple, I'll bet. Don't worry. We didn't run out of them." She whisked an empty tray out of sight behind the counter and brought out another one filled with a dozen plump caramel apples.

"Which one would you like, Miss Val?" she asked.

"I'm sure they're all delicious. You choose for me."

Taryn handed Miss Valentine an apple. She held it in her hand for a moment. "This beauty is absolute perfection, the undisputed star of the Fair." Turning to me, she added, "I'll see you back at the Bell House, Miss…"

"Katherine Kale," I said.

"In about fifteen minutes, Katherine; and then we'll talk about your house. I have to meet a friend of mine first." Squinting into the distance, she added, "I think I see her now, over there at the fountain."

She took a bite out of her apple and walked briskly away, holding the edges of the shawl together with her free hand.

Taryn gave me a friendly smile, but I didn't think she remembered seeing me earlier at the lavender house.

"I'll have a caramel apple," I said, reaching for one in the middle of the front row.

I lifted the apple out of its paper cup by the stick and held it in my hand, as Miss Valentine had done. The tantalizing scent of rich caramel blended with fresh apple was intoxicating. Crumpling the cup, I looked around for a trash container.

The nearest one was several yards away inside the park. Walking in a shower of blowing leaves, I followed in Miss Valentine's footsteps.

Clouds moved northward across a deep azure sky, and red and blue balloons, anchored to low-hanging branches, waved in the wind like flags. A squirrel holding a small piece of corncob in its mouth streaked past me and scampered up a maple tree. Leaves rustled overhead and drifted to the ground, while three giggling little girls played a game of tag around the fountain.

Then in an instant a small part of the scene shifted. Miss Valentine took a faltering step and froze. Around her, the world kept moving. She grabbed for her throat and fell awkwardly to the ground. The ivory folds of her shawl settled on either side of her shoulders in the shape of wings. Her half-eaten caramel apple rolled away into a bed of fall blooming pansies.

All around me, the park burst into frantic action as the people closest to the fallen woman rushed to her aid. The first to reach her side was an older man who had limped over from a nearby bench. He stood above her, balancing himself on his cane. I caught up to the others in time to hear what he was saying.

"Cora? Cora! Are you all right?" He tried to kneel beside her but couldn't manage it. Defeated, he pulled himself up, leaning heavily on the cane for support. "She needs help. Somebody—call 911."

"Here she is, Lieutenant—over here." A tow-headed boy emerged from the crowd, followed by the officer who had been directing traffic and a slender young policewoman. With the commanding air of a man who has assessed and taken control of a crisis, the lieutenant walked over to the place where Miss Valentine lay.

This was more than a fall. She wasn't getting up.

The officer said, "Stand back, Mr. Raycraft." His voice was deep, and his tone authoritative, but the man with the cane stood as still as the statue in the fountain.

"Something's wrong with Cora," he said. "I think she's had a heart attack."

"I can see that. You'll have to move back." The officer's words were like bullets, sharp and distinct in the sudden silence. "The rest of you, too, out of the way. Lacey, take the gentleman away from here."

Everyone in the vicinity hastened to obey. Still Mr. Raycraft hesitated. "Lieutenant, wait," he said. "Did you radio for help? Aren't you going to call an ambulance?"

But the lieutenant had started to perform CPR on Miss Valentine. The policewoman, Lacey, said, "We're handling it, sir. Come along now."

While she took Mr. Raycraft's arm and led him back to the bench, the officer felt Miss Valentine's wrist and throat. He frowned. Long lines appeared in his forehead, and strands of dark hair fell forward from both sides of the part.

Behind me I heard a scuffling and stamping of feet and turned to see Garth MacKay barreling his way through the crowd. Taryn stood at the park entrance, her blonde hair blowing freely in the wind, the black shepherd Tac at her side. Even from a distance, I could see the look of horror frozen on her face.

"Let me take her to St. Andrew's, Lieutenant," Garth said. "I can have her in Emergency in fifteen minutes."

The lines in the policeman's forehead deepened. "The ambulance will do that, Mr. MacKay."

His offer rejected, Garth moved back through the crowd without a word. When he reached Taryn, he put his arm around her. The murmuring of the crowd faded to a deep silence. Then a piping voice cut through the tension like a bell. "The lady was eating a caramel apple."

The speaker was a red-haired little girl whose green shirt was lightly stained with chocolate. "It's in those flowers over there. Lieutenant Gray?"

"What?" The officer looked up and waved her away. "Not now, Sandy. I'm busy."

She wouldn't be so easily dismissed. "The apple. Aren't you going to take it in for evidence?"

Now he heard her. "Yes, I am. Thank you." His grave expression didn't change.

Someone in the crowd laughed, and Lieutenant Gray scowled in the general direction of the sound. "This isn't any place for a little kid to be," he said. "Go find your mother. Lacey, get that apple now."

As amusing as the byplay was, it didn't alter the gravity of the situation. Miss Valentine lay on the ground, still and quiet under her shawl. She needed help quickly. The police were handling it, but nothing had happened yet.

Desperately I wanted her to regain consciousness, to be all right. She had seemed fine a while ago. A little distracted perhaps, but only for a fraction of a second. Then she had talked about Elsbeth's wedding lamp and my house and taken a caramel apple from the tray.

My hand was closed tightly around the stick of the one I'd bought. Quietly I dropped it all into the trash container, crumpled paper cup, napkin, and apple—just in case. Beyond a stand of tall shrubs, I heard two women talking in hushed tones.

"That's one disadvantage to living in the country," one of them said. "It'll take the ambulance a half hour to get here."

"A half hour or a block away, it makes no difference," said the other. "No doctor's going to help poor Miss Valentine now. Did you see her face? She's a goner."

"Oh, my goodness, I hope not…"

Drawn by the sound of splashing water, I walked over to the fountain and sat down on its edge. The statue was very old, most likely another antique, and the part of the arm that rested on top of the vessel was gone. As a cool wind-borne spray touched the side of my face, I watched the drama unfolding in the park and listened to fragments of conversation taking place around me.

"Something was wrong with that apple."

"Oh, no. I just ate one…"

"I got sick from a stalk of bad celery last year."

"But a bad apple? Whoever heard of such a thing?"

"You know the old saying, 'One bad apple spoils the whole barrel.'"

"An apple for the teacher. That's ironic. Didn't Miss Valentine used to talk about irony in English?"

"Do you remember that class? We were always making trouble for her."

"Then we all chipped in and bought her a bottle of perfume for Christmas. I miss those days. There's the siren now. It's about time."

The women moved away, their voices blending into the noise generated by the crowd. So Miss Valentine had been a teacher once, someone to aggravate in a thousand little ways and remember with fondness in later years. I knew the pattern.

As the siren died in mid-wail, I forced myself back to the present. Paramedics streamed out of the ambulance, followed close behind by a state trooper, all three of them hurrying to the place where Miss Valentine lay. She was in capable hands now. It would be all right.

It seemed as if time began to move backward. I kept glancing at my watch. Five minutes passed, and then ten and twenty. Garth MacKay could have gotten Miss Valentine to Emergency by now. That extra time might have made a difference—or not. I couldn't tell. But I didn't think a policeman would allow a citizen to transport a stricken woman to the hospital under any circumstances.

At last the ambulance door slammed shut, and the siren began again. Slowly the crowd began to drift out of the park until only the three children and a handful of onlookers remained. Mr. Raycraft, who had been so reluctant to leave Miss Valentine's side, hadn't gone with her to the hospital. He sat alone on the bench, holding on to his cane as if it were a lifeline. I noticed that he wore a white dress shirt and a navy tie, not exactly fair-going attire. Perhaps he'd only been taking an afternoon walk.

The leaves, balloons, and clouds were still moving, but all other activity had come to a standstill. The feeling of desolation in the park was tangible. Yellow tape cordoned off the area where Miss Valentine had collapsed. Did that mean she was already dead? I would have liked to ask the grim faced Lieutenant Gray, but I'd never seen a man less approachable. Besides he had already left the park. Maybe he was at the hospital with Miss Valentine.

It seemed incredible that on a fine fall afternoon at a country fair a woman could take a bite of an apple and become gravely ill. But why assume that the apple had caused Miss Valentine's illness? Because others did? Mr. Raycraft thought she'd had a heart attack. Still, I was glad that I'd thrown my apple away.

Maybe I shouldn't have done that. If in some way Miss Valentine's apple was responsible for her frightening collapse, the one I'd taken from the same tray might be useful in determining a course of treatment.

It wasn't too late to retrieve it, although the prospect of doing so was unappealing. From where I sat, I could see the container. The apple I'd discarded would still be close to the top. If I didn't remove it quickly, the trash would continue to grow, burying the possible evidence under a mound of soggy cardboard, bits of thrown away food, and even more disgusting matter.

I strolled over to the container and peered inside. The apple lay next to a puddle of melting ice that had spilled out from a paper cup. Grasping the top half of the stick, I pulled it out, wishing I had a paper bag or clean napkin to wrap around it.

Now what? I looked around, hoping to see someone official, the policewoman, Lacey, perhaps, but no capable hands reached out to accept my evidence. I'd have to take the apple to the police station myself, but I couldn't walk there. I'd do it later, when I had my car.

I didn't want to go home yet, and returning to the Bell House with its patron fighting for her life was out of the question. I longed for artificial light, warmth, and the society of the townspeople, even though I would be a stranger in their midst. Even more, I wanted food, something warm and filling to offset the deadly chill that had come over me. A bowl of hot soup, I thought, with pieces of beef floating in it, maybe barley or dumplings, crusty warm bread, and steaming coffee.

Spurred into action by these comforting images, I headed for the Blue Lion Inn.

VIEWED FROM the outside, the Blue Lion was a plain and aging restaurant flanked by a feed and hardware store and a barbershop. Inside, the atmosphere was festive, the décor traditional. Medieval motifs adorned the dark paneling. Bathed in soft, dim lights and held captive within scrolled borders, ladies, knights, unicorns, and lions in stiff, frozen poses encircled the room. The predominant color was red, rather than blue.

Garth MacKay had also come to the Blue Lion for dinner, the second time today we'd had the same idea. He sat with four other men devouring large amounts of food. I'd seen the waitress carrying trays heavy with orders of thick steaks, roast beef, and stew to their table. At the moment, she was bringing them a fresh supply of dinner rolls.

I was happy to find the vegetable-beef soup I'd craved on the menu as one of the day's specials. The entrée was hearty enough to be considered an entire meal, and I didn't leave a drop of it in the bowl. As I finished my coffee, I studied the dessert menu, but only to admire the pictures. Apple pie, cake, cobbler, and crisp—I didn't think I'd want anything made from apples for a while.

I'd wrapped the rescued caramel apple in a large white napkin and set it on the floor, out of sight while I ate. Out of sight, out of mind wasn't working today. Soon, in a few minutes, I'd have to pick it up again.

I didn't think Garth had noticed me until he gave me a half smile from across the room. A few seconds later, just I was ready to leave, he headed toward my booth. The waitress slipped past him, set my bill in front of me, and continued on her way, carrying a tray of desserts to Garth's dinner companions.

"Mind if I sit down for a minute, Katherine?" he asked.

"Not at all." I moved the lawn ornament and candle out of the way. "But I'm finished, and I should let someone else have the booth."

"Nobody will mind if you hang on to it a little longer. This sure was an eventful Fair day, wasn't it? Usually they're quieter."

"Have you heard how Miss Valentine is doing?" I asked.

"I don't know, but she's in good hands. St. Andrew's is a first rate hospital."

"I wonder what happened to her."

"They say it was the apple," Garth said.

"Who are they?"

He shrugged. "Some folks I know. I hope she'll pull through. As a rule, I don't care much for female teachers, but

Cora Valentine is okay. She took an interest in Taryn, talked her into going back to school this fall. That means a lot to me."

This man certainly believed in saying what he meant, even if it was sexist and offensive. He couldn't know that I was one of those female teachers. Should I enlighten him? Definitely. I wanted to see his reaction. But when would be the best time to do it?

"Miss Valentine was my history teacher," he said. "That was a long time ago. She sure made it hard for me." He laughed. "But I wasn't exactly a saint. Taryn is a handful too."

"I hope Miss Valentine will be all right. I only met her today, at the yard sale. She seems like a nice person."

"She still has her bossy teacher side," he said. "Sometimes that woman makes me feel like I'm a kid in trouble again. But she's been retired for years. She lords it over the Historical Society now."

As the waitress passed my booth, I noticed that several people were standing in the entrance, waiting to be seated. It was past five o'clock.

I reached for my purchases and picked the apple up from the floor. The flag colors that swirled through the pillar candle seemed to be moving. It must be the lighting.

"I'd better go before it gets dark," I said.

Garth looked at the candle for what I thought was a long time. Finally, he said, "Nice witch. You'll be all set for Halloween. What do you have in the napkin?"

When I explained how I'd purchased and discarded a caramel apple and then taken it out of the trash again, Garth nodded his approval. "That was quick thinking, Katherine. It may come in handy at that." He took my bill from the tray. "Let me drive you home."

"I can walk," I said. "It's only three blocks from here, and I can't let you pay for my—my dinner."

"A little bowl of soup? It's nothing. Call it a welcome-to-town present."

"Since you put it that way…" I gave in graciously. "All

right. If you're ever in the neighborhood, I'll serve you something. A cup of coffee, maybe."

"A cup of coffee for a bowl of soup." His merry laugh didn't quite match the situation. "Okay, it's a deal."

He walked with me to the front of the restaurant. When he stopped at the table to introduce me to his friends, I saw that he had left half of his Porterhouse steak to cool while we talked. The others were eating apple pie

"Katherine, I'd like you to meet my cousin, Mike. This is Fred. He owns the hardware store next door. Over there's my partner, Greg Sky, and his son, Carrol." He paused to take a breath. "This is Katherine Kale. She's new in town."

The men nodded and went back to their dessert with unflattering haste, apparently more interested in pic than a newcomer to Maple Creek. They appeared to be very much alike, all of them polite, quiet, and hungry.

Garth took my arm and escorted me to the front of the Inn. "Goodnight, Katherine," he said. "Be careful walking home. I'll see you around town."

That you will, I thought, as I thanked him for my dinner. This friendly man with the dark beard and the blue green eyes had captured my interest, but not in a romantic sense. There was something strange about him, something unspoken and slightly mysterious. A certain air, maybe. I didn't know what it was, but I was going to find out.

# THREE

AFTER TAKING MY PURCHASES home, I dropped the caramel apple off at the police station. Lacey thanked me and asked me to return on Monday morning to talk to Lieutenant Gray. Promising to do so, I drove back to Walnut through quiet streets. The only reminders of the day's festivities were the deserted stands around the park.

At my house, I pushed the witch's stake into the soft ground under the bay window and hung the wreath on the door, smoothing the long red ribbon. These simple additions instantly transformed the blue Victorian into my home.

Although the previous owners had left the foundation bare of plantings, the view of the house from the street was still attractive and inviting. Layers of crimson leaves blanketed the grass, providing brilliant fall color, but their time was limited. Next spring I planned to design and plant a perennial garden around the maple tree. Until then lawn ornaments would have to suffice.

Take one season at a time, I told myself. One room at a time. One box at a time.

I opened the door and went inside, turning on lights as I walked through the empty rooms to the kitchen at the back of the house. At present, I had very little furniture. The mahogany sleigh bed and dresser upstairs and the white wooden table and chairs in the kitchen were new. The dining room had an original built-in china cabinet and a window seat. The other rooms were empty, except for the boxes, echoes, and shadows. The cold hardwood floors and the cool white walls created an unsettling atmosphere that was almost eerie. At times I had a strange feeling that I wasn't living here alone.

My home wasn't going to be eerie. Color and flowers would help, and a fire in the fireplace when the weather turned cooler. And I needed to unpack those boxes and take them down to the basement.

I set the pillar candle in the center of the kitchen table and dropped my keys and wallet into my purse. As I filled the teapot with water, the doorbell rang, a clear melodious chiming that shattered the deep quiet. Quickly I retraced my steps. As I reached the living room, the caller rang the bell again. I opened the door to find an attractive woman in a long denim skirt and a bright turquoise sweater that complemented the red glints in her dark windblown hair. She was holding two loaves of bread wrapped in waxed paper.

"Hi, I'm Nell Farmer, your neighbor from across the street," she said. "I just dropped in to bring you these. One white and one wheat."

Their tempting fresh-from-the-oven smell filled the vestibule.

"Oh, thank you. That's so thoughtful of you. I'm Katherine Kale." I reached out to take the loaves. They were heavy and warm in my hands. I hadn't realized that anyone still welcomed new neighbors with baked goods, but then I'd never lived in a small town before.

"I'm trying out my new bread making machine," she said. "They're wonderful."

"I was thinking of buying one. Won't you come in?"

"Only for a few minutes. So—welcome to the neighborhood, Katherine. Are you working in the area?"

"I will be next month," I said. "I'm replacing a teacher in Capac who's going on maternity leave. She doesn't plan to work after her baby is born, so it may be a permanent position."

"This location is ideal for you then."

"It's a little farther north than I'd intended to move. I had a few interviews in Oakland County, but they were in middle schools, and I'd have been teaching in my minor. Capac made the best offer."

"I'm a nurse over at Saint Andrew's," she added. "I have a half hour commute, but it's worth it to live in a country setting."

"Well, I was lucky to find this beautiful old Victorian, and I'm going to enjoy buying antiques for it. I've always lived with borrowed or rented furniture."

As Nell stepped inside, I glanced at the neat two-story frame houses across the street. Probably built in the early nineteen hundreds, they all had distinctive period features and attractively landscaped lots.

"Which house is yours?" I asked.

"The white one on the corner with the columns and the chrysanthemums in front."

I peered down the street. Although the light was beginning to fade, I could make out a bright burst of orange color.

"Come back to the kitchen," I said. "That's where my chairs are."

She followed me. Our footfalls on the hard floor, added to the double echoes and shadows, intensified the aura of strangeness, even though I was no longer alone in the house.

"This is a grand old place," Nell said. "It has genuine atmosphere."

"That's just what I was just thinking. Here's the kitchen, on the right."

This was the one room in the house that seemed like home to me. I'd unpacked the electric percolator and whistling tea-pot first and set patchwork place mats around the table. Now I laid the bread on the counter and pulled out two chairs. "May I offer you something to drink, Nell? Coffee or tea?"

"No, thanks, but I'll take a rain check." She touched the pillar lightly, tracing the swirl of blue down to the base. "What a pretty candle. You must have been at the Apple Fair. Were you there when that terrible incident with Cora Valentine happened?"

"Yes, I was talking to her when she bought the apple."

"I still can't believe it. Cora was someone special in Maple

Creek, a real institution. When she turned seventy last month, the Historical Society threw a party for her at the Bell House."

"I met her today at the yard sale," I said. "She was going to tell me a story about my house."

"Cora was always telling stories. She was my English teacher. I had her for American history too. She taught at Maple Creek High for forty years. I know it's foolish, but we all thought she'd be around forever."

"You're talking about Miss Valentine in the past tense."

Nell lowered her voice. "Rumor has it that she took a bite of a poisoned apple and dropped dead."

I was about to protest Nell's version of the event but stopped myself. Her stark statement was uncomfortably close to the truth. "But that she's dead… It's only a rumor, right?"

Her grave expression gave me my answer. "I wish. I heard it from a pretty reliable source."

"You're saying that someone tampered with the apples?"

"I'd say it's possible," Nell said. "With one of them anyway."

In my mind I saw my hand reaching for a caramel apple and Miss Valentine grabbing at her throat and falling to the ground.

"I took an apple from the very same tray," I said. "For no particular reason. The luck of the draw. When I saw what happened, I didn't eat it, but I never thought about poison."

"Well, that would hardly be anyone's first thought. I ate one myself. So did a lot of people. They were selling like hotcakes. Nobody makes that caramel coating like the folks at the Maple Creek Cider Mill."

If Nell's story were true, that was an understatement, but it didn't seem possible that we were talking about a murder. The twisted individual who believed in killing at random for the thrill of it was an unfortunate part of our dangerous world, but without hard evidence, I had a difficult time believing that was what had happened to Miss Valentine.

But then what did?

"Do you know if anyone else got sick?" I asked.

"So far, no. I'd have heard if they did. It affected Cora almost immediately. Maybe she was the only unlucky one."

"I've heard of razor blades in candy apples on Halloween," I said.

"And arsenic in sample cereal boxes sent through the mail. Remember that?"

I nodded. "And Anthrax in letters, but I think of them as stories on the evening news."

"Life is changing," Nell said. "Now the sickness has come to Maple Creek, Michigan. Poor Cora."

"I hope that apple story is only a rumor."

"Maybe it is," she said.

But I could tell from her tone and the look in her eyes that she didn't believe it.

NELL FARMER'S RUMOR proved to be true, except for one fact. Cora Valentine's death hadn't been instantaneous. She had died ten minutes after her collapse in the park. I read the story in the Sunday edition of the *Maple Creek Tribune* the next morning.

Someone had injected the caramel apple she'd purchased with a deadly, fast-acting poison, not yet identified. Neither Lieutenant Gray's CPR or earlier emergency care would have saved her life. As soon as she'd swallowed her first bite, she was doomed.

Suspecting that other apples at the Cider Mill stand were also contaminated, the police had confiscated them. Over three hundred caramel apples had been sold during the Fair and presumably consumed, but Cora Valentine was the only one to die. All individuals who had been involved in the handling and sale of the apples were being questioned.

That would include Garth MacKay's sister, Taryn.

A memory came creeping back into my mind.

*"Which one would you like, Miss Val?"*

*"I'm sure they're all delicious. You choose for me."*

Taryn had handed Miss Valentine the apple that had killed her. Would she tell the police? Would I?

Of course. This was a murder investigation. And that information would only hurt Taryn if she were the poisoner.

I folded the paper and filled in the missing details. The Maple Creek Cider Mill was in trouble and the murderer who had claimed the life of one of the town's beloved citizens might have killed me too.

Setting this last frightening thought aside for the moment, I turned my thoughts to practical matters. This morning after breakfast I'd driven to a garden center to buy chrysanthemums in assorted colors. Now I had a dozen pots of flowers to plant. Since the weather was still warm and gardening was a time-honored antidote for morbid thoughts, I planned to work outside all day. Maybe handling living plants would help me forget how close to death I'd been.

THE DENSELY SHADED backyard of my house rolled back two hundred and fifty feet to a line of tall firs. Tucked into a corner of the lot, an aluminum tool shed leaned precariously against the low-growing branch of a linden tree. I found a rusty old shovel and set to work digging holes along the eastern boundary of my property where the chrysanthemums would be visible from the street.

Small lavender flowers still sparkled amid long green stalks and ferns that had disintegrated into powder. Trying not to disturb them, I sent the shovel cutting down through patches of grass. The ground was harder than I'd thought. Scattered gravel and pieces broken from clay pots were embedded in the soil, and the shovel's edge was dull.

I made my way slowly to the back of the yard, digging holes and breathing in the smell of fresh dirt and grass, letting my thoughts drift away, until a sound of soft padding on dry leaves insinuated itself into my consciousness.

Something behind me was breathing. I turned around, keeping my hands closed on the handle of the shovel. The collie that had almost dashed to her death in the street yesterday quickened her pace now that she had my attention. She bounded up to me and nudged my hand. Then she began to scratch at a bare patch of the yard, as if eager to dig a hole of her own.

Pushing the shovel deeper into the ground with my foot, I said, "You're a pretty little thing. Don't you have a home?"

She looked up as if she'd understood my question. Her dark brown eyes were intelligent and alert, but her long coat couldn't conceal the fact that she was too thin for a full-grown collie. Since she wasn't wearing a collar today either, most likely she was a stray.

"Are you hungry?" I asked. "Would you like something to eat?"

She yelped once. Now what could I feed her? All I had was Nell's bread. No meat, no groceries at all. Only a six pack of ginger ale. It would have to be a slice of the bread then.

"You stay here. I'll get you some food," I said.

But a squirrel dropped down from the linden tree in a rustle of leaves and fallen branches, and the dog took off after it, a blur of brown in an impossible pursuit. Alone again, I dug the last hole and laid the shovel on the ground. I was about to reach for one of the pots when I noticed a gold glint in the deep depression. It couldn't be a stone, and the color was wrong for clay.

I reached down and drew a cameo brooch out of the soil. Wiping it clean with my fingers, I let it rest in my palm while I examined it. This was the most unusual cameo I had ever seen. Instead of carving the lady's face in profile, the artisan had created a misty ivory head that faced forward against a brown background as smooth and glossy as caramel. The face in the cameo seemed to look directly at me.

The brooch was broken. Something heavy had crushed its lower half, twisting the thin gold frame out of shape and altering the lady's expression. If once she had been regal or serene or pensive, now her smile was malevolent. But that wasn't quite right.

Puzzled, I held the cameo up to the sunlight. She looked

as if she might be screaming in terror, as if she had been buried alive. I'd rescued her, but too late.

What a ghastly thought. In the afternoon warmth, a chill seemed to surround me. I had been out in the sun too long. What I'd unearthed was a buried trinket. If I dug long enough and deep enough in this neglected yard, I might find anything, which was another ghastly thought.

Nobody would ever wear this brooch again, for no amount of skill could restore the lady's original expression. And yet I didn't want to toss it away. I wasn't sure why. I'd never been inclined to keep broken objects and had no sentimental ties to this one. Still, I set the brooch aside on the grass. Then with the pride of a new homeowner, I began to plant the chrysanthemums, arranging them in a waving line of color.

I wanted to send a message to whoever cared to hear it. I lived in the blue Victorian now, and I took pride in my house and garden. Maybe this time I'd found a home I could keep.

WHEN MY WORK was done, I took the cameo inside and rinsed it under the kitchen faucet. I imagined how it would have looked when it was new and shiny, pinned at a collar or above a low-scooped neckline. Cameos were fashionable again, no longer considered quaint, and designers used them in new ways, on belts and barrettes.

But this cameo was old. Who knew how long it had been buried in the yard? I wondered who had worn the brooch and how she'd lost it. Had she looked for it in vain, never knowing that, with every passing season, it sank deeper into the earth? Or had she thrown it away, having no use for broken jewelry, and somehow it ended up outside in the ground? Most of all, I wished I knew what had caused the damage.

Unfortunately, I had no way of knowing the cameo's history. Setting it on a paper towel to dry, I opened a can of ginger ale and took it out to the front porch.

With no other place to sit, I settled myself on the top step and leaned back against the railing. Walnut was a quiet street.

In the Sunday afternoon silence, the only sounds I heard were the grating of a rake moving leaves across concrete and the delicate music of wind chimes. My thoughts slipped back to yesterday and the murder of Cora Valentine.

The idea that a demented killer with a supply of poison was lurking in Maple Creek was terrifying. Of course he could have come from anywhere and might be miles away by now. Maybe somewhere in town another victim lay dead, his body not yet discovered. He'd eaten his caramel apple before Cora's collapse and the warnings on the news.

I couldn't afford to be out of touch with what was happening in the world around me. Later this afternoon or tomorrow, I would go shopping for a television. Then I'd look for a chair for the porch and buy groceries and a small bag of kibble in case the stray collie showed up again.

An excited barking interrupted my mental list making. Halfway down the block, a man walked at a jaunty pace beside a large black dog. As they came closer, I saw that it was Garth MacKay. Suddenly Tac spied a small creature to chase and ran into a driveway. In a gruff voice, Garth ordered his dog back to his side. He waved to me. When he reached my yard, he angled across the leaves up to the porch with a panting, subdued black shepherd at his heel.

"Afternoon, Katherine. Tac, sit! The house looks nice. I hardly recognized it."

"Thanks. I've been planting flowers in the back to make the yard look more cheerful. Now I wish I had a flag. Is there a banner store around town?"

He glanced briefly at my patriotic wreath. "I wouldn't know, ma'am. I'm not a flag waver. Never have been."

*Ma'am?* When was the last time a man had called me ma'am? Never. And Garth wasn't a flag waver? Practically every other citizen in town was flying the American flag these days.

I looked at him more closely. In a roughhewn sort of way, he was attractive, although I'd never cared for beards. His mysterious air intrigued me, but he had just given me two clues to his personality.

"All I need now is a garage," I said. "I don't want to leave my car outside all winter."

"You have room enough to build one. My guess is that the house used to have a garage." He pointed to the ribbon driveway that ended abruptly several feet from the back porch. "Back there somewhere."

"I'll have to find a good contractor," I said, adding one more item to my rapidly growing list of things to do.

"Let me know when you're ready to build. I'll match you up with someone who's honest." Garth sat down close beside me on the narrow stairs. "Tac likes walking on this street." He leaned against the railing, as I had done, and laid his hand heavily on Tac's head. I noticed that his ring was shaped like a lion's head, with black stones for the eyes and diamonds for the teeth. It was a powerful ring on a large, strong hand.

"You know that Cora Valentine is dead, I guess," he said.

"Yes. It's terrible."

"From the way she looked yesterday, I was expecting it. I never saw Taryn so upset."

"Because she sold her the apple?" I asked.

"Partly. Cora was good to her. Taryn is like me. We never forget people who help us."

"Taryn must wish that she'd let Miss Valentine choose her own apple," I said.

Garth looked at me through narrowed eyes. "What do you mean, Katherine?"

I explained how Taryn had selected an apple from the tray for Miss Valentine at her own request. "Didn't Taryn mention that?"

He sidestepped my inquiry. "You don't have to tell the police that." The threat in his voice was barely perceptible, but it was there.

Or was I imagining it? This affable man couldn't be threatening me. He'd only made a suggestion.

"But if they ask me…"

"It's Taryn's story to tell," he said in the voice he used to give Tac an order.

"I don't disagree with you, but I won't lie to the police. I'm not sure what I'll say—if they ask me. But if all the apples on the tray were contaminated, it may not matter."

"I heard they were." Garth sighed. "I wish Taryn wasn't mixed up in this murder. If only she'd stayed at the Bell House with those antiques, but she always likes to be close to the action. This time, it backfired."

"You seem to be very fond of your sister," I said.

"She's my family. I raised her from the time she was four when our mother died."

I was astonished. "All by yourself?"

"I had some help. Once a month a maid came to clean, but mostly I did what had to be done and just let her grow up. Then when Taryn got a little older, she learned to cook."

He frowned and moved his hand down to Tac's shoulders. "Taryn didn't know that anything was wrong with those apples. The killer must have slipped that tray in with the others from the cider mill. It looked the same to her."

"How could he do that in broad daylight without being seen?"

"With all those people around too. I don't know. But that's the only way it could have happened."

"It doesn't seem possible that the killer was targeting Cora Valentine," I said. "How could anyone know that she'd buy any caramel apple, let alone one from that particular tray?"

"They couldn't. Whoever did this just wanted somebody to die. It could have been you or me or anyone. Even Taryn."

"In a way Cora saved my life. If I hadn't been following her and seen what happened, I would have eaten my own apple."

"That's Cora Valentine. She was always helping people," he said. "Right to the end."

It was a simple and touching testimony for a man who didn't like female teachers and had clashed with this particular one when he was in school. But something about it troubled me, and I sensed that it was important.

# FOUR

THE OLD HOUSE WAS FILLED with strange, muted sounds. I lay in bed, exhausted but still awake, trying to identify each one. Once I knew their source, I could relax and stop imagining footsteps on the hardwood floors below or on the stairs. Not that I was afraid of a little midnight noise. Uneasy was a better way to describe what I felt.

My first Saturday in Maple Creek had been fraught with trauma. This heightened awareness to sound was probably a normal reaction. And through it all I kept hearing the deep voice of Garth MacKay making a simple observation about Miss Valentine. Why did his words continue to haunt me?

I fluffed the pillow and listened to the non-threatening outside noises: The delicate tinkling of wind chimes set in motion by the night wind and a train whistle blowing in the distance. Then directly overhead in the attic, a persistent scratching began.

The odd thought I'd had when I held the brooch in my palm came rushing back to my memory, bringing images of the woman in the cameo screaming and tearing at the soil with her fingernails. That was the stuff of nightmares.

I turned on the bed and pulled the blanket up to my neck. Midnight was no time to remember old Edgar Allan Poe stories and let my imagination roam free. Most likely the scratching in the attic was the work of some wild creature that planned to winter in my house. I pictured a small animal that was relatively easy to evict, like a squirrel. I'd never climbed up to the roof to check for openings in the structure. That would be one more task for tomorrow.

Only I would have to buy an extension ladder first. And what about Garth's tribute to Cora Valentine that wouldn't leave me in peace? Would I be able to unravel its significance in the morning?

The next time I saw Garth, he might talk more about Cora. If he didn't, I would ask him. But when would I see him again? Walking Tac? In front of Sky and MacKay Title or at the Blue Lion? My mind fastened on the pleasant scenes of the Fair before Cora ate the deadly apple, and finally I fell asleep.

IN THE MORNING I dragged one of the kitchen chairs upstairs to the smallest bedroom in the house. The entrance to the attic was through a hole cut in the closet ceiling. A loosely fitting square of wood covered the opening, allowing drafts of chilly air to escape into the space below. As I reached up to touch the shelf that I'd have to use as a stepping-stone to the upper-most level, it tottered forward. One of the wood strips on which it rested was broken.

I couldn't track the mysterious scratching to its source until I had a ladder, which would be later today. In the mean-time the scratching noise had stopped. All I heard was rain pattering on window glass. This sound was as normal and comforting as toast and tea in the morning. Moreover, a new day had stripped Garth's words of their mystery. Cora Valentine's last project was the yard sale, which she'd organized to renovate the Bell House. In a sense, she was helping every-one in Maple Creek. Satisfied with this interpretation, I stepped down from the chair and closed the closet door.

In the kitchen I cut two slices of Nell's wheat bread and plugged in the toaster. As I ate breakfast, I planned my day. The only errand I wished I could skip was the visit to the police sta-tion. Now that I'd turned the apple over to the police, I would have liked to leave Cora's death and my own near brush with tragedy in the past and move on. Retelling my experience would keep the memory alive and invite additional restless nights.

Still, I knew that I didn't have a choice. As long as the killer remained at large, so did the threat of another poisoning. Everyone in this small Michigan town of maples and apples was in danger. I didn't know what I could add to my statement, but Lacey said the police would want more details and Lieutenant Gray would be at his desk today to hear them. Cheered by the prospect of an encounter with the handsome officer, I drank my second cup of tea and headed for the station.

LIEUTENANT DALTON GRAY hooked his long tanned fingers together and asked me for the second time, "Was it only a coincidence that you were standing in line behind Miss Valentine at the Cider Mill stand, Miss Kale?"

"I could hardly have planned it."

We were alone in the small police station that shared the new brick building with the fire department. The off-white walls still held a faint odor of paint, and I could see a trace of sawdust in one corner of the room. Every surface was shining, as was Lieutenant Gray. He was as handsome at close range as he'd been standing in the intersection on Saturday directing traffic.

With the exception of the Chief who had the day off, the other seven members of the Department were out on the roads patrolling Maple Creek. From Lieutenant Gray's frequent glances at the window, I had the impression that he would rather be with them than confined to this small space.

"After I left the Bell House, I ran into Miss Valentine again at the Cider Creek stand. I guess we both got hungry for caramel apples at the same time."

He looked at me, silently inviting me to go on. Seeing his raised eyebrows and the hint of doubt in his eyes, I fell silent. In my opinion, I had answered his question adequately.

"Yes," he said. "Now tell me again why you didn't eat that apple."

Feeling more like a suspect than a willing witness, I said, "When I saw Miss Valentine get so sick, I didn't want to eat it. Naturally I had no idea it was poisoned."

"Then you threw it in the container by the fountain. That was a good choice, Miss Kale. Otherwise, you could have ended up like Miss Valentine—dead. And then you decided to pull the apple out of the trash and take it to the station. Very good thinking. Very commendable."

He had made notes as I'd given my statement, written line after line in a heavy dark hand, occasionally frowning and watching me with those disconcerting blue eyes that seemed to say, 'You know more than you're telling me. You know more than you think you do.'

He hadn't asked me about Taryn, and I hadn't mentioned her. So far I'd held my own in this unanticipated grilling, but I was uncomfortable. The station was bright and almost too warm. The rain had turned into a downpour, and I'd left my umbrella in the car. How many yards would I have to walk with only the hood of my raincoat for protection against the torrent? How far was it to the car?

"This rain should take the last of the leaves down," Lieutenant Gray said.

"It seems like they just changed color." I thought of the drifts of fallen leaves under the maple in my front yard already waiting to be raked. I wanted this brief shining season to last a little longer.

And I wanted this interview to be over. The Lieutenant was an extremely handsome man, but he was all business without an ounce of charm. His dark hair fell forward on his face, giving him an attractive boyish look, but I wasn't fooled. He was tough and clever. Unfortunately I couldn't figure out where he was going with his interrogation.

"So, Miss Kale, you moved to Maple Creek on Friday and walked into a murder the next day. What's more, you met the victim and were the last person to talk to her. You followed her to the park. Strange."

His words struck across my nerves like a match. Could he be implying that I was somehow connected to the bizarre incident? I didn't think so, but it wouldn't be wise to hurl a sarcastic response at him or even a bland one like, "It's not so strange." Instead, I told him again about my decision to buy the parlor lamp, even though the price was outrageously high. I waited for him to tell me that was strange too.

He nodded, and his mouth curved into a smile. "Everything at that yard sale was expensive, an easy three times as much as you'd pay somewhere else. Cora Valentine didn't care. 'Anything to raise money for the Bell House,' she used to say."

He picked up his pen and drew three black ink scrolls under the last line. "All right, Miss Kale," he said. "Five Two Eight Walnut. That's the old blue house with the big maple tree in front. It didn't stay on the market long."

"Only a day."

"I saw the flowers you planted as I drove by this morning. Nice colors."

He knew how to throw a person gently off guard. I was about to mention the buried cameo I'd found while planting the chrysanthemums when he tossed an unexpected question at me.

"Since you were the last person to talk to Cora Valentine, can you tell me what you two discussed?"

I didn't know what else to say. "The lamp. Nothing else. I really don't remember, but I told you we'd just met. She was trying to sell one of her antiques. I was a prospective customer. And oh—she said she knew a story about my house. She was going to tell me about it back at the yard sale, but that didn't happen."

"Did Miss Valentine seem upset or frightened? Agitated, maybe? It might be important."

"I can't make a judgment about her state of mind."

With dogged resolve, he plowed on. "Did she say anything about the Fair? The weather? Apples? Someone she was meeting?"

His questions led me straight to two memories. "She told me that the Maple Creek Cider Mill was famous for their caramel apples. Something like that. I can't remember her exact words. Then she said she was going to meet a friend. She thought she saw her in the park"

He leaned forward, elbows on the desk, eyes alert, ready for action. "Did she say who this friend was?"

"No, but why would she? It would never occur to me to ask." I was aware of the edge creeping into my tone. I didn't have anything else to tell him. The rain was tapering off, and I wanted to move on to another activity between showers.

Lieutenant Gray closed his notebook and laid the pen on top of it. "Those old Victorians have real character, don't they? How do you like living in a house four times as old as you are?"

"I love it, even with all the mysterious sounds I keep hearing."

I hadn't meant to say that. I added, "I wonder how long it takes a house to settle. After a hundred years, you'd think it would have done so already."

"What kind of sounds?" he asked.

"Noises in the attic like a squirrel scratching. I'm going to investigate this afternoon."

"You might have bats," he said. "That old Claymore house on my street did."

Was I supposed to turn pale or shriek? Maybe I was misjudging him and misinterpreting his sly smile.

I said, "I never thought about bats. Maybe I'll just call an exterminator."

"Don't you like bats?" he asked.

"They're not my favorite bird—I mean, mammal."

"They've gotten bad press with all those vampire movies. They're interesting creatures. Some people build houses for them."

"Some people will do anything," I said.

From the teasing glint in his eyes, I imagined that Lieutenant Gray had run out of questions or decided he wouldn't learn anything more from me. Probably both. He was now in light conversation mode.

"When I get home, I'm going to call an exterminator," I said.

"If you like, I could come by and have a look. Say tomorrow morning."

I wasn't expecting personal attention from the MCPD. Or was he angling for more information, details I didn't have?

"Is that part of your job?" I asked.

"Sometimes. We take care of all kinds of problems and disturbances like barking dogs, cats in trees, and even bats in belfries. I relocated a possum last week."

"In that case, I accept." I still intended to buy a ladder and go up into the attic myself. Or, rather, I'd stand next to the opening and shine a lantern flashlight over the entire area. If I saw a sinister dark shape flitting toward my face, I'd hurry back down through the ceiling door and trap the creature on the other side, but I wouldn't turn pale or shriek.

Accepting help from a police officer would be more sensible than calling an exterminator, and I couldn't wait to see if Lieutenant Gray maintained his sterling blue appearance in the presence of attic dust and cobwebs.

"Thanks for your offer, Lieutenant." I opened my shoulder bag and felt around inside for my car keys. "I hope what I said will help the investigation."

He stood up. "Thank you, Miss Kale. Every little detail helps. We're determined to catch this killer before he gets to anyone else."

His words and manner inspired confidence. Also his interest in Cora Valentine's conversation and condition, combined with her intention to meet a friend, indicated that the police had a lead. I felt certain that he already knew about the existence of the friend and hoped to learn something new from me.

If only I had asked Miss Valentine who she was meeting. If I'd hurried to buy my apple and catch up to her. If I'd really looked at the people who were standing around the fountain. If she hadn't taken that first bite to begin with...

"Goodbye, Lieutenant Gray," I said. "I'll see you in the morning."

I opened the door and stepped into a puddle of water. Even though the weather was miserable, I was glad to be out-

side and on my way to my next errand. I could only hope that
no one else thought I knew more than I did about Cora Valentine's murder.

# FIVE

THE ONLY MIRROR in the house was in the small second story bathroom. An ornately framed square of glass bracketed by light fixtures, it was fancy but unkind. By the light of the sixty-watt bulbs, my face looked unusually pale, and the blue glints in my black hair had somehow vanished during the night. I needed better lighting, brighter makeup, and a few more hours of sleep.

The scratching in the attic had awakened me again last night and set my imagination racing. With phantom bats flying in the dark space above the wood square entrance and imagined footsteps on the stairs, I had all the ingredients for my own home horror movie.

"There's a story attached to your house," Miss Valentine had said. She hadn't called it a ghost story.

I applied a darker shade of red lipstick, added gloss, and brushed my hair until the blue sheen came back, even though I could hardly see it in this dimly lit room. I might live in a spooky house, but I didn't have to look like a spirit. And I wasn't going to allow nighttime fancies to discourage me from exploring the attic.

Before fixing breakfast, I buttoned a long white shirt over my dress and ascended to the attic again, this time with the help of a ladder tall enough so that I didn't have to rely on the loose shelf. I pushed up the square of wood, stepped onto the floor, and raised my lantern flashlight high. The air up here was cold and filled with dust motes. The faint light seeping in through the vents seemed cold too.

The part of the attic around the entrance had a wood floor,

an apparent unfinished do-it-yourself project. The rest consisted of boards over deep spaces. I took a few careful steps forward. The silence was absolute. No bats came swooping down to entangle themselves in my hair, and no tiny creature dashed away in alarm. In a far corner two trunks cast an ominous shadow. Opening them would be an interesting project for another day, as I had no desire to venture farther into the attic this morning.

Feeling vaguely disappointed, I climbed back down the ladder. I wished I'd refused Lieutenant Gray's offer. He wouldn't find anything except evidence that the new owner of the blue Victorian was imagining sounds in the night. Even if it were true, that wasn't the impression I wanted to leave with anyone.

"HERE YOU GO, Miss Kale. From the archives."

Lieutenant Gray reached down into the darkness between the boards and handed me a magazine. Under a coating of dust, the picture of a well-endowed redhead in a provocative pose blazed across the cover. I was holding a decades old *Playmate*.

"Some kid's secret hiding place," he said. "I guess he forgot about it."

"Do you see anything else?" I asked.

I stood on the floored section of the attic while he walked with ease across the boards, flashing light into the dark corners. I hoped he would find traces of animal habitation or anything to prove that the noises I'd heard were real.

He waited a moment before answering. I watched as his beam of light swept the area once more and then a third time. "Just those trunks over there. Do you want me to see what's inside them?"

"If you will."

He didn't seem to care that he was walking on a treacherous unfinished surface instead of flooring. Anyone would think that he investigated attics every day.

He bent down and tugged open the first trunk. "Nothing in here except old yellow newspapers, and…" He tried to raise the other lid. "This one is locked. Do you want me to force it open?"

"Would you check for animal signs instead?"

"I can do both."

He rocked the trunk back and forth and said, "I think it's empty. Someone must have used the trunks to move and then stashed them up here out of sight. They must have had a hard time getting them through that opening." He walked all around the attic again, seeking out the dark spaces with his flashlight. Finally he said, "You don't have anything living up here that I can see, Miss Kale."

He turned the flashlight to the floor and strode toward me, following the trail of brightness. I stepped aside, but he said, "After you," and I climbed down slowly to the closet floor. What could I say now? Only the truth.

"I'm sorry I troubled you I must have imagined or dreamed the noise."

"Maybe not. I saw a small opening on the northern side of your house just big enough for something to get inside. Your animal may stop in for a spell and go out again."

Feeling vindicated, I said, "I'd better buy a squirrel trap then."

"You could, but it would be easier to hire someone to close the entrance."

"I can do that myself."

"Do you think so? It's pretty high up there. Let's go around to the side of the house. I'll show you where it is."

I closed the bedroom door and waited for Lieutenant Gray to move. He was studying the crown molding in the hall.

"Have you ever lived alone in an old house, Miss Kale?" he asked "Sometimes it's easy to imagine you're hearing things that aren't there, especially when the rooms are empty."

Because I heard only concern in his voice and not the slightest hint of condescension, I couldn't possibly be offended.

"I'm not easily intimidated or frightened," I said. "I've

lived in apartments in foreign cities where everything was strange because I didn't speak the language yet."

His blue eyes lit up in interest. "Did you? Were you a student?"

"No, a teacher," I said and told him about my assignments in Italy and Germany.

"Won't you find life in the Maple Creek, Michigan, too dull and slow?"

"Not at all. This is where I want to be, and as of next month, I'm going to start teaching again at Capac High School."

"We'll keep you safe then," he said. "In spite of what happened to Cora Valentine, we like to protect our teachers. They're hard to come by."

"That's nice to know."

He followed me downstairs and through the kitchen, but once we were outside, I was the one who trailed after him. As we approached the balcony, he came to a stop under the linden tree that grew close to the house. He frowned as he had done yesterday when he was asking me about Cora Valentine.

"What room does that balcony lead to?" he asked.

"My bedroom."

"If I were you, I'd call a tree service and have those branches trimmed."

The linden was full and symmetrical with leaves that had turned a soft shade of yellow. Most of them were on the ground, forming a thick rustling carpet under our feet. I didn't want the tree disturbed in any way.

"Why?" I asked. "It'll shade the balcony in the summer."

"Sure it will, but think, Miss Kale. It's dangerous. Anyone could climb up that tree to the balcony and from there right into your room. I was climbing trees like that when I was six."

I found the image of a miniature police officer perched on a branch amusing, but the Lieutenant was serious now, a man with crime prevention on his mind.

"I didn't think about that, but it isn't very likely," I said.

"It could happen."

"Like the bat invasion?"

He laughed, and the lines about his eyes and mouth deepened. "It never hurts to be careful and prepared," he said. "Make your house burglar and critter proof. You'll sleep better at night." He walked around the corner and pointed upwards. "There's your opening, right under the gutter, about six inches from the roof."

"I can't see anything, but if you say it's there, I'll find it," I said.

"Do you have an extension ladder?"

"Not yet."

"It might be easier to call a professional—say a roofer."

"Maybe I could talk the tree trimmers into doing it."

"No harm in asking."

As we went in through the side door that led to the kitchen, Lieutenant Gray said, "You never know what flaws a house has until you start looking in those out of the way places like basements and attics. But the ones we just found are easy to fix."

He glanced at the crushed cameo on the counter. "What happened to your pin?"

I told him how I'd found the cameo. "First a buried brooch and then a hidden *Playmate*. I wonder what else is lying around waiting to be discovered."

"You never know. That's the fun of living in an old place like this."

He picked up the cameo and held it as I had done. In his large palm, it seemed fragile and almost pathetic in its damaged state. "It looks like a truck ran over it. Why are you keeping it?"

That was a good question. "I'm not sure. The frame looks like real gold."

But that wasn't the reason. I didn't know why I hadn't thrown the cameo away yet. Maybe I'd hold onto it for a while until I figured it out.

"Is there anything new in the murder investigation?" I asked.

"Not much," he said. "Read the paper. These days every other article seems to be about apples."

He set the brooch back down as carefully as if it were still intact and valuable. "Be careful if you decide to close that opening yourself. It's a long way to fall."

"I will. Thanks for your help, Lieutenant Gray."

"You may call me Dalton—Katherine," he said, and with a wave, he walked to the door.

I watched him drive away in his patrol car, feeling better about practically everything. On this visit, he had been helpful and even friendly. In only a few days and with little effort, I had met four new people. I was pleased with my progress until I remembered that one of them was dead.

DALTON'S CLAIM THAT every other story in the *Maple Creek Tribune* was about apples was only slightly exaggerated. In the paper the next day, I read that the people who had handled the poisoned apples, specifically Taryn MacKay and those responsible for making the caramel coating, had been questioned and released, leaving the police without a suspect. In the meantime, apples, especially caramel apples, had tumbled out of grace. At the height of the season, the Maple Creek Cider Mill was losing money.

In a sidebar, the mill's owner proclaimed, "Our apples are safe." Among the day's features were recipes for apple muffins, pancakes, and jams. The industry was making a valiant attempt to distance itself from the murder.

In another part of town, an unidentified man had driven himself to St. Andrew's Emergency, blaming his chest pains on an apple Danish he'd eaten that morning at the Bakery on Main. In the meantime, Miss Cornelia Valentine, so far the only confirmed victim of the poisoner, lay in state at the Carson-Chandler Funeral Home. A memorial service was scheduled for Friday.

I laid the paper aside. The news was depressing, but bright sunshine and another pleasant fall afternoon soon lured me outside. The neighborhood children were still in school, their parents at work, and everyone else apparently inside their houses.

I walked north on Walnut until I reached Lindenwood, a long, unpaved road that led to Hickory Boulevard. Here I turned and continued on past a stretch of woods until I came to a slate gray mansion, embellished with graceful arches and windows. It looked as if it had been among the first houses in town, growing older and mellower every year, as the nearby land was carved up and filled with more modern structures.

Set in the center of a triple lot and enclosed by a high black iron fence, the gray house was surrounded by a green lawn raked free of leaves. Three thinly wooded lots separated it from the brick ranch on its right, insuring the privacy of both homeowners.

With its dull color and austere façade, the mansion should have been drab and cheerless but it had character and signs of young life. In the yard I saw a gleaming wooden sled decorated with holly berries, apparently freshly painted and set out to dry in an island of sunshine.

I was about to move on when I heard footpads on the dry leaves. Turning around, I saw the stray collie following me at a safe distance, wagging her tail slowly as if she were unsure of her welcome. When she reached my side, she nudged my hand with her nose. Her dark eyes seemed to have a sparkle today, but her fur was dull, and her white paws were splattered with mud.

"I wish I knew your name," I said. "Is it Lassie?"

At the sound of my voice, the dog's tail wagged faster. I didn't like to see her wandering freely through town. I should have asked Lieutenant Gray if he knew anything about her. Of course, if I brought her to his attention, he might take her to the pound.

"You're a good dog," I said, petting her gently. She flattened her ears against the sides of her head, soaking up the attention as if she hadn't heard a kind word in a long time. I noticed again how thin she was and how badly her coat needed brushing and trimming.

She followed me to the end of the street where the Boulevard ended at an old viaduct. Then I turned around and retraced my steps. As I neared the mansion again, a man came out of the front door. Although the afternoon was warm, he wore a brown sweater. Using his cane for support, he made his way slowly down the path to the gate.

I had last seen him in the park at Cora Valentine's side and later sitting alone on a bench after the ambulance had taken her away. Dalton had called him Mr. Raycraft. I noticed now that he was strikingly handsome, perhaps about sixty. Except for his gray hair sprinkled with brown and his awkward gait, he had the appearance of a much younger man.

He leaned the cane against the fence and opened the gate, while the collie bounded joyfully toward him. He ignored her.

"Hello," I said.

"Good afternoon." His voice was curt, and he looked away, clearly indicating that he didn't have anything else to say to me. He reached for his cane and walked down the street in the direction from which I'd just come.

Apparently I wasn't going to make a fifth friend today. I kept walking all the way back to Walnut. The collie followed me—unaware or uncaring that she had been rebuffed.

"Come home with me, and I'll feed you," I said. "I bought something special just for you."

If indeed she was a stray and not a lost pet, I was thinking about keeping her. Owning a dog had never been part of my plan, and soon I'd be away from home five days a week and busy with schoolwork; but this pretty creature didn't seem to have anyone to take care of her. I was alone too.

First I had to see if she would accept a meal from me. But the next time I looked down, she was gone. I continued on alone to my own house where I saw another dog lying on the lawn. A familiar man with a beard lounged on my porch step, leaning against a post.

"Hello, Mr. MacKay," I said.

He stood up. The black shepherd surveyed me warily as if I were invading his property.

"Garth," he said. "I thought we were on a first name basis."

"Garth then. Is Sky and MacKay closed for the day?"

"Sky is at the helm. Business is slow. I made a cider run and then walked over to visit you. This is for you." He laid his hand on the gallon of bright amber liquid at his side. "If you're not afraid of poison, that is. I like to give my business to the people at the mill to show my support. Besides, Taryn works there after school."

I picked up the cider. "Who's afraid of a little poison? But I'll let you drink first. Did your sister come out all right when the police questioned her?"

"Sure," he said. "Like I told you, she didn't do anything wrong. Thanks for not telling the police that Taryn chose Cora Valentine's apple for her."

"Well, Lieutenant Gray didn't ask me about it. If he had, I would have told the truth. But all the apples on that tray were poisoned, weren't they?"

"Every last one, but only on that tray."

"So in the end, it didn't matter what I said."

"I'm still grateful to you, Katherine."

I turned the key in the lock. "Come in. We'll sample some of this cider."

He rose and held the door for me, saying in a gruff voice, "Tac, stay."

"Tac can come in," I said. "I like dogs. I was walking with one a few minutes ago. She's a stray, I think."

"That brown collie? I've seen her around."

"Good. Do you know where she lives?"

He shrugged. "Nowhere, anywhere. She just turned up one day. I guess people are feeding her."

"From the looks of her, not much. The poor thing."

Tac followed us into the kitchen, panting heavily as I opened the cider. I filled a bowl with water for him, and he lapped it noisily, and then lay down at Garth's feet. Tac was a good dog. Every house should have one.

"That collie," he said. "Somebody must have dumped her out in the country and left her to fend for herself. Her owner should be shot."

"Maybe that's not how it happened," I said. "She might be a runaway."

"I've seen plenty of so-called runaways in my time, Katherine. That pooch was a castaway."

I poured the cider into the glasses. This was exactly the drink I wanted after my long walk. "Shall we sit here or go out on the porch?" I asked, hoping he'd tell me the reason for his visit.

"This is okay." He pulled out one of the chairs for me. "I came to ask you to have dinner with me. Any night is good for me. I want to get to know you better. I mean, I want us to get to know each other better."

When I hesitated, he said quickly, "That's if you're free to go out with me, if you aren't married or engaged." He looked around the kitchen as if expecting a man to materialize at any minute.

"I'm free, and dinner sounds nice," I said.

"On Saturday then. I'll pick you up around six."

"That'll be—nice," I said. "I was reading about another case of possible poison. Do you think the apple murderer struck again?"

"If you mean that story in the paper, Old Man Evans had a mild heart attack. The doctor says he's going to be all right. Evans used to say, 'An apple pie a day keeps the doctor away.' He's been tempting fate with red meat and fancy desserts ever since I met him. As for that killer, I think he's still around, just biding his time until he targets his next victim."

"I hope you're wrong." I wondered what to talk about next. In our previous encounters, Garth and I had conversed with ease. I hoped that wasn't going to change now that he had asked me to go out on a date with him.

"I see that you broke your pin," he said. "Do you want me to have a look at it?"

For the second time today, I described how I had found the brooch hidden deep in the ground and couldn't bring myself to throw it away. "I don't think it can be repaired."

"Doesn't look like it." He returned the cameo to the counter. "When I moved into my place in the country, I dug up all sorts of things, even bones. Animal bones, that is, not skeletons. Once I came across an old steamer trunk filled with plumbing parts."

"I guess everyone would like to find buried treasure."

"Or money in the attic," he said. "I read about a man once who found five thousand dollars under the rafters. You wouldn't think anybody would lose track of that."

"I haven't found anything else, but I heard strange scratching sounds in my attic. Lieutenant Gray stopped by to investigate. He showed me a place where wild things can find their way in."

"That's bad," Garth said. "Let me take care of it for you."

"Thanks for the offer, but I'm going to do it myself, probably later this afternoon."

Garth looked at me, the disbelief in his expression obvious and unflattering. "That's no job for a lady."

I concentrated on refilling his glass with cider. I was prepared to like this man, and I appreciated his offer of help but not his last remark.

"My father let me help him with all sorts of household repairs from the time I was little," I said. "I know what to do."

"I say it's a job for a man. My offer is still open, Katherine. If I can do anything for you, just let me know."

I couldn't see the point in arguing with him, but I knew that I wouldn't call on Garth MacKay to fill the role of handyman. My house was in good condition, and I was capable of coping with whatever needed doing or hiring someone to do it. I regarded Garth as a friend. How different he was from Dalton who hadn't challenged my decision to climb up to the top of the house, although he had mentioned calling a roofer.

"If you keep hearing those sounds in the attic, you might want a ghost buster at your side, Katherine. A house that's been standing for so long must have a few specters roaming the halls." With a mischievous grin, he drew a card out of his pocket and handed it to me. "Here's my number. Call me any time of the day or night."

He was joking, of course, but I wished that he hadn't mentioned ghosts. At that moment I realized that when I'd been imagining bats and scratching, on some level, I wondered if the blue Victorian was haunted. The idea was preposterous, though, which was why I'd been slow to acknowledge it. I had never believed in supernatural manifestations, and I didn't intend to start now.

# SIX

IN THE SPACIOUS ROOM where Cora Valentine lay in her closed coffin, I stood alone, apart from the mourners, wishing myself a hundred miles away. I knew I didn't belong here among her family and friends, even though the connection I felt to the murdered woman was real and strong.

On two occasions, I had talked to her briefly. In a bizarre way, she had saved my life. I wouldn't try to explain to anyone why I had ventured out on a dreary, rainy evening to pay my respects to a woman I'd hardly known. But then no one would be likely to ask me about it.

I moved silently through the crowd up to the casket, trying not to inhale the potent odors of the funeral flowers, and stood for a moment in front of her picture, saying a silent prayer for her soul. No one came to greet me. Nobody noticed me at all.

Set on an easel beside the casket, a black-framed photograph captured forever the face of a smiling Cora Valentine. In her scoop-necked navy blue dress with a double strand of pearls resting against her throat, her expression was serene. Yet I had the feeling that she had returned from the grave to mingle with the mourners at her own wake. In the eerie glow of the vigil candles, she seemed to say, "Help me, Katherine—please."

Even though my sleeves covered my arms, I shivered. The heavy perfume that emanated from the pink rose casket blanket was overpowering, almost nauseating. I always avoided visiting funeral parlors whenever possible and couldn't wait to leave this one.

I moved away, walking faster than would be considered

proper on this somber occasion. On the wooden table at the back of the room lay the guest book, donation envelopes, and holy cards. By dull yellow candlelight, I signed my name and address and took a card depicting Christ ascending into heaven.

Now, back to the entrance and out the door. But I was too late. Nell Farmer emerged from a group of soberly clad mourners and walked toward me, a subdued smile on her face. Drops of rainwater glistened on her hair and the slick surface of her black coat.

"Katherine, I'm surprised to see you here," she said.

"I guess it wasn't appropriate…"

"No, no, I didn't mean that. Cora was so much a part of the town that everyone either knew her or felt like they did. She didn't have any family left except for her cousin. That's Meg Valentine sitting over there with the Historical Society."

I turned the holy card around in my hands. "I was just leaving, Nell."

"Stay a while. It's raining cats and dogs out there." She scanned the room, peering over the shoulders of people gathered in small groups, some of them with grave expressions, others engaged in animated but quiet conversations.

"Let's sit down for a minute. When Meg is free, I'll introduce you to her. She's a secretary at Maple Creek High School. How have you been? Getting all settled into that beautiful house?"

"Pretty much, but I still have to furnish it. I'm in no hurry. It's livable, and that's what's important. I'm enjoying the bread," I added. "Thank you again."

"You're quite welcome. I love the chrysanthemums you planted. The mixed colors make the house look so cheerful."

"I found a broken cameo the day I planted them," I said.

"You never know what you'll find when you start digging. I read about a man who discovered human bones when he was building a barn. It turned out that his land was once an Indian burial ground."

"I wouldn't want to be him."

"Neither would I. Well, Katherine, are you meeting people?"

I thought of Lieutenant Gray's official visit, the unfriendly Mr. Raycraft, and Garth sitting on my porch, waiting for me to come home. "Yes, a little."

"I'm due for a day off next week," Nell said. "I could throw a party on Saturday night, nothing elaborate, just an informal get-together to introduce you to your neighbors."

"I'd like that, but you'll have to let me help you."

"Okay. That'll be fun. There won't be much work. I'll bake a ham and put together a buffet." She paused and looked toward the casket, shaking her head slowly. "I know that Cora is dead, but I almost said, 'We'll have to ask Cora Valentine. Nobody knows Maple Creek like she does.' That's weird, isn't it?"

"I don't think so. She must have been a remarkable woman, the kind you don't easily forget."

"Cora was important to the town, but I keep remembering back over the years to when she was my history teacher." Nell's voice softened in remembrance. "She was so strict and unbending. A regular Marine sergeant, the kids used to say. No one wanted to be in her class. She didn't let you get by with anything."

"You liked her though," I said.

"Very much."

"That's the kind of teacher I'd like to be, but I don't think I am," I said.

"Well, kids are harder to manage today than they were when I was in school. You'd know that better than I would. I'm sure you're doing the best you can. I remember once when I almost got in trouble with Miss Valentine."

"You were a troublemaker in school, Nell?"

"No, just awkward and clumsy. What happened was an accident. Miss Valentine had a poster board project displayed on a table next to her desk. It was supposed to represent one of the major battles of the Civil War—Gettysburg, I think.

There must have been a million little Yankee and Rebel soldier figures on top of it, cannons and landmarks, everything in its historically correct place.

"One day while Miss Valentine was out of the room, I don't remember why I was out of my seat, but I backed up into it, and everything fell on the floor." She laughed at the memory of an incident that must have been humiliating for a self-conscious girl. "Soldiers flew in every direction. I tried to pick them up and put them back on the poster board, but I didn't know where they all went. I wasn't exactly a scholar."

"Didn't anyone help you?" I asked.

"A few girls did, and we got everything off the floor and were in our seats when Miss Valentine came back into the room. Nobody said anything. At the time I didn't think she noticed the way her figures were all mixed up. Now I'm sure she did. She just didn't say anything. That was the sort of mischief that could have gotten me a few hundred lines or detentions."

"It doesn't sound too terrible," I said.

"Now that I look back on it, it was funny. It stayed in my mind all these years, and I never forgot how scared I was. After that, the kids called me a teacher's pet. I hated that, but most of all, the incident embarrassed me." She laughed softly, glancing once more at the casket. "Dear Cora. Years later I helped her arrange furniture at the Bell House, but neither one of us ever mentioned those days or the flying Gettysburg Project."

"She'd probably forgotten all about it by then," I said.

"I don't know. Cora Valentine had a sharp memory. She never forgot anything she considered important."

We sat together quietly for a while as a steady stream of mourners poured into the funeral parlor. Only a few trickled out. Every now and then a small man in a black suit came into the room, adding elaborate floral tributes and terrariums to the tables and moving those already in place closer together.

"It looks like half the town turned out to pay their last respects to Miss Valentine," I said.

"There's quite a crowd. Let's see. I don't know everybody." Again Nell scanned the room. "That heavy set man in the dark gray suit looks familiar. I think he went to Maple Creek High, a year or two ahead of me. Yes, he was the captain of the football team, but I don't remember his name. And there's Myrold Barren with him. He's the man with the red hair."

The man who had threatened to run over the stray collie. I recognized him. He'd been loud and angry then. He was still loud, but his expression was congenial tonight. It didn't matter. I was prepared to dislike him.

"I've seen him driving in his white convertible," I said.

"Myrold gets around. He wasn't a friend to Cora when she was alive."

"Didn't he like her?" I asked.

Nell lowered her voice. "I suppose he did, but Cora stood in the way of one of his pet projects. Myrold doesn't like opposition. I'll tell you about him later."

Intrigued by this bit of gossip, I studied Myrold Barren. A portly man with a beefy complexion and a short beard, he wore a bulky green and gold sweater that would be more at home on the ski slopes than a funeral parlor. He reminded me of someone, but I couldn't make the connection yet. It wasn't anyone I knew.

Although his voice rose over the quieter murmuring that surrounded him, I couldn't hear what he and the gray-clad man were saying. From their amused expressions, I suspected it was another fond remembrance of Miss Valentine.

Maybe not. If Cora Valentine had stood in his way, Myrold Barren might have wanted her eliminated from the canvas. I could imagine him issuing an order in his booming voice: "Off with her head!"

That was the connection. He reminded me of Henry VIII, as I'd always pictured him. All Myrold Barren needed was a tankard of ale and a drumstick.

Meg Valentine left the sofa to accompany the members of the Historical Society to the door. Noting her departure, Nell said, "We'll catch Meg when she comes back. I haven't offered her my condolences yet. Ah, there's the Police Department, the gallant Lieutenant Gray and the lovely Lacey. They make a nice couple, don't they?"

Looking straight ahead, Lieutenant Gray walked past us with the policewoman, Lacey, at his side. He was in his dark uniform. She wore a shapely black sheath without a single accessory. She didn't need one to look stunning. While she stopped to talk to an elderly woman sitting alone in the last row of chairs, he continued on to the casket alone.

"Are they a couple?" I asked.

"So Lacey says to anybody who will listen. I have my doubts."

I didn't see Garth MacKay or Taryn, and Meg Valentine hadn't returned yet. Maybe she had gone out for a quick dinner. I moved restlessly in the chair, thinking that I should get away from the cloying fragrances. I was about to tell Nell that I'd have to go home soon when she said, "That's Anna Lynde over there with Gerry Raycraft. They were longtime friends of Cora's. Let's go over, and I'll introduce you to them."

I was going to protest that first I needed some fresh air when Anna Lynde waved to Nell. I had no choice but to follow Nell to the other side of the room, and I found that as I moved away from the flowers on the side tables, I could breathe more easily.

"I've already met Mr. Raycraft, unofficially," I said. "He isn't very polite."

"Gerald Raycraft is a private person. You'll like him."

I didn't think so, and when Nell introduced us, Mr. Raycraft acknowledged my presence with a correct handshake and a chilly smile. Then he promptly excused himself and walked slowly away toward the door, his hand gripping the handle of the cane.

Anna Lynde was warm and welcoming. She was a little like Nell herself, although older. I'd guess she belonged to the same generation as Mr. Raycraft and Cora. She resembled

Cora slightly, or perhaps it was only a superficial similarity in height and hairstyle. Mrs. Lynde's figure was slimmer, and her hair was dark brown with the merest hint of gray.

"Call me Anna," she said. "I'm always pleased when a young person moves to Maple Creek. It keeps things in the neighborhoods lively."

Except when a killer decides to take out one of the town's leading citizens, I thought.

"How did you happen to know Cora?" she asked.

I told her about my visit to the Bell House yard sale, omitting the part about meeting Cora again at the cider mill stand and the tragic aftermath.

"I wish I'd bought the lamp that day," I said. "I wonder where it is now."

"The parlor lamp with the dark red roses? I have it. We moved everything I donated back to my garage. Meg Valentine wants to have another yard sale in the spring. The Bell House belongs to her now, and she wants to carry on Cora's work."

"Then you must be the descendent of Elsbeth, the lamp's original owner," I said. "Miss Valentine told me about her."

"Cora liked to know the story behind every antique she handled."

"Did you really want a family heirloom sold?" I asked.

Anna laughed. "I haven't looked at it in ages. I like bright, new modern furnishings. Cora was the one for antiques."

"I only hesitated to buy the lamp because it was so expensive," I said.

"Yes, Cora priced it at seven hundred dollars. Well, I'd hesitate too, Katherine. You can have the lamp for a lot less. The Restoration Fund is in good shape. Come and see me the day after tomorrow, any time after noon." She opened her purse and took out a card. "I'm glad I can take care of some unfinished business for Cora, but nobody in town will ever be more passionate about the Bell House than she was."

"Miss Cora Valentine was one of a kind," Nell said. "She was like a rare and beautiful lamp herself."

"Nice simile, Nell," Anna said. "Very appropriate. Cora would be proud of you. I'll see you on Sunday, Katherine. Maybe you'll find something else you'd like to have."

"I saw a two-tiered mahogany table at the sale. I'd like to have the lingerie chest with the wildflowers painted on the drawers too, and maybe the maple coffee table, but not right away."

"They all belong to me," Anna said.

"On Sunday then." I slipped the card into my shoulder bag, feeling a faint stirring of excitement. After everything that had happened since I'd first seen the lamp, it was going to be mine because I'd met Anna Lynde and happened to mention it. I could almost believe that Fate was playing a part in my affairs, but this was a simple business transaction, the transference of an object from one person who didn't want it to another who did.

Nothing unusual or mysterious was going on here at all. I only felt as if it was.

THROUGH SHEETS OF wind-driven rain, the porch light of the blue Victorian sent out a weak beam that reminded me of the vigil candles burning for Cora Valentine's soul. I imagined the parlor lamp shining in the bay window, giving me proper illumination and a real welcome for all those times I would come home after dark.

On a night like this with rain, wind, and funeral parlor images fresh in my mind, I expected the house to seem spookier than usual. It didn't disappoint me. I unlocked the door and turned on the living room light, but the brightness only brought the shadows out of hiding. The haunting vibes I'd sensed were lying in wait for me. Maybe they had chased the previous owners away.

Impatiently I rejected the nonsensical thought. This was my home now. In the kitchen were tins of Darjeeling tea and Hershey's cocoa, either one of them perfect for combating odd notions and the fall night's chill. I could take a warm bath and go to bed early. Tomorrow I hoped the rain would be gone, and with it these weird ideas.

But Cora Valentine was still dead. Even now, her murderer might be planning his next move. He would use his poison in a different way this time because, except for Garth, with his daredevil streak, few people were eating apples. Or maybe he'd use something else.

As I heated a double serving of cocoa, I remembered the unnerving feeling I'd had when looking at Cora's picture. She wanted me to help her. But in what way? If she was safe in heaven, she didn't need anything else.

The sounds that intruded on the silence of the empty house were outside now, harder to describe than a scratching in the attic or floorboards creaking. It sounded as if someone was at the door, trying to get inside. Maybe Cora Valentine had returned to earth to bring her murderer to justice. Through me she could accomplish this.

This idea was almost laughable. I gave the cocoa mix one final stir and poured the steaming liquid into a mug. I wasn't an avenger, and if I kept adding to this chilling fantasy, I would be awake half the night. Tomorrow evening I would have dinner with Garth. If I were sleepy and irritable, I'd make a poor dining companion and wouldn't enjoy myself.

Still, when I heard the noise on the porch a second time, I opened the door, never expecting anyone to be there. Again, I wasn't disappointed. The street was deserted and quiet, except for the loud clanging of my neighbors' wind chimes. Whatever I'd heard could only have been the wind.

Ordering myself to abandon all unwholesome thoughts, I finished my cocoa and went to bed. Tomorrow, wherever Garth took me, there would be lights and noise and earth-bound pleasures such as good company and food. I hoped they would counteract the dark mood that had overtaken me.

# SEVEN

I CUT A SMALL PIECE OF filet mignon and tasted it. On my un-inspired moving-day diet of sandwiches, I'd had almost forgotten that steak could be so good. With a baked potato, garden salad, and warm dinner rolls, this was a virtual feast.

The lighting in the Blue Lion was as subdued as the noise level, but Garth was a generous and enthusiastic dinner partner. He had entertained me with a series of amusing anecdotes about the town's memorable characters. In his company my gloomy thoughts of the previous evening had all but evaporated.

Garth knew the history of Maple Creek and, through Sky and MacKay Title, the personal history of many of its citizens. He even knew the background of my house, beginning with the early nineteen eighties, but nothing he said sounded like a story.

"Can you remember any more about why the last owners felt uncomfortable in my house?" I asked. "Cora Valentine was going to tell me something, some story associated with it."

"I didn't know the Schaffers very well," Garth said. "I only talked to them a few times."

I sensed that he knew more than he was willing to tell me. "It can't have been the floor plan or the heating."

"Your imagination is already working overtime, Katherine. I don't want to encourage it." A teasing sparkle brightened Garth's blue-green eyes. "Are you still seeing ghosts in the hallway?"

"I never said anything about ghosts," I said.

"Hearing noises then."

"Only the wind."

"If you hear somebody shouting 'Ghosts in the Grave-yard,' it's only kids playing games in the bushes."

"I'll keep that in mind." I took another bite of filet. "About the Schaffers now, I have a feeling you're keeping something from me. If you know anything about my house, please tell me."

This time he didn't hesitate. "Mrs. Schaffer always felt like someone else was living in the house with them. Your hall-way ghost, maybe. It made her edgy and depressed. When the octagonal mansion came on the market, they decided to cut their losses and move."

"You could have told me that before, Garth."

"I didn't want to scare you."

"Well—it'll take more than that. I'm not a fragile Victorian heroine prone to the vapors."

But if another person had sensed something unusual about the blue Victorian, then maybe the strangeness I often felt wasn't entirely my imagination. I didn't intend to let Garth know that his information had affected me. Later, after he took me home, I'd deal with it.

"Thank you. That's—fascinating. This is a delicious steak. How is your Porterhouse?"

"The best," he said. "They have good food here. That's why I didn't take you anywhere fancier."

"I love this restaurant. It has interesting décor and atmo-sphere. I like being surrounded by medieval beasts. On the wall," I added, looking at the wineglass in his large hand and the lion's head ring flashing its black stones and diamonds in the light of the lantern centerpiece.

"The Blue Lion is just an old country inn, but it's my fa-vorite place," he said.

The waiter had greeted him by name. In his herringbone suit, Garth looked at home here. I supposed he ate at the Inn often, as it was close to his title business. He had set the glass down and was studying me with an intensity that made me feel self-conscious.

Maybe my white sweater was giving him the wrong signal, but the beads and rhinestone chips were dressy and appropriate for an evening out. I wasn't going to worry about it.

"You look like you could use a good meal," he said.

"Oh, well…" I shied away from the personal remark and the hungry look in his eyes, reminding myself that I wasn't thinking of Garth in a romantic way. With his beard and barely suppressed rough edge, he really wasn't my type, although I felt comfortable with him and enjoyed his company. "I've been too busy unpacking to spend much time in the kitchen cooking."

"Did you find anything you want me to do for you yet?" he asked. "Around your house, I mean."

I thought of the linden branch growing into my balcony, providing easy access to any intruder who came along with robbery on his mind. I hadn't called a tree trimmer yet. With his powerful arms, Garth could take the branch down in minutes, but I wasn't going to ask for his help unless it became necessary. I didn't want to blur the parameters of our new friendship.

"Nothing yet, but if I do, I'll call on you." In an attempt to steer our conversation away from my appearance and his offer of help, I said, "I went to the funeral parlor yesterday. It seemed like everyone in town was there."

Garth nodded. "That's no surprise. Cora Valentine was a popular lady." He drained his wineglass and reached for the bottle. "While people were paying their last respects, her house was burglarized. I heard it on my police radio."

"That's terrible! It's like robbing a grave."

"Thieves watch the papers for obituary notices. Empty houses are fair game. The rain last night was a good cover for them."

I pictured a masked burglar climbing the trunk of the linden tree. "I'm beginning to think I moved into a high crime area," I said.

"It isn't so bad. People here look out for their neighbors."

"So far the only one I've met is Nell Farmer." I pushed the fleeting thought of Mr. Raycraft to the back of my mind. He didn't live that near to me anyway.

"Yes, Miss Farmer. I know her," Garth said. "Some more wine, Katherine?"

As I said, "Only a little," he filled the glass to the top, sending me a crooked smile.

"Now you know all about my life, but you're still a mystery to me. Tell me about yourself, Katherine. Why you came to Maple Creek, what you do for a living, the things you like—your family." He glanced at my left hand.

"All I know about you, Garth, is that you raised your sister, Taryn, you have a dog named Tac, and you're in the title business." I said. "Exactly what kind of work is that?"

"It's a lot of paperwork. Let's say somebody buys a house. We do a title search to verify proof of ownership, make sure the seller is legitimate. That sort of thing."

"No wonder you know so many people in Maple Creek."

"That's my life," he said. "I'll bet yours is more interesting."

The moment of truth was at hand, and I seized it. "First you should know that I'm one of those female teachers you don't like."

He didn't seem to be surprised or taken aback by my allusion to the casual remark he'd made at our first meeting. Maybe Garth already knew my profession, but Nell and Dalton were the only ones I'd told. I didn't think Dalton would discuss me with anyone; but Nell seemed like a friendly and talkative person, and Garth knew her.

"Are you teaching somewhere now?" he asked. "I ask because I noticed you're home during the day."

I let that pass and told him about my new assignment. "I hope it'll be permanent. The teacher I'm replacing wants to stay home with her new baby when it's born."

He sat back and looked at me for what seemed like a long time. Finally, he said, "I can't see myself disliking you. You're not bossy like Cora Valentine."

I laughed. "You don't know me."

"Not yet, but I'd sure like to. Is this your first year of teaching?"

"It's my sixth. I've been working on army bases overseas, but I was getting homesick for America. I bought a house in Maple Creek because I fell in love with the town, and it's close to my new school. My father died ten years ago. Right now, my mother is on a cruise, but we're going to meet in St. Ignace for Thanksgiving. That's where our family home is. Now you know as much about me as I do."

Except for Germany and Stefan, I thought. Cruising on the Rhine, storybook castles, and German music. The University of Heidelberg. A gold charm on my bracelet for every country I visited. That Army captain with the Texas drawl. Men I'd never see again. Figuratively, I slammed the door on the past. Garth and this evening at the Blue Lion were my present. I didn't want to see into the future. Let it surprise me, but only in a pleasant way.

"Tell me what you like," he said.

"Music, books, antiques, movies—lots of things. And you?"

"I like books too, especially westerns, and some music. Hunting and fishing are my favorite sports. It looks like we're compatible."

"More or less," I said. "But I hate the idea of hunting."

"Ladies usually do. I always eat what I kill, though."

I looked up from my steak. "That's a sweeping generalization, and it's sexist. And good heavens, we're living in the twenty-first century, Garth. You can buy meat in the grocery store."

"Sure I can, or I can eat out, but nothing's as good as fresh venison you've hunted for yourself," he said. "Besides, I like the thrill of the chase."

"I keep thinking about Bambi and his children."

He reached over the table and squeezed my hand. "You're sweet, Katherine."

"And you're infuriating."

"Maybe so, but I aim to be agreeable, ma'am."

The devilish sparkle in his eyes exasperated me, but I decided to retreat gracefully for the moment. I would never like hunting, and Garth would never be convinced that killing a deer was wrong. To him, it was right. But we were having a civilized dinner tonight. We were on a date. It made sense to concentrate on the ways in which we were alike.

"Maybe we ought to change the subject," Garth said. "You won't find Maple Creek very exciting after Europe."

"We've already had an unsolved murder and a burglary. That's a little too much action for me."

"But aside from the Valentine murder, our last killing was three years ago," he said. "No place in the world is guaranteed safe these days."

He was right. I'd had a similar thought, but here in this traditional country inn, terrorists and tragedy seemed far away. That was an illusion, I knew, with no more substance than the air. Disaster could strike at any time and in any place. Between one footstep and the next, as you took a lethal bite of a caramel apple.

I was aware of a sudden strong desire to connect with another human being, probably not the wisest impulse in the present company.

"Would you like dessert, Katherine?" Garth asked. "They have three kinds of apple pie."

I couldn't get away from the apples. None of us could. "I don't think so."

"More wine?"

I folded my napkin and set it beside the empty glass. "No, thank you; I've had enough."

"Then let's get out of here," he said. "I want to show you the lake before it gets dark."

As GARTH OPENED the door of his black Jeep for me, I noticed the shotgun lying on the back seat as casually as if were a pair of binoculars.

"Are you going hunting?" I asked.

"Not until next month."

"Does that gun have ammunition in it?"

He gave me a serious glance, but his eyes sparkled with good humor. "It's against the law to carry a loaded weapon in a car. Watch your skirt." He closed the door and came around to the driver's side of the Jeep. "Don't you like guns, Katherine?"

"Not much. I've never owned one."

He started the Jeep and turned onto the road. "It's a good idea to be prepared for anything when you're living near to the woods. I taught Taryn to shoot when she was thirteen. We used to go deer hunting together."

Not knowing what to say, I settled for the conventional. "She's lucky to have you."

"We're a family, but she's more interested in boys now than in shooting," he said.

"That sounds normal for a teen-aged girl."

"Taryn is almost grown, all right. She was easier to deal with when she was little."

"Everything changes." We passed a small lake surrounded by cottages and then a gray barn with a cupola and a green weathervane. "This is pretty country, Garth. Nice and woodsy. I haven't driven this way before."

"The lake isn't far. There used to be a turn-off to a lovers' lane on this road, but you don't see kids coming around any more. They must have found a new place. Sometimes I like to drive out here with Tac and just sit and look at the water."

He slowed down and steered the Jeep onto a ribbon of a road with thickly layered leaves on the ground and thin woods on either side. Ahead of us, no more than four yards away, a small deer stood at the edge of the woods watching our approach with dark, wary eyes before fleeing back to the relative safety of the trees.

"You see deer all the time around here," he said. "They're almost tame, but they won't let you get too close to them. The best trail to the lake is beyond that weeping willow."

He brought the Jeep to a halt under the tree, and we walked to the water's edge. Beyond the lake rose a breathtaking stretch of autumn-turning forest. Towering conifers, flaming maples, and yellow-leafed saplings glowed in the fading light, their brilliant colors reflected in the smooth blue surface below.

"This is North Mill Lake," he said. "There used to be a mill around, but it's long gone. Isn't this a beautiful place?" He slipped his arm around my waist, drawing me a fraction of an inch closer to him.

"It sure is. I can see why you like to come here."

"In the winter, it's all black and white and silver. If I drive out here then, I stay inside the Jeep."

"It's getting a little chilly," I said.

When I left the house, I hadn't needed anything but my sweater. Now a wrap would come in handy, something elegant like Cora Valentine's shawl. The light was fading, and the air was thickening into a misty dusk, bringing a slight chill. At this time of year, the darkness came quickly. Between one footstep and the next. I wouldn't like to be here at night, even with this burly woods-wise man at my side.

He pulled me a little closer.

"Shouldn't we go back?" I asked.

"We will. Would you like to come here with me some time soon for a picnic or maybe to go fishing? I have a boat."

"It's October, Garth. The temperature is dropping as we speak."

"That's true, but it's been a warm fall. I heard on the radio this morning that they're looking for that trend to continue. It's good to get away from town even for a little while." He added his final and most convincing argument. "The colors are on their way out."

"Well, all right, but only if the weather cooperates," I said.

"We'll go the next warm afternoon. I'll get you home now."

We walked together over the crackling leaves back to the Jeep. Like the golden days of autumn, I felt that we were moving too fast in this friendship. However agreeable a companion Garth was, I was aware of some mysterious element in his psyche that eluded me.

Although he hadn't given me a direct answer when I'd asked him about the shotgun in the Jeep, I was fairly certain that it was loaded. So that Garth could be prepared for anything, like shooting a fragile young deer out of hunting season or defending himself from a rabid coyote? Or something more serious?

If I reached into the back seat for the gun, giving no thought to safe handling, I could imagine him wresting it out of my hand, warning me to be careful in the harsh voice he used to give orders to Tac. Garth's shotgun was loaded. I was sure of it.

I had a feeling that I had just turned down a dangerous road with killer curves. Add a thick autumn fog to limit vision and begin a descent into the darkness. Like…I looked to my right where the ground sloped down so low that I could touch the tops of the trees, if I could reach them. Like that steep drop, a long way to fall.

Garth held out his hand. "Are you coming, Katherine?"

I took it, and the lion's head ring pressed into my fingers. Why not? I thought.

COMING HOME AFTER DARK was the hard part. Again I'd left the porch light on and the small candle lamp in the parlor as well. Still, I knew that beyond the front door the shadows would be waiting for me, along with intense silence broken only by inexplicable sounds. But I didn't plan to see any ghosts in the halls tonight.

Garth unlocked the door and pushed it open. "Goodnight," I said. "Thanks for dinner and the lake tour. I had a wonderful time." I stepped inside. "So—goodnight."

He handed me my house key. "Remember, Katherine. The first warm afternoon, we have a picnic date. I'll be in touch with you."

He strolled back to the sidewalk, and I closed the door and locked it, listening for the sounds to begin. However, they were all outside tonight, on the other side of the door. Reassured, I turned on more lights and stopped in the kitchen for a drink of water.

There on the counter lay the cameo, its crushed face pale inside the glowing caramel colored oval. How many days had it been since I'd taken it out of the ground? And why couldn't I simply toss it into the trash? I didn't have to decide tonight. Opening the drawer, I dropped the brooch inside with scissors, pens, and unrelated bits and pieces of paper.

*Maybe this time...*

I frowned, wondering where those words had come from. *Maybe this time I'd found a home I could keep?* I'd had that thought before, but it didn't apply to the blue Victorian and myself. Having found a teaching job in Capac and the ideal house, of course I was going to stay here. Never again would I have to pull up stakes at the end of a school year and prepare to move to another country.

*Maybe this time I'd found a man I could keep?*

That wasn't right either because I wasn't thinking of Garth MacKay in that way. Besides I didn't want to get married yet, not for years and years.

*Maybe this time...*

I couldn't imagine why my mind had created the phrase or why it refused to finish the idea. It didn't make sense, but as I turned out the lights on the first floor, I considered a disturbing new theory. What if the thought wasn't mine at all but belonged to one of Garth's hallway ghosts?

Now that was an idea to take to bed, guaranteed to bring on sounds in the dark and a nightmare or two. Instead I would think about bringing home the parlor lamp tomorrow. Perhaps the house only needed a little more light.

# EIGHT

"YOU BOUGHT THE BLUE Queen Anne Victorian over on Walnut?" Anna Lynde brushed a fleck of dust from the top globe of the lamp. "This is uncanny, Katherine. You're living in my old house. Do you think the Fates brought us together for some unfathomable reason?"

"It's an incredible coincidence," I said.

"That's putting it mildly."

"And it's the second one of its kind. Cora Valentine told me she used to live there too."

"Cora and I were roommates, Katherine."

Anna's surprise revelation reinforced the sense of strangeness I associated with my house. I felt as if I'd strayed into the Twilight Zone. To anchor myself to reality, I focused on the down-to-earth details of my surroundings: Family photographs in metal frames, arrangements of dried grasses and seashells, a brass plant stand filled with African violets, and the scent of lime drifting down from a silver bowl on the mantle.

When Garth had told me the history of the blue Victorian, he hadn't mentioned Anna Lynde, but then he'd never claimed to know the names of all the previous tenants, and his knowledge began with 1981.

"Did you own the house at one time?" I asked.

"Cora and I and a third girl, Rosalie Grier, rented it for almost three years. That was in the early seventies. Then after Rosalie left town and I got married, Cora bought the small ranch house where she lived until she was killed."

"You knew Cora for a long time then."

"We went to high school and college together. After we graduated, both of us signed contracts at Maple Creek High School. Rosalie moved in during the second semester. Over the years, Cora and I stayed friends. Now, let's see if this lamp still works. I know Cora tested all the electrical donations, but I want to make sure."

She turned the key switch, and soft light flooded the living room, giving the lush red roses on the milk glass an enchanting glow.

"There. From Scarlett's parlor to yours. It should last for another hundred years," she said. "My aunt used to have a pair of matching teacups. I don't know what became of them."

"I can guess. China is easier to break than lamps."

In Anna's twenty-first century living room with its muted sea and sand color scheme, the lamp looked out of place or rather, misplaced in time. It was too lovely to languish in a garage unused and unappreciated, but that was where it had been stored for years. It belonged in a century-old house steeped in period atmosphere.

"Did you have the lamp when you lived there?" I asked.

"No, I didn't inherit it until several years later."

"I'm glad to hear that," I said. "It would really be uncanny if I took the lamp back to its former home."

"The house was already furnished when we moved in. None of us gave a thought to decorating. We were too busy teaching and having fun. That was such a happy time. We were young, and every experience was new. Thinking back on those days makes me feel ancient and a little sad."

In her crisp aqua suit and pearl pendant, Anna Lynde seemed youthful and vibrant. As she bent her head over the lamp, her dark hair fell forward in a stylish swing. I imagined that she would probably look the same for many more years.

Anna turned off the lamp and unplugged the cord. "I don't like antiques. They remind me of the people I've lost—and now Cora. I try to look to the future. I always have."

She began to wind the cord around the base, slowly and

carefully, as if she was afraid that it would break. "You have a genuine feeling for this lamp, Katherine. I can tell."

"As soon as I saw it, I wanted it," I said. "That doesn't happen very often with me and objects."

I had also bought the two-tiered mahogany table, although it needed refinishing. For both antiques, Anna had charged me only two hundred dollars. She insisted that the price was fair. With Cora gone, plans for renovating the second floor of the Bell House had come to a halt, and the Restoration Fund was in healthy shape. Also, Cora had often spoken of leaving a portion of her estate to her favorite project.

"I still have a hard time believing that Cora is gone," Anna said. "It happened too fast. It was bizarre, and there's something so unfinished about her death."

"Because her killer is still at large?" I asked.

"Yes, but there's something else. That day at the Fair, four people told me that Cora wanted to talk to me about something important. She seemed desperate to find me, but before we got together, she died. Now I'll never know what it was."

"She told me she had to meet a friend. Her last words were, 'I think I see her now.' Then she walked toward the fountain in the park."

"That wasn't me," Anna said. "When I heard the siren, I was talking to Myrold Barren in front of the Blue Lion."

She sank into a plush beige chair. "You were with Cora just before the end. This is getting stranger and stranger."

"Especially when you think of the hundreds of people who were at the Apple Fair that day. Cora was going to tell me a story about my house, but she never had a chance."

"I can't imagine what it was," Anna said. "I'd been in Kalamazoo visiting my daughter, Serena. When I talked to Cora on the phone two days before the Fair, we agreed to meet at the Blue Lion for dinner. She didn't say anything about an important message then."

"Something must have come up."

"Yes, but what and when? As soon as I got home on Saturday morning, I changed clothes and walked into town, but I kept running into people I hadn't seen in ages and catching up on the news. When I learned that Cora was looking for me, I tried to find her, but we kept missing each other. I thought we had all the time in the world, but we didn't."

"Did you tell Lieutenant Gray about this?" I asked.

"We've talked several times. He said that if the police knew what Cora wanted to talk to me about, it might help them solve the case. I'd do anything in my power to bring Cora's killer to justice, but how could I know what she was going to tell me?"

"I can see why you're disturbed," I said.

"I feel certain that mysterious message has something to do with her murder."

"Maybe, but you can't know that." Searching for a way to make Anna feel better about a situation she couldn't change, I said, "It might have been something simple like a change in dinner plans. She couldn't make it or she might have wanted to go to another restaurant."

"I'd like to think that, but I'd only be fooling myself. Well, if I keep wondering about it, I'll drive myself crazy. As soon as the funeral is over, I'm going to visit my younger daughter, Sara. I need to get away for a while."

Anna slipped my check in the drawer of her desk. "I'll help you carry the table out to your car. If you change your mind about the other pieces, let me know. Meg is planning another yard sale in May, but until then they'll stay in the garage."

"I should buy a sofa and chair first," I said. "I hope I'll have my house furnished by the spring. Sometimes I feel a little uncomfortable there because the rooms are so empty."

"I can imagine. A house needs pictures on the wall, cozy places to read, and all your favorite things around you. I hope you'll be as happy as I was in the blue Victorian, Katherine. I've had a wonderful life, but every now and then I think back on those days, especially now that Cora is gone. They were almost magical."

She brushed her hand impatiently across her eyes and opened the front door. "Now you see why I don't like to have antiques around me," she said. "Pretty soon I'll be crying."

THE PARLOR LAMP rested on the top tier of the mahogany table, looking as elegant and evocative as a display in an historical museum. When I turned the key switch on, the light made the empty space warmer and more inviting. The bay window with its view of Walnut was the perfect place for a lamp. When the past tenants arranged their furniture, at least some of them must have realized this too.

Although I knew that this particular lamp had never been in the blue Victorian, the arrangement looked almost familiar to me, like something I'd seen somewhere before.

Of course I had. In countless furniture store windows and magazine pictures, and in *Gone with the Wind,* although I didn't think that Tara had a bay window. I was becoming adept at finding mysterious elements in my everyday surroundings.

I remembered my absurd idea that Cora Valentine's spirit had returned to earth to enlist my aid in avenging her killer. Soon I began to wonder if she was lurking among the shadows in the backyard, where she had once gathered leaves for her classroom.

All right, as long as she didn't come inside. Every day I kept adding to this dark fantasy. It took a mid-week visit from Garth, the ghost buster, and Tac to bring me back down to earth.

Keeping the yard clean was a losing battle as the leaves were falling like rain these days, but I enjoyed the exercise and the feel of the sun-warmed wind on my face. I was outside raking when I heard Tac's familiar barking from a block away and Garth giving his rambunctious pet a booming command to heel.

Clearing the last of the leaves from around the witch ornament, I raked my way to the edge of the lawn to wait for them. The black shepherd strained at the leash, impatient to greet me, or more likely to chase the squirrel that was foraging for acorns in the grass. Garth ordered Tac to heel again and crossed my neighbor's lawn, heading toward me.

He wore a camel vest over a dark red shirt, and everything in his way of dressing and his manner cried out "Lord of the Manor." I couldn't suppress a smile at the thought. Lord of Sky and MacKay Title was more like it. Garth could barely restrain his lunging Belgian shepherd at the other end of the leash.

"Hi, Garth," I said. "Won't your master let you run free, Tac?"

Garth brushed the leaves off Tac's coat. "My dogs never run free unless I'm close enough to grab them. You should wait until they're all down, Katherine, and then have a marathon raking session. That's what I do. Do you need any help?"

I'd gone over the entire front lawn, although one would never know it. Garth's advice to rake the leaves all at once made sense. I was going to take it. "Thanks, but I think I'm done for the day. Maybe you can join me for that fall's end marathon."

"Just say the word." He let Tac lead him to the porch and sat down in the manner of one who is a frequent and familiar visitor. "I have the forecast for the rest of the week," he said. "Saturday it's going to be in the seventies. That's good picnic weather."

I'd heard the prediction too and had been anticipating his invitation. "I'm sorry, Garth, I can't do it that day. Nell Farmer is having a little gathering for me to meet my neighbors."

"Day or night?" he asked. "Most parties take place after dark."

"I'm not sure. Nell didn't mention the time, but I said I'd help her get the food together. You'll probably be invited. You live in the neighborhood, don't you?"

He remained silent for a minute, as if considering what to say. "My business is on Main Street, not my house."

"But you've been walking Tac on my street."

"I bring my dog to work every day," he said with a slanted

smile. "Anyway, even if I lived next door to you, Nell Farmer wouldn't be likely to invite me to a party. She doesn't like me."

"Why not?" I asked.

"She thinks I took advantage of her sister. It happened a long time ago."

"And did you?"

"Maybe. Nell says so."

I waited, and when he didn't say anything else, I did. "Aren't you going to tell me about it?"

"No, ma'am. I don't gossip," he said. "If you really want to know, ask Ms. Farmer. She loves to talk. She'll give you all the gory details."

I had noticed Nell's tendency to fill in the outlines of her stories with bright primary colors. She would be a good source of information as well as a friend. "I may do that, but I'd like to hear both versions," I said.

"You would, would you? Maybe I'll tell you some time if you're good." As a wind gust whipped around the maple tree, bringing more leaves down, he said, "That tree is going to be bare before long. Give it another week, sooner if it rains. I think we've already passed the peak color season."

I easily saw through Garth's lament for a vanishing autumn. I was sure that he meant me to.

"What will the weather be like on Sunday?" I asked.

"Nice. More of the same."

"Could we go on Sunday then—if you're not busy, that is."

"I am, but I'll find time for a picnic. Do you want to go out on the boat too?"

About that I didn't have to think. "I'd rather stay on dry land."

"It's a date then. I'll bring the food."

"What can I contribute?" I asked.

"Just yourself." There was that crooked smile again. I was beginning to anticipate when it would appear.

"I'll pick you up on Sunday then, around noon," he said. "Come on, Tac. We'll head on back and let the lady burn her leaves."

I watched them walk down Walnut, back the way they'd come, and then carried the rake to the tool shed. Belatedly I reminded myself of my intention to move slowly with Garth. I had already agreed to the picnic though, and this wasn't exactly a date, just a casual coming together in broad daylight to view the last of the fall color over sandwiches and sodas. Or maybe Garth would provide a more sumptuous lunch with wine.

I was getting as adept at deluding myself as I was in finding mysteries. I had to admit that Garth's allusion to a relationship with Nell's sister had piqued my curiosity. If I did it discreetly, I could ask Nell what she knew about Garth's background without giving her the impression that I was interested in him.

Finding Cora Valentine's killer was Lieutenant Gray's job, and I had no immediate hope of understanding the strange effect the blue Victorian had on me. But I could solve the mystery of Garth MacKay with a few well-placed questions put to Nell Farmer. Fortunately I would have the opportunity to do it on Friday.

# NINE

NELL HELD THE CARVING KNIFE over the baked ham and turned around to face me. "Garth MacKay is a good man to stay away from Katherine. Where did you meet him?"

"At the Apple Fair," I said. "Around. He walks his dog on our street."

"That black beast. I've seen him." The alarm and concern in her voice surprised me.

"Are you referring to Garth or Tac now?"

"His dog's name is Tac? Everything about that man is strange, but I meant the dog."

She began to slice the ham. My counter had all but disappeared under rye bread, lettuce leaves, and jars of mustard and Miracle Whip. I had suggested keeping the ham and bread separate and letting people help themselves, but Nell wanted to arrange sandwiches on a tray in the shape of a wreath.

"I ordered pizzas and a bucket of fried chicken for six o'clock delivery," she said. "I hope we'll have enough to eat."

"That should be plenty. What's wrong with Garth MacKay?" I asked.

"I suppose I shouldn't say anything, but…"

She was going to. I waited, wondering if Nell was about to denounce Garth as the town outcast or a criminal.

"He used to belong to the Michigan Militia," she said. "For all I know, he still does."

"I thought they disbanded."

"Don't believe it. I'm not saying for sure that Garth is a member, only that he used to be. It's no secret. I saw it with my own eyes. We have a lot of Militiamen living around here."

Nell's revelation made sense. I remembered the shotgun in the back seat of Garth's Jeep and his evasive answer when I'd asked him if it was loaded. "I'm not a flag waver, ma'am. Never have been." He'd said that the first day we met. Most telling of all was the air of mystery that surrounded him. I didn't doubt Nell's information, as it fit the impression I'd been forming of Garth all along, but I was curious.

"What did you see, Nell?" I asked.

"When I first moved to Maple Creek, I wasn't familiar with this part of Michigan. One day I took a wrong turn on my way home. The next thing I knew I drove right into a Militia training session. I never saw so many guns in my life, and I can assure you the men didn't make me feel very welcome."

"What happened?" I asked.

"Oddly enough, Garth MacKay came to my rescue. Not that I was in any real danger, but I was frightened. I didn't know what I'd wandered into. Garth said something like, 'I know this lady. She's okay,' and then he told me how to find the nearest road to Maple Creek."

"Aside from the company he keeps, that doesn't explain why you think he's dangerous," I said. "It sounds like he was just being friendly and helpful."

"No matter. Take it from me. That man is trouble." She set the knife aside and handed me the plate of ham. "This is enough to get us started."

"Maybe it's his dark beard," I said.

"You could be right, but a beard makes a man look distinguished—usually."

"Did you ever go out with him?" I asked.

"I was married when I met Garth, but I wouldn't have dated him in any case. He's not my type. I wouldn't say he's your type either."

"So obviously you wouldn't go out with him now?"

"Not now. Not ever. Besides, I've had three failed marriages. A fourth one would be an embarrassment. I'm going to live alone from now on. For a little while anyway."

Apparently Nell wasn't going to volunteer any more information about Garth or his ties to the Michigan Militia. I was the one who had to keep the conversation going if I wanted an answer to my question about Garth and Nell's sister. "Do you know anybody who dated him?" I asked.

From Nell's amused expression, I realized I was giving her the impression that my interest in Garth's romantic past was personal.

"I don't keep up with Garth MacKay's love life, but my younger sister used to go out with him," she said. "I didn't approve of him then and I still don't. He's too rough around the edges. Who knows what else he's involved in?"

"That's all?"

"Most of it." Nell slapped a thick slice of ham down on a rye bread end. "This one's for me. I'm starving."

So there was more. "But your sister liked him," I said.

"All right. Linda was crazy about Garth MacKay. For a few scary days one summer, she thought she was pregnant, but she wasn't. Thank heavens. She stopped seeing Garth after that. She's married to a wonderful man now. They have three children."

"So—that's it?"

"All of it. Why all these questions, Katherine? I hope you're not falling for him."

"Not exactly, but we have a picnic date tomorrow at North Mill Lake."

"Good grief! That's no place to be with a man like Garth MacKay—I'm kidding, Katherine. Don't worry. You'll probably be safe enough. Just don't go near the water. This ham bone will make good pea soup. Do you want to save it?"

"That's a good idea." With a package of split peas, carrots, celery, an onion, and a little water, I would have dinners for a week, but I didn't want to talk about soup making.

"Garth told me he raised his younger sister by himself," I said.

"Yes, Taryn. I guess she turned out okay."

Given Nell's opinion of Garth, perhaps I should consider

myself forewarned. But I liked him, which didn't mean I was falling for him. Forewarned was forearmed. A Militiaman would understand that. And what if Nell had an ulterior motive for discouraging my interest in Garth?

Nell said, "Now if you're looking for a man of substance, I advise you to cast your eye on Myrold Barren. He's coming to the party tonight. Or, if you want drop dead gorgeous, there's Lieutenant Dalton Gray, but you'll have to stand in a long line. I didn't invite Dalton, by the way. I don't know him that well yet. Those are the only two eligible bachelors in town. In Maple Creek we have quality but not quantity."

"You can't possibly know the marital status of every man in town," I said.

She laughed. "Only the illustrious two."

"Well, I don't want to get involved with any man just now, especially Myrold Barren. He was so rude to me the first time I saw him. He said he was going to run over that stray collie if I didn't keep her leashed."

"That doesn't sound like Myrold," Nell said. "He tries to make a good impression on people."

"At the funeral parlor you said something about Cora being an obstacle in Myrold Barren's way. What were you going to tell me about him?"

She joined me at the counter, and I began to transfer ham to rye while she spread mustard on the bread. "That's an interesting story. In a way, Cora Valentine and Myrold Barren weren't so far apart in what they wanted for Maple Creek, but circumstances made them enemies. Have you ever heard of neo-traditionalism?"

"Bringing back old time atmosphere to new development?"

"That's right. Garages are in the back out of sight, porches in front. Turn of the century style houses built close to one another and the street. Hidden driveways and private space. It's a blend of old architectural details and modern features. Myrold Barren is a developer, and Stone Mill Village is his new project. He'd like to see it finished in six years."

"It sounds like a beautiful place," I said.

"It is. I went through one of his model manor houses last summer. Not that I'd ever be able to afford it, but I can dream."

"Did Cora oppose the project?"

"Not at all, but she owned a prime parcel of land that Myrold wanted, and she refused to part with it. That property was part of her inheritance. She was determined to leave it in its natural state, even if the Stone Mill Village came right up to her boundary line. I'm quoting her, loosely. Myrold couldn't make Cora change her mind, no matter how much money he offered her or what arguments he used. Toward the end, they weren't speaking to each other. Meg Valentine says she intends to honor Cora's wishes."

"Do you think Myrold Barren had a motive to kill Cora?"

"Maybe, but I'm sure he wouldn't go that far. Poisoning a woman isn't Myrold's style. He may be blustery and self-centered, but he isn't insane. You'll see for yourself tonight. There." She surveyed the finished sandwiches. "Now to make the wreath."

"Myrold Barren doesn't sound like the man you described a few minutes ago as illustrious," I said. "He seems more like a ruthless developer."

"You're right, but he's a better marriage prospect than Garth MacKay. Myrold is a widower with two teen-aged sons and plenty of money. He plans to move into one of the manor houses when it's finished."

I wrapped the ham bone in aluminum foil and replaced the lids on the jars. Myrold Barren didn't interest me, either as a murder suspect or a potential husband. "That's fascinating," I said. "Now what can you tell me about Lieutenant Gray?"

"Not much. He's sinfully handsome, and he's new in town. He's only been on the Force since last January."

She began to set the sandwiches on the tray in a circular pattern. "I brought a few yards of plaid ribbon to make a bow," she said. "Do you have any scissors?"

"In that top drawer."

"I found them… Oh, what a beautiful cameo!" She lifted the brooch up to the light. "It looks like you mashed it in the blender."

I told her the story of the cameo but not about the hold it had taken on my imagination. "I'm trying to decide what to do with it."

She turned the cameo over and moved the loose pin back and forth. "It doesn't look like it can be repaired. Too bad. You never know what will turn up when you start digging in your backyard. Did you read about the man who discovered human bones when he was building a barn? It turned out that his land was once an Indian burial ground."

"That sounds like the plot of a horror movie," I said.

"I wonder if disturbing a graveyard brought him bad luck."

"I suppose you could find out. Did this happen recently?"

"Seven or eight years ago." Nell cut a length of ribbon and began to make her bow, and I returned the cameo and scissors to the drawer.

I wished I knew more about the man who lived on top of a cemetery. Not facts but feelings and what happened after. Had he walked through his house, haunted by thoughts of the dead? Or did he call the local paper, enjoy a few days of publicity, and finish building the barn?

I said, "I'm not superstitious, but I hope I don't find bones the next time I dig a hole. The last thing I need is an Indian curse."

THE HIGH REDWOOD FENCE that enclosed Nell's backyard provided a lovely and private outdoor setting for a party. On a large picnic table she had set up a buffet. Guests could either sit outside in the lawn chairs, enjoying the warmth until dark, or gather on the spacious back porch.

I sat in a chair, eating a sandwich and listening to silver-haired Eleanor Winters describe the Neighborhood Watch that had been formed after Cora Valentine's murder.

"Even though her killer must have come from some other

place," she said. "No one in Maple Creek could possibly have done such a terrible thing."

"I hope not," I said.

"You've moved to a safe, old-fashioned small town, Katherine. People know their neighbors and look out for one another. Don't they, Arthur?"

Arthur Winters mumbled his agreement and turned back to his pizza.

A hundred Neighborhood Watches couldn't have saved Cora Valentine. Nobody had warned her not to eat that apple. No one could know that death walked with her as she made her way to the fountain in the park.

Nell came up behind me, leading the newly arrived Mr. Raycraft by the hand. He wore a blue striped dress shirt with a dark tie, again too formally dressed for the occasion. He didn't have his cane tonight, and his nod was a few degrees above freezing. That man was the least congenial person I had ever met.

"I've seen this young lady before," he said. "The other day when you were walking your dog, Ms. Kale."

"Please call me, Katherine. The collie isn't my dog. She's just been following me."

I was going to tell him how much I admired his house when he said, "Welcome to the neighborhood, Katherine. You'll like it here. If you ladies will excuse me, I have to speak to Alarice."

He walked away, moving with surprising agility for a man who sometimes used a cane. A chestnut-haired woman in a white blouse and long navy blue skirt, Alarice Crandall was the first person Nell had introduced me to. Alarice had told me that she owned one of the most unique houses on Walnut, assembled by the original owner from a Sears' kit in 1906. When I expressed an interest in its floor plan, she invited me to come over for a tour some Saturday afternoon or Sunday, as she taught piano lessons in her home at other times.

Afterward, when we were in the kitchen together, Nell

mentioned that Alarice and Cora had once been friends but they'd had a falling out years ago over some matter neither one of them ever talked about.

Now Nell said, "Mr. Raycraft can be abrupt. He's that way with everybody. I'll see if the biscuits are done and bring the rest of the chicken out now."

With Nell tending to her buffet and Eleanor Winters talking quietly to her husband, I finished my sandwich and watched Mr. Raycraft and Alarice who were also engrossed in a private conversation. I imagined that they belonged to the same generation, and they looked comfortable together. His manner with her appeared to be open and cordial.

Of the twenty people who had accepted Nell's invitation, Myrold Barren and Mr. Raycraft were already familiar to me, and I felt as if I knew Eleanor Winters, having heard her life story in capsule form. I'd remember Alarice because of her Sears' kit house and the story about her feud with Cora.

As for the rest of the guests, their faces seemed to blur together on a vast neutral canvas. I looked around Nell's yard and gathered a handful of unrelated details from my memory. Linda, the slender blonde in the cream-colored sweater and camel pants, lived in the brick ranch house behind the blue Victorian. She had come to the party with her boyfriend, Jason, who was casually attired in blue jeans and a brown shirt. They sat at the other end of the table close together, holding hands.

Eleanor Winters and her husband owned the large yellow-sided house across the street from me. From Eleanor I learned that my neighbors on both sides were away on extended vacations. Kenneth and Karessa Redmond, who were a generation younger than the Winters, lived next door to Nell. Irene, the attractive brunette in the green dress who had been flirting with Myrold Barren, worked with Nell at St. Andrew's. The woman who had brought the cocoa cake had lived on Walnut since 1965. I couldn't remember her name.

Myrold Barren came down from the porch and began to

circulate through the small crowd. His strident voice drowned out all other sound. Hale and hearty, Henry VIII look-alike, he wore a deep purple sweater. A royal color. He came to a stop at Irene's side, and for the next several minutes they engaged in a lively, flirtatious banter. Then Irene gave Myrold a quick kiss on the cheek and went inside.

Myrold took a beer from the cooler and walked toward me, favoring me with a regal smile. "The guest of honor shouldn't be sitting alone," he said. "You look familiar, Katherine. I've been trying to remember where we met."

I gave him one of my most gracious smiles. "We didn't meet formally, Mr. Barren. You shouted at me from your car on the day of the Apple Fair. The day you almost ran down a stray dog."

"Oh—yes. That day." His momentary flush of embarrassment disappeared in a ready, convivial smile. "I apologize. I don't usually threaten strangers or kill dogs. I'd just had a run-in with an ornery female and took it out on you and your little collie."

"She isn't mine. I saw a dog in need and tried to save her."

He practically radiated good humor. "Let me apologize again for making such a deplorable first impression. It was unforgivable. Now, tell me, Katherine. Why did you come to Maple Creek? I'm always interested in where people move and why."

"I wanted to live near my school, and Maple Creek is a pretty little town," I said.

Myrold pulled up a lawn chair and sat down beside me. "You won't get an argument from me," he said. "I was born here. Everybody is moving northward these days. This is one area where you can still buy land for a reasonable price."

"I'll keep that in mind."

"As an investment, I mean. Once the building boom takes hold, this land is going to be worth ten times more than you'd pay for it today."

He pulled a card out of his pocket and handed it to me. "If

you have any friends who are in the market for a new house, tell them to drive out to Stone Mill Village. The first condos will be completed by the spring. You come too," he said. "I'll give you a personal tour."

My dress didn't have a pocket, and my purse was inside the house. I turned the card around in my hands twice, wondering what to do with it. "I just bought a house," I said.

"So Nell tells me. It's the blue Queen Anne down the street. Keep the card anyway. In a year or two you may decide that you'd rather have something more modern. Anyway, you're welcome to tour the Village. It's going to be the first one like it in this part of the state."

Apparently Myrold's inability to acquire Cora Valentine's acreage hadn't made a dent in his plan. "I'll consider myself invited," I said.

"Myrold?"

Irene was back with two pieces of cocoa cake and a smile that generated enough warmth to melt the icing. "Am I interrupting something?" she asked.

I summoned a polite smile. "No. That cake looks delicious. I think I'll try some."

Myrold reached for one of the plates. "Nice talking to you, Katherine. Glad we cleared up that misunderstanding about the dog."

"Yes," I said, and I guessed that we had, with an apology for a bad day and no lasting harm done.

I had been sitting in one place too long, and the cake did look good. But what I wanted was to talk to people, meticulously matching outfit with name, and name with residence. I hoped to forge an acquaintance with every person who had come to Nell's party to welcome me tonight. Perhaps in time they would become my friends.

LONG SHADOWS fell across the yard, and soon the lanterns Nell had strung across her porch glowed like miniature beacons in the dusk. In the mild breeze, the wind chimes began to stir. The month was October, after all, a time of fleeting warmth and early darkness. The autumnal chill couldn't be far behind.

The party had wound down slowly, with people leaving in pairs or small groups until only the Winters and the Redmonds were left outside, happily discussing their planned cruise to Alaska. I walked past the remnants of the buffet. All that remained of Nell's sandwich wreath was the ribbon. Cake, pizza, chicken, and biscuits had also vanished, leaving only crumbs and a stray slice of pepperoni to scent the air.

Myrold's voice and laughter drifted out of the house. I found him in the kitchen deep in conversation with Nell.

"I think I'll head on home, Nell," I said. Thanks so much for arranging this party. Everyone made me feel welcome tonight."

She hugged me. "We're glad to have you in our town, Katherine."

"I'll see you safe to your front door, Katherine," Myrold said.

I reached for my purse. "It's just down the street. I'll be fine."

"I won't hear of you walking home alone in the dark. After what happened to Cora, we can't be too careful with our newest resident."

His dictatorial tone rankled. "I thought the consensus was that Cora's killer came from out of town."

"We can't know that for sure. If the mad poisoner is lurking in some shadow, I'll take care of him." Myrold shook his large fist.

"Go along with Myrold," Nell said. "I'll feel better knowing you're in good hands."

I picked up my purse. "Really it isn't necessary. The streetlights are on, and if this poisoner appears, I'll scream. We're close enough so that you'll hear me."

In the brief awkward silence that followed, I realized how ungracious I sounded. Myrold would think that I hadn't forgiven him for the incident with the collie, which wasn't true. "All right," I said. "It'll be nice to have an escort."

"Good. That's settled then." He laid his heavy arm across

my shoulder. "Thanks for including me, Nell. We'll get together soon. All ready, Katherine?"

I struggled to keep my manner and tone of voice agreeable. "Whenever you are."

At that moment I felt as if a malevolent force were sweeping me along into the center of a whirlwind. What a strange thought to be having after a pleasant evening. It had everything to do with the man who had cleverly maneuvered his way into a place at my side. Somehow and as soon as possible, I was going to find out why.

# TEN

LAMPLIGHT STREAMED OUT over the flagstone walk, cutting through the blackness like a laser beam. On either side of the blue Victorian, the houses were dark, but across the street, lights burned in the Winters' first story windows.

Following the trail of brightness, I walked up to the porch with Myrold Barren close behind me. I didn't want him to come any farther and didn't intend to give him an opportunity to invite himself in.

"Thanks for the escort, Myrold," I said. "Goodnight."

"You're welcome, Katherine. You know, you're living in a pretty isolated location here."

I glanced back at the Winters' lights. "I don't think so. I'm in the middle of the block with houses all around me."

"The lots are far apart. At night you might as well be alone in the middle of a forest."

I fumbled in my purse for my key while Myrold leaned against a porch post, as Garth often did on his visits.

"Now you're trying to scare me," I said. "Main Street is an eight-minute walk away. What about the Neighborhood Watch?"

Before answering, he surveyed the empty street and deserted sidewalk. "I don't think they're on duty tonight. In Stone Mill Village, people live close to one another and still have their own private space. When you're alone, being part of a planned community is a real advantage."

So here was the underlying reason for Myrold's insistence on accompanying me to my doorstep. He wanted to make another pitch for his pet project. I rushed to the defense of my choice.

"I like places that are genuinely old, not just built to look that way," I said.

"You have a point." He tapped the spindle work ornamentation on the railing. "Solid wood—over a century old. The downside is that for years all those people have been making grooves in the floors, painting over hinges until the doors don't fit properly, and wearing out the appliances. In my units everything is brand new, state of the art, and the walls are freshly painted."

The loop of my key chain was wound around my brush. I freed it and quickly unlocked the door. I didn't want to listen to a sales talk at this time of night, or any time for that matter.

"The last owners renovated the house completely and painted inside and out. So far I haven't found anything broken," I said.

"These old houses look good from the outside, but sometimes their floor plans are inconvenient, and the rooms are small and cramped."

That sounded like the prelude to a request to come inside. "That's not the case here," I said. "The last owners knocked down a wall to make a master bedroom out of two, and the other rooms seem large enough to me."

In only a few minutes the air on the porch had turned chilly. I left my hand on the doorknob, opening it a crack, and said again, "Goodnight, Myrold. Thanks again."

"Promise me you'll drive out and have a look at the Village anyway," he said. "You might like what you see."

"I'll do that." I added a smile, and as soon as he turned around, stepped inside and closed the door. I had no intentions of touring Stone Mill Village. Let Myrold Barren keep his precious planned community. Living in the blue Victorian gave me a sense of history and belonging. I was the last in a parade of unknown people who had called this house their home, and that was important to me.

Not all of the former residents were unknown, though. Anna Lynde and Cora Valentine had once lived here with a girl named Rosalie Grier, and the house was over seventy years old then.

As I turned on the upstairs light, I wondered what it would be like to be the original owner of one of Myrold Barren's units. Everything from the crown molding on the walls to the floors would be brand new. No faucets would drip, and knobs would stay attached to cabinets. If by chance a flaw appeared in the structure, the builder would take care of it promptly, especially since I knew him and he seemed sincere enough.

But no builder could furnish a Stone Mill Village unit with atmosphere and ghostly vibes. Wishing I had thought to say that to Myrold, I shut the door of the linen closet and turned on the hall light.

AN HOUR LATER, as I lay in bed, reviewing the party and anticipating tomorrow's picnic with Garth MacKay, a thought dropped into my mind with the soft thud of a stone falling on frozen ground. When I'd walked past the linen closet, the door had been partially open, about four inches. I hadn't left it that way.

Or had I? I couldn't remember. I'd been in a hurry. Puzzled, I replayed the hour before I left for the party. I saw myself taking a washcloth and towel out of the linen closet and then closing it. After countless coats of paint, the door never stayed shut. Still, it couldn't have swung four inches forward by itself.

I didn't think the ghost of Cora Valentine had helped herself to a towel as she passed by on a stroll through her previous house. Once the image formed, however, I couldn't get rid of it, and it made me feel uneasy.

I almost got out of bed to see whether the door had opened again. Instead I willed my body to relax and tried to fall asleep. At this late hour, investigating restless closets was a self-defeating activity. Unlike the previous owners, I wouldn't be driven out of my house by a feeling. I could deal with anything in the sunlight, and the next time I went to the hardware store, I'd buy a supply of ghost-proof magnetic latches.

But in the morning, I discovered that my blue and white bath towels were out of their alternating color arrangement. Three blue towels lay together on top of the stack. Yesterday I'd been in a hurry to put the laundry away, my mind on making sandwiches, the party, and Garth's association with the Michigan Militia, rather than on what I was doing. So had I failed to separate the towels?

Possibly. But who could remember such a trivial matter? I didn't need to find a new mystery in the linen closet. Ghosts didn't use towels and certainly wouldn't care about coordinating colors.

I wondered if I was manufacturing excuses for the inexplicable, but I didn't have time to worry about it now. I was going to be late when Garth came to pick me up if I kept puzzling over every mysterious happening or deviation from the norm.

Like the bone. When I went outside to water the chrysanthemums, I saw it lying on the grass, picked clean and dull gray, except where clumps of earth clung to its surface.

Recalling Nell's graveyard story gave me a momentary start, but I soon realized that this unappetizing object was an old soup bone that had been buried for a long time. That pesky stray collie must have dug it out of the earth, leaving a deep depression in my flowerbed.

I was certain that she'd be back for her treasure. The next time she appeared, I was going to lure her onto the back porch and from there into the kitchen. For the first time in years, I felt a strong need to share my home with a dog.

"I'M GOING TO CALL her Vicky," I said.

Garth spread a red and green plaid blanket on the ground while I opened the picnic basket. "That's a nice name, Katherine. Any special reason?"

"When I was a little girl, a brown collie used to wander into our yard to visit me. Her name was Vicky. I have a picture of her with me and my Dad."

"Do you think she's going to let you adopt her?" he asked.

"We'll see. Food is a powerful lure…" I broke off as I spied the contents of Garth's old picnic basket. He had packed a veritable feast of fried chicken, strawberries, chocolate angel food cake covered in plastic wrap, and a bottle of white wine. I'd been expecting beef and cheese on rye with soft drinks and maybe a side of potato chips. I suspected that Garth had more than one surprise in his repertoire.

"Did this elegant lunch come from the Blue Lion?" I asked.

"No, Taryn dreamed up the menu and packed the basket. She loves to cook. When I told her where I was going, she insisted on making the lunch."

"You have a remarkable sister," I said. "I've never had chocolate angel food cake."

"Taryn found the recipe in one of our Grandma's old cookbooks."

"I'd like to meet Taryn some day," I said. "I've seen her twice now, once with you and once at the cider mill stand, but she doesn't know me."

I paused, realizing that I shouldn't have reminded Garth of his sister's inadvertent part in the tragedy. He didn't seem to mind.

"Taryn isn't working at the mill any more," he said. "After the poisoning scare, the owners laid off their part time help. So many people lost their appetite for apples that it brought the sales way down. That's why she has a little extra time on her hands."

"That's too bad," I said. "I hope things turn around for them."

"So do I, but it'll be too late to save the season."

"There's always next year."

I unwrapped the paper plates and served the chicken, while Garth uncorked the wine and poured it into two large plastic cups.

"I'm sorry they're not crystal flutes," he said. Handing one to me, he raised his cup and said, "To another fall, Katherine."

I added, "As beautiful as this one."

I couldn't imagine a more ideal setting for a private picnic. The trees that shadowed the lake burned the sky and the landscape with rich fire colors, and the water was as still and smooth as blue stained grass.

We had North Mill Lake to ourselves this afternoon. At any moment, I expected someone to come along with a camera or picnic basket, but that didn't happen. I couldn't remember when I'd ever been more at ease with a man. Then, lulled by the spell of water, woods, and leaves, I said the one thing that I should have kept to myself until Garth and I knew each other better. "Nell tells me that you belong to the Michigan Militia."

Instantly I regretted my impulsive words, but Garth's expression didn't reveal surprise or cloud over with anger. He took another piece of chicken and said, "Nell is right. I do."

In the silence that followed, I shifted uneasily on the blanket. The rustle of leaves underneath it seemed unusually loud. I felt as if I had broken some unspoken code. Definitely I'd violated good sense and courtesy. What could I do now? Apologize for my lack of discretion? Tell Garth about my new interest in Militia activities?

"I remember once you said you weren't a flag waver," I said.

I suspected that I'd blundered again. I'd better keep quiet and let Garth lead the conversation. Or maybe ask him about fishing or Taryn. I poured the last of the wine, dividing it between the two of us. When I looked up, Garth was smiling, that slanted smile that told me I hadn't offended him at all.

"That's true about the flag, Katherine, but it doesn't have anything to do with the Militia," he said. "I love my country. It's the government I don't like—and their symbols and laws."

"I always assume that if you live in America, you accept the government," I said.

"Speaking only for myself, I don't agree, but I'm not breaking any laws now. Did you notice my license plate? I have one."

"I did notice." And I'd wondered about it. I knew that Militiamen didn't see the need for them. Garth had picked me up in an old blue Buick with a bent and weathered plate that looked legitimate. I hadn't noticed whether or not he had one on the Jeep.

He was still smiling, apparently enjoying himself immensely. The teasing gleam in his blue-green eyes was brighter than the stones in his lion's head ring.

"Do you still keep a loaded shotgun in the back seat?" I asked.

"The last time I looked, it was in the trunk. I didn't think I'd need it today."

"You won't."

"When I have to, I can protect what belongs to me," he said. "I don't need anyone else to do it for me. Not the Army, not the police. No one."

He might as well have said, 'That's the way I am. Even if you don't understand, accept it.'

"That's good to know," I said.

"I could protect you, too, Katherine, the next time that ghost comes around."

"I have no ghosts bothering me." Or, none that I cared to talk about at the moment.

I intended to avoid discussing the reality of Garth's ties to the Militia until I knew how I felt about this newly revealed side of him, and supernatural talk was strictly off limits. We needed a change of topic, something less controversial.

"Do you think Cora Valentine's killer is going to strike again?" I asked.

"Some folks think so, around Halloween, unless he was only out to get Cora Valentine."

Why Halloween? I wondered. Then I remembered. Razor blades in apples, drugged candy—all the horrors that had killed a child's traditional night to wear costumes and have fun. Halloween was only days away.

"Maybe he just wanted to kill once for the thrill of it or to see if he could get away with it," I said. "Besides, wasn't Cora well loved in Maple Creek?"

"So you'd think, but she had her enemies like everybody else."

With that sweeping statement, he handed me the saltshaker.

"I don't think I have any enemies, Garth," I said.

"You might have one you don't know about somewhere. Maybe not. You're pretty nice. Cora was always meddling in other people's business. A few years ago she told me that I was too lenient with Taryn. I didn't like that very much."

"Were you?" I asked.

He stared across the water at the leaves trembling in the lightest of breezes.

"I didn't think so at first, but then I gave the idea some consideration and came to the conclusion that she was probably right. I set up some ground rules, and Taryn followed them sometimes. Cora became a mentor to her. After a while, she let Taryn help out at the Bell House. They used to read a book a week and then talk about it. I have to say that Cora was good for my sister."

That was the strangest and most touching tribute I'd ever heard. I hoped that wherever she was, Cora knew how Garth felt about her.

"A man who would put poison in an apple someone was going to eat would have to be out of his mind," he added.

"Or a woman.

"Do you think a woman could have killed Cora?" he asked.

"It's possible. Do you remember the wicked queen in *Snow White?* 'She made a poisonous apple. It was beautiful to look upon, so that anyone who should see it must long for it, but whoever ate even a little bit of it must die.'"

I couldn't decide whether I was seeing admiration in Garth's eyes or amazement.

"I used to read *Snow White* to Taryn when she was a little girl, but I couldn't quote from it," he said.

"I'm an English teacher, remember. My students were too old for fairy tales, but sometimes I used a Grimms' story or a fable in writing assignments."

"I don't think Cora knew any wicked queens, but someone may have had it in for her."

"Someone like Myrold Barren?" I asked.

"Everybody knew there was no love lost between those two. Their feud went way back, and it was about more than Cora's land. But Barren would have nothing to gain by killing her. With Cora alive, he could always try to get her to change her mind about selling him that land or trick her."

"Do you know what the feud was about?" I asked.

"It began when she kept him from graduating with his class. He had to go to night school."

"But that was a long time ago. He's so successful now."

"Some things you don't forget," Garth said. "Over the years, plenty of people tangled with Cora, more after she retired and got involved in civic affairs. Whatever she did, she still thought she was running a classroom. But I'd rather talk about you than Cora Valentine. Tell me about your travels. When you were working overseas, did you get to see the British Isles?"

Already my month's vacation in England before leaving for home seemed far away in time as well as space, but I willingly took out my memories of castles, London, Shakespeare, and the Thames and shared them with him.

"I'm glad I had those years, but I learned an old lesson," I said. "There's no place like America."

"No place like home. Now, that's something we have in common, Katherine."

He peered into the basket. "We ate all the chicken. Let's try Taryn's cake and then we'll do whatever you like. Walk around to the other side of the lake or go for a drive in the country."

A leaf drifted down onto the blanket and was lost in the red squares of the plaid. Before long, the colors of the countryside would fade to black and white, and, with luck, Cora's killer would be behind bars. In the meantime what was I doing on a picnic in a secluded romantic place with a man who flaunted the law of the country by carrying a loaded gun in his car?

Garth MacKay had a whole other side. He had read fairy tales to his younger sister and possessed an undeniable charm. In spite of myself I liked him. The realization didn't cheer me. Associating with Garth MacKay could be as dangerous as living in a town where a demented killer might even now be preparing for his second strike.

But was I going to stop seeing him? I didn't think so.

# ELEVEN

I STOOD IN THE MIDDLE OF the upstairs hall, listening to the rain falling against the old windows and trying to figure out what was different about the house tonight.

It wasn't mysterious noises. No floorboards creaked under ghostly steps, and no unseen creature scratched at the attic boards above me. All I heard was my own breathing and the splattering of raindrops on glass, but the feeling that someone was in the house with me was too strong to ignore.

Something hinted at an alien presence that existed just beyond my range of perception. It might be a faint scent of cologne, some subtle alteration in my surroundings, or a sliver of a shadow. I couldn't decide.

Maybe someone had broken into in the house while I'd been out with Garth. An invasion by a flesh and blood intruder made more sense than my imagination or the spirits I persisted in thinking about.

Still, I glanced at the door of the linen closet to make sure that it hadn't swung open the moment I'd looked away. It was as I had left it, closed but not completely.

The intruder would have been able to wander through my house at his leisure for I had been gone most of the day. After our picnic, Garth had taken me on a long drive through the countryside and then to a country inn for a late dinner. To my surprise, we found so much to talk about that we scarcely noticed time passing.

We headed back to Maple Creek, driving through darkness and rain, and said goodnight in the vestibule, both of us dripping with water after our mad dash from the car to the house.

He kissed me in the light of the parlor lamp, and nothing seemed the least bit unusual until he left.

If someone was hiding in the house when we came home, he would have heard Garth's voice and waited silently for him to leave, perhaps assuming that a woman alone would be easier to slip past or subdue. He was going to find out that he was wrong—if he existed.

Cautiously I opened the door to the spare bedroom and turned on the light. The room was a vast expanse of ivory walls and bare windows. On an impulse, I opened the closet and looked up. The wood square that led to the attic was in place, and the space above was silent.

In the bathroom I found the same clutter I'd left behind this morning. My nightgown trailed down from a hook in a cloud of white cotton, and a scarf hung over the bathtub rod. Reassured, I moved on to my bedroom. The quilt covered the bed in smooth folds, but so many brushes, makeup, and perfume bottles crowded my dressing table that I couldn't possibly tell if anything had been disturbed.

Next I opened my jewelry box. Except for the gold bracelets that I had bought in Italy, I had nothing expensive to tempt a thief, nothing of any value except to me. Everything appeared to be here. Since I'd taken my purse with me, the little cash I kept on hand and my credit cards were safe.

Who would break into a house to steal a bottle of French perfume or a compact? When he saw how little I had to take, an enterprising burglar would have abandoned his search, in which case I didn't have anything to worry about.

The French doors that led to the balcony were locked. With no evidence to support it, the theory of the burglar began to fade, along with the feeling that I wasn't alone in the house. The image of myself prowling through empty rooms looking for a person who didn't exist was almost amusing.

Still, I made a systematic search of the rest of the upstairs and then moved slowly through the first floor, turning on lights as I passed by. I didn't find anything out of place. My kitchen was so pristine and organized that anyone would think it was never used. Finally, only the basement was left to search. That would be a good hiding place for a thief surprised in the act of robbing a house. I should have looked there first.

At the top of the stairs to the lower level, I turned on the three switches. Simultaneously, lights came on over the landing below me, in the section of the basement directly under the stairs, and outside. I looked down, and there in front of the door that opened onto the driveway was my evidence, clearly illuminated in the feeble light of a dim overhead bulb.

One corner of the rug that I'd placed in front of the door was folded over and moved closer to the wall than it had been when I'd last seen it. That was the kind of giveaway detail a sharp burglar would never overlook, the kind that could trap him. Therefore my invader must be inexperienced or careless.

I straightened the rug and turned the doorknob to the right. The door was locked. Nevertheless, now I was convinced that someone had broken into my house, tripped over the rug, and apparently failed to notice it.

I peered down the remaining stairs at the section of tiled floor illuminated by a bare bulb. The rest of the basement was dark and ominous. Although I didn't hear any suspicious sounds, I decided to call the police. Let a trained officer finish the investigation I'd started, just in case an intruder was hiding down there.

LIEUTENANT GRAY'S handsome face was grim. He had just come inside from a tour of the grounds, and raindrops glistened in his hair and on his dark jacket. He flashed his light down the stairs once more, although he had already made a thorough search of the basement and gone through every room in the house, as I had done.

"There's nothing around that I can see," he said. Then, with a hint of the sardonic humor I remembered, he added, "You're not hearing any more noises in the attic, I take it."

"No, Lieutenant Gray, whatever creatures were there must have found a new place to nest."

I hesitated, wondering if I should mention the linen closet. The lieutenant probably already had me categorized as a woman who thought her attic was haunted. On our last meeting, when he'd come to the house to investigate the scratching sounds, he'd asked me to call him Dalton. Tonight he appeared to be in a less familiar mood.

In the end, I decided that the open door might be relevant, a sign of someone searching for an unknown object in an unlikely place.

I told him what I'd seen and added, "I might have imagined it. The door is warped, and there's nothing in a linen closet that a thief would want. Only towels, but…"

I had nothing to lose. "It looked as if someone had been moving them around. They weren't exactly the way I had arranged them."

"Let me have a look," he said.

I followed him back upstairs and waited while he shone his light into the closet on rows of towels, washcloths, sheets, and pillowcases, everything neatly folded, nothing out of order.

He ran his hand along the sides of the closet up to the ceiling. "You don't have any secret panels," he said. "You don't keep envelopes of money under shelf paper, do you?"

I couldn't tell whether or not he was serious, although the idea of stashing an emergency fund in a secret place had occurred to me.

"I had all my cash with me tonight," I said.

He opened the door to the spare room and checked the attic opening. "How many entrances does the house have?" he asked.

"Besides the front and side doors, there's one that leads to the back porch and the French doors to the balcony. All of them were locked. I remember you mentioned that anyone could climb up my tree and get inside through the French doors."

"Yes, that's a dangerous setup. I see you didn't have that branch taken down yet." He assumed the stern no-nonsense tone of a city inspector on the trail of code violations. "How about that opening under the eaves? Did you fix it?"

I tried to remember how many days had passed since his last visit. It couldn't have been that long ago, not more than a week.

"Not yet," I said. "I've been doing other things. I'll get to it the next nice day…"

"Do it," he said. "That balcony is where you're most vulnerable, and I think we've just had our last nice day for a while. It's too dark on that side of the house. Besides the maple tree in front and the linden, your neighbors' shrubbery is overgrown. You might as well hang up a 'Welcome Burglar' sign."

"I'll make one that says, "Only if you're young and agile. About the rug…"

"How can you be so sure you didn't trip over it yourself?" he asked.

"I like articles centered, shelves leveled, each thing in its proper place—it's like a compulsion."

"I see. Somebody must have been inside the house then. You say you aren't missing anything."

"Not that I know of. I don't have much to steal yet."

He glanced around the empty room and nodded. "Your burglar wouldn't know that until he got inside. We had a break-in at Cora Valentine's house around the time of her funeral. So far as we know, nothing was taken there either, but Cora's cousin couldn't tell us everything that was in the house."

"Someone told me about that burglary. I hope there's no connection."

"That I can't determine at this time."

"What I can't understand is how anyone would know I was gone," I said. "My car was parked in the driveway all day. Unless he'd been watching the comings and goings of the people who live on the street."

"That could be it," Dalton said. "We'll keep a careful watch on Walnut for the next few weeks."

"I wish I knew how he got in."

"Any number of ways. No house is impenetrable."

He took one long last look around the hall and then started down the stairs to the first floor. "My advice is still to get that tree trimmed, Katherine. Don't put it off. It's important. Maybe change the locks. Keep your French doors if you like them, but be aware that they provide easy access. Let your neighbors know when you're going to be away from home for long stretches of time."

For now that meant Nell and the Winters, those congenial people across the street. Dalton's advice was sound, but I wasn't sure I was going to follow it. I wanted to keep my personal life private. Today I'd only planned on spending a few hours with Garth, but our date had lasted all day. That was my own affair.

"That just about wraps it up here," he said. "Call again if you find anything missing tomorrow, or if something else suspicious happens. Two burglaries in Maple Creek are too many, especially after what happened to Cora."

The murder was on everyone's mind these days, lying just below the surface, along with a fear of apples and a second surprise strike.

"What does a burglary have to do with Cora Valentine's murder?" I asked.

"Maybe nothing, maybe something." He shrugged. "We can't make any assumptions at this point."

"Are there any suspects in custody yet, Lieutenant?" I asked.

"No."

As we walked to the front door, he nodded approvingly in the direction of my lamp. "That's what you need," he said. "Women who live alone should have a lot of light. That bulb in the upstairs hall can't be any more than twenty-five watts. You might think about having a sensory motion lamppost installed in the front yard."

*"Will more light and higher voltage keep the ghosts and burglars at bay?"*

I wished I could say that, but it sounded too frivolous, and I didn't know Lieutenant Gray very well yet. Maybe I never would. I imagined that he didn't like responding to a burglary call from a woman who had heard mysterious sounds in her attic. I'll bet he couldn't wait to be back in the warm, dry police station drinking coffee and gobbling doughnuts.

I reined in my uncharitable thoughts. Lieutenant Gray had done nothing to merit them. I was tired, and a headache was starting above my left eye. I was glad that it had held off this long and more than ready for the day to be over.

"Good night, Lieutenant Gray," I said. "Thanks for coming."

He gave me his first smile of the evening. "It's Dalton."

I closed the door. Once again I was alone in the house, but I had searched it thoroughly. As an added measure of safety, a trained professional had done so as well. I should be doubly safe. I had a feeling that I would sleep well tonight, even if someone had broken into my house earlier.

THE STRAY COLLIE lay on a bed of soggy leaves alongside her newest hole and an uprooted chrysanthemum plant. A shredded orange petal resting on her brown head betrayed her guilt. At her feet lay the large, mud-encrusted knucklebone she had dug out of the ground.

"Vicky," I said softly.

As I approached her, she didn't move. In spite of her scrawny frame and dull coat, she was beautiful, and her dark eyes were strangely proud for a canine in need. I longed to fling the disgusting bone back into the hole, and cover it with dirt, but I couldn't do that while she was looking at me. Although she seemed good-natured, I didn't know how she would react if I went near her food.

"If you're hungry, I have a real bone for you inside," I said. "A ham bone. Vicky, would you like it?"

I hadn't made the pea soup yet and was willing to sacrifice one of the essential ingredients for this abandoned dog.

"It has nice pieces of meat on it," I added.

She didn't stir, but she licked her chops. As I turned slowly and walked back to the house, I felt her gaze on me.

I wanted her. After last night's break-in, I needed a dog. This tenacious stray would be a source of security in a dangerous world, a touch of warm velvet fur, and a companion. She was practically watching my house now, but I wanted our bond to be official. The ham bone would be an effective lure. Later I'd leave a pan of water for her at the foot of the stairs and a crust of bread on the top step, followed by a tasty meal on the porch tomorrow, and ultimately a tub of warm water.

That was my plan to win her confidence, but when I came back with the bone, she was gone again. Obviously adopting her wasn't going to be as easy as I'd thought. With a sigh, I laid the bone down beside the hole. I had no doubt that she would find it. If she began to associate me with food, in time she would trust me.

Although the ground was muddy, I moved as much of the dirt as I could back into Vicky's hole, making sure that the disgusting knucklebone was well covered. Of course now, there was an unsightly gap in my wave of chrysanthemum color, and it was too late in the season to replace the damaged plant. But with the events of the past weeks, that might well be the least of my worries.

# TWELVE

"I'D LIKE TO LOOK AT that cameo again, Katherine," Nell said. "I've been wondering if I'd ever seen it before—a long time ago."

She had stopped by to return my tray and stayed for a cup of coffee and a little gossip about Myrold Barren. Her friend, Irene, had observed Myrold at the Blue Lion having dinner with Cora Valentine's cousin, Meg. Since he'd never shown any interest in Meg before, Nell thought this was part of his latest scheme to acquire Cora's acreage.

Then she had made her request in a casual tone that belied her interest.

She scooped a teaspoon of sugar out of the bowl and stirred it vigorously into her coffee. "Now that I've said that out loud, it sounds far-fetched. When you first showed the cameo to me, just for a moment I thought there was something familiar about it, but I wasn't sure. I'm still not."

"Where do you think you saw it?" I asked.

"In my American history class years ago. Cora Valentine used to wear pretty old-fashioned blouses with lace and ruffles. She always pinned a brooch to her collar. I remembered that the other day. I used to sit in the front row and couldn't help noticing what she wore."

"Cora used to live in this house. It's possible that the cameo belonged to her," I said.

"That's right. I'd forgotten. I used to wish I had a blouse like hers, but my family couldn't afford anything fancy. I guess you can't find them today."

"Only in vintage clothing shops, or maybe Victorian catalogs," I said. I tried to imagine Nell in the kind of frilly blouse she described, but her style was more contemporary than antique, with long sweeping skirts and form fitting sweaters in colors to complement her dark hair with its red glints.

I opened the drawer and reached into the jumble of pens, nails, and small tools I'd tossed inside. The cameo wasn't there. "That can't be," I said. "I don't see it."

Pushing everything toward the front, I pulled the drawer open as far as it would go and ran my hands along the back. It was no use. The cameo was gone.

"I saw you put it there," Nell said. "Unless you moved it and forgot about it."

"No, I haven't even thought about it." I frowned, as I made an obvious connection. "On second thought, maybe it isn't so strange." I told her about the break-in. "The thief must have taken it."

"My God, Katherine. If you'd been home, you might have been hurt. Did he get anything else?"

"So far as I can tell, only this."

"That's funny. I don't know what to say. We've never had a burglary in this part of town before."

"I'm beginning to lose faith in that Neighborhood Watch," I said.

"We'll have to reorganize and plan. Now that Halloween is almost here, we need to be more vigilant—this year especially."

Halloween was a week away. As concerned as I was about children wandering around on dark streets and the ever-present threat of dangerous treats, my thoughts were centered on the burglary and the missing cameo.

The disappearance might be significant. The gold bracelets in my jewelry case upstairs were more valuable than a broken brooch that could never be repaired. And why would a burglar look for valuables in a kitchen drawer, unless he was searching for one particular object? If he was the same person who had gone through my linen closet, he had been in the house before. That was a truly frightening thought.

"I wonder why anyone would steal a broken pin," Nell said.

"Because that unusual face just caught his eye."

As it had mine with the haunting, crushed smile. I recalled the eerie effect the cameo had on me when I first held it in my hand. The eyes that seemed to look directly into my own, the image of a screaming woman being pulled alive from her grave, and my reluctance to discard it all came back to me.

A sly whisper worked its way into my mind. *Perhaps the intruder was Cora Valentine come back to claim her cameo.*

Thank heavens I hadn't said that aloud. "Maybe the burglar came here specifically to look for the cameo. You, Garth MacKay, and Lieutenant Gray are the only ones who knew about it." Realizing that I was practically accusing Nell of theft or complicity, I added quickly, "I didn't mean that the way it sounded."

"Oh, dear," she said. "I might be to blame, though. I'm afraid I mentioned it at the party the other night. Alarice and I were talking about gardening. She said that every time she tries to use her bulb planter, she can hardly break through the ground because of all the stones. Then I told her about the cameo you'd found, and one thing led to another. Anyone could have overheard us."

"You think that one of our neighbors is a thief?" I asked.

"One person might have told somebody else, and so on. I'm sorry, Katherine. I would never have said anything if I thought it was important."

"Until a few minutes ago, it wasn't. Don't worry about it. There has to be another explanation."

Nell sighed and looked down into her empty coffee cup. "I wish I could have seen that brooch one more time. I didn't think about it for years. Now I can't get it out of my mind."

"Cora might have owned a similar pin," I said. "You could ask Meg Valentine. Cora's jewelry belongs to her now."

She brightened. "That's a good idea. I'd like to talk to Meg anyway. Is there any more coffee, Katherine?"

I poured the rest of the coffee into our cups and sat back to reflect on gossipy neighbors and cameos. I suspected that

Nell was as curious about Meg's new relationship with My-rold Barren as she was about the cameo. Making inquiries about Cora's jewelry collection would give her a perfect opportunity to add to her knowledge.

Because the cameo had been stolen from my house, my interest in its original owner went beyond curiosity. As for myself, I was going to talk to Anna Lynde who had once shared this house with Cora. As young women living together, they would have been familiar with each other's jewelry. Because the piece was so unusual, Anna might remember it. Also I felt as if I knew Anna already, while I had only seen Meg Valentine at the funeral parlor.

In the meantime, I intended to drive out to the police station and report the cameo stolen. I felt certain that it was important in some as yet unknown way.

THE RAIN continued to fall well into the afternoon, bringing down a torrent of leaves and saturating the ground. The house, along with my lawn witch and chrysanthemum bed, appeared to be sinking into a sea of mud.

Vicky had allowed me to lure her onto the back porch with a dinner of kibble and leftover roast beef. To keep her from feeling trapped, I propped open the porch door so that she could leave whenever she wanted to.

She wouldn't come any farther, although she watched me with keen interest as I moved around the kitchen drying dishes and putting them away. I knew she would venture into the house when she was ready. Until then she would be well fed and dry on the porch. Most important, she was almost in the house. I didn't quite have my companion yet, but it felt as if I did.

Deciding not to go out in the miserable weather, I left a message for Lieutenant Gray, who was out of the station on a soggy patrol of Maple Creek, and another on Anna Lynde's answering machine. My plans for the day derailed, I decided to clean house, thinking that I might come across some other missing item, but everything was accounted for. Of all my possessions, only the brooch was gone.

Aside from that, all was as it should be in the blue Victorian, but all was not well. My thoughts kept returning to Cora. I couldn't let go of the idea that once she had pinned the cameo to the lace-trimmed collar of her blouse. I could almost see her image in the hall mirror, stepping back to see whether she had it on straight.

Then, wearing that dressy blouse, would she have gone outside to plant flowers in the yard where it would come undone and fall unnoticed to the ground? I suspected that I was heading in the wrong direction. I had to find out more about Cora's life. Perhaps that knowledge would help the police solve the mystery of her murder.

Although I found it hard to believe that one of my neighbors had stolen the cameo, I couldn't rule it out. Thanks to Nell, the story of my discovery might have reached the ear of the one person who had a special interest in it.

Why wouldn't she simply have knocked on my door and told me that she'd heard about the cameo brooch and thought it belonged to someone in her family? I'd gladly have given it to her.

The answer was obvious. Because she had something to hide, she had to retrieve it in secrecy.

I didn't know why I was now thinking of the burglar as a woman.

Taking a few steps back, I approached the mystery from a different angle. I had found the cameo the day after the Apple Fair. The burglary had occurred almost three weeks later, long after Cora Valentine had been killed. How could the theft possibly be connected to the murder?

I had no answer. Presumably, the cameo had been buried in my yard for a long time, perhaps for decades. An expert would be able to determine how long. The police department or the university would be able to refer me to someone who specialized in dating buried objects. But I was forgetting that I didn't have the cameo any longer.

The need to be doing something productive, anything, held me in a steel grip. I glanced at the silent telephone. Would Lieutenant Gray ever return my call?

I considered checking with Nell to see if she'd had any luck contacting Meg Valentine but then remembered that she was working a late shift at the hospital. The day seemed to be lasting forever, and the rain and my confusion were having an adverse effect on my mood.

Finally I checked on Vicky who was sleeping peacefully on her blanket and decided to go out for a light dinner. In spite of the inclement weather, I didn't want to stay home tonight and create variations on the cameo theme.

Quietly I closed and locked the kitchen door. Through the window I saw Vicky stir and then lay her head down again. With security, lights, and a dog on the back porch, I should be safe.

Before leaving the house, I doubled checked every lock and turned on my parlor lamp so that I wouldn't have to come home to darkness. From now on, this was going to be my ritual.

I MET DALTON in a small restaurant on the highway about twenty miles north of town. Named the Country Cabin, it was a plain white-sided bungalow bursting with lights that penetrated the rapidly forming fog.

He was sitting alone at a table toward the front, positioned so that he could see the door. His air of authority and constant surveillance inspired confidence, and his friendly smile held an unspoken invitation. He seemed a little older tonight, almost careworn. This wasn't surprising, as he had the responsibility of keeping Maple Creek safe, which must have been a relatively easy task until the murder.

Not wanting to interrupt him with official business while he was on a dinner break, I said, "Good evening, Lieutenant," and prepared to sail past his table.

He put out his hand to detain me. "If you aren't meeting somebody, Katherine, how about joining me?"

"Well…" I looked around. The place was filled with empty tables, and I saw only a handful of diners, no more than a dozen. I'd arrived at an in-between time before the dinner crowd. With no reason not to accept his offer, especially since I didn't want to eat alone tonight, I said, "Thanks, I will."

He got up and pulled out a chair for me, and I unbuttoned my raincoat. With both hood and umbrella, my hair had stayed dry and held its shape. I was glad that I was wearing a new dark red shade of lipstick.

"They have the best ribs in town here," Dalton said. "Everything's good, and the service is the fastest in town."

He had scarcely finished the sentence when a plump, smiling waitress appeared at the table with a menu and a glass of water. "Coffee, Miss?"

"Please," I said. "I know what I want. I'd like a bowl of soup…"

Quickly I scanned the entrees. Wednesday's special soup was cream of mushroom. They also had clam chowder. "I'll have a bowl of chili instead, with a salad and a small ginger ale."

As she started to write the order on her pad, Dalton said, "A good choice, but you'd better make that a large drink. Their chili is hot. So are the ribs."

"That's perfect. It's chili weather. A large ginger ale then," I added.

"Have things been quiet in the old blue house on Walnut?" Dalton asked.

Encouraged by his inquiry, I told him about the missing cameo and added Nell's suspicion that it had once belonged to Cora Valentine. "I left a message for you at the station," I added. "It was about the robbery."

"That's an odd thing for a burglar to take," he said. "Are you sure you didn't just move it and forget?"

"I'm positive."

But if one more person asked me that question, I would begin to doubt it.

"Did you find anything else missing?" he asked.

"No, not yet. What do you think the chances are of finding it?"

"Sometimes we recover stolen property, but in your case, I don't think that's going to happen. A pin so small could be anywhere. Whoever took it might have decided that it wasn't worth keeping and thrown it away."

"Do you think there could be a connection between the cameo and the murder?" I asked.

He appeared to be considering this seriously, but from the amused look in his eyes, I wondered if he was only humoring me.

He said, "Anything is possible, but I wouldn't think so. Do you like to read mystery stories, Katherine? That sure sounds like one." The teasing look in his blue eyes softened the condescending words.

I said, "I love mysteries, but I know the difference between fact and fiction. If the cameo did belong to Cora Valentine and somebody wanted it badly enough to commit a crime to get it, I'd look for a connection—if I were investigating the case."

That caught his attention. "That's conjecture, Katherine. I think what we have here is a coincidence. A bizarre one, I'll grant you."

"Even a coincidence could be relevant," I said.

"I agree. All right. Until we have the killer safe behind bars, we won't discount anything. First we'll need to identify the owner of the pin. Since we don't have it and there's no way of knowing when it was lost, that's a tall order."

"It's an almost impossible task," I said. "The house dates back to before 1900."

In a quick turnaround he said, "But the homicide detectives are up to it. Ah, here comes our dinner."

The steaming chili and barbecued ribs smothered in thick sauce filled the air with a heavy scent of tangy tomato and seasonings. I hadn't realized how hungry I was.

Dalton said, "You won't find a better place for ribs in Michigan. This reminds me. Did you hear about that man who dug up all those bones in his backyard? Turns out his house was built on top of an old Indian cemetery."

I listened to the story again. It varied from Nell's version in only one way. Dalton knew what had happened to the homeowner. He had written a series of adventure books for children based on his discovery and now had a lucrative new career and a measure of fame. Indian curses made good horror stories.

I promised myself that I'd concentrate on the facts and confine fantasy to leisure reading, but in order to gather those facts, I had to make contact with Anna Lynde.

# THIRTEEN

AFTER THE REAL LIFE horror of the poisoned apple murder, anyone would think that Halloween decorating in Maple Creek would be subdued this year. But as the end of October drew near, the same homeowners who had decked their houses in patriotic colors brought witches and skeletons out of storage. They hung them on doors and in trees where they moved in the wind with the flags. R.I.P. stones turned lawns into graveyards, and it seemed as if carved pumpkins glared down from the porch of every house on Walnut.

The Winters' neighbors had transformed their gray-gabled house into a virtual mansion of horror in which most of the inmates were in a state of constant motion. A wooden spider made its way up a giant black cobweb that dropped from the roof down to the ground. Under the picture window, a life-sized witch stirred her brew, while ghosts encircled the trunk of a tree. More macabre figures appeared every day.

The only one that made me uneasy was the bust of a screaming woman nailed to a tree trunk. Her face was a sickly shade of green, and her hair was blown back as if caught in a cruel vise-like grip. Her terror-filled expression reminded me of the lady in the crushed cameo.

More frightening than any Halloween trapping was the brief story in the morning edition of the *Tribune*. The police were questioning a fifteen-year-old boy in connection with the murder of Cora Valentine. As an assignment for his creative writing class, he had written a first person account of how he had planned and carried out the crime. Probably he never intended to give the paper to his teacher, but he left it unattended in his locker where an unidentified friend found it and took it to the police.

As I raked my front yard, I couldn't help thinking about the boy. I hoped he had an explanation for the incriminating story. Perhaps he was an aspiring true crime writer or a troubled kid looking for attention. Let him be anything but a cold-blooded murderer and his story only a tasteless work of fiction.

I looked up just as Garth MacKay and Tac materialized on the sidewalk in front of me. I hadn't heard them coming, having been too lost in my thoughts to be aware of my surroundings. That wasn't wise, even on my own street in broad daylight with the alleged killer in police custody.

"Hello Katherine," Garth said. "Your neighbor's place is like a funhouse. I wouldn't want to look at it all day."

"Hi, Garth. I don't intend to. I keep busy."

I reached down to pat Tac who was sitting at his master's feet without being told to do so. I wished I could bring Vicky out so that the two dogs could get acquainted, but as soon as the rain had stopped, she'd vanished. Now she only appeared for her evening meal. I didn't know where she slept.

"What have you been doing?" Garth asked.

"Well, a lot of things. Yesterday I drove to Grand Rapids and ordered a sofa and chair for the living room, I called a tree service to trim the linden, I've been looking all over for that cameo…" I trailed off.

I had also bought a new fall wardrobe for school and a television, but I didn't think that Garth would care about that. Nor would he be interested in hearing about the dinner Dalton and I had shared at the Country Cabin.

"That doesn't sound like much," Garth said. "Where did you lose the cameo?"

I told him about the burglary. "I'm only humoring Lieutenant Gray. I don't think for a minute that I moved it and forgot where."

Garth's expression was grim. "You should have called me

back that night, Katherine," he said. "I thought everything was all right when I left you."

"We had no reason to think that it wasn't. I called the police."

We were still standing in front of the blue Victorian, I with my rake in hand and Garth holding Tac's leash. Although we had parted on more than friendly terms, for some unknown reason, I felt ill at ease with him today. Should I continue our conversation in front of the house or invite him inside?

I laid the rake against the maple tree and walked slowly up to the front porch. Garth followed me and sat down on the top step, leaning against the railing.

"You were out with me," he said. "It was my responsibility to see you safely home."

"And you did. The burglar was gone by the time we got back."

"I don't like this," he said slowly. "Why would anyone break in and steal an old broken pin you found buried in the ground? Who even knew about it?"

I couldn't resist teasing him. "You for one."

His face darkened briefly. Then he said, "We were together when the break-in happened."

"I know that, Garth. I was only kidding."

"You should have a dog like Tac to watch the house," he said.

"I have Vicky—almost. She's adopted me at mealtimes."

"I'm talking about a real guard dog. I know someone who has a nice litter of Belgian shepherds for sale. Tac looks gentle, but he would give up his life to protect me."

Tac looked up at Garth, his expression a mixture of adoration and curiosity. 'Protect you from what?' he seemed to ask.

"Tac is a beautiful dog, but he looks anything but gentle to me. I'll keep trying to tempt Vicki inside. Anyway, if this intruder found what he wanted, he's not likely to be back."

That was what I hoped. I didn't want to admit it to Garth, but I had a premonition that further trouble awaited me in the near future. The theft of the cameo might be only the first phase.

"Like I said, Katherine, if ever you feel threatened by anyone or anything, call on me."

Once he had said, "I can protect what belongs to me."

Garth's generous offer made me as uneasy as the bust of the screaming woman on the tree did. For a minute, it seemed as if he were saying something else. Almost staking a claim? No, that couldn't be. We hardly knew each other.

"Thanks, Garth, but I think I can handle whatever comes along." With a little help from the Police Department, I added to myself.

"All right. Don't forget. I mean what I say."

"Did you read the story in the *Tribune* about the suspect in Cora Valentine's murder?" I asked, in an attempt to change the subject.

"That's Josh Cameron's kid," he said. "Terry is a little weird, but I don't think he did it. Probably got the idea on the Internet."

"If it turns out to be a hoax, he's going to be in trouble."

"Terry is always in trouble. Josh doesn't believe in discipline for his kids. This may change his mind. Katherine…" Garth paused, straightening the leash that had gotten twisted around Tac's throat. "Would you like to go out with me again? Have dinner at another place I know?"

I hesitated, thinking that a second date so soon was unwise, but when I started my new job next month, I would be too busy to socialize for a while. Besides, how could I refuse after Garth had just offered me his help?

Easily, with a sincere-sounding fabricated excuse—if that was what I wanted. I said, "That sounds like fun. When?"

"This weekend. Saturday night, about six?"

That was only a few days away. I had no other engagements except for lunch with Anna Lynde tomorrow.

"Saturday night is fine," I said.

"Good. Then I'll let you get back to your leaves. Tac, Come."

They turned around and walked back toward Main Street. So Garth had come to the blue Victorian specifically to ask me to go out with him again. I reminded myself of my plan to proceed slowly in this new friendship. I thought I knew his secret now, but something about him continued to trouble me. If he posed some kind of risk, I was falling into his trap by continuing to accept dates with him.

Well, I was growing accustomed to danger. It seemed as if I was destined to encounter it at every turn. The up side was that if this danger involved Garth, it also held the promise of fun.

AFTER A LUNCH of chicken salad and warm rolls, Anna Lynde and I moved to the living room to drink our tea and eat the fresh strawberry tarts she had bought at the Bakery on Main. When we were finished with dessert, she took an exquisite bracelet out of a jewelry chest and handed it to me. It was surprisingly lightweight, even with five large pink cameos joined by thin gold links.

"I broke the safety clasp years ago, but I was never afraid of losing it," she said. "I'd notice something that large slipping off my wrist."

I set the bracelet down on the coffee table beside the tea tray and studied the patrician heads carved in profile. Some of the faces were flushed with delicate pink; others were the color of thick, rich cream. The cameos were about an inch and a half long and perhaps an inch wide, larger than the one I'd found.

"I haven't worn this in years." Anna clasped the bracelet around her wrist and held her arm up to the light that streamed in through the arched window. The combination of pink, white, and gold brought instant sparkle to her soft gray dress.

"That's the most lustrous shade of pink I've ever seen," I said.

"One summer Cora, Rosalie, and I toured Europe. We bought our cameos on the Isle of Capri. Cora's bracelet was like this one, only smaller and lighter. She bought a matching pin and earrings for herself. Rosalie had a brown cameo similar to the one you described and a matching bracelet, but I'd have to look at it to be certain."

"I wish you could. I'm afraid it's gone forever."

"That's so strange. Buried for years and then found, only to be lost again. I don't know what to tell you, Katherine."

In Anna's cool, sunlit living room, the vague dark strands I had been trying to tie together were dissolving. Spirits and buried clues were easier to think about in an old atmospheric house than in this crisp, contemporary setting.

"So the cameo I found couldn't have belonged to Cora," I said.

"That's a stretch, but let me think. In those days we used to share clothes and jewelry, everything, even boyfriends. Cora may have borrowed Rosalie's cameo. I don't remember, but I am pretty sure that Rosalie never lost it. The one you found was unusual but it couldn't have been unique."

I had been hoping that Anna would be able to identify the crushed cameo, as the one Cora had owned, based on my description and her memory of decades-old possessions. And then what? I would take the information to Lieutenant Gray who by now would have discovered that Terry Cameron's story was a ruse intended to bedevil the police force. The facts weren't cooperating with my theory.

"I had some idea that the cameo might tie in to Cora's murder," I said. "I guess I'll have to give it up."

"That Cameron boy confessed. I don't think he knows what a cameo is. Poor Cora helped so many troubled kids. She didn't deserve to be killed by one."

"I'm going to think that he's lying for some reason until I hear otherwise," I said.

"That's a good idea. So will I."

"You said you used to share boyfriends. Did you mean that literally?"

Anna laughed. "Let me clarify that for you. When we rented the old Victorian, four boys were living in the house next door. That's the one to the east. Gerry and Jon had been in college with Cora and me, Nathan taught chemistry at Maple Creek High, and Ross was in graduate school. They used to help us, and we were all friends together."

"That sounds like fun," I said.

"We did have good times. We used to chaperone dances and football games at the school and then go out to dinner. In the winter the boys helped us with that old fireplace and shoveled our drive. We were so helpless then—or we pretended to be."

"Did you all stay just friends?"

"For a time, but then I realized that Cora was in love with Gerry. They went out on a few dates, and their relationship showed signs of turning into a romance. That's Gerry Raycraft, the man who was talking to me at the funeral parlor. His uncle owned the house the boys lived in. Later Gerry bought it."

She unclasped the bracelet and laid it gently back in the velvet lined jewelry chest. "That was so long ago. Jon is a defense attorney in Detroit now, and poor Nathan was killed in the Vietnam War. I don't know what happened to Ross. He moved out West somewhere. Gerry and I are the only two of the old crowd left in Maple Creek."

Cora's obituary hadn't mentioned a husband. "What happened between Cora and Gerry?" I asked.

"Rosalie happened. She was pretty, very sweet, something of a flirt. She and Gerry started seeing each other and seemed happy together."

"Cora must have been devastated to lose Gerry to her own roommate," I said.

"She wasn't happy about it, but she had to accept the inevitable. Then a dashing Southern boy came to town and swept Rosalie off her feet. She married him and moved out of Michigan, but by that time, whatever had existed between Cora and Gerry was gone."

At the Bell House yard sale, when I was lingering over the lamp, I remembered Cora Valentine saying that when she wanted something in life, she took it. Apparently she hadn't wanted Gerry enough. But of course no woman could acquire a man as if he were a lamp, especially if his affections belonged to someone else.

Anna said, "In those days, Cora had other problems. For those first few years of teaching, she was having a hard time with her classes. She was too easy going, and some of those ninth graders were little hellions. She took everything too much to heart. Her real name was Cornelia, but the kids used to call her Corny Valentine. She disliked that nickname so much that she insisted on being called Cora instead of Cornelia."

"Corny Valentine. That's sort of cute. If she had ignored them, it would have died a natural death."

"But the name bothered her, and so did her rowdy classes. I didn't think Cora would stay in education, but even with all the chaos she had, she really liked teaching. In her second year, she changed her personality and her methods. It worked. By the time she retired, she had won several awards for teaching excellence and earned a reputation as a martinet."

As interesting as Cora's metamorphosis into strict master teacher was, I still wondered about her broken relationship with Gerry Raycraft.

"If Cora and Gerry lived in Maple Creek all these years, didn't they ever get close again?"

"No, but they remained friends. Sometimes I thought they would, but it didn't happen. Then there was Alarice. Gerry squired her around for a time, but nothing came of it. Maybe Cora didn't care as much for Gerry as I thought she did. As for Gerry, he's a hard man to like, but you've met him. You know what I mean."

"But apparently Rosalie liked him," I said.

"He was a little friendlier when he was young, but he was always on the quiet side. Well, Katherine, I've enjoyed this stroll down memory lane, but I don't think I've helped you much." She lifted the lid of the teapot and peered inside. "Cora gave me this teapot one Christmas. Shall I make more tea?"

"I'd like some," I said. "I wanted to ask you something else, Anna. It's about my house. When you were living there, did you ever notice anything unusual about it?"

"Unusual in what way?"

"It's difficult to explain. Strange sounds in the night, a feeling that you weren't alone..." I shrugged. "Thoughts about ghosts?"

"Do you mean, did I ever think the house was haunted? It

never occurred to me, but we didn't stay home very much. If there were such a thing as a haunted house, though, that old blue Victorian fits my idea of one."

"Garth told me that the woman who lived there before me felt a presence, something that made her uneasy enough to want to move out of the house quickly. I wonder if that story Cora was going to tell me was about ghosts," I said.

"It could be. Cora may have met the previous owner through her antiques. That's the kind of story she loved to tell."

"I just wondered," I said. "Since the burglary, I've been a little uneasy. And even before that."

"I can understand that," Anna said. "But there's no way you can know what Cora was going to say, no more than I can figure out the mystery message. Well, we're left with these current troubles. I'm glad the police are going to give special attention to your street. Now tell me, have you been meeting any eligible men?"

"A few. I don't know how eligible they are."

"It always helps to have some attractive prospects on hand. I wish you could have four handsome young men living next door to you to look out for you like we did."

Anna meant well, but I could build a fire in my fireplace and shovel my own snow. I said, "That would be nice, but these aren't the seventies. I don't think I need a man to look out for me."

"I'm sure you're very capable, Katherine. I was just remembering all the fun we used to have. Now that I'm alone, sometimes I have to force myself to focus on my future. My girls have their own lives, and I still miss my husband. It's so easy to want to go back to the past, especially when it was such a happy time."

"Maybe some happy times are waiting for you in the future," I said. "I'll help you make tea." Taking her empty cup and my own, I followed her into the large streamlined kitchen where every appliance imaginable was lined up on the counter.

I had thought of Anna as a very capable woman herself and wondered if she was really poised on the brink of unhappiness. Apparently she visited her daughters frequently, and I was under the impression that her husband had been dead for some time, about ten years.

I thought it strange that her thoughts seemed to return to those days when she, Cora, and their other roommate, Rosalie, had lived together in the blue Victorian, next door to four friendly, helpful boys, rather than to the early years of her marriage.

Very strange indeed. I was curious, but there was no way I could ask about it; nor would I. I didn't like people prying into my own affairs. Certainly I wasn't going to invade anyone else's privacy.

# FOURTEEN

I STOOD UNDER the linden tree in a bright stream of October sunshine. Forester's Tree Service had trimmed the dangerous branches and fed them to the chipper. Now no one could climb up to the second story and enter the house through the French doors without making a Superman leap from a distance of twelve feet. I never thought this was likely to happen, but it made sense to follow Dalton's advice in case I had to call the police again.

Vicky lay at the far end of the chrysanthemum bed watching me. When the tree trimmers had appeared, she'd emerged from some unknown place and stayed to bark her annoyance at the crashing branches and ear-splitting roar of the chipper.

I raked the last of the crushed twigs and leaves toward the sidewalk. I'd had a productive morning, supervising the sealing of the small opening at the top of the house by Skylight Roofers and then cleaning the entire yard. While I was working outside, I had gone over Anna Lynde's recollections. Although they were interesting glimpses into her past, they didn't take me into new territory.

What I had was a jumble. Still, I felt as if I were overlooking an essential clue, a single fragment that should have been obvious. Not finding any ready answers, I moved on to another activity.

Even with the missing branches, the tree still gave the balcony a measure of privacy, or would do so in the spring when the leaves came back. I glanced at the property next door, wondering if the owners would return any time soon. The house had the look of a residence that had been left to its own devices too long.

A traditional two-story white frame with a small side porch and large addition on the back, it had dark green shutters and a spacious redwood deck blanketed with leaves. The old evergreens around the foundation were tall, unshapely spires. Planted too close together, they vied with one another for space and light. Once a week, a lawn service came to cut the grass and blow the leaves into the street, but no one ever pruned the shrubs.

Thirty years ago, they would have been small, or, more likely, didn't exist yet. Four fun-loving young men had lived in the house then. The deck looked fairly new, but the grill and ancient picnic table had probably been in the yard for decades. Using Anna's memories, I tried to visualize a scene that might have taken place there in the early seventies.

The season would be the same, the maple trees ablaze with color overhead and the scent of burning leaves in the air. For a typical barbecue, hamburgers would sizzle on the grill in a cloud of charcoal, while hot dogs roasted over a bonfire. The impressions tumbled over one another in their haste to appear: A sudden chilling breeze, green and gold cashmere sweaters, ice cubes clinking against tumblers, and shadow figures wandering among the trees.

Three of the figures were more than shadows. I could almost see them. A pretty longhaired girl in a short brown dress sat on a swing, smiling up at a handsome, earlier version of Gerry Raycraft. He wore a bulky sweater with a Varsity letter emblazoned on the sleeve, and his dark hair didn't have a single strand of gray in it.

In another part of the yard Cora walked toward the picnic table carrying a large bowl of potato salad. She looked away from Gerry and Rosalie, as if trying to hide the pain she felt at the sight of the man who should have been hers falling under the spell of another woman.

This past memory that wasn't my own seemed so real and personal that I almost felt as if it belonged to me.

Years later at the yard sale, Cora had said, "When I see something I want, I take it." I knew that she wasn't talking about antiques.

No woman could take a man and make him hers when he had already given his heart to another. Surely Cora would have known that. According to Anna, she had accepted the inevitable. What else could she do? Then or now, the answer was the same. Nothing.

Uneasy with my strange re-creation, I looked away from the house, allowing the scene to evaporate. I could almost feel the autumn chill I'd conjured. The winds were picking up, blowing the raked leaves back onto the sidewalk. The temperature was changing again, slowly but perceptibly. I had worked outside long enough. I felt as tired as though I'd lived through a long, disappointing party, trying to keep my tears from falling and my mouth frozen in a smile.

"Vicky, come inside," I said a little too sharply.

From the saucy tilt of the dog's head, I knew that she heard me, but she didn't move. After all, it was hours until her dinnertime, and she didn't care about blowing leaves or falling temperatures. She ignored me and stared at the new hole she had dug in my flowerbed when I hadn't been looking.

"Well, I'm going in," I said. "Stay outside if you want to, but don't dig any more."

I turned to open the porch door.

*Maybe this time...*

Like a voice wailing in the wind, I heard those three words again, that haunting phrase. Or maybe I'd only thought them. That had to be it. They'd been gone for days now, but here they were again, dropping into my mind for no known reason.

All right. Instead of obsessing about this thought, I would try to complete and understand it.

*Maybe this time I've taken the right precaution to keep intruders out of my house?*

*Maybe this time it's my turn to be happy?*

Inexplicably, the face and the voice of Garth MacKay were

with me. I looked back to the sidewalk, half expecting to see him walking with Tac, crossing the yard, his blue-green eyes flashing like the stones in his ring. I would tell him, "Isn't it strange, Garth? I was just thinking about you."

No one was there. Thoroughly spooked at the turn my wayward imaginings had taken, I left the rake and the ladder on the ground and went inside, calling Vicky one more time.

But she was gone again. I left the door to the back porch open for her but closed and locked the inner door that led to the kitchen.

How had I managed to see that ghostly barbecue party from the past? More to the point, why? Most likely it had never happened that way, with Cora watching the girl who must be Rosalie and young Gerry Raycraft, all three of them frozen in that haunting, telltale tableau. Anna's description hadn't been vivid enough for me to build the scene in such graphic detail, and she had never mentioned a swing.

I had known for some time that the blue Victorian could set my imagination whirling into motion. Now it seemed that the backyard had similar powers.

SOAP AND WARM WATER also had power. In the bathtub, I washed the dirt of the yard out of my hair and body and let it all drain away, along with the tension and anxiety that had come upon me. A fluffy dry towel, clean clothes, and a spray of light gardenia perfume worked their magic, making me feel new and energized again. As I blow dried my hair in front of the dressing table, I wouldn't have been surprised to see the tear-stained face of the young Cora Valentine behind me, but the only reflection I saw was my own.

With my black hair, blue eyes, and fair skin, I supposed I was reasonably attractive except when I looked serious or troubled, as I did now. I dusted powder and blush on my face and outlined my lips in Glazed Rose. There. That was a little better.

From now on, I intended to cast off all melancholy

thoughts and enjoy the leisure moments and parties of my own life, beginning with my weekend dinner with Garth MacKay. Perhaps some day Dalton would ask me to go out with him. I sensed that his friendship went a little beyond official business. As for Cora's murder and the mystery of the missing cameo, they would either be resolved or not. In any event, I didn't know what I could do to affect the outcome.

With the linden branches gone, my bedroom looked brighter, suggesting new ways to savor the coming days. Next summer, I would begin each morning by filling a tray with comfort food and having breakfast on the balcony. French toast with bacon, warmed maple syrup, and fresh orange juice. Forget calories and cholesterol. I would sit high above the ground and look down on a garden of flowers in full bloom, eating slowly because I wouldn't have to leave for school in ten minutes.

Maybe a handsome man would share the breakfast with me. Dalton—or Garth. Perhaps someone I hadn't met yet. Dalton, I thought. Deciding to entertain myself by creating another fantasy with a happier tone and ending, I opened the French doors and stepped outside. The wind blew my hair into my face. If only it could blow away the aura of mystery and gloom that lingered in the old house.

The size of the balcony was exactly right for a small café table and two chairs, with enough room left for two people to move around. From this different perspective, I looked again at the house next door. The blue Victorian was larger and higher, closer to the sky. The balcony would be an ideal place to relax and dream, almost like being magically suspended in space.

In the sunlight the railing had the sparkle of fresh white paint. I leaned my hand on it. Without warning, with hardly a sound, the whole front section gave way, toppling downward and breaking apart as it hit the ground.

My palm was suspended in mid-air, and my heart was spinning like a planet wrenched out of orbit. For a heart-stopping instant, I imagined myself falling forward. In a frantic struggle to regain my equilibrium, I grabbed the side railing. Miraculously it held. Trembling in every part of my body, I held fast to the posts and moved my body away from the edge as my mind tried to register the grim reality.

I had nearly plummeted to the ground with the unstable section of railing. At this moment I could be lying under the linden tree, crushed like the brown cameo. No one had come out to investigate. Anybody who heard an unusual noise would assume that the tree trimmers had returned, while I lay broken and dying on the ground, or badly bruised with fractured bones.

Leaning back against the cool wood of the house, I tried to stop shaking. My heart was beating normally now, but my mind insisted on replaying a reel of myself reaching out to touch the railing and going down with it.

It didn't happen that way. But it might have.

From a safe distance, I surveyed the edge of the balcony. The posts appeared to have been sawed smoothly away from the floor and then fitted snugly back into place, held there by the side sections. To the casual observer, it would look as if nothing was wrong until someone put his weight on the railing. Because the balcony was located outside my bedroom, I would be that person.

I had only been on the balcony once before and hadn't touched the railing on that occasion, so I couldn't tell if it had been this way when I'd bought the house. But if this dangerous flaw had existed at that time, wouldn't the inspector have discovered it?

Someone had tampered with the railing after I'd moved into the house, hoping that eventually I would lean on it and fall, but his possible motive eluded me. In my view, that person could only be the nameless, faceless burglar. No enemy is more dangerous than the one who is unknown.

The wind that shook the leaves was stronger now. I had to move, to go inside, before a strong gust blew the French doors shut, trapping me on the balcony two stories up with no way to get back inside the house. I hadn't seen any sign of life on the street, and Vicky wasn't in the yard now. To be stranded on the balcony until somebody passed by on Walnut would be an inconvenience but not deadly. Still, I wanted to avoid any further disruption in my day.

Quickly I stepped back into the bedroom and locked the doors. Now I had to call the police to report one more bizarre incident and then find someone to repair the damage as soon as possible. My newfound euphoria had gone over the edge of the balcony with the railing section.

LIEUTENANT DALTON GRAY closed the French doors and turned around to face me. His expression was grim, but his tone was cool and professional, inspiring confidence. The minute he had walked into the house, I'd felt that the harrowing incident was in the best possible hands.

"I agree with your assessment, Katherine," he said. "Now we have to find out who did this."

"I'm completely clueless. I don't have any enemies."

"No irate former husbands or stalkers in your past? Nobody you might have provoked without meaning to?"

"Not a one."

I didn't care for the direction Dalton was taking with his questions. My trouble had begun when I'd moved to Maple Creek. If I had acquired an enemy before that, I had no knowledge of it. The danger originated in this town.

I said, "I've hardly been back in the states long enough to attract any attention to myself."

"How about someone who might have followed you home from the Continent?" he asked.

"Lieutenant Gray," I said, "I'm not living in a suspense novel. My life in Europe was very ordinary. I'm an ordinary person. I don't expect that to change."

It had though, on the day of the Apple Fair when Fate had arranged for me to meet Cora Valentine in the last few hours of her life. While I'd been settling in, getting to know my neighbors, raking leaves, and making dates with a new man, something dark and dangerous was going on behind the scenes. Someone was determined to turn my humdrum days deadly.

The only person in my life who could be considered remotely dangerous was Garth MacKay, Michigan Militiaman. Now that I thought about it, wasn't his interest in me too sudden not to be suspicious? I reminded myself that Garth wasn't the kind of man I would be attracted to in normal circumstances. Wouldn't the same be true of him? If so, why was he pursuing me? Also, when I had planned to go slowly in my relationship with him, why was I doing the opposite?

And could Garth's attention to me be in any way connected with his desire to protect his sister? I didn't think so, for presumably the police had cleared Taryn, but I didn't know the whole story.

I had no intentions of confiding in Dalton about this personal matter. "I don't understand what's going on," I said. "The person who stole the cameo must be responsible for this."

"Not necessarily." He held the bedroom door open for me and stood at the top of the stairs, surveying the landing as if he hoped to find a clue hiding in the shadows. "If someone is out to get you, this was a hell of a random way to do it. Most people don't use their balconies at the end of October. Why should anyone think you'd be an exception?"

"I don't know how to answer that. Could this possibly be a twisted Halloween prank?"

"I hope not. We're expecting a quiet Halloween, but we'll investigate that angle."

We were still on the second floor landing. He glanced at the linen closet that now remained closed with the help of the magnetic latch. "Did you find anything else missing or out of place?"

"Not that I've noticed, and I did look all over for that cameo. It's gone."

"I guess about now you're wondering what you moved into," he said.

"Well, this isn't exactly my idea of peaceful small town living. After only three weeks, I must have a thick file at the MCPD."

"It isn't so thick."

"Maybe the railing wasn't tampered with on the day of the burglary," I said. "It could have happened at any time."

"Yes, and with all the overgrown greenery, no one would notice any unusual activity around your house. That's the kind of set up robbers love. I'm glad you had those branches taken down."

"Is there anything else I can do?" I asked.

"A couple of things. First, I'd have that railing fixed without delay. Have another inspection done too. I've already looked the place over and didn't find anything suspicious, but a second go-through can't hurt. You want to make sure you don't have any more booby traps lying around."

As we walked down the stairs, he pushed on the banister at intervals, but nothing moved. When he turned into the kitchen, I followed, reluctant to have him leave but unable to think of any additional questions. All his visit had accomplished was another page of notes for my file. Still, while he was in the house, I felt better, almost reassured. Nothing could harm me when the police were on the premises.

He had his hand on the doorknob now. "Those basement stairs are dangerous, Katherine. They're too narrow and steep, and your lighting is bad."

I sighed. Was nothing right with my house? When the realtor had showed me the historic blue Victorian, I thought that everything about it was perfect. "That's the way most basement stairs are built," I said. "I could change the light bulb, though."

"That would help. Incidents like this often happen at home. Say you're watching television and decide to make a quick trip to the basement between commercials. You don't bother to turn the light on, so you don't notice that the three bottom steps have been removed. You fall and lie there unable to move, hoping one of your neighbors will remember that he hasn't seen you lately."

"I see what you're saying."

And I didn't like it. In a few sentences, Dalton had created a nightmare scenario. I imagined that his purpose was to encourage me to follow his advice.

"Did you notice anything wrong with my stairs other than the way they're built?" I asked.

"No, I gave you one of my favorite examples. You should be aware of what can happen. Everybody should."

"I'll do everything I can to protect myself, but it might not be enough."

"We're on call twenty-four hours a day," he said. "In the meantime, we'll try to find out who's behind the break-in and this latest incident. Take care."

And he went through the door. He might just as well have wished me luck. I was going to need it.

# FIFTEEN

"THIS IS MY HOME, and I will not feel afraid in it."

My words sounded hollow in the cool, gloomy basement. Kneeling on the hard floor, I shone my flashlight into the dark recess under the stairs. All I could see were cobwebs.

I had taken Dalton's frightening anecdote to heart. After making an appointment with E-Z Home Improvements to replace the missing railing, I had embarked on my own inspection of the house, intending to work my way up to the attic. If anything looked the slightest bit suspicious, I would take care of it immediately.

I had also changed the light bulbs in the basement as well as the one in the landing fixture. Even with the added illumination, this lowest level was the least inviting part of the house. The walls were painted a light shade of blue, and sand-colored tile covered the floor, creating a curious underwater effect. A large fruit cellar occupied the northwestern corner. All of the shelves were empty, except for one. It held a lone can of diced tomatoes.

Besides the washer and dryer, the previous owners had left a refrigerator and an ancient gas stove behind. Both were in good working condition, but I doubted that I would use them. The models in the kitchen were only two years old and more than sufficient for the amount of cooking I intended to do. For a large family, though, or someone who entertained on a grand scale, having these extra appliances would be ideal.

Satisfied that all was well in the basement, I turned off the flashlight and climbed the stairs to the kitchen, the one room in which I always felt at home. Everything appeared to be all right here, too, familiar and cozy. Slowly I worked my way through the first and second stories up to the attic, ending my inspection with a quick glance into the darkness beneath the roof. As far as I could determine, all was well everywhere. Apparently, the only dangerous part of the house was the balcony, and that was going to be repaired.

I should have been reassured, but I kept wondering whether I had missed a possible death trap set by my unknown adversary. If only I could call Dalton back, but without good reason, I would never do it.

"These aren't the seventies," I'd said to Anna Lynde. How superior that must have sounded. Still, this one time only, it would be a pleasure to pretend to be helpless and turn the dual problems of my home invader and would-be killer over to a capable man.

Wait! Was that my thought? It couldn't have been. Anna had said something similar the other day. I was only echoing her sentiment.

A walk in the afternoon sunshine would be a perfect way to rid myself of these alien notions. Tying a bulky navy cardigan over my shoulders, I checked to see if Vicky was in the yard. Through the porch screens, I saw her lying beside her hole in the flowerbed. This time when I called to her, she ran around the side of the house to the front. She was waiting for me there, prancing around in the leaves and wagging her tail as if she really were my dog.

"Let's go for a little walk," I said.

She yelped twice and dashed across the street ahead of me. Fortunately no cars were coming, but I couldn't let her continue to run free. It was a wonder she had survived this long. I called her name, and she stopped at the garish Halloween house and looked my way, waiting for me to catch up to her.

Since the last time I had seen it, the yard had acquired more decorations. Today a life-sized Dracula lay sleeping in a coffin, a scarecrow dangled from a tree, and a malevolent green frog as large as Vicky guarded a pool made of small gray stones. But the mummy on the porch was the most impressive of the newcomers. It looked so real I would have sworn it was authentic. And something was different about the bust of the screaming woman. It appeared to be a little lower on the tree, closer to the ground. Perhaps it had been moved to make room for one more monstrosity.

I intended to turn on Lindenwood and walk down the street where Gerry Raycraft lived, but when I saw Nell in front of her house, I changed my mind. Once again Vicky ran on ahead of me and circled Nell, playfully nipping at her rake.

"Hi, Katherine," she said. "Who's your partner?"

"Her name is Vicky. I'm trying to adopt her."

"Well, good luck. She looks a little wild."

"As soon as I coax her into my house, I'm going to make it official."

"If you really want her, you'd better get her a license," Nell said. "I'm surprised Dalton hasn't picked her up."

"You're right, but he must have more important things on his mind."

"I haven't seen you lately," she said. "Did you start your new teaching job yet?"

"Not until the week before Thanksgiving."

Nell rescued the rake from Vicky's mouth and set it aside. Shading her eyes, she peered down the street. "Isn't the Rawson house hideous?" she asked.

"It's really too much. Do they have young children?"

"Two girls, but they're in high school now. The Rawsons just like to decorate. You should have seen all the elves and reindeer they had out for Christmas."

"No Santa Claus?"

"He was on the roof."

Nell's own yard was in pristine condition. It didn't look as if she had missed a single leaf. Her fading fall flowers were resting in a bed of fresh redwood bark, and her only decoration was a flag waving in the light breeze.

"I'll be so glad when Halloween is over," she said.

"Any particular reason?"

"I hate all this diabolical stuff blocking my view. I just don't like vampires and spiders. Especially spiders."

"Well they're all plastic," I said. "Speaking of horrors, something happened to me this morning."

As I described my experience on the balcony, Nell's face registered disbelief and then shock.

"Oh, Katherine, how terrible! You must be the unluckiest person in town."

"I wonder if anyone else has had bizarre accidents or burglaries lately."

"I haven't heard, but I'll bet it has something to do with Halloween. Look at what that Campbell kid did to Cora."

"May have done, Nell. There's something unreal about that confession."

"Maybe. He's always been a troublemaker, though. I think he's the one who decorated my trees with toilet paper last year. Do you know how hard it is to clean up a mess like that? I think there's still some up there."

"From last year? I don't think so." Nell's tree was almost bare, except for a large nest.

"Are you going to have that railing repaired?" she asked.

"Tomorrow morning."

"Good. If you can get through Halloween without any mishaps, I think you'll be home free."

"I'll try," I said. "Goodbye for now, Nell. Vicky? Let's walk."

HOME FREE. I liked the sound of that phrase, but unlike Nell, I didn't think my near accident had anything to do with Halloween. With what then? An enemy whose name and grudge I didn't know? A lunatic prankster? I would rather focus on the imaginary barbecue scene, which was intriguing and scary but not potentially lethal.

I didn't want to share my re-creation with anyone when I didn't understand it, but I needed more facts. I had to find someone to talk to, ideally a person who wouldn't leap to the conclusion that I was delusional. Logically that person would be Anna Lynde who possessed first hand knowledge of the time and the people involved.

I was going to ask her a few specific questions. First, had there ever been a swing in the backyard of the house next door? That was an unusual inquiry. I would have to think of a reason for mentioning it. Then, did she have pictures of her friends dating from the seventies? I wanted to know if Rosalie's hair had been long and if Gerry Raycraft had ever worn a sweater with a Varsity letter on the sleeve. If Anna verified the details, that meant they hadn't originated in my mind. I wasn't sure I wanted to explore this possibility, but I had to do it.

Also, was it only a coincidence that after concocting this fictitious event, I had almost fallen from the balcony? Anyone would think so, but after my recent experiences, I was ready to question every unusual happening.

A tap, tap, tapping sound on pavement broke my concentration. Vicky, who had reached the wooded acreage that adjoined the Raycraft house, dashed around the corner and back again to alert me to some momentous happening, just as Gerry Raycraft appeared. He was walking with his cane today, stepping carefully over a section of sidewalk that was raised to a dangerous height by the roots of an old oak tree.

Hoping that he wasn't going to rebuff me, I smiled at him.

"Katherine," he said. "Good afternoon. I see you're enjoying this beautiful fall day with your little stray."

He was beaming, his eyes almost sparkled, and he actually came to a stop alongside me, leaning forward on his cane. He was so unlike the man I'd encountered previously that I wondered if I was talking to his twin brother. In manner, if not in appearance, he reminded me of the young Gerry Raycraft at the barbecue party, aged now and wearing a tweed jacket.

I could see why Nell and Anna had defended him when I'd commented on his unfriendly nature. Perhaps some days were better for him than others, although I'd have thought that a day when he had to use his cane couldn't be all that good.

"Some of these sidewalks are treacherous," I said.

"That they are. Watch your step."

I assured him that I would be careful and walked on, listening to the tapping sound growing fainter. Vicky deserted me to run into the Raycraft woods, and I stopped at the iron fence to admire the freshly painted dollhouse drying in the sun.

Like the blue Victorian, this miniature mansion reflected the Queen Anne style of architecture. Painted pale yellow with moss green roof and trim, it blended authenticity with fancy. From the twin turrets to the gingerbread-trimmed gables, it was a child's fantasy in wood.

On second thought, it might be intended for a collector. When I talked to Anna, I could ask her about Gerry Raycraft's unusual hobby. The sight of the exquisite dollhouse, along with his courtly attitude, softened my earlier impression of him.

Ready to move on, I called to Vicky, but she didn't come. I needed a leash and collar as well as a dog license, and, at some time in the future, a course in obedience training. If she was going to be my dog, she had to stop disappearing at will.

THE NEXT NIGHT Garth MacKay glowered at me from across our table in the crowded Red River Steakhouse. He looked exceptionally handsome in a herringbone suit and shirt of fine blue cotton. His dark beard was neatly trimmed and his eyes had radiated with merriment and good will until I told him about my brush with death on the balcony. Then his mood quickly evaporated, and a scowl replaced his smile.

"I thought you trusted me enough to let me help you if something happened again," he said.

"The railing has already been replaced. I know you're busy in your title office. I wouldn't dream of imposing on you."

"I'm not too busy for you, Katherine."

I looked down at my steak for a moment, considering how to answer him. These significant words were in keeping with Garth's manner toward me this evening. Beginning with the bouquet of yellow roses he had handed me when I opened the door, I'd sense a change in him.

First the roses, then extravagant compliments on my simple beige dress and single strand of pearls, progressing to a strong hand resting on my shoulders and moving up to my neck in a caress. I didn't need a romance barometer to realize that Garth no longer regarded me as a casual friend—if he ever had.

But something about him continued to trouble me, and I still hadn't figured out what it was, unless it had something to do with the Michigan Militia. He seemed to consider my calling the police when the railing broke a personal affront. Could the source of his annoyance be a dislike of Dalton or, more likely, of the police in general? That would be in keeping with his Militia beliefs.

"I can take care of what belongs to me," he'd said. I didn't doubt it, but that didn't include me.

About the real Garth I was clueless. He was a man of mystery who guarded his secrets well. Most people wouldn't be aware that he had any. Still, even if he was now thinking of me in a romantic way, he wasn't ready to reveal his private thoughts to me.

Or was I imagining this other, darker side of Garth, as I had created the barbecue? And what did it matter since I'd never thought of him as a possible lover?

He was waiting for my response. I had to say something.

"It's nothing I'd bother a friend with. I appreciate your concern, though, Garth. I really do."

I thought I had found the right words, the perfect words, to set us firmly back on a friendship plateau, which was where I wanted us to be.

"I look on you as more than my friend, Katherine," he said. "Much more. And I know about building. Sky and MacKay Title is only a block away. I could have been at your house in five minutes."

The Red River Steakhouse on Saturday night was no place

to have a serious conversation. All around us people were en-joying good food and engaging in lighthearted conversation with their dinner companions. I should launch us on a discus-sion of Halloween trivia or Devil's Night customs in Maple Creek, but it's never easy to deal with a man who insists on missing the point.

"The next time something dangerous happens, you'll be the first to know," I said. "I promise."

Apparently this concession satisfied him for the moment. Naturally I hoped that nothing else would happen, although I was still caught up in the spell of the blue Victorian. What would Garth say if I told him that sometimes I imagined Cora Valentine's spirit walking the halls of my house or that I'd inadvertently opened a door to the past and observed a fragment of an event that might have occurred a long time ago—or not?

I wished I could tell him, but that was the secret I was keep-ing from him. "If a ghost slithers by some night, I'll call you to come hold my hand," I said.

"I'll hold your hand any time, ma'am, and we don't have to wait for those ghosts in the hallway. They're not the ones who cut the railing anyway. How about if I come by tomor-row and make an inspection of your house?"

"The police already did that, and so did I. The place has been doubly inspected and guaranteed safe. I'd like to forget about it for now. Couldn't we please talk about something else?"

"We sure can, Katherine." He set his knife and fork down on his plate. A devilish smile replaced the scowl on his face. "What I'd like to talk about is us."

Well, I'd asked for a change in subject. Now I had another problem to deal with. It shouldn't be too hard to solve, how-ever, once I found the right words. Because I didn't have them at the moment, I fell back on repetition.

"About us, Garth?"

"You and me," he said.

"I wasn't thinking of myself as part of a twosome."

"That can change."

"We haven't known each other very long," I said. "It's only been a few weeks."

"Since the Apple Fair. I looked up and saw you coming toward me. You were wearing a red dress. Then you spoke to me, and we got acquainted. I don't need any more time to know that I want you."

This was going to be more difficult than I thought. Garth's appeared to be sincere, and his words were direct. I had to be direct too, and diplomatic, if I could manage it.

"You're an incredible man, Garth," I said. "You're attractive, kind, easy to talk to, sexy; I could go on and on. You're everything I want in a man someday. But I'm not ready for a relationship—not for a long time. I only just came back to the states. I haven't furnished my new house yet or even started my job. Besides, I don't know everything about you."

I only thought I didn't know how to answer him. I had said way too much.

"What do you want to know?" he asked. "Ask me."

Here was a perfect opportunity, but I couldn't very well say, "There's something about you that troubles me. I can't explain what it is, but it's there."

"Your ring," I said. "It's so unusual and striking. Is it an heirloom?"

He raised his hand up to the light. "You might say that. It belonged to my father. Is there someone else in your life, Katherine?"

"There's no one. I just need to be free for a while."

*Make that a long while.*

He found my hand across the table and squeezed it. The band of the ring pressed hard against my fingers, and he loosened his grip.

"I can wait, Katherine. I just wanted you to know what's on my mind."

Oh, no. I didn't want Garth to wait for me. How had I gotten myself into this predicament? More to the point, how could I extricate myself from it without losing him as a friend? Maybe I couldn't.

But the merriment came back to his eyes. He released my hand and said, "When I want something or someone, I don't like to wait. Life is short, and you never know what's waiting for you down the road."

"That's certainly true."

Garth's philosophy was hauntingly similar to Cora Valentine's, and Cora was dead. But what did that have to do with his surprising declaration?

"I respect what you're saying, Katherine," Garth said, "but I'm sure I can change your mind."

He was smiling, and his words were romantic, but at the same time something hidden in his tone made them sound like a threat.

# SIXTEEN

THE FRAGRANCE OF ROSES followed me down endless halls and twisting garden paths. I couldn't outrun it. From some distant place I sensed that it was gathering strength. Soon I would be overtaken, overpowered, and lost forever. The haunting was growing stronger, bringing back the sweet scent of summer roses on a cold fall morning.

I was lost.

I turned once on the bed and came out of the dream, waking to see Garth's yellow roses crowded into a creamy pitcher on my nightstand. So much for a new haunting. The bouquet represented my real dilemma of how to deal with Garth's intentions toward me.

The flowers were fuller this morning, with the last tight buds opening into petals that glittered like gold against lacy green ferns. They were lovely. I was touched by Garth's romantic gesture, although I didn't let it blind me to the reality of the situation. In a sense, this magnificent gift was a bribe, given to promote his cause. And when had I become so cynical?

Even if I were deeply attracted to Garth MacKay, I couldn't imagine building a life with him. We were too different. He was a staunch Militiaman who had broken one law that I knew of and probably many more. I loved my country and wouldn't even jaywalk on a small town street. I didn't like guns. He carried a rifle in his car. I knew my own worth and was secure in the life I was carving out for myself in Maple Creek. He had another plan for me.

Last night he had ended our evening with a lingering kiss that brought forth a reluctant response from me. He didn't remind me that he had the power to change my mind; he didn't have to. The memory of his beard scratching against my face, his ring pressing on my skin as he caressed me, and the scent of shaving lotion laced with the freshness of the woods and the air had powers of their own.

I reminded myself that Garth hadn't said anything about building a life together. "Want" was the word he'd used.

The arrogant bastard.

The next time Garth MacKay invited me to have dinner with him or accompany him on an excursion that even remotely sounded like a date, I intended to be unavailable. But I would keep the roses.

I brought them down to the kitchen where I could enjoy their sunshine color and fragrance in the morning light while I scrambled eggs for breakfast. Today was Halloween, and I'd thought of a legitimate reason to visit Anna Lynde. My new living room furniture was going to be delivered on Monday. When it arrived, I wanted to have the antique coffee table polished and ready to set in front of the sofa. I'd decided to buy the lingerie chest as well. Maybe I'd move Garth's roses to the living room. They really were a thoughtful gift.

ANNA LYNDE FILLED a teapot with boiling water and gave the loose leaves inside a stir. She brought two teacups painted in a nostalgic chintz pattern out of the china cabinet and a plate of sugar cookies from the kitchen. My mission to acquire the antiques and knowledge had turned into a tea party.

"Back then, we all wore our hair long," she said. "It was the style. Our skirts were unbelievably short." She touched the edges of her peach knit dress that dropped to the middle of her knees. "Even with a hemline this length, I would have considered myself dowdy and unattractive."

With a soft laugh, she added, "I had nicer legs in those days. I always used to get compliments on them. Now I like to keep them covered."

"I love today's long skirts and dresses," I said.

Anna's dining room table was littered with old photograph albums. The one we were going through was filled with color pictures of Anna and her friends when the girls had lived in the blue Victorian. In spite of Anna's avowed reluctance to revisit past times, it had been her own idea to bring out the albums. She wanted to show me how my house had looked thirty years ago.

I pointed to a picture of Cora in a white dress that resembled a baby doll nightgown. "If I wore an outfit like this, I'd feel naked."

"Not if all the other girls did." Anna turned the page. "Here we are in front of the house. Gerry Raycraft took most of the pictures. He was quite an amateur photographer in those days."

Besides the maple, which had been a mere sapling in the seventies, I counted five more trees in my front yard.

"Everything looked so much greener," I said.

"There were more trees on Walnut then and fewer houses. Across the street from your house, at least half the block was wooded acreage."

She lifted the picture out from the black corners that held it and handed it to me. "You may keep this one, if you like, Katherine. I have an envelope of duplicates somewhere."

Three decades ago the Victorian had been painted a lighter shade of blue with deep navy trim. In the picture, Cora and Anna stood on the porch, while a third girl sat on the steps, leaning against the railing. I thought I would recognize the girl on the swing from my barbecue re-creation, but I didn't, except for her long blonde hair.

"That's Rosalie Grier in front of us," Anna said. "She was always happy, always smiling."

"Do you remember if there was a swing in the yard next door?" I asked.

"The boys had one on the front porch. That was a romantic place to sit in the evening."

"I didn't mean that kind," I said. "Just a board with ropes tied to a tree branch."

"Oh, yes. Gerry made one for the backyard. He was always good with wood and building things." She turned another page. "These were taken on Capri the day we bought our cameo jewelry. And here's one of Rosalie and Cora picking strawberries. We only did that once."

Anna's picture collection captured the faces and the spirit of the years that interested me, and as she flipped through the pages, her commentary became increasingly detailed and sentimental.

"Now these were taken out West. We spent a summer in Colorado taking courses toward our Master's degrees. I always meant to go back there. Maybe I will some day. This was taken in the Maple Creek High auditorium. Cora and I bought white dresses to chaperone the Snowball Dance. Gerry and Ross went with us. We had so much fun that night. Now, here's Gerry cooking something one day when the boys invited us over for dinner. It's a stew or baked beans. I don't remember. Maybe barbecue sauce. He had a recipe with a secret ingredient."

Gerry Raycraft wore a sweater with a Varsity letter on the sleeve.

"Here are the boys raking leaves. We used to have the grandest bonfires. All of us at the lake. Ross had a boat. And…"

Anna's voice faltered. "Cora at the very first Apple Fair. Oh, my God…"

"What?"

"She's in front of the Cider Mill stand with a caramel apple in her hand. They always set up at the same site. It's a tradition. How very sad and ironic."

In Anna Lynde's comfortable living room, with the heat from the gas logs wrapping around me, I felt a chill. Cora young and happy in the picture, had smiled into the camera, not knowing that she was standing in the place where three decades later she would take her first bite of the poisoned apple that would kill her. Around me, the chill turned to ice.

"And prophetic," I added.

Anna appeared to be aware of the figurative temperature drop too. With a shudder, she said, "I don't think I want to look at pictures any more today, Katherine. We'll finish them another time, if you're still interested. There's just one more thing…"

She turned to the back of the album where two color photographs encased in plastic occupied an entire page.

"Here are Cora and Rosalie. A professional photographer took these photographs for the faculty section of the school yearbook. Oh, look, Katherine. I'd forgotten that."

In her picture Rosalie wore the kind of ruffled white blouse Nell had remembered Cora wearing. At the collar, a brooch added a charming old-fashioned touch.

"It's her brown cameo," Anna said.

"That's the same one I found. It has to be."

Anna opened a drawer in the china cabinet and took out a large magnifying glass. "I think so too, but look closely."

I did, and there wasn't the slightest doubt. Under the powerful glass, the lady in the cameo smiled up at me, intact and incredibly lovely, her face undamaged and her expression serene.

"When was this picture taken?" I asked.

"The fall of 1972. We went to Europe that year."

"So Rosalie could have lost the cameo any time after that."

"Rosalie left the following year at the end of the summer. It's odd that she never mentioned losing the cameo, but she was always leaving her possessions strewn around, always misplacing something. I remember that the safety chain on her bracelet broke too. I don't think she wore it after that, but she loved her cameo brooch."

I mulled over these facts, hoping to weave them together in a way that would shed light on the mystery. "That means the cameo was probably buried in the backyard from 1972 or 1973 until I dug it up."

"It seems likely."

"What happened to Rosalie?" I asked.

"She left town to get married. Actually, she eloped, but where she is now I have no idea. We lost touch years ago. At the time, she and Gerry were going together, but then this boy from Georgia came to town to visit his cousin. I don't remember where Rosalie met him, but he swept her off her feet.

"We didn't dream they were serious until we found Rosalie's goodbye note on the kitchen table. She'd moved out without giving us notice. Cora and I had to pay more for rent and utilities after that, but when Rosalie sent us a letter telling us how happy she was with her new husband, we forgave her for leaving without saying goodbye. Cora and I each received a Christmas card that year, but after that nothing."

"That's a strange story," I said.

"I thought so at the time, but over the years, I've lost track of many people that I considered good friends. They move away, get involved in their own lives, and don't spare a thought for the ones they left behind."

I nodded. "I've had the same experience. Now that I'm back in the states, I don't think I'll ever hear from my friends in Europe again."

And I knew that in time, after years had passed, they would be only images in an album, names barely remembered, faces frozen forever in my memory as they were at the precise moment their pictures were taken.

"Rosalie always had plenty of dates and male attention, but Cora and I were her only close women friends," Anna said. "I guess we weren't as close to her as we thought. Just before one of our high school reunions, Cora wrote her a long letter. It came back stamped "Moved—Address Unknown." I wanted Rosalie to be one of my bridesmaids."

She closed the album and said. "The following year I got married myself and moved down to Rochester, and Cora bought a house of her own in Maple Creek. The boys stayed on Walnut a few more years, but that wonderful time was over. Then when my girls were small, my husband and I came back to Maple Creek and bought this house. Now, I'm a widow and I'm thinking about moving again. My heavens…"

Anna looked at her watch and then at the clock on the mantel. "Whenever I start going through these old albums, time flies. I don't know how it got to be so late."

"You get lost in the past," I said. "It's easy to do."

"That's it, but I want to stay right here in the present. Let's go out and get your coffee table, Katherine. I'll send the lingerie chest along with a handyman I know who'll only charge you a few dollars for delivery. Then would you like to join me for dinner in town? I love to eat out at the Blue Lion, but I dislike going there alone."

"I would," I said. "I don't feel like cooking."

Now for the second night in a row I didn't have to. Remembering that the Blue Lion was Garth's favorite restaurant, I could only hope that I wouldn't see him there.

I WASN'T DESTINED TO BE lucky tonight, perhaps because it was Halloween, and a full moon was shining in the sky. On this night of trick or treat, Fate was playing a trick on me. Or maybe it was a treat.

Garth MacKay was having dinner with his partner, Greg Sky, at a table uncomfortably close to the booth Anna had requested, and he looked devilishly handsome, like an eighteenth century rake. Why hadn't I noticed how very attractive this man was? I tried to call back the negative feelings that had assailed me this morning but found that I couldn't do it. I kept thinking about yellow roses.

Damn the man.

Anna intercepted the smile he sent my way. "I didn't realize you knew Garth MacKay," she said. "I'd be very careful around him, Katherine. He's a good man to stay away from."

"For any particular reason?"

"For one, he belongs to the Michigan Militia."

"So he told me, but he doesn't talk much about it. Is there anything else?"

"He's supposed to be dangerous, but no, I can't think of anything specific. In fairness, I shouldn't talk about him. Where did you meet him?"

"At the Apple Fair," I said. "In front of Sky and MacKay Title. He was feeding a hot dog to his Belgian shepherd."

"That was a significant smile he just gave you. You might call it a possessive smile. Stop me if I'm prying into your life."

"No, it's all right. Garth walks his dog on my street. We've gotten acquainted, a little."

"That's right. Sky and MacKay Title is on the corner of Walnut and Main. He lives in an old farmhouse out in the country. Cora took his sister, Taryn, under her wing. That's all I know for certain about Mr. MacKay, but if a man has a reputation for being dangerous, there's probably a good reason for it."

"Maybe it's all because of the Militia," I said. "He can be charming, and he's very thoughtful, not to mention handsome. At least I think so."

"That's the kind of man to watch out for. But I forget I'm not talking to one of my daughters. I'm sure you know what you're doing."

"I wish I were."

I didn't want to say anything more about Garth MacKay. I didn't want to think about him or about the roses on my kitchen table, filling the house with their haunting fragrance. I hoped that Garth would concentrate on his dinner and whatever conversation he was having with his partner.

"I'm going to have a corned beef sandwich and save room for dessert," Anna said. "They have the most marvelous chocolate cheesecake here.

I'd been considering soup and a salad, but Anna's choice sounded more appealing, especially the cheesecake. It was Halloween night, a holiday of sorts, and no time to count calories.

"That sounds good," I said, noticing that Anna was looking over my shoulder, staring intently at something or someone. She was frowning.

"I don't believe this," she said.

"What?"

"Gerry Raycraft just came in with Alarice. He rarely leaves his house. Neither does she. Don't look, Katherine."

But I had already turned around. As Anna had said, Gerry Raycraft stood in the entrance, holding his cane as if it were an umbrella rather than a necessary aid. In front of him stood the woman I'd met at Nell's party who lived in the Sears' kit house. She wore a navy polka dot dress with a white shawl wrapped around her shoulders. She was smoothing its long fringe, untying it and tying it again, giving the impression that she was ill at ease in this den of iniquity she had just entered.

"I'm astonished," Anna said.

I could tell that, and she didn't look very happy either.

"What's wrong? Is one of them married to someone else?" I asked.

"No, they're perfectly free to see each other. It's just that since Gerry had to start using a cane, he likes to spend most of his time at home, and Alarice used to have that disorder... I can't think of its name. The one where you're afraid to leave your house."

"Agoraphobia. Well, something brought them out tonight, maybe Halloween," I said. "But Alarice came to Nell's party."

"She's a little better now. She goes out sometimes to shop and keep appointments, but she never stays very long. All her life she's given piano lessons in her home. Once a year, she has a recital for her students, but it's always short, and she's usually the first to leave any affair she attends."

"What a terrible disorder."

"They found a table. Good. They didn't see us. Gerry used to take Alarice out years and years ago, but I thought that was all over."

Anna opened her menu and appeared to be studying the dessert selections, but since she'd already made her choice, I assumed she wanted to avoid having to speak to Gerry and Alarice. I didn't understand this, as from what Anna had said previously, I thought she had high regard for Gerry Raycraft and fond memories of him.

Perhaps her feelings for him went beyond fondness. Of course. That was it. Anna was a widow, and Gerry was bachelor. She didn't like to see him in the company of another woman. Whatever the case, I was certain that Anna was greatly affected at the sight of Gerry with Alarice. For the rest of the evening, she did her best to avoid speaking about them.

# SEVENTEEN

I, ON THE OTHER HAND, did my best to learn more about Gerry Raycraft whose mercurial personality puzzled me. After our sandwiches arrived, when Anna was discussing the pros and cons of buying one of Myrold Barren's condominiums, I slipped in a question about the dollhouse in the yard of the Raycraft mansion.

"Gerry used to repair broken toys for needy children," Anna said. "Years ago, he started making them from scratch. He's going to donate the dollhouse to the Church Charity Raffle. Ah—that's why those two are together."

"Did I miss something?" I asked.

"Alarice sews doll clothes for little girls who wouldn't have a Christmas present otherwise. She creates entire wardrobes."

"Gerry and Alarice do have something in common then."

"Only that. Gerry is such a good man. He's never been properly appreciated by anyone. He took care of his old uncle for years until he died. Then Gerry had a stroke. He's entitled to a little peace and joy in his life, but Alarice isn't the right woman for him. He needs somebody who can make him happy."

"And that somebody is me," she might as well have added.

"Oh—your friend is leaving, Katherine," Anna said. "I thought he'd come over and say something to you. I guess he thinks that smile was enough."

"I'm not encouraging Garth MacKay," I said, trying to add a little conviction to my voice.

But I was a bit baffled because I'd been expecting Garth to stop by our booth and say "Hello," "Happy Halloween,"

"How are you tonight?" Anything. Maybe ignoring me was part of his game plan. Maybe this time I'd met my match.

*Maybe this time…*

A shiver of apprehension froze the thought in mid-sentence as I recalled how that phrase had haunted me on previous occasions. But this was a night made for haunting. Maybe this time I'd be able to complete the thought.

Just then the waiter appeared with our cheesecake, reminding me of the candy bars waiting to be handed out and the coffee table I had to unload from my trunk.

Like the unfortunate Alarice, suddenly I couldn't wait to get home.

TWINKLING PUMPKIN LIGHTS outlined the windows of the Rawson house, casting an unearthly glow on the bust of the screaming woman and her dark companions. Dracula, now awake and sitting up in his casket, had his own spotlight, but the effect of the lawn display was mitigated by the deafening noise coming from inside. The rock music and laughter were loud enough to drive away the boldest of spirits, blasting Dalton's prediction of a quiet Halloween into the atmosphere.

Whatever happened to shivery recorded sounds and ghost stories? Deadly silence and fear complemented each other. If it weren't for the gruesome decorations, this would be just another teen party.

I eased the coffee table carefully out of my trunk, not wanting to add still another scratch to its surface, and carried it across the crackling leaves to the house. The glass top made it heavier than I'd thought, but I could manage. Up over the porch steps, one at a time—there. I set it down and opened the door.

I'd left the porch light and parlor lamp on. Still, I had an urge to rush through the house, turning all the lights on until the blue Victorian was as bright as the Rawson place. And I wanted to change into something more comfortable than the green knit dress I'd worn to visit Anna.

Even with the front door closed, the blaring noise from across the street intruded, but the sound was happy, a welcome change from the silent waiting halls. Would I ever be able to come home without running into this sense of unease? No matter what I'd done to turn it into a home, in a sense, the house still wasn't mine.

In the kitchen, I peered through the window to the porch. Vicky's nose was pressed to the door, her dark eyes filled with reproach, no doubt because her dinner hadn't arrived at its accustomed time.

I opened the door wide, but she remained on the porch. "Vicky, you poor hungry little thing," I said. "Come in."

She wagged her tail slowly but stayed where she was, riveted to the floor mat.

Quickly I spilled two cups of kibble into her dish and moistened it with warm water. "It'll be ready in just one minute, girl."

In that time, I could slip out of the dress and into a pair of jeans and a sweater. I hurried to the staircase. I would light a few candles in the bay window, too, the orange ones...

"Trick or treat!" The high, young voices shrilled from the front porch.

I picked up the candy and opened the door to a diminutive ghost, an angel in white, and a black-clad witch wearing a tall peaked hat. All three little girls had long flaxen hair that reminded me of Rosalie in the yearbook picture.

A woman in a black hooded raincoat waited on the sidewalk, while two boys, a little taller and older, ran out of the darkness. In garish rock band costumes, they were too young to mingle with the teens in the party and almost too old to go trick of treating, but not quite. I passed out candy to all. Then, not seeing anything except the police cruiser coming slowly down the street, I closed the door.

Now, if I did it quickly, I could change clothes before the next group arrived.

A soft, pleading whine from the back of the house reminded me that Vicky's dinner was more than ready. I set her dish on the floor a few feet inside the kitchen and watched her inch her way longingly toward it.

Again, I headed for the stairs, only to hear "Trick or Treat." This time the deep male voice was familiar. Reversing my direction, I opened the door. In a circle of lamplight, Dalton stood on the porch, tall, dark, and official. He had parked his patrol car in front of my house.

"Happy Halloween, Katherine," he said. "I was in the neighborhood and thought I'd stop by to see what you're giving away."

"Nice costume, Dalton. It's Baby Ruth miniatures."

He stepped across the threshold and scooped four candy bars out of the dish. "Caramel and nuts—my favorite. Is everything all right here?"

"I'm not expecting trouble. I have three packages of bribes."

"We got a call that someone was shooting firecrackers from the Rawson place at the houses across the street."

"They have the wrong holiday. It's only the music."

"The kids promised to tone it down a little for the early-to-bed crowd. Believe it or not, there's a chaperone on the premises."

"That's asking a lot," I said. "Once a teen party gets going, it's hard to keep it down."

"I'll swing around this way again. I'd rather have kids partying in one place than getting into trouble all over town. It's mostly the little ones who are out on the street with their parents tonight." He looked up the staircase where the downstairs light struggled to reach the landing. "Did you have that railing repaired yet?"

"It's as good as new, but from now on I'll test it before putting my weight on it."

"Good idea. I'm on my way to Grover Street. Another party complaint."

He appeared to be enjoying himself. If a little noise was

the only problem the police had to deal with, the evening would be a success. I opened the door for him and listened, trying to decide whether the rock music was any softer. It sounded the same to me. "Thanks for stopping in to check on me," I said.

"I wanted to make sure you weren't under fire."

He looked up at the night sky where the shimmering full moon rode high above the trees. I wouldn't have been surprised to see the silhouette of a flying witch sketched across its surface.

"That moon is sure an amazing sight tonight," Dalton said. "Makes me wish I wasn't on duty."

That was an unexpected observation from a dedicated police officer like Dalton. It could have a variety of interpretations, although the gleam in his blue eyes and his rakish smile were fairly easy to read.

"It'll still be there when you're done for the night," I said.

"I don't think so. I'm on duty till late tomorrow morning. There won't be another full moon on Halloween again for almost two decades."

"Then we'll have to enjoy this one tonight," I said, trying to match his light mood.

"While it lasts," he added. "Have fun, Katherine. Stay safe."

FINALLY THE BLARE of rock music gave way to deep night silence and more familiar sounds like wind and chimes. But once I heard the cry of a night creature so piercing and fright-filled that it might have come from a vampire's victim. All along Walnut, lights went out, and houses settled back in the comforting darkness. Eventually even the Rawson place grew quiet, although the outdoor illumination continued to wash over the lawn decorations.

At eleven thirty I turned off my lamp, blew out the candles, and took the empty candy dish into the kitchen where Vicky lay sleeping alongside her food bowl. She got up when she saw me and scrambled back out to the porch. I held the outer door open for her and watched her melt away into the shadows that filled the yard.

From the back of the house, the moon appeared to be swelling and gaining in brightness, like an orange party balloon cut loose from a tree branch. On this enchanted night, I thought I could almost reach up and touch it.

I sat on the top porch step and leaned against the door thinking about Dalton's parting words and the blue gleam that I was so sure I could interpret. The man was gorgeous. I'd thought so from the first moment I'd seen him directing traffic at the Apple Fair. I wouldn't mind going out with him— if he were to ask me, that is. Once or twice only, a movie and dinner, nothing intense. I already had intense with Garth.

But what of Lacey, the policewoman, Dalton's partner? I had almost forgotten about her. I hadn't seen her since I'd gone to the police station to report the burglary. Maybe she had been transferred, or her hold on Dalton wasn't as strong Nell had implied. Tonight he'd stopped by to see if I was all right.

Don't read too much into that, I cautioned myself. He's only doing his job, and if he throws in a little flirtation, who has to know or care except you?

Relationships, always tricky, were especially convoluted among the quirky inhabitants of Maple Creek. I would have thought Anna well satisfied with her life, but she also appeared to be romantically interested in her old friend, Gerry Raycraft who had dated two of her roommates in the distant past.

Did he return her interest? I couldn't tell, having seen them together only once before tonight.

I recalled that longstanding feud between Cora and Alarice. Could Gerry Raycraft have been the inadvertent cause of it?

Anna thought that he deserved a woman who could make him happy. Still, he had emerged from his gray mansion to seek the company of Alarice who had an aversion to going outside. How different Alarice must be from Cora and Rosalie, and from Anna herself, now that I thought about it. I would like to get to know Alarice better.

Unlike Anna, I didn't see anything unusual in Gerry's choice. Years ago, a smiling, happy woman had failed him. Perhaps he was looking for something else now, or perhaps no one at all. He might be content to remain a bachelor with an occasional female dinner companion.

Then there were Myrold Barren who was dating Meg Valentine, according to Nell, to secure a coveted piece of acreage, and Nell herself who would consider a fourth marriage failure an embarrassment. Woven throughout these interactions was a mysterious and dangerous thread that had begun on the day of the Fair with a plump, juicy Michigan apple laced with poison.

These were only a few of the fragments in the tapestry. I wished I knew how to tie them all together.

Life in Maple Creek was like a dark soap opera. Since Garth had revealed his intentions toward me, I considered myself a part of it, one of the quirky townspeople who lived in an old haunted house and amused herself by spinning stories in the light of a full Halloween moon.

If only I could know how they would play out—especially my own.

A cold nose nudged me. Vicky came out of the darkness at the back of the yard. Tail wagging, front paws on the first step, she waited for me to invite her inside. We were making progress. In a few nights, she might decide to make her bed in the kitchen. The house wouldn't seem so lonely then.

I laid my hand on her head and murmured, "Good dog. It's time for bed."

THE LUMINOUS DIALS on my alarm clock pointed to one-thirty. I lay in bed listening to the wind tear through the trees and whip around the house. Although I was tired, my mind refused to shut down. Did all of the sounds originate outside, or was someone walking up the stairs? Once I thought I heard something scratching at the boards in the attic again.

*Some vile thing.*

That was impossible. The opening had been closed. Nothing could get inside the house. It had to be the wind or my imagination.

*Wake when some vile thing is near.*

Why should I remember that quotation from *The Book of Fairy Poetry* at this particular time? What possible relevance did it have to my life? None.

I would have to check the attic one more time, in case Dalton had missed another opening. Soon, but not tonight when the wind was blowing and I was wearing a nightgown.

I couldn't understand why I always imagined Cora Valentine's spirit roaming the halls of the blue Victorian. If I were to consult a medium, would Cora be able to come through and tell me why she couldn't rest? Only in a ghost story. And where would I find a medium? Probably not in Maple Creek, but it didn't matter because I wasn't going to look for one. The wind was creating the noise, not a restless spirit.

As I turned from one side to the other, my thoughts, like the sheets, became increasingly tangled and uncomfortable. I wished I could harness the images that flashed on and off in my brain.

Think about pleasant things, I told myself. Love and roses and swings…

I pulled the sheets straight up to my chin, and moved my head higher on the pillow. Now let those lovely thoughts come.

The strange romantic pairings of Maple Creek began to play through my mind like clips from a sentimental old love movie. Gerry and Alarice; Gerry and Anna; Gerry and Rosalie; the unknown Southern boy and Rosalie…

Why not add Garth and Katherine? Or should it be Dalton and Katherine? And don't forget Myrold and Meg.

This was like counting sheep, and at last my body and mind began to relax. I turned once more on the bed and eventually fell asleep.

# EIGHTEEN

ON THE MORNING AFTER Halloween smashed pumpkins littered Main Street, and at Maple Creek High School a suspicious white substance sprinkled across the front entrance gave the students an unexpected day off. Capricious nature caused the only other damage, sending high winds that brought down temperatures, branches, and one power line.

Otherwise, the night had been quieter than anticipated. So claimed the *Tribune* editor in the early edition, with a heartfelt note of thanks to the police, the Neighborhood Watches, and parents who had supervised their children's activities.

But on the radio I heard a disturbing report. Terry Cameron had recanted his confession, admitting that he'd written the story about killing Cora Valentine on a dare and to see if his teacher would grade it or call the police. Now he wanted to be left alone, but that wasn't going to happen. At the very least, he would have to undergo extensive counseling.

This latest development in the Cora Valentine case meant that the killer was still out there...out there...out there...

The possibility was as chilling as the deteriorating weather conditions. As I raked the last of the leaves and fallen twigs into the street, the words echoed in my mind. Perhaps the real life horror was scheduled to occur after Halloween when people weren't expecting it.

I had one more chore to do, and then I could go inside. My maple tree had lost a large branch in the wind. It lay across the walk, blocking the stairs to the porch. I bent down, intending to drag it out to the curb but found that I couldn't budge it. At this precise moment, I looked up to see a familiar man in a dark green jacket walking down the street with an exuberant black dog.

For a brief moment I wished myself anywhere but outside in the yard, visible and approachable. But Garth and I were the only two people on the street, and he was obviously headed for my house. Anyway, I didn't really want to avoid him, even though it might be wiser for me to do so.

When he reached my side, he dropped Tac's leash and lifted the branch as easily as if it were a dried sunflower stalk. "Let me help you with that, Katherine," he said. "The windstorm played hell with trees all over town."

Tac lunged toward me. Ordering him to Sit and Stay in the gruff voice he reserved for the dog, Garth deposited the branch in the street next to the leaves.

"Thanks, Garth," I said. "Did you close your office early?"

"The power's out on Main. It was supposed to be back on by noon. Maybe that's noon tomorrow. We decided to call it a day."

He looked toward the bay window where soft lamplight streamed out into the gloom, issuing a silent invitation. "I'm getting a sore throat. Must be coming down with a cold. I was hoping you'd offer me a cup of coffee before I head on home. The Blue Lion is closed or I'd stop there," he added.

How could I refuse? There was no way, and he must know it.

"I could do that," I said. "Don't you have a generator?"

"Yes, but we weren't busy anyway. No power is a good excuse to leave work early. I'll finish up out here for you while you make the coffee."

I'd already raked the yard, and Garth might be coming down with a cold. Possibly he was. I noticed the package of throat lozenges in the pocket of his jacket. Maybe. He had been working in a house without heat for hours.

"This is all I'm going to do for today," I said. "Thanks again for hauling that branch out for me."

"Anytime, Katherine. Anything."

I countered this sweeping, generous offer with one of my

own. "One cup of coffee coming up then—or would you prefer hot chocolate?"

"I'd like a cup of black coffee, nice and hot. I've been drinking cold orange juice all morning."

He looped Tac's leash over the porch railing and reminded him to Stay. Following me into the house, he stood in a circle of light, a picture of male health and vigor. Was this a man felled by a sore throat? He could be. Lately I was getting too suspicious.

"This is better," he said. "Bright and warm."

"Let me take your jacket."

"Thanks, but I think I'll keep it on for a minute. I see you bought that coffee table from the yard sale. I had my eye on it too. It looks like one my grandmother used to have."

"Anna says it dates from the nineteen thirties."

I had moved the yellow roses to the center of the table. Reflected in the glass surface, they filled the room with color and fragrance—and a memory of the last time Garth and I were together on this very spot.

"I bought a hand-painted lingerie chest from Anna, too, and I'm having a new sofa and chair delivered today," I said. "Pretty soon this will be a real living room."

"Your house is starting to look downright homey."

"It may not be a decorator's dream, but I'm buying furniture I really like."

I looked around, satisfied with what I saw: An antique lamp, two distinctive vintage tables, and a pitcher of roses, everything classy and inviting. I'd made a good beginning at putting together a comfortable home.

Whenever someone was with me, the blue Victorian was simply a gracious old house, at the moment sparsely furnished, but nevertheless my home in progress. Neither mysterious sounds nor supernatural vibes contradicted the effect. Those disturbances belonged to the night and usually waited to appear until I was alone and vulnerable.

At the moment I was with someone and safe.

"Let's go back to the kitchen," I said, leading the way through the hall. "I have a kettle of chicken soup simmering on the stove. Would you like some with your coffee?"

"Yes, if it isn't too much trouble."

As I lifted the lid and gave the soup a stir, Garth came up behind me. "That sure smells good. I didn't think you were the domestic type, Katherine."

"Usually I'm not, but I like to eat, and today seemed like a good day to make soup. It's hot and nourishing, the ideal way to ward off a cold, if you believe in folk medicine."

"I'll accept your offer with pleasure," he said. "I've been eating in restaurants for a week."

"Did your sister lose interest in cooking?" I asked.

"Taryn's gone away for a while. She's in Tennessee visiting her cousins for Thanksgiving."

Which was three weeks away. Something in Garth's tone and his careful phrasing piqued my curiosity. "Won't she miss too much school?"

He shrugged. "Her teachers gave her some reading and assignments, but I don't know if she'll do much without me around to remind her."

"So you're alone. Do you cook for yourself?"

"Not with the Blue Lion right around the corner from my business."

"That makes sense. Well, this soup isn't a meal, but it may help your cold."

I filled the new coffeemaker and then swirled the ladle through the steaming golden liquid, scooping up bits of celery, carrots, and pieces of shredded white chicken into a bowl, while Garth sat down and took off his jacket. The sleeves of his red striped shirt were rolled up twice on his brawny arms. As always, I was drawn to the flashing black stones and diamonds in his ring.

"Here's a spoon for you and some crackers." I took two cups out of the cupboard and then sat down across from him. "I'll have a cup of coffee with you. I guess you heard about Terry Campbell."

"Yeah. It didn't seem to me like he did it. Things are bad enough in the world today without kids pulling stunts like that. He needs a trip to the woodshed. It's long overdue."

"That's an outdated, unenlightened view, Garth," I said. "You talk like you're a hundred years old."

"I'll stand by my beliefs, Katherine. Terry gave the cops a false lead and let the real killer off the hook. Look what happened in Maple Creek last night. Orange pulp and seeds all over the road, and kids playing at being terrorists, shutting down a whole school. Mrs. Winters nearly caused an accident when she swerved to avoid a pumpkin."

I couldn't argue with that, although the image of my neighbor steering past a pumpkin into a vehicle had to be comic exaggeration. "Did they ever find out what the white substance was?" I asked.

"Powdered sugar and salt, and they cleaned up the street, but that problem Terry Campbell caused won't go away so easily. It doesn't say much for the future when we let the kids take control. I'm in favor of the traditional family and a steady diet of discipline," he added.

I decided to let that go. This was one more way in which Garth and I were fundamentally different, and I didn't want to argue with a man at my dinner table, especially one who was coming down with a cold. "Didn't you ever have any trouble raising Taryn?" I asked.

I wouldn't have noticed his slight hesitation if I hadn't been watching for it. "Some. Mostly little things. Taryn was always well behaved, more than I ever was, only she never did like going to school. I want more for my sister, and she's going to have it."

"There's no reason why she shouldn't," I said.

Taryn was fortunate to have a brother who cared so much about her. I supposed Terry Campbell's father cared about him too, but sometimes all the caring in the world wasn't enough.

The coffee was ready. I remembered Garth's preferences. No sugar, no cream; just hot and black. As I poured it, I reflected that Garth was easy to please. The role of nurturer was a new one for me. I wasn't sure it suited me, but I enjoyed seeing the gratified look on his face as he finished the soup in record time.

"This is great," he said. "I can't remember when I had anything so good."

I filled the bowl again. "I'm a little out of practice. While I was in Europe I ate out most of the time."

"What I like best is to eat at home. Even a can of beans tastes better when you're in your own house. Tell me, Katherine. Did the police ever find that burglar?"

"Not that I know of."

"I saw that your railing was fixed when I came up the walk. Did they catch the person who did it?"

"No, but the incident is over. I want to forget about it."

And for a while I almost had until he reminded me.

"You shouldn't do that," he said. "Suppose something happens again?"

"I hope it won't."

"So do I, but I wish you'd let me conduct a private inspection, just to make sure everything's in order. The police aren't giving you any help, and I've had a lot of experience working around old houses. You should have seen Sky and MacKay Title when we bought it. The place was a regular death trap."

"So far my house has been inspected three times. That's counting the official one, before the closing."

"A fourth walk-through won't hurt."

"I thought you were coming down with a cold," I said.

"I am. Your good soup revived me."

"Well…"

I could see that I was going to lose this battle, but Garth did have a point. An additional inspection might reveal a problem we'd all overlooked. Maybe the scratching noises I'd heard and the footsteps on the stairs weren't entirely figments of my imagination.

I wished I could believe that they were.

"I guess you could have a look in the attic," I said. "It's a little awkward for me to walk up there."

His face lit up with pleasure. I felt as if I'd awarded him a contract or prize.

"Good. I'll check the basement out too, and the house has its original windows. Could be there're not as safe as you'd like."

"While you're up in the attic, you might check to see if there's any way a creature could get inside. I'm thinking about a bat, something like that. I had one opening sealed, but I still hear a scratching sound."

A teasing smile crossed his face. "Are you still hearing ghosts?"

I squashed my impulse to deny it and said in a forced light tone, "One or two. They come out at night when the wind blows."

For some reason, he found that amusing. "If anything got in, I'll send it on its way," he said.

I STOOD IN THE SMALL, empty closet listening to Garth's boots stamp down on the skeletal floor above me as he crisscrossed the attic. At the entrance, dust motes floated in the light of the lantern. The air pouring down through the square opening was frigid and stale. I shivered and buttoned my cardigan up to my neck.

With the lack of light and ventilation and the boards spaced so far apart, this was the last and most difficult stop on Garth's inspection tour.

"Do you see any openings?" I asked.

Apparently he couldn't hear me. I climbed up the ladder and rested my elbows against the shelf. "Do you see anything at all, Garth?"

He walked over to the opening, covering his mouth as a fit of coughing came over him. "Nothing with wings. You need more insulation up here, Katherine. What's in those trunks over in the corner?"

"Nothing. They came with the house."

"I'll go have a look anyway."

As Dalton had done on his first visit, Garth tugged open the lid of the first trunk. "It's empty, except for some papers," he said. "And this one…" Unlike Dalton, he opened it with no trouble. "This is empty too. Wait, here's something." He knelt down behind the second trunk, coughed again, and came up with a small square article in his hand.

I hoisted myself up to the attic floor. "What did you find?"

"A blue book. It looks like a missal or small Bible."

Taking giant steps to navigate the attic boards, he came toward me and held the volume up to the light of the lantern. "It's *My Diary*. Why do you hide your diary in the attic when you live alone, Katherine?"

"Because…" I couldn't go on. "You don't really want me to answer that, do you?"

"No." A dark smudge marked his face like a scar. With his black beard and devil-may-care grin, he reminded me of a pirate. "Let's go back down. You'll get all dirty if you stay here." He handed the diary to me and turned me gently around.

Excitement gripped me as I clutched the cold gritty book. Maybe the diary held an explanation for the scratching sounds or, better still, for the entire haunting.

A more likely theory was that my imagination was running amok. Still, words written long ago would provide a glimpse of the past, whether it proved to be mundane or wonderful.

Garth picked up the lantern. "Down you go now. Don't fall."

"Really, Garth, I've climbed ladders taller than this."

But I descended slowly to the hardwood floor, with Garth close behind me. In the small, empty bedroom, he turned on the overhead light, and I opened the diary.

Quickly I leafed through the little book, raising more dust. The thin pages were filled with lines written in green ink. A few of the words were smeared, but the handwriting was neat and the text was legible. Inside the cover I looked for a name or year, but all I saw was a quotation: "The day with its possibilities lay before me."

"When Lieutenant Gray checked out the attic, he found an old *Playmate* magazine," I said. "Someone else must have left the diary, probably a young girl. Exactly where was it, Garth?"

"Behind that second trunk, down between the boards. You're not going to read somebody's diary, are you?"

"Sure, if it holds my interest. The owner won't be coming back for it at this late date. But I can't help wondering. Who would go to the trouble of hiding a diary in an attic and then leave it there?"

"She must have forgotten all about it."

"That's probably it. I wish I knew how old it is."

"Maybe you'll find a date in one of the entries," he said.

I opened the diary again. "It starts on February 10th. There's no year."

"If you read this girl's writings, you may find a clue to the time somewhere. Maybe she still lives in Maple Creek and you can look her up and return it to her. Do you want me to carry those trunks outside for you?"

His voice was raspy. I felt guilty for doubting that he had a sore throat. "Not now, Garth. You've done enough, and look at you. Plowing through all that dust in the cold probably made your throat worse. You can wash your hands in the bathroom."

He turned off the light and followed me into the hall.

"It's all for a good cause, Katherine, but I didn't do anything. Your house passed inspection with flying colors."

I'd known that would be the outcome. Now he did too. But what caused the sounds, and where did my sudden feeling of impending disaster come from? As I opened the linen closet, I remembered when I thought some spirit hand had disarranged the towels on my shelves. Whatever haunted the blue Victorian was alive and well. Probably not alive.

I handed Garth a blue towel and washcloth from the top of

the stacks. "So the house won't kill me. I didn't think it would."

"But something else might," he said.

# NINETEEN

GARTH CAME INTO the kitchen smelling faintly of lavender soap. All traces of his foray into the attic were gone from his face and arms, but he still looked a little like a pirate. The unknown, dangerous quality that mystified me was never far away.

"Do you really think someone might be planning to kill me?" I asked.

"It could be. I don't understand what's going on here, but I don't like it."

"Well, you didn't find anything suspicious in the house. That's something."

"The danger comes from outside. Just be careful. During the day I'm only a few houses away, and at night…"

"You're a thoughtful man, Garth, but if anything else were to happen, I'll call the police again," I said.

"I'll give you my number at home anyway."

With each word, his voice grew progressively more hoarse. Again, a feeling of guilt tugged at me. An hour ago, Garth had stopped in for a cup of hot coffee, and then I had allowed him to roam through the damp basement and cold attic, breathing dusty air. He must be concerned about me or he would have finished his coffee and gone straight home to fight off his cold. He must care.

I brought my largest mug down from the cupboard. "You sound terrible. Sit down. I'm going to make you another warm drink. It'll be hot tea with lemon and honey this time."

He touched my shoulder gently. "You're the thoughtful one, Katherine."

Loud, angry barking from the front porch almost drowned

out the shrill whistle of the teakettle. "Oh… We forgot about Tac," I said.

"I didn't. He's fine on the porch. He's used to waiting for me."

Garth sat down at the table, just as I heard a sharp rapping at the side door. Through the window, I caught a glimpse of Nell, with her long hair flying around her face in the wind.

"It's Nell Farmer," I said. "I think you two know each other."

As I opened the door, leaves from my neighbors' yard blew in with a rush of wind. I pushed them back outside with my foot. "Come in, Nell."

"Hi, Katherine," she said. "I didn't want to go anywhere near that ferocious black dog."

"That's Tac, Garth MacKay's shepherd."

"Oh, right. As I said, ferocious." She smiled at Garth as warmly if he were a friend she hadn't seen in a while, someone she'd never warned me about.

"Hello, Mr. MacKay. Nice to see you again. It's been a long time." She handed me a plate covered with orange plastic wrap. "We had a Halloween party at the hospital yesterday, and I set some cookies aside for you. Well…" She looked at Garth and then at me again. "I'm sorry. Am I interrupting something?"

Quickly I said, "Not at all. Garth stopped to help me with a heavy branch that fell. I'm making tea. Come join us."

But she was already sitting down, patting her windblown hair back in place, taking the cover off the cookies. "How's the title business these days, Mr. MacKay?"

"Good, ma'am, but we lost power today."

"It's getting pretty breezy outside. I think we'll have another windstorm tonight," she said.

Garth nodded his agreement and pulled the package of lozenges out of his jacket pocket. "From now on, it's downhill all the way, weather wise."

"At least we had a nice warm fall."

With this bland weather observation, conversation floundered to a standstill. I poured the tea, cut the lemon, and found the container of honey shaped like a bear, all the while wondering what new topic to introduce. The tension in the kitchen was like a live wire on the ground, sparking, smoking, and deadly to touch. Obviously Nell's moment of courtesy didn't reflect her true feelings about Garth, but she seemed determined to appear sociable. As for Garth, he was unusually reticent. He hadn't opened the lozenges yet.

"What kind of cookies did you bake, Nell?" I asked.

"Pumpkin chocolate chip. They're orange, very seasonal."

"They sound delicious." I handed Garth the honey bear. "Squeeze a little of this into your tea, Garth. He has a sore throat, Nell."

"Well it's cold and flu season, as we say at the hospital," Nell said.

Garth added a dollop of honey to the mug and took a swig of tea. "I never get colds."

"Mmm. You have one now."

"As a nurse, do you know of any secret remedy, Nell?" I asked.

"There's no cure. Plenty of liquids and bed rest will make you feel better temporarily, but you have to let it run its course. You could try one of my cookies, Garth. They're spicy."

Garth finished his tea in a gulp. "No thank you, ma'am, not now. That was good tea, Katherine. I'm on my way. Nice to see you again, Nell." Four short sentences, and he was standing up.

"I'll see you out," I said.

In the hall he opened the front door and enveloped me in a crushing bear hug while Tac barked in unbridled joy at his master's reappearance. "Thanks for everything, Katherine, and take care of yourself. I'll be around."

"I hope you feel better soon," I said.

With a wave for me, Garth untied Tac's leash and led him back to the sidewalk, as I closed the door. What Nell had called a breeze was a strong wind, and it felt much colder than it had when I'd been outside working.

Now I was having a weather conversation with myself.

In the kitchen, Nell was sampling one of her cookies. "I'm really sorry for intruding, Katherine," she said. "I recognized the dog, but there was no point in walking back home with the cookies. I didn't realize that you were seeing Garth."

"It isn't like that. As I said, Garth was walking by with Tac, and he carried that heavy branch out to the curb for me. He has a cold. I made him a cup of coffee."

I felt that my own short sentences revealed enough of the afternoon's events to satisfy her. Garth's visit really was spur of the moment, and, remembering how Nell had told Alarice about the crushed cameo, I didn't intend to mention my latest find to her. Not that I thought telling Nell about the diary would lead to a second burglary. For now I just wanted it to be my secret.

"Wasn't it tea that you served Garth?" she asked.

"First I made coffee."

"Oh. Coffee *and* tea. Love must be in the air. I finally met up with Meg Valentine. Myrold Barren sent her flowers yesterday. Plain daisies. Like he couldn't afford anything more expensive. He doesn't have his hands on Cora's property yet though."

"Maybe Myrold doesn't have an ulterior motive," I said.

"Myrold always has a reason for what he does, but Meg is no fool. With Cora's money, she has freedom now. She doesn't have to stay in that dreary high school job anymore. Myrold won't get anything from Meg that she doesn't want to give. By the way, she showed me Cora's jewelry," she added. "Cora owned a pink cameo pin, but it isn't like the one I remember."

"Oh, about that…" I had almost forgotten Nell's interest in the crushed cameo and seized the opportunity to steer the conversation away from men, love, and flowers. "That mystery is solved."

I told her what little I knew about Rosalie Grier, the cameo's owner.

"I didn't know that Cora and Anna had another roommate," Nell said.

"Rosalie taught at Maple Creek High for a while, but that might have been before you were a student there. Anna says she moved out of the state years ago."

"Leaving her pretty cameo behind. That's odd."

"Maybe not so odd. We think she lost it. I don't see how we'll ever be able to learn anything more."

"Well, who cares? I'm more interested in what's happening now." She took another cookie and passed the plate to me. "Garth MacKay looked right at home in your kitchen, Katherine. Do you think he might be sending you flowers one day?"

I smiled at her, thinking about the yellow roses in the living room. "You never know. More tea, Nell?"

SOON AFTER NELL LEFT, the van from the furniture store pulled up in front of the house. As I hurried to the door, I heard a dog's soft whining on the back porch. Soon after that, Anna's handyman arrived with the lingerie chest. By the time I'd settled on the best location for the sofa and chair, fed Vicky, and reheated chicken soup for a light dinner, the last of the daylight was fading.

The wind had increased, bringing with it a cold rain. I made a fresh pot of tea, built a fire, and settled down near the fireplace to read the diary. At last. I'd wanted to do this ever since Garth had placed the small blue book in my hand.

*It was a dark and stormy night,* I thought. Perfect for a ghost story. Because the diary had been hidden in the attic for so long, I'd convinced myself that it must hold some tantalizing secret, perhaps a tale of mayhem and murder. But this wasn't a Gothic novel. I was about to read events from the real life of an unknown person who had once lived in the blue Victorian.

Maybe the writer was someone who had entertained two unlikely guests in the kitchen, fixed a meal for a dog, and sat before a fire with an engrossing book of her own. I read the quotation again: "The day with its possibilities lay before me." What a wonderful sentiment that was for the beginning of a day, or a diary, for that matter. If only the writer had included a complete date. Turning the page, I began to read the first entry, dated February 10th.

FEBRUARY 10—THIS DIARY is my birthday present to myself. So many wonderful things are happening to me now that I want to make sure I'll never forget them. It's like I'm at the real beginning of my life. Everything is new for me here. I have friends, I'm living in a beautiful house, and I know where I'm going. I finally have everything I've worked so hard for.

I bought a new shade of fingernail polish called Frosty Peachmist today. I'm wearing it as I write this. Now I have to find a lipstick to go with it. I'd like a soft orange color. I don't know when I'll find time to go shopping again. I have too much schoolwork to do. I wish I could read faster.

February 11—"The day with its possibilities lay before me." I found that sentence in a musty old novel somebody left in this room. From now on, I'm going to look at my life that way. Each new day equals new possibilities. I love the saying, but the story is as musty as the book. I couldn't finish it. I like modern novels.

Last night after dinner we had a chocolate cake from Sanders for my birthday. I didn't think anyone would remember. My friends gave me a bottle of cologne that smells like carnations, a pair of gloves, and a record.

Today after school, I went shopping for a red dress to wear to the Valentine Dance. The one I wanted was too expensive, but I couldn't find anything else as nice. I'm going back to buy it tomorrow.

February 12—It snowed all day today. I stayed inside and painted my bedroom a pretty shade of cornflower blue, like a summer sky. My borrowed furniture looks almost new against the fresh background. I got a lot of paint on myself too, but it was worth it to have pleasant surroundings.

February 13—It's morning. Another *boring* Sunday. Nothing ever happens on Sunday. I have to keep reminding myself of my new motto. There will always be another day and more possibilities.

Will it ever stop snowing? I'd like to go back to bed and sleep till noon, but I have more schoolwork to do. Later we're going to a movie. Tomorrow it's school again. Five more days before another weekend. I can't wait until spring.

February 15—We built a snowman in the front yard and had a snowball fight. Juvenile, but fun. Cocoa afterwards.

February 18—We all saw *Little Big Man* and then went out for pizza. The movie was good but too long. The pizza was great!

February 19—Went to a party. Wore my red dress with my pearls. No one interesting there. More snow.

February 27—I decided to start buying sterling silver for my future home when I get married. I saw a pattern I liked in a magazine. It has a pretty name, Carolina. The spoons have graceful scalloped edges and a swirling design. I'm looking at china patterns too.

March 1—Another month begins today. It doesn't look like spring will ever come to Maple Creek. It's snowing again! I hope we won't have one of those chilly summers. This year I want to live at the beach, get a tan, wear something sexy, and *really* start to live. Maybe I'll meet my future husband this summer.

March 5—This morning, I saw daffodils in the backyard. The snow didn't kill them after all. Maybe spring will come in spite of this hateful winter weather.

Now I have some real news to write about. I've found someone I like very much. He's dark-haired, cute, and *very nice!* He was here all along, and I liked him when we first met, but I thought he was taken. Now I'm not so sure, but it doesn't matter because he's interested in me, not her. I can tell.

I LAID THE DIARY DOWN, amused to have encountered weather observations even on these old pages. Having read thus far, I assumed that the writer was a schoolgirl absorbed with thoughts of makeup, clothes, and boys. That she wanted to wear something sexy at the beach suggested that she was in high school, perhaps a junior or senior. Or maybe she was in college, dreaming about an early marriage rather than a career, writing about a boy she liked, and fussing about the weather that no one has ever found a way to change.

I shouldn't leap to judgment about her. If I were to record the events of my own life today, I'd write about the branch that I couldn't lift, Garth's offer of help and how it had led us into the attic, a strange tea party, and the weather.

In truth, I was a little disappointed in the diary. I'd hoped to be drawn immediately into an enthralling adventure from yesteryear. I had to remember that nobody's life reads like a story unless the author is writing fiction.

My cup was empty, and so was the teapot. I carried them into the kitchen and almost fell across Vicky. She lay on the threshold, farther into the house than she'd ever ventured before. I was making progress indeed. The next step was a collar around her neck.

"Good dog," I said "Good Vicky."

She rose, stretched, and wagged her tail, following me up to the sink as I filled the teakettle again; but she jumped when the phone rang and backed up to the wall.

"It's only the telephone, Vicky," I said. "It won't hurt you."

As I picked up the receiver, I noticed the business card for Sky and MacKay Title on the counter. Garth had scrawled a number under his name and left it near the phone. When had he done this? I thought I'd been watching him all the time. Obviously he had a sly side.

"Kale residence," I said. "Hello?"

"Katherine? It's Lt. Gray—Dalton."

My heart skipped a beat. "Is anything wrong?" I asked. "Did you find out something?"

"Whoa, Katherine. This is a social call. I'm off duty. Would you like to take in a movie with me? Maybe we could have a burger after."

My instincts about his interest in me had been right, and

this was exactly the kind of evening with him I'd envisioned. But for some reason, Garth's face came to my mind. What was wrong with me? A date with Dalton was what I'd been waiting for. Wasn't it?

"That sounds like fun," I said, pushing aside the intrusive image. "When?"

"Tonight."

I hesitated and set Garth's card down. I didn't realize I'd picked it up.

"I know it's short notice, but I don't get much time off," he said. "It'll be casual. Like the time we had dinner together at the Country Cabin."

It had been raining that night too. A quick glance at the clock told me that it wasn't as late as I'd thought, only a little after six.

Because this was extremely short notice, I should turn him down. But wait! That was just an excuse. Why not accept? Then instead of continuing to wonder about him, I would know whether he was a gorgeous sometime traffic cop who most likely deserved his reputation as a player or the kind of man I'd like to have a relationship with some day.

"So what do you say?" he asked.

"Sure," I said. "What time should I be ready?"

# TWENTY

*His face was as lean as his body, chiseled in sharp attractive angles, and his smooth dark brown hair gleamed in the afternoon sunlight. One strand fell forward on his forehead from a center part, brushing the top of his eyebrow.*

And his eyes were blue, a true, pure cerulean more often seen on the cover of a romance novel than a human face. Except I hadn't been able to see their color that day at the Apple Fair because he was stationed in the intersection directing traffic while I stood at the corner, mesmerized by the sight of this exceptionally handsome officer.

So why wasn't I dazzled now? Dalton sat across from me in a rollicking down home restaurant on the outskirts of town, hungrily devouring his second steak sandwich while country music blared loudly in the background. If I was feeling slightly let down, it was because my expectations had been too high.

Dalton was still gorgeous; he was charismatic and entertaining, but no small town policeman could fill the boots of the larger-than-life figure my mind had created. I should have known that from the beginning. On some level, I suppose I did.

It was the dark policeman's uniform. Conveying strength and power, it had been a definite turn on. That was why Dalton intrigued me. Tonight I was out with the real person, and he wore a cobalt blue sweater that accentuated the color of his eyes. I'd already discovered that Lt. Dalton Gray was an ordinary man.

You'll have more fun with an ordinary man than a hero, I reminded myself.

"I like good food," he said. "'Eat, drink, and be merry, for tomorrow you may be dead.' That's my philosophy."

I smiled, thinking about Myrold Barren in his role as Henry VIII, with a drumstick in one hand and a beer stein in the other. Until this moment I hadn't seen Dalton that way. "That doesn't sound like a policeman's philosophy."

"I follow it when I'm off duty. During my shift, it's 'Speak softly and carry a big stick.'"

"That's more like it."

I was relaxed with him now, although the evening had gotten off to a shaky start. The movie, a supernatural thriller heavy on blood and special effects, had left me feeling slightly queasy and edgy. As soon as I stepped inside the Old Barn, however, visions of thirsty vampires went slinking away.

"Are you sure you wouldn't like another sandwich?" he asked. "Maybe another beer? Anything else?"

"No, thanks. This was plenty."

"I found this place last year when I transferred to Maple Creek," he said. "It's the liveliest restaurant for miles around."

"Where were you working before?" I asked.

"Up in Saginaw. This was supposed to be a two-year stop on my way to the big city. Until the Valentine murder, nothing ever happened here except for routine traffic violations and run-ins with the Militia. All that's changed now."

"Do you think you'll stay on the Force?" I asked.

"For a while. The town grows on you, and people here are polite to cops. Sometimes even the bad guys are." He poured the last of his beer. "Yes, I think I'll stay in Maple Creek for a few years, only it's a long drive to the concerts."

I hoped to learn something new about Cora Valentine's murder from Dalton, although I suspected that he would never talk about it, except in a general way. Still, there was no harm in asking. "Do you think the homicide detectives are going to find Cora Valentine's killer soon?"

"I don't know about soon. Say one of these days. As a cop, I hate pick to up a newspaper and read that a certain case has the police baffled. Eventually the killer will be behind bars and the town will be safe again, no matter how long it takes."

"In the meantime, someone else may get killed."

"True, but that hasn't happened yet. We got through Halloween without major trouble."

"I still don't know who wanted me to fall from my balcony, and you never caught the burglar," I said.

"No, not yet, but there haven't been any other burglaries that I know of." A dark frown shadowed his eyes. "I like the challenge of unsolved murder cases. Sometimes it takes years to find a killer. You keep the files open, keep on working and making connections, and hope for a break. It's going to happen here."

Until it did, I had to dodge a murderer. For how long? I'd read about a serial killer who was captured eighteen years after his last murder, long after everyone except a dedicated policeman and the mother of one of the victims had given up hope. Still, Dalton sounded optimistic, even though the loss of Terry Campbell as a suspect must have bounced the investigation back to square one. I might as well believe him.

"How about you, Katherine?" Dalton asked. "Are you going to stay on in Maple Creek after those incidents?"

"Oh yes. I love my house, and the town isn't responsible for what happens here. It's a person, and he's going to be caught—or she is. You said so."

Dalton's frown turned to a broad smile of approval, and he raised his empty glass. "Here's to a long healthy life in the little town of Maple Creek."

"For both of us," I said.

"That's enough shop talk, Katherine. We're supposed to be enjoying ourselves tonight."

"That's the idea."

"Good." He reached for the check. "Now—how about moving on to another activity?"

Another activity? I was ready to go home. Dalton had picked a fair restaurant, but that was about it, and I hadn't learned anything worth watching him shovel in sandwiches.

Or maybe I had, I realized, as Garth's image reappeared in my mind.

"Much as I'd like to continue the evening, I'm ready to call it a night," I said. "It's late…"

He turned a knowing blue gaze on me, waiting. "It's only ten. If you'd like to live a little dangerously, I know a new club on the lake."

"I don't think… Not tonight."

"Okay," he said. "If you're sure."

"I am, but thanks for dinner and the movie."

"Some other time then, Katherine," he said. "We'll have to do this again."

ALL THAT NIGHT and throughout the next day, it rained, a jarring change from bright lights and country music to dull endless gray. Vicky slept, and I spent long, restless hours rattling around in the old blue house alone or watching the rainfall.

It dropped down from the sky in torrents, pouring out of the gutters and turning the foundation around the bay window into a mud stream. My witch ornament lay face down alongside a fallen bird's nest, and stark black branches, stripped of their last leaves, reached up to the swollen clouds as if to protest the deluge.

The rain was expected to last all week, changing to a rain-snow mix for the weekend. I turned on lights and kept the fire blazing and water boiling for tea. This morning, between one swallow and the next, I had become aware of an ominous scratchy feeling in my throat.

The single happy outcome of the miserable weather was Vicky's decision to come into the house. I looked up to find her lying between the kitchen and the hall, resting her head on her paws, watching me.

"You can come in, Vicky," I said. "Come, girl."

She came and lay down close to the fire. When I slipped a lightweight chain around her neck, she didn't resist.

"Good dog," I said in my softest voice. "Vicky is such a good dog."

I took a large Milk-Bone biscuit from the box and set it in front of her, telling her once again how good she was.

Did I say I was alone? No one who has a dog ever lacks for company.

Once again I settled down in front of the fireplace. This was an ideal day to read the diary. Opening the little blue book, I turned a page and found myself with the writer in April.

APRIL 30— SPRING at last! At last! Today I bought a new swimming suit and a white cover up that's so pretty I could almost wear it as a dress. Whenever I pass Graham's, I look at the engagement rings in the window. Spring is a great time to be in love.

May 6—Our school play is *A Midsummer Night's Dream*. Everywhere I look I see signs of spring. The weeping cherry tree in the front yard burst into blossom overnight. The flowers are pink and very delicate. The branches droop down to the ground, making the tree look like a bridal veil. They won't last long.

We're reading Robert Frost's poetry in English II this week. He wrote, "Nothing gold can stay." That's true, but it's so sad.

I'd love to have an outdoors wedding in front of the cherry tree when it's in bloom next spring, but I don't want to wait that long to be married.

May 14—I ran into Gerry in town today. He invited me to have lunch with him at Fontaine's. We had egg salad sandwiches and double chocolate sundaes.

At last we had a chance to be alone. For the first time in ages, we could talk privately. He said that he'd like to take a trip around the world on a tramp steamer some day. I told him I'd like to visit faraway exotic cities too. That isn't really my dream, but it could be because I love him.

There's a pretty ranch house with rosy colored bricks for sale on our street. I could see myself living in that house with

Gerry and being very happy. I wish I'd told Gerry my dream, but the time wasn't right. I will some day.

I'm collecting pictures of wedding gowns. There's a beautiful one on the cover of the *Journal* this month. It's simple white cotton, almost like a sundress, but it's elegant and romantic too, just perfect for a backyard wedding.

HIS NAME WAS Gerry.

I set the diary down on the coffee table and picked up the mug of cocoa next to Garth's roses. The flowers still held their bright yellow color but seemed to have lost their fragrance. My head was beginning to ache, and my sore throat had gone beyond scratchy. I really should get up and fix something hot for dinner and then go to bed early. Instead I stared into the flames, sipping the lukewarm drink and thinking.

Gerry Raycraft? Maybe.

The language and details of the entries had the flavor of the seventies. Obviously the writer had lived in the blue Victorian. There was no cherry tree on the property now, but I knew they weren't long lived. If the writer's love interest was Gerry Raycraft, she could be Cora Valentine who had been in love with him before he turned to Rosalie. Or she could be Anna Lynde who was still romantically interested in Gerry. Rosalie Grier was a third possibility, but based on my previous idea that Cora's spirit roamed the house, I thought the diary most likely had belonged to Cora.

What a coincidence it would be if Cora's spirit had used the scratching sounds in the attic to lead me to her old diary. On this gloomy, rainy day I had no trouble believing it. Perhaps that had been her plan all along.

But why? To bring her killer to justice? How could the small book accomplish that? Besides, apprehending killers was the responsibility of Dalton and his associates. That didn't mean I couldn't do a little investigating on my own.

I needed a sample of Cora's handwriting. Anna Lynde might have kept a letter or postcard she'd written. Meg Valentine certainly would. If the diary belonged to Anna, I'd simply return it, and we would have a lively discussion about courtship and marriage custom then and now, and I could let go of all the ghostly connections that were clamoring to be made.

Let the diary belong to Anna and not Cora. I didn't want to deal with the spirit world.

Turning back a few pages, I reread the soda fountain entry, marveling that at one time a young woman would consider abandoning her own dream for the love of a man.

Although she hadn't exactly said that. The writer had allowed Gerry to believe that she wanted to be a world traveler when what she really longed for was to settle down with him in a little ranch house in Maple Creek, Michigan.

It would never occur to me to change my dreams to accommodate the desires of a man. Any man. That wasn't the twenty-first century way. Nor would I collect pictures of wedding gowns.

At present I didn't have a man in my life, but I had so many things: This beautiful blue house, my own dog, memories of Europe, Dalton, my friendship with Garth, and school in a few more weeks. In spite of the undefined threat that hung over me like a rain cloud on the verge of bursting, I would be completely happy, if only I wasn't getting sick.

I turned around in the chair in order to watch the fire and slowly drained the mug. Vicky was sleeping on her side now, her bright new tag shining in the light. I wished I had somebody to mull over this new development with. The one drawback to a canine companion was that she couldn't talk.

Hoping to distract myself from physical discomfort, I went back to the diary. Although I loved my world and my own time, this fragmented glimpse into the past had its own charm.

This time, instead of reading every word, I skimmed the pages, looking for entries that dealt with the writer's romance. She tended to skip days, making entries only when the spirit or a significant event moved her. Still, a clear picture of her life began to emerge. During the week she was busy with schoolwork. On weekend nights, she went to the show with her friends. Sometimes she dated other boys, most of whom she didn't bother to name. Whenever she had an opportunity to be with Gerry, she took advantage of it and came home to write several pages about their encounter.

They met again at Fontaine's for sundaes. Frequently they attended the same parties. On one of these occasions, he stayed by her side all evening, even though they hadn't come together. One Saturday they went to a carnival in another town, and once he asked her to go to a concert as his date. She told him that she was keeping a diary, and he bought her a leather bound book with blank pages, as a surprise gift in case she ran out of space.

Sometimes instead of whole sentences, she wrote fragments: Rehearsal tonight. Pizza on the way home. Umbrella broke. Have to buy a new one. Movie date with a jerk. I won't go out with him again. Haven't seen Gerry all week. *Where is he?*

Then I turned a page and found a longer entry:

SOMETHING TERRIBLE happened today. A lightning bolt set the garage on fire. Luckily my car was in the shop, and the girls were away. I was terrified that the house would burn down. I was trying to find the phone directory to call the Fire Department when I heard the sirens.

The sky was filled with clouds of billowing black smoke. I could hardly breathe. I stood outside with the crowd gathered across the street until a fireman made us all move back to the corner.

"But I live there," I said.

"Move back! Move!" he shouted. He wasn't even listening to me.

I heard someone say, "It sounded like an explosion." One woman asked me if I was inside when the lightning struck. She said, "Don't cry. It's only wood. You can always have a new garage built. Just so the fire doesn't reach the house. That's the important thing."

I wasn't crying. The smoke was making my eyes water. I

watched the flames come closer and closer to the house. It looked like they were aiming straight for my bedroom.

Suddenly I had a scary feeling that I was going to lose everything I loved, if not today, then some other day when another freak accident would tear my world apart. There was nothing I could do to stop it. Everything I loved would go up in smoke.

Then the first raindrops started to fall and I saw Gerry coming through the crowd. He put his arms around me and held me close. I'll never ever forget his words. "Don't cry, honey. It's going to be all right. I'm here now."

# TWENTY-ONE

THE LAST ENTRY explained the missing garage. No one had ever rebuilt the one destroyed in the fire. Also, in my interpretation, it seemed to signal a turning point in the writer's relationship with Gerry.

The shrill ringing of the telephone summoned me back to my own world. At my feet, Vicky stirred and raised her head drowsily but didn't follow me into the kitchen. Letting the edges of my shawl fall free, I picked up the receiver.

"Kale residence. Hello?" My voice sounded ragged and faraway, like that of a stranger.

"Hello, Katherine. It's Garth MacKay."

Shivering in the abrupt transition from fireside warmth to cool air, I swallowed past the painful lump in my throat. "Garth. How are you feeling today?"

"Much better. I just called to thank you for taking such good care of me yesterday."

"I only gave you coffee and tea," I said.

"Don't forget the chicken soup. It was plenty, and it worked. Are you all right?"

"Now I'm the one with the sore throat. I'm trying to discourage it."

Cradling the phone on my shoulder, I pulled the edges of the shawl together across my chest. The air in the kitchen was icy. I glanced at the window above the sink, wondering if I'd left it open. It was closed, but a cold draft was seeping in above the windowsill, fluttering the ruffled edge of the curtain.

"That isn't good," he said. "I hope I didn't give it to you."

"I don't see how you could have."

The concern I heard in his voice sounded sincere. Was it possible that he really cared? I'd thought so briefly yesterday, but his response just now had been fairly routine, the kind I might make myself.

"Maybe Nell brought some germs with her from the hospital," he said.

"It's probably the change in weather. This interminable rain."

I moved Garth's business card around on the counter in a circular path and imagined leaping flames while I waited for him to come to the real point, if he had another point. In the lengthening silence, I could hear the hum of the refrigerator, and if I listened very carefully, the crackling of the flames from the living room.

With a cell phone, I could be sitting beside the fire and talking to Garth at the same time. An answering machine would be even better. Then I wouldn't have to use my voice at all.

"I'll let you get some rest," Garth said. "That's what worked for me. Goodnight, Katherine. I'll see you soon."

"Good night."

*Thank heavens.* I replaced the receiver and poured a glass of grapefruit juice. In a way I was pleased that Garth had called, but I didn't feel like talking to anybody tonight. Each word I uttered seemed to tear another piece away from the lining of my throat. I didn't have any lozenges in the house, or any of that miracle liquid a person could drink to cure a cold while getting a good night's sleep. Besides the leftover chicken soup, my only cold-fighting remedies were aspirin and honey-lemon tea.

It wasn't too late to go out and try to find a drug store open. I could bundle up, wear my raincoat, and take the umbrella. Both were in the hall closet, within easy reach, but in the end I decided to go shopping in the morning. By then the rain might taper off and, with luck, I would feel better. For tonight I'd try tea and bed rest.

My mind backtracked. Garth had been thoughtful to thank

me for the tiny part I'd played in his recovery, but I sensed
that he had another reason for calling me tonight, one that he'd
abandoned when I mentioned my sore throat. Well, if it was
important, I would know about it eventually. If I hadn't been
feeling so miserable, I would have told him about the contents
of the diary. With details gleaned from the entries and his
knowledge of Maple Creek history, we might have been able
to color in the outline.

That was a project for another day. I made an omelet for
my dinner and fed Vicky. All I wanted to do was go to bed.
In the living room I smothered the flames and marked my
place in the diary. Then I let Vicky out one last time for the
night. Maybe, like Garth, I would improve by morning.

*Maybe this time...*

Impatiently I shut the words out of my mind. I refused to
think about the haunting tonight or about anything except
getting better.

EIGHT O'CLOCK WAS a ridiculous hour to go to bed, but it had
been dark since six, and the rain was still falling steadily. Time
was immaterial. With a backward glance at Vicky who lay
asleep by the stove, I filled a carafe with cold water for the
long night and climbed the stairs to the landing where I'd left
a small lamp burning.

Here I paused and contemplated the door to the spare bedroom. I always kept it closed, perhaps in a subconscious desire to create a barrier between the attic and the rest of the
house, which was foolish. Nothing was up there now except
for two empty trunks.

*And something that made a scratching sound in the night.*

Could Garth have overlooked another object that had fallen
between the boards? I should investigate again.

If both Dalton and Garth could navigate my attic with ease,
then so could I. Tomorrow or the next day when I had more
energy, I resolved to take another look around in the dim, secret places. It occurred to me that I was more like the women

of Anna's generation than I wanted to believe, allowing men to do what I didn't want to do myself.

No more, I vowed. Opening the door to the spare bedroom, I crossed to the window that overlooked the driveway. This must have been the writer's room, directly across from where the burned garage had stood. Decades later, white paint covered the cornflower blue walls, without a shadow of dark bleeding through.

I imagined a young woman sitting at her desk, recording the highlights of her days on thin pages in green ink. She had crammed her new spring wardroom into the small closet and dreamed of rings, wedding gowns, and cherry blossoms. Then at the end of the day, she'd made her way up to the attic to hide her diary, first throwing a cloth over the rack to keep dust from falling down on her clothes.

Why would she do that? A younger girl would want to conceal her innermost thoughts from a snoopy brother or prying mother. But surely the writer wouldn't live with roommates whom she didn't trust to respect her privacy. Perhaps she had another reason. Like a secret so important that she couldn't take a chance on its being discovered?

Then why write about it? Each unanswered question led to another one. Quietly I closed the door. If I didn't stop thinking about the diary, I would be awake for hours; but later, as I lay in bed, another thought came to me. Why hadn't the writer mentioned a cameo brooch or bracelet?

I now had a fascinating mini-mystery to ponder. I could think of a few possible explanations. Perhaps the trip to Italy hadn't happened when she was writing the portion of the diary I'd read, or, assuming she already owned the jewelry, its novelty might have worn off. Or describing accessories might not have been important to her. If I were writing about my date with Dalton, for instance, I wouldn't have written that I'd worn a rhinestone pin shaped like a star on my mint green sweater.

She had mentioned wearing pearls with the red dress, though. Perhaps she'd write about the cameo in future entries.

Think about it tomorrow, or you'll be awake all night, I told myself.

I didn't keep a diary. It might be interesting to begin one though. I'd call it a journal and write about everything that had happened to me since I'd moved to Maple Creek, beginning with Cora Valentine's murder. Then, thirty years from now, someone would find it and wonder about me.

I AWOKE TO ANOTHER rainy morning and a dog's persistent whining downstairs. Ah, the joys of dog ownership. I swallowed tentatively. My throat was a little less raw, but still sore, and my headache was gone. Reminding myself that a cold is always worse at night, I decided that I'd better make the most of the daytime hours.

Vicky was in the kitchen, lying in front of the door to the back porch. She'd stopped whining as soon as she heard me moving around upstairs. I let her out and fixed breakfast, all the while thinking about the diary. Over hot tea and dry toast, I remembered fragments from the dream I'd had last night: Footsteps on the stairs, mysterious sounds above my ceiling, thunder and lightening.

In my dream, I went up into the attic, climbing stairs that didn't exist, and saw a figure in a long dress that was neither green nor gray. She sat on one of the trunks, and although she faced me, her features were a blur. At her throat she wore a cameo pin. I saw it as clearly as if I were holding it in my hand. The intricately carved head with its ivory features and serene smile faced forward. Then the woman in the gray-green dress whose features were hidden spoke to me.

"I haven't minded living up here in the attic, Katherine. I always knew you'd come some day."

At that point, the dream ended, or I couldn't recall any more of it.

Dear God. That was a genuine nightmare, and why had I just remembered it?

The fear that I'd known in the dream attic was with me now,

as sharp and real as the sound of thunder outside and the lightning flash that sent splinters of illumination through the narrow ventilation strips.

No. I was getting confused. That was in the nightmare. This morning's rain was constant and miserable, but it didn't include thunder and lightning.

Get a grip, I told myself. Stop thinking about that appalling dream. You have to go to the store. It's eleven-thirty already.

*She'd said, "I haven't minded living up in the attic, Katherine."*

A dog was barking outside. The sound came from the front, which was puzzling. Usually Vicky stayed in the backyard. It was raining harder now. I had to let her back in the house.

I was never going to set foot in that attic again.

*"I always knew you'd come some day."*

Prepared to dodge a wet dog, I hurried to open the front door. There stood Vicky, still barking, and behind her Garth MacKay, balancing a black umbrella and an armload of packages. Vicky slipped past me, water falling off her coat, and shook herself vigorously in the hallway. Garth stood in the shelter of the porch, large and powerful, a towering figure against the mist and rain.

"Morning, Katherine," he said. "I brought a carry-out lunch from the Blue Lion for us. I thought we could eat it together."

"Why—thank you. Come in…" I couldn't think of anything else to say except, "Did you walk all the way from Main Street in the rain?"

"Sure. There's no point in driving this little distance."

I reached for the largest of the packages. "This is so nice of you, but—I didn't expect you—anyone that is—to do something like this. What's inside?"

"Things that are good for you, and I like to keep my women guessing."

"Oh, you do?"

I felt as if we were frozen in place, Garth dripping water

on the floor of the porch, while I stood inside holding a container of something that smelled delicious. I'd asked him to come in, but he hadn't moved.

In my best hostess voice, I said, "Let me take your coat."

"I'll leave it out here on the porch. You don't need any more water in your house." He draped his raincoat over the railing, leaned the umbrella against a post, and stepped heavily inside. The brief awkward moment had passed.

"I didn't think you'd feel like cooking for yourself, and there I was at the Blue Lion about to order lunch," he said. "Today's special is roast chicken with stuffing and mashed potatoes. I thought, I'll bet Katherine would like that, and here I am. I didn't bring anything to drink though."

"I'll make some tea," I said.

Restored to health after a one-day cold, Garth was a vision of energy and vigor. The raindrops that lay on his hair and beard gave him a becoming boyish look that contradicted my image of Garth MacKay, Militiaman. Then my gaze fell on his lion's head ring. He was the same man in a different setting with a new set of props.

"Is your power on?" I asked.

"Everything is back to normal, except business. It's slow."

"Come, let's get these boxes open."

As we walked through the living room en route to the kitchen, he paused in front of the sofa. "That furniture looks nice and comfortable."

"I spent a few hours sitting in the chair last evening, enjoying the fire, but I haven't tried out the sofa yet."

He was looking at the coffee table. The yellow roses were more beautiful and fragrant than they'd been as a fresh bouquet. I realized that I could smell them this morning.

"I see you've been reading that old diary," he said. "Did you find anything interesting in it?"

"Yes, I think so." In the kitchen, I whisked my empty cup and saucer off the table, and opened cartons. It seemed that Garth had brought enough food for the entire block. "I'll tell you all about it later, but first, I wanted to ask you something. When you were up in the attic, did you see anything else?"

"Just those two trunks. Nothing alive, no openings. Why?"

"I'm just curious. Old attics fascinate me. You never know what you'll find when you start rummaging through them."

"Some attics maybe, but not this one."

He settled himself in a chair while I set the table and filled the teakettle with fresh water. As Nell had observed, Garth looked at home in my kitchen, and he'd only been here twice before.

"Like I told you, Katherine, you need more insulation up there. It should be warmer in the house unless you have the thermostat turned down."

"No, I turned it up a few degrees."

"Well, there. Let me know if you decide to have it done. I can put you in touch with a good contractor."

"I may do that," I said.

The house would hold the heat better, and workmen tramping across the boards with their loud voices and powerful lights should chase away the haunting airs. Or seal them in? That could happen too.

I ordered myself not to think about that now, to concentrate on this magnificent spread.

Besides roast chicken, stuffing, and mashed potatoes, Garth had brought rolls and side orders of green beans with large pieces of cherry pie for dessert. Everything still felt warm in spite of his short walk in the rain.

He'd bought two orders—or three. I hoped he was hungry because this was more like a Sunday dinner than my usual noontime cup of soup or sandwich. "It all looks wonderful, but I don't think I can eat very much," I said.

"Yes, you can. What's that old saying? Feed a cold and starve a fever? Or is the other way around?"

"I don't remember."

"Well, let's eat while it's good and hot."

I tried a little of the chicken and discovered that I was hungry. My order of mashed potatoes was twice as large as Garth's, by design, I was sure. Nothing could be smoother or more soothing to eat when you had a sore throat, unless it was my chicken soup. Garth had remembered that.

Vicky whimpered from the doorway where she lay watching us intently but not exactly begging.

"It looks like you finally have your little watch dog," he said.

"Vicky let me know you were at the door."

"She was wagging her tail the whole time. But you're a good dog, Vicky, almost as good as Tac."

He waved a bit of chicken in her direction. In an instant she was at his side, wolfing it down, waiting for more.

"It's incredible how fast they learn," I said. "From now on she'll be at the table when I eat."

"I guess I shouldn't be spoiling your dog."

"That's all right. Everyone needs a little spoiling." I looked at my empty plate and all the leftover food. "I'm amazed that you would go to all this trouble." Too late I remembered that I'd already said something similar.

"It's no trouble. Like I told you, I was there for lunch anyway, and I wanted to bring something for you."

"But why?"

"Call it reciprocation," he said. "When a lady does something nice for me, I don't forget it."

In a short time, the atmosphere in the kitchen had gone from homey and casual to serious. Attempting a light tone, I said, "Is that such a rare occurrence? For a lady to be nice to you?"

"Naw. It happens all the time. I didn't say that right. What I meant was…"

"That's okay," I said quickly. "I think I can figure it out. Let me tell you about the diary."

He listened politely as I summarized the entries and explained my theory that the diary had belonged to one of the young women who had lived in the blue Victorian during the seventies.

"Cora, Anna, or Rosalie," I said. "My guess is Cora."

"That doesn't sound like the Cora Valentine I knew. She must have done a lot of changing over the years."

"People do change."

"I guess Cora wouldn't mind you reading her diary, wherever she is. Maybe Meg Valentine would like to have it when you're through."

I'd forgotten about Meg. My first thought had been to call Anna. That still seemed like the best idea, again because I knew her.

"First I'm going to finish reading it and then I'll call Anna Lynde. Cora is dead, but some of the people she mentioned may still be alive. Gerry Raycraft, for one. I suspect he's the man the writer was in love with."

Garth frowned into his teacup and then picked it up and drained it. "I sure wouldn't like to be mentioned in any woman's diary. I don't think I am."

"That's something you have no control over. And you're not likely to know about it if you are."

"I guess you're right." He fixed me with a shrewd glance. "Okay, now you've told me about the diary. Suppose you tell me why you asked me about overlooking something up in the attic. Are you looking for Volume Two or is there some other reason?"

I hadn't planned to speak about the strangeness I'd sensed in the house, especially not to Garth who had a tendency to tease me about hallway ghosts. However, the intimacy of sharing a satisfying meal with a kind, caring man was my undoing. After all, I'd wished for a confidante many times and in my present weakened state, I was susceptible.

That's what I told myself. It sounded good.

I brewed a fresh pot of tea, and while we ate our dessert, I told Garth about the haunting of the blue Victorian.

# TWENTY-TWO

"THESE OLD HOUSES are filled with sounds," Garth said. "I didn't know you were letting them bother you. It's no wonder you're having nightmares."

In his view, that was what my haunting amounted to. Sounds blended with impressions and feelings. By adding a giant measure of imagination, I'd managed to create something frightening out of nothing. I was trying to believe this.

"I only had one nightmare," I said.

"About someone living up in your attic. If she was there, I didn't see her. Taryn used to be afraid of our attic when she was a little girl. She always thought she'd get trapped inside and die there."

"Didn't she know you'd never let that happen?"

"Not when she was five or six. She still won't go up there. Now it's because she doesn't want to get dirty."

"Well, I'm not a little girl, and I'm not afraid of my attic."

Garth hadn't mentioned his sister lately. I'd been curious about her absence and also his silence. Usually Taryn was one of his favorite subjects. "Is your sister still down South?" I asked.

"Yes. Now, Katherine, let's break this haunting down into small parts. There's nothing in your attic to make a scratching sound. You must have heard something else like a tree touching the house."

"That might have been true before I had the linden trimmed."

"A branch in the gutters, then. Maybe a small bird trapped in a downspout. Before I leave, I'll have a look outside."

"How would you explain footsteps on the stairs?" I asked.

"Are you sure there wasn't a real person on the stairway?"

"Positive. They say an old house has to settle. Maybe the explanation is that simple."

He laughed. "Give it another hundred years, Katherine. Let me see. Footsteps. How about your imagination?"

"That would explain the first time," I said. "I heard them more than once."

"Then let's go with the house settling. That's an easy answer when you can't think of another one. I don't believe in ghosts. Cora Valentine is dead and buried. It's funny the way that cameo disappeared, but it doesn't have to be a mystery."

I didn't agree with everything Garth said, but his down to earth approach made me feel better. In my kitchen, sitting under the light with this practical, no-nonsense man, the very thought of ghosts prowling through the house by night seemed far-fetched.

"You're just anxious about the break-in and that balcony scare," he said. "That's natural. It's enough to make anyone jittery."

"Even you?" I asked.

"Any woman, I was going to say." The implied insult got lost in his mischievous smile.

"I'm glad you didn't," I said.

"Some people like living in old houses. They come with history and sometimes objects other people left behind like the diary. That's part of the vintage home package."

"I know that, but I can't get over the feeling that something extraordinary is going on here."

"Something is, but it's a live person you have to worry about, not a ghost. I take that back. You don't have anything to worry about as long as I'm around."

"Spoken like a hero," I said. "I may take you up on your offer some day."

"When you do, I'll be right on your doorstep faster than the police."

I imagined that he would. All I had to do was ask. But that

might not be wise. Definitely it wouldn't be wise. Garth's allusion to the police reminded me of something I tended to forget. He was a man who lived his life somewhere beyond the law. That was a place I didn't want to visit.

"Let's hope there's no more trouble," I said.

"Let's hope." He got up and gave Vicky a quick farewell pat on her head. "And now I have to get back to work. Are you going to stay in out of the rain and take care of your sore throat today?"

"I plan to build a fire and read all afternoon. I'm feeling so much better, thanks to you."

"I didn't do anything except bring you lunch."

"You listened to my ramblings. That's important to me."

"I'll listen to you any time, Katherine," he said.

He pulled me close to his chest and hugged me tightly. "Any time at all."

AFTER GARTH LEFT, the rain tapered off to a cold drizzle. I drove to the drug store where I filled a basket with cold medication, throat lozenges, boxes of tissue, and ginger ale. At the last minute, I added butter rum lifesavers. I really was feeling better, but didn't intend to be caught unprepared again.

Since I had no reason to linger outside in the inclement weather and something interesting to do at home, I hurried back to the blue Victorian. Within twenty minutes, I was settled in the chair by the fire, wrapped in my shawl, with the diary on my lap and Vicky at my feet.

This time, as I read, I intended to look for familiar names and clues. Now that I was alone in the house again, the mystery seemed alive and well. Although breaking the strange occurrences in the house down into parts made sense, I strongly suspected that they were related. At this moment I might be holding the connecting key in my hand.

I opened the diary to June 18th and started to read.

JUNE 18—THE SUMMER with its possibilities lay before me. Tomorrow evening we're celebrating the end of school with a barbecue in Gerry's yard for the seven of us. I can't afford a real vacation this year, but it doesn't matter. My future is here.

June 20—The day the garage burned down, Gerry told me that he would always take care of me, but he didn't say he loved me until last night. I thought he did, but a girl can never be sure until a man says the words. This is my summer dream come true!

June 30—Gerry's bachelor uncle, Jack Raycraft, took us out to dinner at an expensive restaurant to celebrate his sixtieth birthday. There's a slight family resemblance, but Mr. Raycraft is gruff and grouchy. He looks older than sixty and walks with a cane. Maybe the reason he's in such a bad mood is because he's often in pain.

Mr. Raycraft doesn't like me. He didn't say so, but I could tell. I have no idea why. I've always been polite and respectful to him. It could be because I'm dating his nephew. He thinks that girls today are too independent, not like they were when he was young.

Later I told Gerry I was sorry that I'd made such a bad impression on his uncle. Gerry loves him and wants us to be friends.

He said, "Uncle Jack does like you. That's his way with everybody."

"What did he say about me?" I asked.

"Not much. Only that you're very pretty, but a little too young for me."

The mystery deepens. Gerry and I are the same age.

"Nothing else?"

"I think you remind him of a girl he wanted to marry a long time ago."

"What happened to her?" I asked.

"She married someone else." He kissed me. "You'll win him over. Everybody likes you. Just give it a little time."

I hope he's right.

July 4—We had a barbecue for the Fourth of July and invited our friends and everyone on the block. Even that shy little Alarice came. She acts like she has a crush on Gerry, but she doesn't go out much, so I don't consider her competition.

After dark, some of us walked down to the park for the fireworks. Afterward, Gerry and I sat up half the night on the swing, just talking and looking at the stars. It was the best way to spend a summer holiday.

July 5—I asked Gerry to tell me about the girls he dated before he met me.

"There weren't many," he said.

"How many?"

"An average number. They're all in the past. You're the best girlfriend I ever had. You're the only one I want."

That was the best compliment I ever had.

July 6—Gerry hasn't actually asked me to marry him yet. He will. There's a seamstress in town who can make a pattern and sew a wedding dress if you show her a picture. I saved that *Journal* cover so that I'll have it when the time comes.

Gerry and I are going away together this weekend, but we're not telling anyone. I'm afraid of jinxing what we have and that some day Gerry's uncle will try to break us up if he knows how serious we are.

"Don't worry about it," Gerry said when I told him. "That's not going to happen. We belong together. Nothing is going to separate us."

July 9—We had a wonderful time!!! Everything is perfect now.

July 12—Anna came home from her trip today wearing the most beautiful engagement ring I've ever seen. I wish I had a diamond ring. I have to convince Gerry that he'll never be happy unless he has me in his life forever. I know exactly how to do that.

July 14—Back when I was first attracted to Gerry, I suspected that Cora liked him too, but she never said anything about it. This afternoon she talked to me about him for the first time ever.

She told me how happy she was that we were dating. "You two have a lot in common," she said. "Gerry and I were just friends. I want to concentrate on my career. Having a boyfriend now would just complicate my life."

I'm glad I didn't take Gerry away from Cora. I honestly like her and would be sorry to know that I'd hurt her. She was always the best of friends to me. Anna too. But I wouldn't do anything different. I couldn't. I had to have Gerry.

SO THE WRITER WASN'T Cora but Rosalie Grier, the third roommate about whom I knew very little, only what Anna Lynde had told me.

Laying the diary down for a minute, I set about gathering my impressions. I felt as if I were drowning in a sea of superlatives and romantic excess. Rosalie's way of writing had made me picture her as a much younger girl. It must be all those exclamation marks.

Of course when she wrote her lavish descriptions of Gerry and the paragraphs charting the stages of their love affair, she couldn't know that one day someone would read them and critique her style.

I tried to ignore a bothersome twinge of guilt. Reading the diary of a dead woman was one thing. Invading the privacy of the living was quite another. To be sure, for some unknown reason, Rosalie had left her diary behind years ago, which suggested that she didn't care what happened to it. Did that give me the right to read it?

Probably not, but I was going to do it anyway. Rosalie and I would never meet. Still, just for a moment, I had a feeling that she was in the living room, standing behind me in the shadows, pleading with me to read between the lines.

In a way, Rosalie was more interesting than either Cora or Anna. I tried to remember everything Anna had said about her. Rosalie had owned and lost the brown cameo. She had taken Gerry away from Cora who said that she didn't mind. Assuming that Rosalie had recorded Cora's words accurately, this didn't ring true. Most likely, Cora was trying to salvage her pride. No one likes losing, especially when the prize is a perfect man like young Gerry Raycraft.

Also, didn't Cora's backing away contradict her philosophy about taking what she wanted? Perhaps after losing Gerry to Rosalie, she had changed her way of looking at life.

What else did I know? While dating Gerry, Rosalie had surprised her friends by eloping with another man who was apparently more perfect still. The Southern boy, Anna had called him. How could that have come about?

The answer lay in the diary. Eager to know the reason behind Rosalie's change of heart, I turned to the next page, only to discover that she had let several days go by without making a single entry. Then, on August 23rd, she wrote a lyrical description of the missing summer days.

AUGUST 23—THIS IS absolutely the most beautiful summer I've ever known. The days seem to go on forever, the sun shines, the rain comes at night, and the nights are magical. As I write this, I think that Maple Creek, Michigan, is a lot like Camelot this year.

Gerry and I have been together every day except for one weekend when he had to accompany his uncle on a business trip. Nothing seems important to me any more except the hours we spend with each other, but August is almost over. School will be starting soon. If only this summer would never end, not yet anyway. It's too soon.

August 25—It happened!! When Gerry came to pick me up to go to the show, he said, "This is a present for you. I found it in an antique shop."

I was pleased but puzzled because he never gave me a gift before.

"For what occasion?" I asked.

"Because I love you."

He took my hand and set a small walnut-stained music box in my palm. "It plays 'Greensleeves.'"

I lifted the lid, and the poignant familiar strains drifted out into the air, as sweet and clear as fairy bells. Inside on a bed of blue velvet lay a glittering diamond engagement ring in a white gold setting.

"Will you marry me, Rosalie?" he asked.

At last! At long last!

I can't remember what I said, but it must have been "Yes!!!"

I TURNED THE PAGE, eager to know what followed. Kisses to seal their agreement, I imagined, or perhaps a night of lovemaking, for that was what I assumed Rosalie had alluded to in one of the entries. Or maybe wedding plans, as she had already chosen her gown. But in spite of her resolve to write in her diary faithfully, the next entry was dated three days later. It consisted of eight hastily scribbled lines.

AUGUST 28—MY LIFE has taken an unexpected turn. Last night at a party that we almost didn't go to, I met the one man I've waited all my life for, and I'm *so glad* we met while there's still time.

But maybe it's too late. I don't know what I'm going to do—if there's anything I can do."

DRAWN ON BY the entry's cliffhanger ending, I turned a page and then another. They were both blank. The rest of the diary contained only empty sheets. This couldn't be the last of the entries. I kept turning pages in the hope of finding one that I'd missed, but there was nothing more. Rosalie had ended her story with this sparse account of a fateful meeting.

I closed the diary with a sigh, feeling as if I'd been reading an engrossing romance novel, only to find that the last chapter had been torn out. In a way, though, I knew the sequel. Rosalie had married her new true love and moved out of the state, while Gerry Raycraft lived on in Maple Creek and, over the years, turned into a replica of his gruff uncle.

But so much was missing.

Not only had I failed to find any connection to the mystery, but now I had a new set of questions. The one person who might have the answers was Anna Lynde. Perhaps when she read Rosalie's diary, she would remember more of her story.

# TWENTY-THREE

I DIDN'T HAVE A CHANCE to talk to Anna until two days later because she was busy with appointments and prior engagements. By that time, the long rainy spell had given way to a rare warm November day that made me long for the vanished summer. My sore throat had never reached the cold stage, and I could swallow without any pain now. I felt better, and looked better too, with a healthy color in my face and a bounce in my hair that had been missing for days.

At eleven I slipped into the red rayon dress I'd worn to the Apple Fair and added a beige cardigan. Anna and I were meeting at the Blue Lion for lunch, and I was eager to hear her impression of the diary. I couldn't explain it, but I had a feeling that time was running out. But for whom? My feeling didn't give me a name.

Anna was settled in a booth with a cup of coffee when I arrived. She wasn't alone. Myrold Barren sat across from her, a tall drink in his hand, as always boisterous and regal. He was wearing red too, a glaring fire engine shade. I hadn't realized that he and Anna knew each other that well.

Perhaps they didn't. Anna's warm smile held a hint of relief when she saw me.

"Katherine," Myrold said in his booming voice. "Where have you been keeping yourself? I haven't seen you since— when was it? Nell Farmer's party?" He rose and stepped out into the aisle, ushering me into the space next to the wall.

The man was overwhelming, and the color of his sweater almost blinded me. Remembering our last encounter and his impassioned promotional pitch for his village, I braced for another one.

"I've been around," I said.

"I stopped by your house on Tuesday morning, but you didn't answer the door. You're not trying to avoid me, are you?"

"I must have been in the attic checking on the insulation."

"I wanted to show you an artist's rendering of Valentine Park," he said. "That's our latest addition, dedicated to the memory of our dearly departed Cora Valentine. I'm going to have twenty new units up by spring, ten on either side of a winding stream with a nice view of the woods for atmosphere."

So he had acquired Cora's property after all.

"That invitation to tour the Village is still open," he said. "I'll leave you ladies to your lunch and gossip. Anna, you let me know when you're ready to make a move." He patted her arm in a familiar manner. "Don't wait too long."

"I'll let you know as soon as I decide," she said.

As he went roaring away to greet another diner, Anna's sigh was audible. "I'm glad you weren't late, Katherine. That man has so much energy he wears me out."

"He's too much—of everything."

"That's a good way to describe Myrold Barren. I made the mistake of telling him I was thinking about moving. Now I'm not so sure, but he won't let it alone. The moral of the story is 'Don't take his Village tour.'"

"I don't intend to. I love my house."

"I can't wait to see the diary," Anna said. "Where did you find it?"

I told her about Garth's inspection of my attic and the reason for it. "I was afraid some creature had gotten inside."

"Those old houses can be hard on your nerves," she said. "Sometimes I hear strange noises in mine. It comes from living alone."

Remembering that Garth had a similar explanation for the sounds, I opened my shoulder bag and took out Rosalie's diary. Its cover felt warm and smooth, as if it had acquired a life of its own. "You can probably read it while we're waiting for our lunch," I said. "About half of the pages are blank."

I hadn't told Anna anything about the contents, only that I'd come across an old diary that had belonged to Rosalie Grier and thought she'd find it interesting.

"I can't understand what it was doing in the attic," Anna said. "Rosalie couldn't have thought we'd snoop in it. Oh—unless it's filled with unflattering comments about Cora and me."

"Not at all. She mentioned that Cora was her best friend, and you were too."

"So I was an afterthought. Well, I'll admit I'm dying of curiosity. After Rosalie's cameo turned up, I started thinking about her for the first time since my letter came back all those years ago. I wish I could return the diary to her."

"There must be some way you could trace her," I said.

"With a private investigator, I suppose. But it doesn't make sense to go to all that expense just to return a diary." She shook her head. "Thirty years is a long, long time. Rosalie could be anywhere. Ah—here comes our waiter. I'm going to have the Blue Lion Turkey Club."

I had been living on leftover chicken soup since my last Blue Lion meal, the one Garth had provided. Anna's choice, pictured on the cover of the menu, looked like a one-course banquet to me. "I will too."

We placed our order and, while Anna began reading, I drank a cup of coffee, studied the lions and unicorns on the wall, and thought about Garth MacKay. This was his favorite place. He might come here for lunch today. He might be here now.

I didn't see him, but Myrold Barren was sitting somewhere near. I could hear his foghorn voice, blaring through the softer conversations of the other patrons. The man was magnetic, blatantly drawing attention to himself, as well as an occasional annoyed stare from a fellow diner.

Anna looked up from the diary, a frown creasing her forehead. "I remember so much of this, but something isn't right."

That was exactly the kind of reaction I'd hoped Anna would have, a realization of something that didn't quite mesh, perhaps the connecting key.

"Do you have any idea what it is?" I asked.

She marked her place with a napkin. "This all happened a long time ago, but I didn't realize that Rosalie and Gerry were so serious about each other. They kept their secret well."

The way Anna's voice softened to the consistency of pudding when she said Gerry's name told me that her own interest in him wasn't all my imagination. What was it about that irascible, rarely congenial man that made him so fascinating to women?

"Gerry took me out to dinner last night," Anna said. "It's certainly strange to read about him from the perspective of an impassioned young woman."

"Was he as perfect as Rosalie thought?" I asked.

"At the time, I wouldn't have said so, but I was in love with my future husband. I suppose I didn't notice half of what was going on around me. Obviously I didn't know Gerry as intimately as Rosalie did, but I know the man he is today. He's reserved, but when you get to know him, you'll find that he's cultured and charming, a true gentleman. When you're my age, cultured, charming gentleman companions are a rare commodity."

"That's true at any age." I thought of the men I knew: Handsome, effervescent Dalton, raucous Myrold Barren, and Garth MacKay, thoughtful, protective Militiaman. Could any of these men be called cultured and charming? Maybe Dalton, if one wanted only a dollop of culture.

"Gerry was as devastated by Cora's murder as I was," Anna said. "He hasn't gotten over it yet. They were good friends."

"But not lovers?"

"If we can believe Rosalie, no, although I think Cora might have been downplaying her interest in Gerry."

"Maybe later, after Rosalie went away, Cora and Gerry grew closer."

"Who knows? I wouldn't say so. As the years went by, Cora valued her independence and privacy more and more. I think Cora's death took Gerry back to those days when we were all friends and had our whole lives ahead of us."

"Yes, like Rosalie's quotation. 'The day with its possibilities lay before me.'"

The arrival of our lunch brought a temporary halt to our discussion. Anna finished her sandwich quickly and went back to the diary, reading quietly while I drank another cup of coffee.

"Here's something funny," Anna said. "I don't remember Rosalie ever having an engagement ring. If Gerry had given her one, wouldn't you think she'd have shown it to us? The girls made such a fuss over my diamond."

"Keep reading. The last entry may be relevant."

She did, turning the pages in search of more as I'd done earlier.

"So that's how Rosalie met her Southern boy," she said. "I always wondered. August 28th was only a few days after she accepted Gerry's proposal, and she eloped with another man on the first of September. When I heard the news, I couldn't believe it. Now that I know Rosalie and Gerry were engaged, it makes no sense at all, even though the evidence is here in Rosalie's own handwriting.

"This sounds like a plot for a romantic comedy," I said. "In real life the man could have been a serial killer, a bigamist, a wife abuser, anything. You've referred to him as a Southern boy?"

"That was Cora's description of him, based on what Rosalie told her, but Rosalie never said anything about planning to elope with him. That's why Cora and I were shocked when she just left."

"Do you remember his name?" I asked.

"Let me think. Stephen…Seymour…Stuart? I'm not sure."

"Wasn't Rosalie under contract at Maple Creek High School?" I asked.

"I understand that she sent a letter of resignation to the

Board of Education. The principal wasn't happy because he had to start interviewing replacements a few days before school was scheduled to open."

"That was irresponsible," I said. "I wonder why she was in such a hurry."

"So did everyone. And here's something interesting. Gerry never said one word about proposing to Rosalie."

"Given what she did, I can understand why."

I sat back, mulling over the events of that long ago summer: A chance meeting, a whirlwind courtship, and a hasty elopement. I could understand falling under the spell of an attractive, charismatic stranger at a party, although that tended to happen primarily in songs and movies. But would a woman leave her entire life behind to run away with a man she'd met only recently? I didn't think so.

I said, "Rosalie's story reminds me of an old folk ballad about a woman who deserted her family to sail away with her lover. He turns out to be the Devil, and he takes her to hell."

"How Gothic," Anna said. "I hope Rosalie ended up in a better place."

THAT AFTERNOON, I changed into jeans and tennis shoes and carried the ladder up from the basement to the attic entrance. If Rosalie had left anything else behind, I intended to find it. Since both Dalton and Garth had already covered the area, I knew that further discoveries were unlikely, but I had to be certain. After all, both men had been looking for signs of invasive wildlife, rather than an abandoned memento.

I climbed the ladder and pushed up on the panel. Chilly air gushed out through the opening, and tiny dust particles drifted down in my face. Without a doubt, this was the most unpleasant part of the house. I couldn't imagine Rosalie stealing up here at the end of a writing session to hide her diary away from prying eyes.

Setting the lantern flashlight down, I stepped onto the finished floor and from there to the nearest board. Faint light filtered through the ventilation slits. It did little to illuminate the vast shadowy space and nothing to warm it. The cold penetrated my cotton shirt, and the thought of my fireplace waiting for me downstairs when I completed my search propelled me into action. I took a deep breath and swallowed, suddenly aware of an unwelcome prickly sensation in my throat.

*Not again. Please. I just got over a sore throat.*

Nothing could live for long in this environment. Pulling my flashlight out of my belt, I quickly formed a plan of investigation. I would crisscross the attic as Garth had done, moving from east to west, shining the light into every hidden place. Then I'd examine the empty trunks again myself.

I turned the flashlight on and walked slowly toward the front of the house, ducking under low ceiling beams, and always watching where I stepped. The most treacherous area of the floor was the unfinished section. Here were uneven board ends with long nails sticking out like crocodile teeth. I kept as far away from them as possible.

Turning around, I made my way to the back, looking for something, anything that a previous tenant might have left behind. Back and forth, over and over, I moved awkwardly, balancing myself on the boards. Covering every inch of the attic in this way had the added benefit of stripping away its air of secrecy. After seeing what was here, or rather, what wasn't, at close range, I'd never have to lie in bed again, wondering if a restless spirit was trapped at the top of the house.

Not that I ever did that.

I opened the lids of the trunks and leaned over each one to run my hand along their inner surfaces. As Garth had reported, they only contained gritty yellow newspapers. By now I was filthy, breathing in dust, and trying not to cough because my throat hurt. My reason for embarking on this fool's errand seemed trivial and faraway. With less than half of the attic still to search, I had lost enthusiasm for the project.

Then I should bring it to an end for today. I could come back another time. As I turned, my foot came down hard on something that wasn't wood. Bending down to investigate, I saw a small cylinder covered in a drift of cobwebs.

The object was a tube of lipstick, as cold and hard in my hand as an artifact retrieved from a tomb. At one time it had been encased in silver and decorated with alternating stripes of blue and cream. Graceful scrolls framed the cylinder at each end. Now it was badly tarnished, its shine dulled.

Holding it up, I flashed the light on the discolored label. I could barely make out the words. Yardley…Sonnet Peach… Frosted Lipstick. The color was a soft pale orange. I removed the case and inhaled the faint herbal fragrance. Although the lipstick must have lain in the attic for years, the perfume was still delicate and fresh.

Questions clamored through my mind. For how many years, exactly? And how long did a lipstick retain its scent? Most important, was there any possibility that this was Rosalie's property, accidentally dropped as she passed by with her diary in her hand? I was thinking about the Peachmist fingernail polish she'd mentioned in one of the entries.

That scenario seemed unlikely. A girl would hardly go to the attic to apply makeup, but it might have fallen out of her pocket or purse. I had no way of knowing. Still, I considered myself lucky to have found the lipstick before giving up my search for the day.

The questions began again. What did this discovery mean and what else, if anything, might I find? But I was getting ahead of myself. Any female resident who had ever ventured into the attic of the blue Victorian over the years could have lost her lipstick here.

No longer aware of discomfort now that I'd had a measure of success, I picked up the lantern flashlight and headed back to the opening. Before climbing back down the ladder, I reached up to make sure the entrance panel was securely shut.

Back in the bedroom, I carried the lipstick over to the window to examine it again in the sunlight. Someone had used it a few times, but not enough to wear down the softly curving top. In spite of its apparent age, it looked relatively new, and that was truly weird.

The only Yardley products I'd ever seen on shelves were soaps and perfume. Finding out when the company discontinued their lipstick line would be fairly simple, involving a brief search on the Internet. I could use one of the computers in the Maple Creek Public Library. And then, what would I do with this knowledge?

Besides trying to find out whether or not Rosalie had once owned a tube of Sonnet Peach lipstick, I didn't have the answer yet. Today's discovery was a small part of the murky larger picture.

Slipping the lipstick into my pocket, I turned the doorknob. With a start that sent an icy chill racing through my bloodstream, I remembered that I hadn't closed the bedroom door. Trying not to give in to panic, I turned the knob to the right once again.

To no avail. It was useless. I couldn't do it. *Dear God*.

While I had been up in the attic, someone had come into the house, closed this door, and locked me inside. I didn't even know a key existed, but I should have. If the intruder had a key to this room, why not one to the house? Dalton had advised me to have the locks changed. I berated myself for not having done it.

Now what?

This isn't good, but there's no need to panic, I told myself. What can you do?

At the moment, I couldn't think of a thing.

# TWENTY-FOUR

THERE HAD TO BE some way out of this predicament. I was locked in a room, not trapped in a flooded cave. All I had to do was open the window and shout for help until someone heard me. Since this was the first pleasant day we'd had all week, that might happen at any moment.

Once again, I decried my absent neighbors, but they weren't the only people in the neighborhood. Surely at least one person would take advantage of the warm weather and go for a walk.

I tried to raise the window, but it refused to budge. After years of disuse, the frame was frozen in place or painted over. Then I'd have to break the glass using—what? Because I planned to set up a computer in this room, I'd left it empty. The only objects I had with me were the flashlights, the ladder, and the lipstick, all inadequate hammer substitutes.

Ignoring a surge of panic, I punched the window several times as hard as I could, but the old glass remained intact. Staring at my reddened knuckles, I realized that my best option had just disappeared. What now? I didn't even have a chair in this room, or a small stool.

*Don't despair. You can always go back into the attic and sit on one of the trunks.*

I wasn't that desperate yet, but I didn't have access to drinking water. That was important. I touched my throat, hoping that the prickly sensation wouldn't turn into pain, and tried to erase the visions of ice cubes dancing crazily through my mind.

I wouldn't think about physical discomfort or ailments. I'd try to break the glass with the flashlight. It might be an inadequate hammer substitute, but it was all I had. If that didn't work, I'd do what I could, even if that meant pounding on the glass until my knuckles bled. I wouldn't stop until I attracted someone's attention.

A row of scarlet burning bushes grew alongside the drive, forming a natural fence between the houses and ending in my neighbor's front yard, where three giant boulders formed a semi-circle around a small fruit tree. Above them, the windows were dark and silent with half-drawn shades and drapes.

I had a clear view of a small section of the sidewalk. Even if no one came along, maybe one person who knew that I was home would call and wonder why I didn't answer the phone. Myrold might stop by with his artist's rendition of Valentine Park. He'd know that I was inside because my car was parked in the drive. Being the persistent kind, he'd keep knocking on the door until it occurred to him that something was wrong.

Or maybe Anna would remember the name of Rosalie's Southern boy and hurry over to share the information with me. Or Garth would take Tac for a walk after he closed Sky and MacKay Title. One concerned person was all I needed.

Anna, Myrold, and Garth. Nell would be at the hospital. How could I know so few people who would investigate if I suddenly vanished? In retrospect, not to tell anyone what I planned to do today had been foolhardy, since it involved a trip to the attic. But when did I ever discuss my activities with other people?

I had Vicky. Soon she would start fussing for her dinner. When I didn't appear at the door to call her, she would sound the alarm.

*Dog to the Rescue. Stray Saves Trapped Owner.*

Dream on, Katherine. Your dog won't do that.

Where was Vicky anyway? Before going up to the attic, I'd let her out into the yard. Usually she lay outside near the back porch, waiting for me to bring her back inside. Today she must have wandered away because she hadn't alerted me to the intruder's presence.

If she were in the vicinity now, with a canine's superior sense of hearing, she would react to the loud sounds at the window and come around to this side of the house to investigate—unless someone had disposed of her.

*That didn't happen. Focus.*

I walked to the window again and ran my hand over its surface. If I could break it, I would increase the chances of someone hearing my cries for help.

I unbuttoned my shirt and pulled it off. Shivering as the chilly air in the room hit my flesh, I wrapped the white folds around my hand, picked up the flashlight, and, targeting the upper right corner, pounded with its sharp edge on the glass.

To my surprise, it cracked and then a large section broke, sending a shower of shards in every direction. Cool air poured in through the opening. Bit by bit, I chipped away at the window, pausing only to sweep the fragments to one side with the flashlight.

Now I was slightly better off, if still isolated and a long way from the ground. Stepping away from the window, I put on my shirt again and called for help until I was hoarse and my throat ached. Finally I sank down on the hardwood floor, worn out by the unaccustomed stress and exertion.

What else could I do? Waiting for a dog to come looking for her dinner or a curious passerby was too passive. I had to figure out how to free myself quickly. Maybe if I sat quietly and thought, I could come up with another idea for saving myself. Maybe…

*Maybe this time…*

Oh, no, not now. I couldn't deal with a haunting phrase and being captive in my own house at the same time. First, I had to get out of this room.

I had been trying not to think about the person who had locked the bedroom door. Now I couldn't seem to stop. What was his motive? Did he know his next move already, or was this meant to be the last one, the final stage of a larger plan that had begun with home invasion and was scheduled to end with my death?

And where was he now? Could he somehow know that I'd broken the window?

*Keep thinking. Maybe you'll figure it out. You don't have anything else to do except wait for the rescuer to appear.*

But I'd already done everything I could. Nothing was left to do.

*Maybe this time after all these long bitter years, someone will figure it out.*

Unbidden, the rest of the thought had come to me. When I was concentrating on my escape, the phrase that had haunted me for weeks had completed itself. Although its meaning eluded me, I was certain the words were correct. That was good, but for now I had to set it aside, as it wasn't going to get me out of this room. What would?

IN NOVEMBER, even unseasonably warm days end early. Some time later, when the sky was darkening, I heard Vicky barking at the side door. I hurried to the window. If she continued to disrupt the neighborhood quiet, sooner or later someone might call the police. Dalton would be fast to respond. As soon as he arrived, he'd know that something was wrong, and I wouldn't have to spend the night locked in a dark and empty room.

But it was Garth's voice I heard, not Dalton's.

"Katherine! Where are you?"

He was standing beneath the window, looking up while Vicky pranced around him and pawed at the door.

"In the spare bedroom, Garth. I'm locked in."

"You've got to get out of there now!"

The next instant I heard a crash of glass shattering and heavy footsteps on the stairs. Garth was on the landing, outside the door, turning the knob, and pounding on the door, as I had done on the glass. "We have to get out of the house!" he shouted. "Where's the key?"

"I don't know. There's no key."

"Stand back out of the way." His large foot came crashing through the wood, and the door swung forward, hanging on one hinge.

"Come with me," he ordered. "Out of the way, Vicky."

At once I saw the reason for his melodramatic entrance. Rather, I smelled it. A sharp unpleasant odor filled the air beyond the door. Already it was drifting into the room.

Grabbing my hand, Garth said, "It's gas. Stay with me, Katherine."

He practically dragged me down the staircase, pulling me up when I stumbled, wrenching my hand away from the banister when I reached for it.

I caught my breath. "There's a gas leak? In the neighborhood?"

"It's in your house. Leaking out from under the side door. I'll get you outside and then find out."

"No—I'll call Consumer's Energy."

He didn't answer, but we were on the first floor now, where the odor was stronger. Through the kitchen, at the broken side door, out into the blessed fresh air—we were safe

Garth flung me into the scarlet bushes and ran back inside. I tried to stop shaking and spoke softly to Vicky to quiet her. Another dog was barking now. It must be Tac, left on the front porch, wanting to join us.

Slowly reality caught up with me. While I'd been trapped in a locked room, a torrent of gas had made its way through my house. I could have died. Again.

A small slight figure in a long red raincoat rushed across the street. It was Mrs. West, welcome but too late. Before she reached the house, Garth was back. As he drew near, I felt an unfamiliar, overwhelming desire to throw myself into his arms and weep.

"It's okay now," he said. "The burner on that old stove in the basement was on. I turned it off. A few more hours of breathing those fumes, and you'd have gone to sleep for good. How did you lock yourself in that room?"

Did he really think I'd be so careless? "Someone else did that."

Garth's eyes narrowed, and his voice took on a stony edge that I'd never noticed before. "Tell me what happened."

Breathless and flushed, her hair in a mass of loose curls, Mrs. West hugged me, "Katherine, are you all right? I just heard Mr. MacKay shouting at you."

"I'm fine…"

"She will be," Garth said. "I'll open the windows and carry that stove out to the curb for you."

"No, wait!" I grabbed Garth's arm before he could take off again. "It has to stay here. I'm going to call the Gas Company and the police. Thank God you came by when you did, Garth. And Mrs. West, thanks for being so observant."

"I'd have come sooner, but I was under the hair dryer," she said.

"Why get the police involved?" Garth asked.

"Because someone tried to kill me. That stove you want to move is evidence."

ALL THE WINDOWS in the house were open now. The toxic fumes had begun to dissipate in the fresh evening air, but a faint unpleasant smell still lingered here in the kitchen, which was the room closest to the basement.

I had fed Vicky and praised her lavishly for leading Garth to the window. She was lying on the back porch, as far as she could get from the last of the fumes and still remain in the house. Garth had left Tac on the porch tethered to a post. Both dogs were quiet now that the rescue was complete.

While Dalton and Garth glared at each other, I scooped ice cubes into a tall glass, filled it to the top with cold water, and drank great gulps. Dalton had just come upstairs after examining the rogue stove, the first step and also the last in his investigation.

"Mr. MacKay," Dalton said. "What exactly is your business with Miss Kale?"

I'd never heard Dalton speak in such a scathing tone, but Garth didn't appear to take offense.

"I'm Katherine's friend, Lieutenant Gray," he said. "I was walking by with my dog and heard her dog barking." His subtle emphasis on Dalton's rank was a mild insult. Dalton gave the impression that he hadn't noticed.

"Garth got me out of the room," I added.

"I see." Dalton's gaze strayed to the broken side door. "Okay, Katherine. Here's the deal. Mr. MacKay's prints smeared the underlying ones. There's no sign of a break in, nothing we can use. Same as before."

"My house is trying to kill me," I said.

"Someone is using your house to do that. Who would have a key to the place?" Again, his gaze fastened on Garth MacKay.

"No one that I know of, but I never had the locks changed. I kept putting it off; then I forgot about it."

"In this case, procrastination could have been deadly." He looked around the kitchen and glanced down the stairway to the basement. The essence of the brusque, capable, efficient officer, Dalton hadn't actually done anything, but it appeared that he had. "If you don't need that old stove, you should get rid of it. Now, you'd better get yourself over to St. Andrew's for a check up."

"There's no need for that. I'm all right—that is, no worse than I was before this happened."

"Nevertheless, do it. And one more thing," he said, with another look at Garth. "You should review your list of acquaintances and friends. See if anyone has a motive for wanting you out of the way."

"That's an outrageous suggestion," I said.

Now Dalton's withering look fastened on me.

"But I'll do it."

"I'll be in touch. Don't forget to go to Emergency," he said. "I'll stop by there later and check on you. Goodnight, Katherine. Mr. MacKay."

As Dalton went out through the broken door, the temperature in the kitchen began to rise. I rinsed the glass and filled the teakettle with water for tea.

"That man doesn't like you, Garth," I said.

He shrugged. "That's nothing new. Gray is a cop. But he likes you."

"Maybe. I've been a challenge to him because of the murder and these incidents at my house."

"He hasn't done anything to stop them that I can see." Garth leaned over the sink and closed the window halfway. "After you have your tea, I'll take you to Emergency. This broken door is an invitation to burglars. Would Mrs. West stay here for a few hours until we get back?"

I knew that he'd heard me. He was proceeding as if I'd never voiced my intention. "I'm sure she would, but I'm not going to the hospital. And about the door, I have Vicky. She proved herself tonight."

"Your friend from the MCPD said he'd check on you."

"I'll go in the morning. I feel good—sort of—but I'm tired."

And every now and then I realized anew what could have happened to me tonight. I needed to regain my lost sense of security. That was the real problem.

Garth came closer to me and tilted my head back. As he studied my face, the band of his ring touched my skin. It felt hard and cold.

"Just sort of good?" he asked.

"My sore throat came back."

"It's no wonder. If I'd known you wanted that attic checked out again, I'd have done it for you," he said. "All you had to do was ask."

At that moment I remembered the lipstick. I pulled it out of my pocket. "It was an impulsive decision, a whim. Here's what I found. Yardley's Sonnet Peach, a shade from the seventies. I wish I knew who left it in the attic."

"That's what almost got you killed?"

"Look on the bright side, Garth. If I hadn't been up in the attic, I might have been downstairs when the murderer let himself in."

Garth wasn't smiling. "We have to get to the bottom of this, Katherine. Dalton is useless."

"I don't know what else I can do."

"Gray said to look to your friends and acquaintances."

"That's Anna, Myrold, Nell, and you. You've all been in and out of my life from my first days in Maple Creek, but I don't suspect any one of you of trying to harm me."

"I'm glad you don't think I'm the villain," he said, with a smile. "It makes my job easier."

He moved closer again, too close for our present situation.

"I'll stay with you tonight, Katherine."

How deftly he'd slipped that into the conversation.

"No you won't."

"It's dangerous for you to stay alone in a house with a broken door."

"I have Vicky."

"How about spending the night at my house then? You can use Taryn's room."

Not in a million years, I thought. Not in a billion years. Still, Garth had a point. If the invader came back, he wouldn't need his key. However this dilemma had several solutions, none of which included Garth.

"I think I can patch the door up until tomorrow," I said.

"That'll work, but I'll do that for you tonight."

This constant dialogue was beginning to annoy me. It seemed unending. I was grateful to Garth for his part in saving my life, but now it seemed that he was trying to take control of it. Still, I decided to let him repair the door. After all he'd broken it—to save me. I had to remember that. When had our relationship become so complicated?

A while back, only a few weeks ago, I'd made up my mind to keep him out of my affairs. Somehow I'd let the opposite happen. Soon I'd have to sort out my feelings for Garth and either move forward with him or pull away. To continue as we were was unfair to both of us.

"If you do that, I should be safe enough for the time being," I said. "I don't think he'll be back tonight."

"Then tomorrow I'll change the locks," Garth said.

"And I'll stop at St. Andrew's."

"Between us, we'll make Lt. Gray happy."

I nodded. "And thwart the killer."

Was this conversation going to go on forever? Suddenly I wanted desperately to be alone in my own house. With the afternoon's harrowing events, I hadn't had time to think about the lipstick and the mystery involving Rosalie's departure, which might be related to what was currently going on in my life.

I wanted to think about that now, and I needed a warm bath, a hot drink to soothe my sore throat, a little time by the fire, and my comfortable bed—in that order. But I had to wait for everything and be gracious to this man who had done so much to help me.

"If you're sure you have the time, I'd appreciate it," I said.

He laid his hand heavily on my shoulder. "Like I told you once, Katherine. For you I'll always make time."

# TWENTY-FIVE

A WARM BATH, HOT COCOA, and the comfort of sitting by the fireside worked their magic. A long night's sleep would complete the restoration, and tomorrow, the day with its possibilities lay before me. In other words, I was ready to take on the unknown adversary who had dared to threaten my life in my own home.

An intelligent woman would be long gone from this house, trading all the authentic period features for safety. I could list the house and buy another one closer to my school or perhaps in Myrold Barren's Village. I considered myself an intelligent woman, but I refused to run away. Besides, since the danger originated beyond the walls of the blue Victorian, it might well follow me to a new location.

For what seemed like the hundredth time, I traced the strange happenings back to their beginning and always found myself at the Apple Fair, meeting Garth in the yard of Sky and MacKay Title, and following his directions to the yard sale where I met Cora Valentine.

Then Cora was murdered, and I unearthed the crushed cameo. The real beginning was Rosalie's cameo buried in the backyard of the house, which she'd left under mysterious circumstances. All of that was ancient history. Rosalie was gone, Cora was dead, and deep down I knew that nobody haunted the house. And yet...

A certain presence still seemed to shadow me whenever I walked up the stairs, and lately a delicate, fresh fragrance haunted the living room. It reminded me of the bars of lavender soap tucked among the sheets and towels in my linen closet. Curiously, the lipstick I'd taken out of the attic was in my closed purse on the coffee table next to Garth's roses. How could the scent escape from there into the air around me?

I set my imagination free to speculate. What if the spirit who walked the halls of the blue Victorian and haunted the attic wasn't Cora but Rosalie?

*Maybe this time after all these bitter years, someone will figure it out.*

Perhaps the voice that whispered this silent wish in my mind was hers.

All along I had imagined Rosalie living an ordinary life in a Southern city with a family and a husband she still loved passionately. She never thought about Gerry Raycraft. He was part of her past. Her children would be grown by now. Most likely she'd never given the diary another thought after she left Maple Creek, and the lipstick probably belonged to someone else.

That was one possibility. Could there be another?

I wanted to find her. In the morning, after making my requisite visit to St. Andrew's, I intended to call Anna. Together we could brainstorm and perhaps come up with a way to do it.

ON MY WAY HOME from St. Andrew's, I drove by Anna's house to tell her about my latest narrow escape and to show her the lipstick. She was sitting in her airy, whitewashed sunroom reading the morning *Tribune,* but she was already dressed for the day in a long gray skirt and a silky peach blouse. She listened in horror as I described my frantic attempts to attract attention to my plight and the chilling realization of the real danger.

"Are you going to be all right?" she asked.

"I'll be fine. I only went to the hospital to humor the police."

"Thank heavens. That stove is ancient. I'm not surprised that it malfunctioned."

Apparently I hadn't made myself clear. "Somebody turned on the gas deliberately. The same person who cut my railing, I think."

"Oh, my God. You should get out of that house, Katherine."

"I'm afraid that wouldn't help. If Garth MacKay hadn't happened to come along when he did, I would have died in that room. I was lucky."

"I should say so. Mr. MacKay has been around your house a lot since you came to town."

"Well, his business is on Main Street."

Anna slid over that obvious fact. "He's an attractive man, but do you know anything about him?"

"A little," I said.

"I mean, about his family. Who he dated before, if he ever had a serious relationship—if he's still a member of the Michigan Militia... Things like that."

"I know about Taryn and Tac."

And that Garth had once dated Nell's sister. And that he had vowed to make me change my mind about wanting him. Naturally I would never tell Anna that.

"Garth doesn't talk much about himself," I said. "He's a very thoughtful man, and he's only a friend." Realizing that I'd said more than I intended to, I handed Anna the lipstick. "This is what I found in the attic."

She held it against the sleeve of her blouse. The soft orange shades were almost identical.

"My, this is pretty." She waved it under her nose. "And the scent is heavenly."

"Do you suppose Rosalie used Yardley products?" I asked.

"You want to know if this could have belonged to her. Katherine, I can't even remember what brand of cosmetics I wore in the seventies." She handed the lipstick back to me. "It's possible."

"I wish you could remember the name of Rosalie's husband," I said.

"Last night I lay awake for a long time thinking about it. His first name may be Stuart."

"Did Rosalie tell Cora where he came from?"

"Yes. Some place in Georgia."

"Stuart from Georgia. That should be next to impossible to trace."

"I'm sorry, but this happened thirty years ago. Maybe it'll come to me."

"I guess you don't know the name of the relative Stuart was visiting in Maple Creek then," I said.

"If Cora knew that, she never mentioned it."

Having this conversation was like cruising down a dead end street. But Anna had lived with Cora and Rosalie. She might know more than she realized. Now I'd see how she would react to my theory.

"Did you ever wonder if Rosalie really did leave town with Stuart?"

"I'm sure she did. She left a note. I was the one who found it."

"Let me play Devil's Advocate. It was all so hurried. Couldn't she have changed her mind at the last minute and done something else?"

"If that happened, she would have come home."

"Maybe not if she was too proud to admit she'd made a mistake."

"No, Katherine. You have an intriguing theory, but you're wrong. If her plans changed, Rosalie would have come home where she had friends and a job. And don't forget the letter she sent us from Georgia. Oh—I remember now. She mailed the letter from Savannah.

Stuart from Savannah. We were making progress.

"Do you remember anything about the day Rosalie went away?" I asked.

Anna folded the *Tribune* neatly and said, "I haven't forgotten anything. Let's sit over here where it's brighter."

Her sunroom resembled a garden with green wicker furniture, a bubbling indoor fountain, and flowering plants. In this relaxing setting, I could easily imagine myself transported back to the time Anna was reliving.

"A few of us girls were going to Stratford to see a Shakespearean play, for a last outing before school started," she said. "Rosalie didn't leave with Cora and me. She had a hairdresser's appointment. She was supposed to drive her own car and meet us there, but she never showed up."

"Weren't you worried?"

"Not really. We assumed she'd changed her mind and decided to do something with Gerry instead. That wasn't unusual for her. We were a group of girls. Rosalie liked activities in mixed company.

"Cora and I got home around two or three in the morning and went to bed. The next day I found Rosalie's note on the kitchen table, under the sugar bowl."

"Was it in her handwriting?"

"Only the signature. Rosalie always wrote notes and letters on her old portable typewriter. She signed the note in that green ink she liked, the same kind she used in her diary."

"The signature was definitely hers?"

"It must have been. I never doubted it until you brought it up. Katherine, you're turning an ordinary event into a scary mystery. It never occurred to us that Rosalie didn't do exactly as she said, especially since we never saw her again. Her car was gone," she added.

I couldn't tell if Anna doubted it now, but her face seemed a little paler under the light natural makeup.

"That morning, I went up to Rosalie's room," she said. "Her bed was made, and all of her personal possessions were gone. I remember how sad I felt, but like everything, in time the feeling passed."

"What did Gerry say when you showed him the note?" I asked.

"He already knew. Rosalie had left a letter for him in his mailbox. Gerry was so hurt. For a few days he talked about going after Rosalie and bringing her back, but he did never did. Now that I think of it, that should have told me how much she meant to him."

"Rosalie's story sounds more like a historical romance

novel than a movie. *When a young girl elopes with a handsome rake, her true love pursues her, determined to win her back.*"

"To my knowledge, Gerry never did anything like that. It was all talk. Why would he, when Rosalie left of her own free will with the man of her choice? When she wrote to us from Savannah, Cora showed him the letter. As I recall, Gerry said he was happy for her."

"Didn't she write to him too?"

"If she did, he didn't tell us."

I couldn't believe that Rosalie's friends hadn't delved more thoroughly into her sudden departure, but then they'd known her. My perspective was deeply colored by my growing suspicions.

"Did you keep the note and letter by chance?" I asked.

"Only for a while. I'm sure I threw them away years ago."

"This story keeps getting stranger. Anna, we have to try to find Rosalie. We have a first name and a city. I know it won't be easy, but maybe we'll have luck."

Anna nodded. "I agree, Katherine. I'll feel better knowing that Rosalie is all right."

"Then the two of you can get together for a reunion and talk over old times."

"Wouldn't that be wonderful? The next time I see Gerry, I'll ask him if he remembers Stuart's last name," she said. "If we know that, maybe we can contact her. And Katherine, I'm sorry if I sounded negative about Garth MacKay a while ago. I only have your best interests at heart."

"It's all right," I said.

"In my experience, men don't do thoughtful things for women without expecting something in return."

"How cynical you are, Anna."

"I'm worldly wise. I've been through a few similar situations with my own girls. Just be careful."

I had heard this warning before from Anna and also from Nell. Someday I might decide to heed it. "I'm always careful. But I believe that if something is destined to happen, it will."

"Just like with Rosalie and Stuart," Anna said.

THAT EVENING the blue Victorian came alive with sound. Upstairs, Garth pounded the last nails in place, while in the kitchen, Vicky and Tac barked at the noise, and two Porterhouse steaks sizzled on the broiler.

In the meantime, I tossed a green salad and wondered why I still didn't feel safe with a strong man on the premises, not to mention two dogs and three new locks on the doors.

All afternoon, my suspicion that Rosalie had met with foul play had been playing through my mind. I could almost add sentences to the haunting phrase that was now a complete thought: *You're getting warmer. Keep going in this direction, and soon you'll reach the fire.* But I was still floundering.

Anna had promised to call me if she learned anything new from Gerry Raycraft, which meant Stuart's last name. With this information, I imagined it would be fairly easy to trace Rosalie by calling Savannah Information—unless his name was Smith or Jones, or he had an unlisted number. I had to consider the strong possibility that he might have moved. After all, how many people remained in their hometown all their lives, assuming Savannah was Stuart's hometown?

Common sense told me that I might be cruising down yet another dead end street, but curiosity urged me to try.

Garth came stamping down the stairs and crossed to the landing where he had set out a variety of cases containing enough tools to build a small addition. He began putting them away quietly and efficiently, each item in its own section.

"All done, Katherine. No one will be able to get in now, unless he comes through a window." Laying an array of shiny new keys on the counter, he said, "I made three duplicates for each door. Keep them in a safe place. They're already marked."

"I don't know how I can ever thank you." Even as I uttered the words, I realized that I should have phrased the statement in another way. Maybe Garth wouldn't notice the wording.

"Consider it a favor for a friend. This dinner is thanks enough," he said.

"You're such a fast worker. It won't be ready for another half hour."

"I'll sit and watch you. I like to see women cooking."

"Oh you do? Well, you won't see this often."

I had insisted on paying for the materials, but with matching determination, Garth refused to accept payment for his labor. He agreed to stay for dinner, and fortunately I had two steaks in the freezer.

"I wish I could find out who tried to hurt you," he said.

"To kill me."

"Okay, you're right. Kill you. I'd take care of him."

"Lieutenant Gray didn't call," I said. "I'm not expecting him to."

"Like I keep telling you, Katherine, don't count on the MCPD. They're good for local color but don't trust your life to them." He may as well have added, "Count on me."

"I hope you're wrong."

Garth sat down in his usual place, with Tac on one side and Vicky on the other. I set the table and pondered the pros and cons of sharing my thoughts about Rosalie with him. He'd probably think I was letting my imagination run wild, but I wanted the input of somebody who hadn't known Rosalie.

I didn't have anything to lose since Garth already thought I was overly imaginative. "Do you know of any people in Maple Creek whose parents came from the South?" I asked.

"My partner, Greg Sky, for one. His mother was born in Nashville."

"A little farther south. Georgia, maybe."

"Let me think."

His laid his large hand on Tac's head and rubbed his fur in an absent manner. If only Garth could give me a few names, I'd have another lead, although who would remember an out of town guest at a party held over thirty years ago? I didn't even know what kind of party it was.

"I can come up with a list of names for you, Katherine. What are you going to do with it?"

Incredibly, Garth sounded suspicious of me, but I had to admit that my request was rather unusual. In truth, it was downright strange. I told him my theory and my plan and prepared to hear him blast it to pieces.

But all he said was, "That's sure going about it the hard way, Katherine. If this lady got killed thirty years ago, what does it have to do with you today?"

"I'm not sure. It may be irrelevant."

"It would be better to go back to Cora's murder. Who killed her? Right after that is when your trouble started."

"I just have a feeling that one happening relates to another."

"And if you find out that Rosalie is alive and well in Georgia, where does that leave you?"

"Square one. I've been spending a lot of time there."

He took a small notebook out of his pocket. "I'll give you some names, but I want you to let me help you with whatever you're going to do."

"You're already doing that."

"Yes, well, a few of these folks aren't particularly friendly. They'll tell you more if I'm with you."

"That sounds alarming. It's only information I want."

"Even so," he said. "Have you given any thought to what you're going to say?"

"The truth—or part of it. I'm trying to locate a man called Stuart, last name unknown, from Savannah, Georgia. He visited his cousin in Maple Creek about thirty years ago and may have attended a party while he was here."

"That's like looking for a needle in a haystack, but we may find your man. The population in this town hasn't changed much over the years, except for births and deaths. We can start with Eleanor Snow over at Eleanor's Herbs. Her father moved to Michigan from Georgia in the seventies or eighties. His name was Jeff Karinton."

"Possible cousin of Stuart Karinton," I said. "It has a certain ring."

"Don't get your hopes up, Katherine. There's Dan Carolin, Willston Everett, and Esther Bell. We'll end up at Bell's Country Kitchen just in time for lunch. Esther's mother is another transplanted Southerner."

"When can we do this?" I asked.

"How about the end of the week on Saturday morning?"

"Saturday will be perfect," I said.

"And we can make another search of the attic, if you want to be sure there's nothing else up there."

"Only if you have the time to spare for all that," I said. "I did have another small area to cover."

"I look on it as fun, like a Hardy Boys adventure."

The doorbell rang out, its clear notes sending both dogs racing to the front door. Garth called Tac back to his side in the sharp tone that commanded instant obedience, but Vicky darted ahead of me through the living room as if she were determined to greet the visitor first.

Nell stood on porch, still wearing her white uniform. She had a small American flag pin on the collar.

"I heard you were in the E. R. this morning, Katherine," she said. "Is anything wrong?"

"Not any more. Come on in and I'll tell you about it."

"Whose truck is that in front of your house?"

"It belongs to Garth MacKay. We're going to have dinner together."

"Here? Oh, no. I'm intruding again." She stepped back.

"Don't be silly, Nell. It isn't like a date. If you haven't eaten yet, please join us."

Hastily I reviewed my menu. I had two steaks, but I never ate a whole one, plenty of French-fried potatoes, a large bowl of salad, and rolls from the bakery. Not plenty, but enough for three.

"I had a late lunch, but I'd like a cup of coffee or tea, only if you're positive I won't be in the way," she said.

I assured her that she wouldn't and led the way back to the kitchen, both of us following Vicky now.

"You're little stray has taken over your house," she said. "Oh, hello, Mr. MacKay. How nice to see you again."

Garth rose and flashed her a smile that certainly looked sincere. "Hello, Miss Farmer."

Hoping that this encounter would be easier than their last one, I gave Nell a scaled down summary of my experience with the gas stove, ending with the unnecessary trip to St. Andrew's. I made sure to emphasize Garth's heroic contribution.

"I can't believe something terrible happened to you again," she said.

"I'm learning to expect the unexpected."

"You've had more than your share of trouble since you moved to our town, Katherine," she said. "I hope this is the last of the incidents."

"I'll second that," Garth said.

"I had another reason for stopping by," Nell said. "I hate to bring more bad news, but I thought you'd want to know. There's been another poisoning case. This time the victim is Gerry Raycraft."

# TWENTY-SIX

"HOLD ON TO THAT black beast, Mr. MacKay," Nell said. "I don't like the way he's staring at me."

Garth gripped Tac's collar. "Okay, ma'am, but he won't bite you. Only my enemies have to be afraid of him. Now what's this about Gerry Raycraft?"

I filled three mugs with hot black coffee, watching the steam rise into the air, passing my hand over them because suddenly I was very cold. First Cora and then her old friend, Gerry, and...

"Mr. Raycraft says he bought two apple fritters at the Bakery on Main this morning and got sick as soon as he ate them," Nell said.

...Cora had eaten the poisoned apple exactly one month ago.

"Then he's still alive," I said.

"His prognosis is fair. He's convinced that the pastries were contaminated at the bakery. Naturally they deny it. I hear that Mrs. Tattersall ate one herself to prove they were safe. Anyway, he's talking about suing them, so I'm guessing he's going to be okay."

I set the mugs on the table and moved the creamer and sugar bowl closer to Nell. "Cora was murdered a month ago today. Doesn't anyone remember that?"

Nell said, "I'm sure the police do." She poured a liberal amount of cream into her coffee and stirred it until the color changed to a smooth, rich caramel.

Along with everyone else in Maple Creek, I had been expecting Cora's killer to strike again. Then Halloween had passed, November came, and my own brush with death pushed that fear to the back of my mind. Everyone knows that terrible things can happen when you least expect them—and sometimes on a one-month anniversary. I made a mental note to keep that in mind.

"Wasn't a similar case reported right after Cora was killed?" I asked.

"Old Man Evans and the Apple Danish," Garth said. "He brought that one on himself."

"I have to warn you, Garth, I bought the dinner rolls at the same place."

"I'm not going to worry. I know Mrs. Tattersall. There's never been any trouble with her baked goods until now."

"Well, in that case, I won't worry either. Are you sure you won't stay for dinner, Nell? You don't have to eat the rolls."

"Another time. This is good. Invigorating." She finished her coffee and set the mug on the sink. "I haven't been home yet, but after that balcony accident, I was concerned about you. We'll have to get together and talk. A ladies' night out," she added, glancing in Garth's direction.

"We'll do it soon," I said.

Garth said goodnight to Nell, and she gave him a civil if cool farewell smile.

"Don't burn your steaks, Katherine," she said. "I'll let myself out. Have fun, you two."

As soon as we heard the door close, Garth said, "You heard the lady."

"About the steaks, yes. I tend to get distracted. If they're too well done, we'll call them Louisiana blackened."

Garth got up and peered over my shoulder. "They're fine, Katherine. Do you need any help?"

I checked on the French fries. In another few minutes, they'd be ready. Salad, rolls, sharp steak knifes, saltshaker, and pepper mill were on the table. All I had to do was tip the potatoes out of the fryer onto a paper towel and pour them into a serving dish. I didn't have any dessert, only the chocolate ice cream in the freezer. Well, that should be safe.

"No, everything is under control," I said. At least with my dinner it was.

I realized that I was glad to have a companion to share this meal with, happy to feel safe in my own house with its strong new locks, and grateful that so far I had escaped death. Not that Gerry Raycraft was going to die, but someone had tried to kill him. Somewhere, perhaps in a dark basement, at this very moment the poisoner was whipping up a lethal mixture for his next victim.

None of these thoughts were conducive to a good digestion. "If you're ready, we can eat," I said.

THE STORY IN the *Tribune* was sketchy. The apple fritters that Mr. Gerald Raycraft had bought were suspected to be laced with enough poison to make a person deathly ill but not kill him. Mrs. Tattersall had turned over the remaining pastries to the police. She claimed that her helpers were innocent of any wrongdoing. No one else had gotten sick.

In that sense the scenario was similar to that at the Apple Creek Cider Mill in October. The *Tribune* reporter included a reference to the one-month anniversary of Cora Valentine's murder and speculated that the same person was responsible for both crimes. The last paragraph of the story was the sketchiest of all, detailing the progress made by the homicide detectives in capturing Cora Valentine's killer. Dalton would be unhappy to read one of his least favorite sentences: *At the present time, the police have no suspects in custody and no leads in the case.*

Now that I knew Gerry Raycraft was going to recover, my thoughts turned to the search for Rosalie. I began to wonder if Anna had talked to Gerry before he made his fateful trip to the bakery. I dialed her number and left a message on her answering machine, but the afternoon passed without a single phone call.

Before dark, on an impulse, I drove past Anna's house. Her car wasn't in the drive. Maybe she had gone away again, or she might be visiting Gerry at the hospital.

At present I couldn't learn anything from Anna, but in four more days, Garth and I would visit the people in town who had Southern connections. I didn't allow myself to be too optimistic, but maybe I'd have success.

*Maybe this time, after all these bitter years, someone will figure it out.*

I'll do what I can, I thought.

THE NEXT AFTERNOON I moved the lingerie chest to an empty corner of my bedroom opposite the balcony. After giving it a thorough cleaning, I planned to line the drawers with pastel paper, as soft and pleasing as the colors of the wildflowers painted on the smooth maple surface.

Standing in the sunlight that spilled through the French doors, I fell in love with the piece again. Stalks of Viola, Buttercup, Lavender, Queen Anne's Lace, and pink Loosestrife adorned the front of the chest. The pattern continued on each of the five drawers, with the flower's name lettered in neat Gothic script above or below its picture. Slight variations in the shape of the petals and leaves attested to its originality.

I imagined that the artist was a talented amateur who had decorated her furniture for her own pleasure. Cora would have known who had owned the chest, along with its history, and sold it to me for three times Anna's generous price.

I polished the wood and brass knobs until they shone. Then I took a clean cloth and wiped the inside of the drawers, a tedious chore but one I wouldn't have to do too often.

The third drawer stuck. Gripping the knobs, I forced it open. Something concealed inside layers of lavender tissue paper rolled a few inches forward. I unwrapped the object and stared in shock at a bracelet of five cameos joined by delicate gold links. The forward facing heads were encased in glossy brown ovals with gold frames as thin as threads. I was looking at Rosalie's cameo times five, before the damage and in a different form.

I could assume that the chest had belonged to Rosalie, or,

remembering a line in her diary, that she had borrowed it from one of her friends, most likely Anna.

An illusive something tugged at me. Then I realized what it was. The tissue paper appeared to be new with no sign of yellowing or age, suggesting that someone else had come across the bracelet recently, wrapped it, and left it here.

In a chest that was part of a yard sale? I had no way of knowing exactly when this discovery had taken place.

I did know about the bracelet though. According to Anna, Rosalie had purchased it in Italy, but after the safety chain broke, she rarely wore it, preferring the cameo pin. In spite of the broken chain, the bracelet was still wearable and valuable. Why would she leave it behind?

I could think of only one reason. Rosalie hadn't gone from the blue Victorian voluntarily. How to prove this was going to be a challenge. Whatever the nature of her departure, she had left bits and pieces of her life strewn around in the house. Perhaps I would find more of her possessions up in the attic.

And, if my theory was correct, who had been the first to find the bracelet and wrap it carefully in lavender tissue paper?

Once again, I longed to share my discovery and ideas with Anna Lynde. Leaving the chest as it was but taking the bracelet with me, I hurried to the phone and dialed her number. She still hadn't returned, which left me no choice but to proceed on my own.

HISTORY REPEATS ITSELF.

Cora Valentine dies after eating a poisoned apple, and the next day I unearth the crushed cameo. Gerry Raycroft survives a similar murder attempt, and the next day I find Rosalie's bracelet, exquisite and intact.

Of course, if I'd opened the drawers, I could have known the bracelet was in my possession any time since the chest had been delivered. Procrastination was a necessary by-product of my extended vacation. Once I started teaching again, I would revert to my usual efficient ways, but now I had time to devote exclusively to untangling the mystery. That was my plan for the evening, and I had a new idea.

I had been overlooking someone. While Anna and Garth were temporarily unavailable, presumably Alarice was still in her Sears' kit house giving private piano lessons every week-day morning. After that, she would be free until late in the afternoon.

Alarice had known Rosalie and once had a crush on Gerry Raycraft. Since she had attended the Fourth of July barbecue, she might also have gone to the party and noted Rosalie's new interest. Maybe she knew Stuart's last name.

I could visit Alarice around two or three and ask her if she had time to give me a tour of her house today. I'd take her a loaf of pumpkin bread and bring up Gerry's ordeal, which must be a popular topic of conversation in Maple Creek today. Then, when the time was right, I would ask my question. If she had some relevant knowledge, I meant to possess it.

ALARICE'S HOUSE WAS a small gray brick ranch set farther back from the street than its neighbors. Thick overgrown shrubbery shrouded much of the façade. In the spring when the untrimmed trees were in leaf, a thick curtain of green would hide the house from view.

Alarice greeted me warmly, almost as if she'd been expecting me. I cast off this strange thought. Until this morning, I hadn't known I was going to visit her.

"Come in, Katherine," she said. "I was hoping you'd stop by some day."

"Are your piano lessons over for the day?" I asked.

"Not quite, but I'm free until six."

I handed her the pumpkin bread, wrapped in transparent orange paper but still filling the air with fragrant, seasonal spices. "All those leftover Halloween jack-o'-lanterns inspired me to bake."

"How kind of you. Here, have a seat."

She removed a stack of sheet music from the small sofa that vied for space with busts of composers, overflowing bookcases, and end tables crowded with figurines. While she searched for a place to set the pumpkin bread, I looked in fascination at her distinctive décor.

A mahogany Baby Grand piano filled a third of the living room. The walls were covered with vintage prints of women playing musical instruments. Alarice had found space for her sewing machine and several baskets containing patterns and snippets of material. The most unusual decoration was the large statue of a Greek god leering down from its high white pedestal.

"It's Dionysus," she said. "I fell in love with it."

"You have some very unique decorations here," I said.

Alarice had crammed so many objects into this living area that I was afraid I'd soon have difficulty breathing. How could she prefer these rooms to the outside world? Already the walls seemed to be shrinking and moving closer, and for me, the house was too warm. The thermostat must be set at seventy-five degrees.

Alarice didn't appear to notice the heat. She wore a paisley shawl over her long sleeved navy dress, an austere outfit brightened only by the silver of her dangling cleft note earrings.

Find out what you need to know and get back outside quickly, I told myself.

"So many really interesting things. I've never seen such a collection." I focused on the statue of Dionysus. "It's almost like sitting in a museum."

"They're a source of great pleasure for me," she said.

"Did you hear what happened to Gerry Raycraft?" I asked.

"Yes, and I was so upset when I read about it," she said. "That poor man has had one setback after another. He didn't deserve this one."

"I was shocked to hear that a second person was poisoned," I said.

I wasn't the least bit surprised when Alarice ignored my allusion to Cora's poisoning death. How I wished I knew what had caused their rift. But that was a question I didn't feel I could ask her.

"Nobody's safe any more." Alarice surveyed her room, as if to find reassurance and comfort in the overwhelming closeness of her possessions. "I swear, Katherine, it's getting so I don't want to leave my house."

"If you let yourself feel that way, you're giving the killer power over you," I said. "You're allowing him to steal this beautiful fall day away from you."

She neatly sidestepped the point of my observation. "We won't have many more days like this before winter sets in. Katherine, I'm sorry. This isn't the best time for you to see the house. It's a mess. I've been a bit under the weather the last few days, and you know how housekeeping wears you out."

"I do indeed. Well, that's all right, Alarice," I said. "Whenever you're able will be fine."

"I just try to keep this room neat."

But that, I imagined, was a formidable task. Now for my question before Alarice excused herself, pleading illness.

"I wondered if you'd help me solve a little mystery," I said. "The other day I came across an old diary in my attic."

I thought I detected a slight shift in her expression, but I couldn't be sure.

"It belonged to a girl named Rosalie Grier. Years ago, she used to live in my house. That's the blue Victorian on Walnut."

"I know, and I remember Rosalie. I'll never forget her. She was a sweetheart, so nice and kind. Everybody loved her. But she moved out of town ages ago."

"That's right. It's been fun reading about life in Maple Creek in the seventies from her point of view."

"You should call the *Tribune*," Alarice said. "I'll bet they'd do a story about it."

"I may do that." I zeroed in on my objective. "In one entry

Rosalie wrote about a Southern man she met at a party. His name was Stuart."

"That would be Stuart MacPhearson," Alarice said. "I'll never forget him either."

# TWENTY-SEVEN

SOMETIMES SUCCESS, like death, comes along when you aren't expecting it. I hadn't held any real hope that Alarice would remember Stuart's last name. With a silent thank you for the impulse that had brought me to her house, I asked, "What made Stuart MacPhearson so memorable?"

Her voice and eyes radiated with enthusiasm. "He was polished and courteous, a real Southern gentleman. I'd never met anyone like him."

"Was he handsome?"

"I thought so, but it's his personality that I remember. How can I explain Stuart? He was from the South, so different from the boys around here."

"Like an exotic plant?"

"That's it. Katherine, you have a genuine gift with words. Stuart was like a tall rugged plant, a wildflower. He was charming. I was charmed."

"You're gifted in the language department yourself," I said. "So Stuart had charisma."

"I didn't know that word thirty years ago, but yes, that's what it was. Stuart gave a girl the impression that she was someone special. He was a botanist, but he had a second major in musicology. We talked about music. I was studying at the Institute of Musical Art in those days and didn't get invited to many parties, but I knew his cousin, Jess, from high school. She wanted me to meet him."

"Was Rosalie charmed by Stuart too?"

"She ended up marrying him. I knew that once Stuart saw Rosalie, I wouldn't have a chance with him. And that's what happened. But I couldn't begrudge Rosalie the happiness she found with Stuart. I truly liked her."

Alarice drew her shawl closer around her. "Rosalie arrived late that night with Gerry Raycraft. Jess introduced her to Stuart, and it must have been love at first sight. When Stuart went home to Georgia a week later, he took Rosalie with him."

"That was incredibly fast."

"I guess Rosalie and Stuart knew what they wanted." She sighed. "Sometimes I wish I were young again with a party to go to and a man like Stuart MacPhearson to meet. And no pretty girls around." Her furtive glance at Dionysus seemed almost forlorn.

"Did you see Stuart or Rosalie after that night?"

"No. Jess and her family moved to the West Coast later in the year, and I never heard from any of them again. Well, it's all in the past now."

That was true, but, as Alarice had talked about her encounter with Stuart, it had seemed immediate to her. For a moment I wondered why she would speak so freely to a relatively new acquaintance, but I supposed that teaching piano at home didn't give her much opportunity for interaction with other adults. She was probably glad to have someone to talk to.

I had my information now: Scottish heritage, a fairly common surname, double majors in botany and musicology. Stuart MacPhearson had just become more traceable, and I couldn't wait to begin my search. Still, I didn't want Alarice to think that I had only visited her because I wanted something. Looking around the room for inspiration, I said, "I've been admiring your statue, Dionysus. Where did you find it?"

"In a garden catalog. Maybe I'll move it outside in the spring."

"It's certainly impressive. You can almost tell what he's thinking."

A smile transformed her plain features. "You noticed that too? I thought I was the only one."

However exquisite the statue was, I wouldn't care to share my living space with a pagan god. What a strange choice of decoration this was for the quiet woman who sat in front of me, mourning her vanished opportunity and seeking warmth from the folds of her shawl. Strange, and yet at the same time, it was fitting.

As if she had heard my thought, Alarice said, "Make the most of your youth, Katherine. The time when you're young goes by too fast. I'm satisfied with my life, but sometimes I wonder what it would be like if I had made different choices."

SEVERAL HOURS LATER I sat by the telephone with a pen, a scratch pad filled with notes, and a map of the United States. Using one of the library's computers and Stuart's twin interests as a springboard, I had traced Professor Stuart MacPhearson from Savannah to Atlanta, down to Fort Worth and Galveston, Texas, and back to Savannah where he was currently living and teaching botany in a small private university.

He had written books about Southern gardens and invasive plants, as well as a biography of Stephen Foster. With the help of a friendly librarian, I learned that he lived in a renovated plantation house with his wife who taught elementary art and owned a gallery.

I now had the telephone number of Stuart's university, but it was too late to call him tonight. I'd do it in the morning. When I knew for certain that Rosalie was living with her Southern husband, as I'd assumed before my imagination took over, I could look for Cora's killer in the here and now, which was a more sensible approach than chasing yesterday's phantoms.

In all, this was a happy outcome for a visit that had ended in a heavy sense of time passing.

I rose and stretched, just as the strident ringing of the telephone at my elbow jarred me back to my own life. Picking up the receiver before it could ring again, I said my usual greeting. "Kale residence. Hello?"

"Katherine, it's Garth. I'm just checking on you. How are the locks?"

"They're working fine and so far keeping the burglars out."

"That's great. We didn't talk about time the other night. I'll pick you up at seven on Saturday morning."

"Oh—Garth. I was just going to call you. We won't have to go after all. I just found out where Stuart is." I told him about my visit to Alarice and the results of my subsequent telephone search. "If I'm lucky, I'll be able to talk to Professor MacPhearson tomorrow."

"That's fast work, Katherine, but how do you know that you have the right man?"

That thought had never crossed my mind. "I'm pretty sure." I circled Stuart's name on the last sheet of the pad and began to draw a series of daisies under it.

"Then that's great news. So—I still have Saturday free. Would you like to do something with me anyway?"

"In the morning?"

"I have the whole day. We could drive up to Port Huron and have lunch on the lake. Or dinner. We'll celebrate your successful detective work."

This had turned into the kind of encounter I'd sworn I wouldn't have with Garth again, but that was a while back. I'd seen more of him in recent days that I would have if we'd been dating. In this time, our relationship had changed so subtly that I'd scarcely been aware of what was happening.

*Be honest with yourself, Katherine. You were completely aware. Every minute.*

"I'd love to go," I said. "Let's hold off on the celebration though. This lead might blow up in my face."

His hearty laugh dispelled the lingering aura of sadness that had followed me home from Alarice's house. "It wouldn't dare," he said.

I could visualize Garth's eyes lighting up. They'd be as

bright as the stones in his ring in anticipation of the pleasure to come. At the prospect of my company, that is. I joined my daisies with long swirling links.

"I'll be ready by seven," I said. "A nice long drive by the lake is exactly what I'd like."

"And we'll be taking advantage of the good weather while it lasts."

He had made a similar comment when he invited me to a picnic shortly after we met, and the temperature was still warm for November—wonderfully, unseasonably warm.

"I'd like to know what Professor MacPhearson has to say myself," Garth said. You've got me curious about Rosalie. What if your suspicions are right on target and there was another murder that no one ever knew about?"

*What if…?*

I underscored my daisies with heavy jagged lines and tried to retrieve the thought that had just sailed by. Cora, Gerry, Anna, Alarice. Something about the four old friends when they were young…

"Katherine? Are you still there?"

Some connection that joined them like a daisy chain, one that bridged the decades…

"I was thinking. I haven't heard from Anna Lynde yet," I said. "She was supposed to ask Gerry Raycraft if he remembered Stuart's last name and then call me. Maybe something happened to her."

"Whoa! Now you're getting carried away. That's not the Maple Creek Poisoner's M.O. He likes a splashy display and publicity. Besides Raycraft was in the hospital. Mrs. Lynde probably just got busy doing something else or maybe went out of town."

Everything that Garth said was true, and he was very convincing. I wanted to believe him, but I didn't. Not entirely.

"I have an intuition that something is wrong," I said.

"They can be unreliable. I know mine are."

"I don't have them often. Cora, Anna, and Gerry Raycraft

were all part of the same crowd back in the seventies. So were Rosalie and Alarice. Well, Alarice was on its fringe. What's going on now may have its roots in some past event that involved all of them."

"That's interesting but vague," Garth said. "What do you think it is?"

"I have no idea, but if I'm right, Anna may be in danger. Alarice could be next."

"But where do you fit into this scheme?" he asked. "Or don't you think your incidents are related?"

"I'm not sure. Maybe I'm just an observer or a meddler. Someone in the way. A catalyst?"

"I wouldn't take that theory to Lt. Gray," he said. "He'd laugh you out of town."

"I'm not going to do that. I'm only telling you, as my friend."

I realized that I had just taken sides and chosen an ally in Garth over the dashing Dalton. Last month I wouldn't have thought it possible.

"Wait until you talk to the professor to come up with more theories, Katherine. We can discuss it tomorrow at lunch. I'll bring sandwiches from the Blue Lion."

"That sounds good," I said. "Thanks for calling, Garth. I'll see you around noon."

I hung up the receiver and closed the scratch pad on the dancing daisies, trying to catch every random thought as it slipped by.

Bizarre revenge plot, elaborate cover up, mindless slaughter, madness, apples...

This wasn't a choose-the-best-answer test question. I had to find something that Cora, Gerry, Anna, and Alarice all had in common, besides once belonging to the same social group. Unlike my search for Stuart, this task wasn't going to be easy, and I really should be getting ready for bed.

I found Vicky sleeping on the back porch. When I spoke her name softly, she got up, stretched, and stood with her nose pointed toward the door. I let her out and watched her blend into the shadows beyond the porch light.

With its tall trees and sinister dark spaces, my deep wooded yard must have looked the same when the blue Victorian was built, and not too different thirty years ago. As I stared into the blackness, listening for the clink of Vicky's tag against her chain, I felt certain that something evil had once happened in this place, for it was here that I had found the crushed cameo buried in the ground. Somebody was planning an encore.

Suddenly aware that all the locks Garth could install would be worthless if I continued to stand in the light of the porch lamp, making an easy target of myself, I called Vicky's name sharply. She materialized out of the darkness, tail wagging, eager to come inside.

I shut and locked the door, hoping to keep the evil things away for one more night.

IT HELPS TO SLEEP on a new theory, except I was still awake two hours after I'd turned out the light and slipped under the covers. I was a little apprehensive about calling Professor MacPhearson in the morning. I realized that I might either find myself at Square One again or right in the middle of an old murder mystery. Neither place was appealing.

But hadn't I been a part of the past events all along, even though I hadn't known it until now?

You don't know it yet, I told myself. The reality may be something like this:

*Rosalie MacPhearson lives with her husband in a renovated plantation house. She teaches elementary art in a Savannah public school and owns the gallery her husband bought for her on their twenty-fifth anniversary.*

In an alternate version of the reality, Rosalie was murdered in Maple Creek by a clever killer who covered up his crime for thirty years until something happened to make him kill again at the Apple Fair.

But what could it have been?

I turned around on the bed, fluffed the pillows, drank a half glass of cold water, and settled down to think. If I had a murder, I'd have to add a murderer, and this person could well be a woman. Since I wasn't a member of Dalton's team, I didn't have to be scientific or even logical as I reviewed my collection of possible suspects.

First was Myrold Barren with his fanatical attachment to his growing Village. He had coveted Cora Valentine's acreage and ultimately wrested them from Meg. "Coveted" and "wrested" were strong verbs, but I thought they described Myrold's desire adequately. Even before the volatile land conflict, Cora had prevented Myrold from graduating with his class, which must have humiliated and enraged him.

How long would a successful builder hold a grudge against his old teacher?

The obvious problem with Myrold's possible involvement in the Rosalie mystery was that he belonged to my generation. He couldn't have any connection to Rosalie or even any knowledge of her. Or could he? My instincts told me not to discard a single idea, since I didn't have all the facts.

I moved on to Alarice. Would she kill the woman who usurped the attention of the charming man she had just met? Would any woman do that? I rejected this idea as ridiculous. Alarice claimed that she had liked Rosalie. Besides, how could a young music student plan and execute a murder in a week, let alone devise a cover up?

If something is important to a woman, however, she'll find the time to do it. In a short week, Rosalie and Stuart had met, made a commitment to each other, and eloped, according to Anna and Alarice who should know, having been there at the time.

That left me with Anna and Gerry Raycraft. Anna was one of the most innocuous people I'd ever met and a friend to both Cora and Rosalie. As for Gerry, he was an ill-tempered man who sometimes remembered to be polite, but since he was the poisoner's second victim, I considered him harmless too.

Finally I came to Garth, the man people loved to warn me about. A member of my generation and also the Militia, Garth had no qualms about breaking the law to serve his own purposes, but he must care about my safety. He'd installed strong locks to protect me from whatever danger lurked outside my door. Certainly he couldn't be the source of that danger.

I'd better stop thinking and go to sleep. Tomorrow promised to be an interesting day, and I wanted to be rested and ready for whatever it brought. Closing my eyes, I felt myself drifting off to sleep, with Garth's image burning in my mind.

# TWENTY-EIGHT

STREAKS OF LIGHT were breaking through the dark sky when I awoke the next morning. Outside my quilt, the air was chilly. Resisting the pull of the soft flannel sheets, I reached for the alarm.

Six o'clock and four hours before I could call Professor MacPhearson at his university office. Then, armed with whatever information he provided, I would know which direction to take.

And the day with its possibilities lay before me: Learning that Anna had merely gone on a day trip to visit one of her daughters, finally knowing Rosalie's whereabouts, enjoying one of my last free days before I started school—and Garth.

I had gone to sleep with his name and face in my thoughts. How strange it was that I felt more comfortable with him than I ever had with Dalton, since Dalton was the man I'd preferred in the beginning.

I would keep Dalton frozen in my memory as I'd first seen him at the Apple Fair, a gorgeous action figure but not a man I would ever truly know. It occurred to me that Alarice had immortalized Stuart MacPhearson in the same way, freezing him in time and building a cherished remembrance based on an encounter at a long ago party.

But I wasn't Rosalie, and Garth wasn't a visiting Southern gentleman. He was a local man whom I wanted to know much better.

That's well and good, I told myself, but don't overlook the dangerous side of getting involved with a member of the Militia.

Standing quietly at the side of my bed, Vicky nudged my

arm with her nose. She was trustier than the alarm clock that I'd forgotten to set. The night had been still and therefore peaceful. I'd had enough sleep and felt prepared to meet the day's challenges, whatever they might be, but I stayed in bed a little longer, remembering the unfamiliar voice I'd heard in my dream.

*Don't try to recall it now. Instead, think about all the sounds you didn't hear.*

No mysterious scratching in the attic, no wind or rain pounding on the old windows, nothing trying to force its way inside. Only a silence as deep and thick as a treacherous November fog. The silence of the grave.

*That's another thought you don't need to have.*

The house at sunrise was quiet too, except for the voice from my dream. I couldn't stop myself from remembering. The words forced themselves into my mind. I could almost hear them now, as a whisper originating somewhere above me:

*Two more steps, Katherine, maybe three, and then you're there, but don't be afraid. I'll be with you.*

Did I dream the eerie words last night or hear them? I couldn't be sure, but for the sake of my sanity, I hoped I'd dreamed them.

Someone or something was going to be with me, and I didn't have to be afraid. But I was. The day's possibilities had suddenly evaporated, leaving behind a vast murky void. I couldn't afford to be hesitant or fearful today. I decided to fill the hours until ten with activity and take Vicky for a long walk in the fresh air to a place where the Voice couldn't follow me.

And if I didn't get a grip, I was going to go completely over the edge and burn out like a star.

In the kitchen, I gave Vicky a large dog biscuit and fixed a breakfast of tea and toast with strawberry preserves for myself. The familiarity of this room where everything was simple and practical always brought me back down to earth. In the gradually increasing morning light, I saw Garth clearly as he was, with all the Militia trappings. I was going to proceed very, very slowly.

I'd said that before. This time, I meant it.

Vicky licked the last biscuit crumbs from the floor and walked up to me, whining. When I got up, leaving the last quarter of toast on the plate, she raced ahead of me to the back porch. As soon as I opened the door, she dashed outside.

I waited for her, watching her tear through the ruined chrysanthemum bed. In the hours after dawn, the yard didn't look the least bit sinister. The haunted place was only a deep lot with bare trees, remnants of dead plants, and the ghosts of bright fall flowers.

*...but don't be afraid. I'll be with you,* the Voice had said.

The message was optimistic and encouraging, a veritable mystic pep talk. Still, I'd give anything to forget it. Not to have heard it at all would be better still.

Eventually Vicky wandered back to the door and stood there waiting for a new diversion, reminding me of the power and comfort of routine for both woman and dog.

"Let's go for a walk, girl," I said.

In only three more hours, I could call Savannah.

AS WE PASSED THE WOODS that adjoined the Raycraft estate, Vicky began to whine and tug on her leash.

"No," I said, trying to imitate Garth's sharp tone. "Vicky— heel!"

Running free was no longer an option for Vicky now that she had an official owner. Besides, the brush was filled with burrs that quickly became embedded in fur. As painful to touch as tiny blades, they were almost impossible to remove without subjecting a dog to a massive grooming session.

Vicky obeyed me reluctantly, her eyes fixed on the beckoning trees. When we reached the edge of the woods where the Raycraft estate began, I stopped. Through the high black spires of the fence that surrounded the property, an enchanting carousal horse painted in pale rainbow colors stood patiently in the sun, absorbing the first warm rays.

Gerry Raycraft must be home from the hospital then and

well enough to work on one of his charity projects. No sooner had I completed the thought then he came out of the house. Noticing me, he waved. Slowly and awkwardly, using his cane, he walked across the grounds, while Vicky barked a raucous welcome.

Since I'd last seen him, his face had grown gaunt. The brown suede jacket he wore seemed too large, and the harsh morning sunlight accentuated his unhealthy pallor. I imagined that a severe case of poisoning would do all that, but at least he was alive.

"Good morning, Katherine," he said. "I see you're walking your shaggy dog again. You're very faithful to that animal."

"Mr. Raycraft, I'm so glad to see you've recovered."

"I wouldn't go that far, but I'm living."

He leaned his cane against a post, and steadied himself on the fence. "You're going to wake the dead with all this racket, Canine."

"Vicky, be quiet!" I pushed down gently on her shoulders, forcing her into a sit, which she promptly turned into a down.

"How are you feeling, Mr. Raycraft?" I asked.

"Like I've been put through a wringer. I have a long way to go."

"I hope they catch the poisoner."

"That won't undo the damage done to me—and to Cora."

"No, but then he won't be free to do it again. I've been admiring your beautiful horse. All the colors give it such a cheerful appearance."

He smiled, in my experience of him, a rare phenomenon. "It did turn out nicely. You can bid on it at the charity auction coming up next week."

"If I had any children, I would," I said.

"You may have a child one day. If you buy my horse, you'll have a Raycraft original all set up in the nursery."

The man was beginning to sound like a milder version of Myrold Barren promoting his Village.

"I don't need to start buying toys yet, but I will go to the auction," I said. "Have you seen Mrs. Lynde lately?"

"Not for a while—no. It's impossible to keep up with Anna Lynde's comings and goings. I didn't realize you two were friends."

"I got to know Anna when I bought her great-aunt's parlor lamp. She's a lovely person."

"You'll get no argument from me there. Well, you're a young woman, Katherine, and Mrs. Lynde is young at heart. You two should get along well together."

Could Anna have forgotten her promise to question Gerry Raycraft about Stuart? Or was it possible that she had deliberately misled me?

No I decided. Not Anna, the innocuous. But then where was she?

Gerry Raycraft pulled a snowy handkerchief out of his jacket pocket and mopped his brow. "I think I overextended myself this morning, but I wanted to go back to work. I was afraid my days of toy making were over. Happily, they aren't. Enjoy your stroll, Katherine."

So saying, he took his cane and limped back to the mansion.

Tugging gently on Vicky's leash, I coaxed her up, and we walked on. I couldn't help but admire Gerry Raycraft's spirit, even though he wasn't my favorite person in town. He didn't offer fellowship to the world, but he created beauty and magic. If he'd only carved and painted this one carousal horse, I considered it a significant contribution.

I pushed my sleeve up and looked at my watch. Now I had less than two hours until I could call Savannah. That gave me ample time for an extra long walk. On the way, I could rehearse what I was going to say to Professor MacPhearson.

THE PROFESSOR'S VOICE was like smooth golden honey warmed in a Georgia sun. It made me feel as if I were talking to an old friend. I liked him instantly, which made it easier for me to explain why I had called. He listened as I described the articles I'd found after moving into the house where his wife had once lived. I didn't mention the crushed cameo.

"The bracelet looks valuable, and I thought she'd like to have her old diary back."

After a brief pause, he said, "There must be some mistake, ma'am. My wife never lived up north."

"Not even a long time ago?"

"Never. You have her confused with another woman. Where in Michigan is this house located?"

"In Maple Creek. That's in Lapeer County."

"Now that's a coincidence. My aunt used to live in Maple Creek. I visited her once, but I wasn't married at the time. I'm still confused. Why do you think this bracelet belonged to Doreen?"

Since my suspicion had proved to be true, I saw no point in going into greater detail.

"I guess I received some false information," I said. "I'm sorry to have disturbed you, but I have another question. Did you ever know a young woman named Rosalie Grier?"

"Let me think. Rosalie.. Yes, when my aunt lived in Michigan. That was around 1970 or 71. Rosalie was my cousin's Jessica's friend. How is she?"

"I'm not sure," I said. "Did you know her well?"

"Hardly at all. We met at a party and went out to lunch one day—oh, wait, that was another girl. You're going back a long time, ma'am. My memory's a trifle faulty."

"I think the bracelet may belong to Rosalie then," I said. "Someone told me—I mean, I had the impression that your wife's name was Rosalie. Thank you for your time, Professor MacPhearson."

"I wish I could have helped you. If you run into Rosalie, give her my regards."

"I'll be sure to do that."

I hung up the receiver and watched one version of my reality come tumbling down. Now I had to follow the alternate reality to its conclusion, and that was a dark and dangerous way.

"Rosalie," I whispered. "What happened to you?"

AT NOON GARTH SET the contents of the Blue Lion take-out bag on the kitchen table and stepped back to survey the spread.

"I brought roast beef with cheese, ham on rye, and chicken salad. There's two of each. Do you have any horseradish, Katherine?"

"I think so." I opened the refrigerator, found the mustard, and looked for the horseradish among the array of jars and bottles on the third shelf. "Yes, here it is, behind the gherkins." I added the pickles, completing my modest contribution to the lunch—condiments and relish.

"This is a lot of food, enough for a whole dinner," I said.

"I wasn't sure what kind of sandwich you'd like. We'll give some to Vicky and save the rest for Tac."

I should have been hungry since I hadn't eaten anything since breakfast, but my churning thoughts had driven all thoughts of food out of my mind.

*Two more steps, maybe three, and then you're there...*

"We have beer and ginger ale," he said. "I'll get the glasses and ice cubes."

I felt certain that Professor MacPhearson's revelation was the first step. Reaching for a bottle of Vernors, I said, "We're all set then. Sit down, Garth, and I'll tell you what I know."

As we ate, I related what I'd learned from Professor MacPhearson.

"Somebody is lying," I said. "It has to be either Anna or Alarice. Or they're mistaken, but that doesn't seem possible."

"You know how facts get garbled when people gossip," he said.

"Anna told me about Rosalie's elopement herself. She saw the note, but it was typewritten. Anyone could have written it and forged Rosalie's signature."

"Let's eat. Then we can try to sort this out." He handed me one of the sandwiches. "Chicken salad with dried Michigan cherries?"

"That sounds different."

I stepped back from the mystery long enough to take a bite of the sandwich. "This is delicious," I said. "Now we know that Rosalie didn't elope with Stuart MacPhearson. I don't think she ever left Maple Creek. She was murdered here."

Garth, well into his ham sandwich, nodded. "You're a very imaginative lady, but in this case, I'd say that sounds right."

"So the killer is lying to cover up his guilt."

"Or to protect someone," Garth said.

"Yes, that would be a reason to lie. How far would a person go to protect someone he loved?"

"If it was me, I would go all the way. I'd do whatever it took."

I looked at him, thrown into confusion by his vehemence. My question had been purely rhetorical. I didn't expect his quick reply, or the blaze of passion in his eyes.

The air in the kitchen seemed to grow perceptibly cooler as the minutes on the clock stove ticked by. The ice cubes in my glass and the draft seeping in through the old window chilled me and cast a cool pall over the closeness that had sprung up between us.

"Would you define 'whatever it took' for me, please?" I asked.

"Just what it says."

"Even murder?"

"Theoretically."

"Well…" I could have predicted his answer. I wished I hadn't asked the question.

"I never killed anyone, Katherine," Garth said. "But I told you once that I'd do anything to protect what belongs to me."

"Does that include people?"

"Especially people. Who do you think could have killed Rosalie?" he asked.

Happy to leave the realm of theory for a while, I said, "Alarice maybe, because she was jealous of her."

"That sounds like a motive out of a story book, Katherine, and Alarice is a respected member of the community. She teaches piano lessons to little kids."

"That doesn't make her exempt from suspicion. How about Cora or Anna?"

"If you suspect Cora of killing Rosalie, then who killed Cora?"

"That's a good question."

"You're friends with Mrs. Lynde. Tell her what you suspect. Watch her reaction."

"I'll do that as soon as I talk to her. This affair is getting so complicated I'm thinking about turning it over to the authorities."

Garth scoffed. "Why should the police take on an old murder case? They can't even get to the bottom of the one they have."

"If someone in Maple Creek was killed, even if it happened years ago, the police would want to know about it. Dalton told me that he likes the challenge of unsolved murders."

"Did he? That sounds like a kind of personal thing to say."

I glanced at him, trying to gauge his mood, but he was unwrapping his second sandwich, spreading extra horseradish liberally on the rye bread.

"I ran into him one night at the Country Kitchen," I said. "We had dinner together. That's when he told me."

"You two are getting pretty chummy."

"I wouldn't say that."

"Good. While I'm here, do you want to go up and have another look in the attic in case the vanished lady left more of her stuff behind?"

He had a white dress shirt on today and a handsome navy and green tie. "You're not dressed for the attic," I said.

"It doesn't matter. I won't go crawling around between the boards. I'll just have a quick look. You can hold the lantern."

"Okay. I guess it wouldn't hurt."

He gave Vicky a piece of his sandwich and gathered up the cartons and paper. Now that the dangerous part of our conversation was over, his mood was miraculously restored.

"This is the best lunch I've had in days," he said. "Pretty soon you'll be in school. I'll miss having you home when I walk by."

"Well, this extra vacation was only temporary. I have a career and a house to pay for. I'll have weekends off, though."

I looked up just in time to see the mischievous smile on his face.

"So we're friends again, are we?"

"Definitely."

"More than friends?"

"Possibly. It's too soon to tell."

I bridled at the look of triumph on his face, remembering with chagrin my many resolutions to proceed with caution.

His smile was broader now and devilish.

"I told you I could make you change your mind," he said. "Before we go up to the attic, I'd like to do something else."

He pulled me into his arms for a long kiss that turned into many, sending waves of desire thundering through my body. As he pushed my hair back with his hand, the lion's head ring scraped my temple, and his beard scratched across my face. I was dimly aware of only the most fleeting discomfort. The kitchen felt as warm as if I had left the oven on, and the air drifting through the windows was red hot.

"Let's go up to the bedroom instead," he said.

This was the most tempting offer I'd had in a long time, but I said, "Let's not." The cool, clipped words had a greater cooling effect than the draft that had returned.

I was using my head rather than my heart. Garth MacKay was ready to share everything with me, except that secret part of him that he hid so well. That was something he would never give away.

"I'm not going to let you go," he said.

His strong hands were surprisingly gentle as he caressed my neck, but his eyes and his voice burned.

"You'll have to," I said. "You can't leave Jeff Sky all alone to handle the workload."

"He won't care. I'm the senior partner. You said we were still friends, Katherine."

"We are. *Friends*, Garth."

"No more?"

"Maybe in the future. Not now."

He kissed me again, moving his mouth slowly down my neck. "I don't believe you."

"The distant future," I whispered. "There's so much more that I need to know about you."

"You know everything there is to know about me. You have for a long time."

A long time? I'd only known Garth for one month, and in that time, I had been filled with doubts about him. In truth, he'd told me very little about his life.

Trapping me against the wall, he said, "All right. Ask me what you want to know."

That was what he said, but the look in his eyes contradicted his words.

"What aren't you telling me?" I asked. "What are you hiding?"

He pulled back. "You're not accusing me of murdering Cora Valentine, are you, Katherine?"

"No, but there's something…"

He looked away, toward the window, and then turned to face me. "Yes, there is, but I can't tell you, honey. It isn't my secret to tell, and it doesn't have anything to do with what's been happening to you. I'll do anything to protect you."

"Anything except confide in me?"

"I can't. Some day maybe I will. Not today."

He kissed me again, but the fire that had leaped so high moments earlier had turned to smoldering ashes.

"Are we still on for Saturday?" he asked.

At the hesitancy in his voice, I almost wished that I could go back and relive the last few minutes. I'd say something else, or the same thing in a different way. Probably it wouldn't make any difference, because I knew that I would never give myself completely to a man who insisted on keeping a secret, especially since I suspected that it involved something illegal or possibly Taryn.

"If you still want us to be, yes, of course," I said.

"I'll pick you up at seven then."

"Thanks for bringing lunch," I said.

And how inane that sounded after all we'd talked about. But Garth didn't appear to notice. Now that we'd set things right between us, more or less, his natural good nature regained control. He was my good friend again, helpful, reliable, capable.

"Get the lantern flashlight, Katherine,'" he said. "If there's anything more up in the attic, we'll find it," he said.

As I followed Garth up the stairs to the second floor, I felt that we were a team, both of us working to solve the mystery that had clouded my days in the blue Victorian. One day we might be much more. Perhaps during a long, relaxing drive by the lake I could persuade him to tell me the secret he was harboring. If that happened, then the greatest barrier between us would be down.

# TWENTY-NINE

IN MY DREAM, it was October again, and I wandered through the Apple Fair, experiencing its wonders for the first time and thinking about the handsome officer I'd just seen directing traffic on Main Street.

A sweet scent moved toward me, creating tantalizing images of caramel apples as it traveled through the warm air. The rich fragrance surrounded me. Apples grown in Michigan orchards, covered with caramel sauce made in the local cider mills, they were irresistible and at the moment what I wanted most in the world.

I found my way to a booth where a pretty fair-haired girl presided over the trays. The woman ahead of me in line said, "Maple Creek Cider Mill turns out the best caramel apples in the state. They define the season for me."

I recognized Anna Lynde, which was strange because we hadn't met yet. At the collar of her white ruffled blouse, she wore a crushed cameo.

"That's such a beautiful pin you're wearing," I said. "What happened to it?"

She touched the carved face lightly, almost self-consciously. "It met with a little accident, but I couldn't bring myself to throw it in the trash."

"No, of course not. I couldn't either."

The mistress of the stall smiled brightly at Anna. "Hi, Mrs. Lynde. Plain or nutty today?"

"Nutty, please."

"Good choice. I made these myself this morning."

Anna chose an apple from a full tray and handed the girl

the correct change. When she turned around, I saw to my horror that the cameo was dripping blood down on her blouse. Apparently, not noticing that anything was wrong, she walked off, holding the apple in her hand.

"For you, Miss? Plain or nutty?"

Suddenly the caramel apples lost their appeal for me. Buying one of these gooey confections was a bad idea, one of the worst I'd ever had. My throat was beginning to hurt again. The sharp nuts would only irritate it more. I needed something warm and soothing. Maybe I should just buy a gallon of cider and take it home. I could heat it on the stove and add spices…

Behind me I heard a loud, impatient sigh. I was holding up the line. I had to make a decision, to say something.

"I'm sorry. I changed my mind."

The fair-haired girl's smile disappeared. "But you can't. You have to buy an apple."

"I don't want one."

I looked for Anna in the crowd. I had to stop her from eating the apple, but I didn't know why.

She was just entering the park. Pushing my way through the balloons tied to low hanging tree branches, I tried to catch up to her, but the closer I came, the faster she walked. My feet felt heavy, as if I were wearing shoes made of concrete.

With a sound like gunfire, a blue balloon burst behind me, blasting me into another part of town. Ahead I saw a charming lavender Victorian with deep purple trim. In the front yard a man sat on a rustic bench feeding tidbits to a large dog that looked like a wolf. The man's blue-green eyes glowed, and the black stones and diamonds in his unusual ring sparkled in the sunlight.

As I approached, he said, "Katherine, I have something for you. It's a caramel apple laced with strychnine."

I held out my hand to take it…

and came out of the dream. For a moment I thought I could still smell the scent of caramel, thick in the close air of my bedroom, but the eerie sensation passed. Pure morning light washed away the residual terror, but one element of my dream was real. My sore throat was back. I swallowed, hoping that I was mistaken, but it was definitely there, still at the scratchy stage.

I was ravenous. Usually I didn't wake up hungry, but when I did, I tended to crave muffins or coffeecake, something sweet. Now I began to imagine steaming black coffee and scrambled eggs with crisp dry toast and a jelly doughnut—comfort food. This morning for a change I decided to have breakfast in town.

It was easier to think about food than the nightmare.

I knew that dreams were reflections of impressions, fears, and desires, nothing but fragments of the previous days transformed in terrifying or wonderful ways. Perhaps they were more. If I could call the dream back and dissect it, I might be able to discover its meaning.

First I isolated the facts, as I believed them. Garth would never harm me. Taryn didn't do anything wrong. Anna was the most innocuous player on the canvas. And of course, Cora Valentine had been the one to die after eating the poisoned apple, not Anna Lynde.

But in the dream, how did Anna come to have the crushed cameo? More to the point, why would she wear a damaged pin? Add one more impossibility. How could she wear the brooch when the clasp was broken?

*This was only a dream; by nature, it's illogical. Remember Alice in Wonderland?*

Swinging my legs over the edge of the bed, I searched for my slippers. I didn't have to look far. Vicky had taken possession of them. She lay under the window, awake but drowsy, guarding them with her paw.

As I walked across the floor in my bare feet and reclaimed them, she yawned loudly, got up, and stretched. I sat on the edge of the bed and thought about Garth.

Could my dream be trying to warn me about him? Not for a minute did I think he was the infamous Maple Creek Poisoner, working with his sister-apprentice, Taryn, but he could hurt me in other ways, if I gave him the power to do so.

He probably would, for I longed to feel his arms around me again, to surrender to him completely, and to accompany him on an unknown road to some future place.

That would be quite a trip, but how melodramatic was that sentiment. I'd just cast Garth in the role of the demon lover. Garth was far from evil, but he had a devilish smile. Since I'd moved to Maple Creek, I'd taken one risk after another. Why not add one more that might end in pleasure?

That was an irresponsible thought, one more suitable to the romantic young girl Rosalie had been than to Katherine Kale who had her life somewhat in control.

It didn't matter. I was only thinking, filling in the first fragile hour of the morning with fantasy before beginning the day.

AS I WAS GETTING READY to walk to town for breakfast, the phone rang. Hoping that Garth was calling to check on me, I picked up the receiver and recited my customary greeting.

"Good morning, Katherine," Anna said. "I got in late last night and found all these messages from you. Is anything wrong?"

So she was alive and apparently well. Garth had been right about my imagination. I had to rein it in. Breathing a sigh of relief, I told her how I had traced Stuart MacPhearson and what I'd learned.

Her reaction was surprisingly vehement.

"But that's impossible. Rosalie eloped with Stuart. Your professor must be lying. If Rosalie is dead, maybe the professor killed her and is covering it up. You probably had the wrong man. Stuart is a common name."

"I don't think so. This Stuart MacPhearson visited his aunt and cousin, Jessica, in Maple Creek. The time is right, and everything else matches."

"It still doesn't add up, but I have another concern. Could you come over this morning? I'd like you to see something in my garage."

"More antiques?" I asked.

"Evidence, maybe."

"That sounds mysterious. I'll be over in about an hour. I'm just on my way out for breakfast."

Instead of walking, I drove to town, lingered over a ham omelet, and then doubled back to Anna's house, all the while wondering if Professor MacPhearson could possibly be lying. On the way I constructed a third version of reality.

Stuart convinced Rosalie to elope with him, but for some unknown reason, he murdered her on their honeymoon. Afterwards he returned to Savannah, keeping his hasty marriage a secret. When he asked Doreen to marry him, he didn't tell her that she would be his second wife. In the meantime, because of the farewell letters, Rosalie's friends assumed that she was happily married to Stuart.

Could that friendly man with the honey-sweet Southern accent be a killer? I didn't think so.

I could fashion a dozen such stories, each one more outlandish than the other, and all of them having great potential as suspense fiction, but I wanted to concentrate on real life developments. I still didn't know if Anna's absence was ordinary or had something to do with the strange goings on in Maple Creek. And what kind of evidence had she found? I had a feeling that I was very close to the answers.

IN ANNA'S COOL, shadowy garage, the antiques seemed to melt into a dark and hulking mass. On my previous visits I hadn't noticed how spooky the place was. Now I could almost imagine the ghost of Cora Valentine moving through the narrow rows, touching the surfaces of her beloved tables and telling their histories in a shivery spirit voice.

The furniture was arranged as it had been in front of the Bell House, on either side of a wide center aisle, with barely enough space to squeeze between the rows. I didn't see the china or other small items. They were probably packed in the boxes stacked at the back.

My lingerie chest had been sandwiched between an old Singer sewing machine, circa 1900, and a roll top desk to the right of the window. Two handsome mahogany chairs occupied the space now, and the turn of the century prints previously set out on the matching buffet were nowhere in sight.

"Did you move the chairs there after I bought the chest?" I asked.

"No; I'm glad you noticed that," Anna said. "This isn't the way we left the garage."

"Where are the prints?"

"On the piano bench with the sheet music. I found them there this morning. Wednesday was the first time I've been in the garage since you bought the table and chest."

My mind flashed back to a memory of blue and white towels left out of order in my linen closet and the edge of a rug kicked aside at my door.

"My daughter, Sara, drove up from Rochester," Anna said. "She wanted an antique mirror and magazine stand for her new apartment. I noticed the chairs as soon as I opened the door. There are other pieces in the wrong place, too, little changes that only I would notice."

"Whoever was in here didn't leave the garage in a shambles, but he wasn't very careful. Were you with your daughter the last few days?"

"I helped her move. I apologize, Katherine. I meant to leave you a message, but I forgot."

"I was afraid something had happened to you," I said.

"I really am sorry. It didn't occur to me that you'd be worried."

"Is anything missing?" I asked.

"I can't tell. There's so much stuff in this garage. Cora was supposed to have an inventory list, but Meg couldn't find it. I think your mysterious burglar is targeting me now."

"You may be right. I wish I knew what he was looking for and if he found it."

"If we knew that, we'd be on our way to identifying him. Or rather the police would. I want to keep as far away from this as possible."

"I don't know if we can."

I reached down and picked up the prints, arranging them in the shape of a fan on the mahogany buffet, the way they'd been. "He's looking for something he didn't find in my house."

Anna moved to the window, weaving her way through a set of brown wicker furniture. "This lock never worked properly, but no one ever showed any interest in what I kept in the garage before."

As she turned around, for a moment I thought I saw a crushed cameo at the collar of her white silk shirt, but it was only a trick of the light or my imagination again.

She brushed her hand across her throat. "I'm not making any accusations, but my neighbor told me that Myrold Barren was prowling around my yard," she said. "She saw him looking in the windows."

"Could she be mistaken? Myrold seems too direct to skulk. Maybe he just wanted to give you another sales talk."

"I'm going to ask him about it, or maybe it would be safer to tell Lieutenant Gray when he gets here."

"I'm glad that you notified the police."

"I called them the first thing this morning, but I wanted you to see the garage, to corroborate my story. With everything that's been happening around here lately, I wondered if I was losing my mind."

"It's still going on. Did you hear about Gerry Raycraft?"

"Yes, I did. Poor Gerry. I talked to him last night. My God, another poisoning victim—another one of my old friends."

"At first he thought the pastry he ate was contaminated at the bakery," I said.

"Not any more, but he's as mystified as we are. All this tension is making me ill. When I was away from Maple Creek, I found myself relaxing again. I'm seriously thinking about listing this place and moving to Rochester."

"What will you do with all these antiques?" I asked.

"Store them until spring. Then Meg will take them for the

next yard sale. It's time someone used this garage to park cars again."

"You might be happier living near your daughter. I only wish the police were more help."

I rested my hand on the buffet. A few scratches marred the red mahogany stain, but the three wide drawers would make a good storage place for china and silver in a house without a dining room.

"Shall we go inside and have some coffee?" Anna asked. "I haven't had breakfast yet, and I need to settle my nerves."

"I'd like that, and I have a few more things to tell you."

Running my hand over the shiny top of the buffet, I tried to grasp a stray idea that had just surfaced, something connected to this burglary. In a heartbeat, I had it.

Over the years I doubted if Anna had given much thought to the antiques stored in her garage, but prior to the Apple Fair, Cora would have dusted each piece and checked to see that the drawers were empty. Suppose she had found something as I had, maybe the same bracelet I would find a month later.

On the day of the Apple Fair, Cora had been desperate to talk to Anna. Did she plan to tell her what she'd found? Possibly, but since she and Anna kept missing each other, she might have told someone else whom she trusted. If that person had killed Rosalie and thought the bracelet would incriminate him or her, Cora might have signed her own death warrant.

I could never know for sure exactly what had happened, but my scenario made more sense to me than the possibility of a random case of poisoning by an elusive town lunatic.

Whatever happened had begun at the Apple Fair and included my discovery of the crushed cameo. I was on the right track now. I knew it.

Anna shut the garage door and locked it. "This is a pointless precaution. That old window is easy to open from the outside. That's how the burglar must have come in."

As we walked back to the house, I said, "In all the excitement of looking for Stuart, I almost forgot to tell you about Rosalie's bracelet." When I described the matching cameos, Anna's face turned pale.

"The lingerie chest was part of the bedroom suite I lent Rosalie. Why wouldn't she take that beautiful bracelet with her?"

"Or her diary and lipstick."

"I'm beginning to understand why you think something happened to Rosalie," she said slowly.

Rosalie's bracelet was now in my possession stashed in a drawer of my own. If my reconstruction of the past events was accurate, I might be in even more danger than I'd thought.

I needed one last piece of verification. "Do you know if Cora ever used lavender tissue paper?"

"Yes, she must have bought fifty packages for the yard sale."

"That's what I thought. Now I'll tell you the rest of my theory," I said.

# THIRTY

I CONCLUDED MY hypothetical version of Cora Valentine's murder and sat back in Anna's elegant mahogany chair to wait for her response.

"It might have happened that way," she said. "I could never figure out why Cora was so eager to see me that day, but if she'd found Rosalie's old bracelet, she'd want to tell me about it."

As Anna lifted the heavy silver coffeepot, her hand shook. A few drops of the coffee missed the cup, splattering on the dining room table. "This brings the murder right into my home. And poor Rosalie…" She took a deep breath and added, "I'm sorry. I don't have anything to go with the coffee."

A lack of cookies or cake was the least of our worries. "It's all right," I said. "I just had breakfast."

The coffee was too strong for my taste, but the hot beverage soothed my throat, and I welcomed the fortification it provided. "Why did you think Professor MacPhearson was lying?" I asked.

"Because it's so hard to believe. As I recall, at the time Cora was a little suspicious about the way Rosalie left, but she didn't pursue it. It never occurred to us that Rosalie didn't write those letters herself."

"I wish you still had them."

"So do I, but I remember what they said. Anyway, when one of your friends drops out of sight, you don't leap to the conclusion that she was murdered."

"I was almost ready to believe that about you," I said. "I'm going to stop at the police station on the way home. I don't think Lieutenant Gray will laugh at me when I tell him what I suspect."

She frowned. "Why would he do that?"

"It's just something Garth said."

"Oh." She passed me the sugar bowl. "Are you still seeing him?"

"Off and on. We're going out to dinner tomorrow."

"How much of this does Garth know?" she asked.

"Almost all of it. You're the only one I told about the bracelet, though."

"That's good. I know you're fond of Garth MacKay, but I don't trust him."

I knew that and saw no point in discussing Garth with Anna again since we were never going to agree. I gave a noncommittal response. "Sometimes it's hard to know whom to trust."

"The people you've known the longest are the safest, I believe. Well… It's all too much for me." She took a sip of coffee and leaned back in her chair like a rag doll that had lost half its stuffing. "What are you going to do now, Katherine?"

"Give my theory to Lieutenant Gray and then go out with Garth tomorrow and have a good time."

*And hope nothing else happens and that Garth doesn't betray me.*

"That's as good a plan as any. Wouldn't it be wonderful if you helped the police solve Cora's murder?"

"I don't aspire to be an amateur detective. I'm only going to tell them what I think and let them do all the work. I just want to live my life in peace and have a little fun along the way."

"But none of us can relax until the killer is behind bars."

"That's true. If a murderer has gone unpunished for thirty years, it's time he pays for his crime," I said.

That was an understatement. It was long past time for retribution. Maybe I was meant to be instrumental in solving the case. Could Fate have sent me driving through Maple Creek on the very day the beautiful Queen Anne Victorian went on the market?

Maybe, I thought.

*Maybe this time someone will end the long deception. Maybe it's going to happen today.*

MY HOUSE WAS waiting for me, washed in the late afternoon sunshine, a blue jewel set against a backdrop of cloudless blue sky. In spite of the accidents that had plagued me within its walls and on the balcony, this was my home, my safe haven, and I loved it.

Feelings of well-being overwhelmed me as I realized how fortunate I was. I had my life, this glorious November day, and everything a woman could wish for except a roughhewn, bearded man with blue-green eyes who demanded my affection, while he kept his secret from me.

Garth MaKay belonged to the future. I could see him there as clearly as if he were sitting on my front porch, leaning back against the railing, waiting for me.

My visit to the police station had gone well. After listening with great interest to my ideas, Dalton promised to make sure that they were incorporated into the investigation. For the first time in weeks I felt that everything was going to come out all right.

I unlocked the door, and Vicky yelped a greeting as I walked through the vestibule to the kitchen. Her boisterous presence had helped to diminish the house's ghostly aura. The new furniture also did its part, and the attic was definitely empty. Yesterday, after a thorough investigation, Garth had assured me that nothing else could possibly be hidden between the boards.

*Maybe it's going to happen today.*

And maybe not, I thought. The day was almost over. The railing on the balcony was repaired, the gas stove had been hauled away, and I was safe behind locked doors, thanks to Garth.

At that moment of comfort and security, I suddenly remembered the bracelet. Suppose the intruder with an agenda had stolen it while I was away from home?

Even though the doors had new locks, and I had Vicky to watch the house?

It was unlikely, but I had to be sure. Hurrying up the stairs, I opened the bottom drawer of the lingerie chest. The diary, the lipstick, and the bracelet were still there, hidden under my summer nightgowns, waiting for Dalton to collect as evidence in the morning.

So all was well. I stood in the hallway outside my bedroom for a minute, realizing that the attic had lost its power to unnerve me now that the scratching noise was gone. I still didn't know what had caused it.

"Don't worry about it, Katherine," Garth had said in that practical, down to earth tone he used sometimes. "I go back to my original idea. The sounds you heard were a combination of wind and branches."

"We didn't find any branches touching the house," I reminded him.

"No, they fell down and got raked up with the leaves. That's why you don't hear anything up there any more."

I listened now. The entire house was steeped in a deep silence, a good and comfortable absence of any threatening sound. Then from downstairs raucous barking broke the spell into fragments of noise. Vicky was sounding the alarm.

The door to the spare room, once Rosalie's bedroom, was open. I stepped inside and crossed to the window. Instead of the still life view of my neighbors' shaded windows and the deserted sidewalk, I saw Gerry Raycraft sitting on the middle boulder in the front yard of the house next door. Leaning heavily forward on his cane, as still as a garden statue, his gaze was fixed on the ground. Although his face was turned away from me, his posture suggested pure dejection. Or could it be distress?

He must have gone for a walk and become tired or fallen ill. I didn't think this dignified and aloof man would trespass on someone else's property unless he had no other choice. Whatever the situation, I had to help him.

Calling to Vicky to be quiet, I rushed down the stairs again to the kitchen, where she was frantically pawing at the side door. Opening it just enough so that I could squeeze through, but leave her in the house, I walked slowly over to Gerry Raycraft. He turned his head slightly at my approach.

"Mr. Raycraft," I said. "What's wrong?"

"It's nothing, Katherine. Just a little weak spell. It'll pass."

"Maybe you left the hospital too soon."

His wry smile accentuated the lines in his face. "I didn't have any say in the matter. They claim I'm recovered, so I guess I have to be."

The mansion was only minutes away by car, but to someone in Gerry Raycraft's weakened condition, the distance could be insurmountable. It didn't seem as if he could move at all.

"Your neighbors won't mind if I borrow their stone, will they?" he asked.

"They're on vacation. What can I do for you?"

"I'll be fine. I just need to rest for a few minutes. Go back to whatever you were doing."

I laid my hand on his shoulder. "And leave you out here like this? No, I'll…"

Do what? Hastily I reviewed my options. Nell was a nurse, but she would be at the hospital. That left me and 911. "Let me do something," I said. "Isn't there someone I could call?"

"I'm afraid not. Like so many people my age, I'm alone in the world."

"How about your doctor then?"

"No. I've had enough of doctors to last me a lifetime. They never did me a bit of good, except for—there's a pill I can take for my heart condition. It's at home. I shouldn't have come out without it."

I could help him then. "Let's go inside. I'll get you a glass of water or a cup of tea. Then I'll drive you home and you can take that pill."

If his condition worsened, I'd call 911 or St. Andrew's. They'd have an ambulance here in… Half an hour. When

Cora Valentine had collapsed in the park, I remembered someone in the crowd lamenting the distance between Maple Creek and the hospital.

"I don't want to inconvenience you," he said.

"You aren't. The kitchen is just beyond the door. Do you think you can make it that far?"

"If you help me, yes."

He rose and took a few steps forward. Putting my arm around his thin shoulders, I helped to support him. "Okay. It's a dozen more steps and then you can sit down in a real chair while I get you something to drink."

As we neared the house, Vicky set up a new clamor.

"That dog..." he said.

"You aren't afraid of dogs, are you?"

"Not usually. It's just that I'm not very steady on my feet just now."

"Wait outside for a second. I'll put her on the porch.

He slumped against the side of the house, holding onto his cane with a tight grip that whitened his knuckles, while I went inside and shooed Vicky onto the back porch.

"Just for a little while, girl," I said. "It's all right."

I closed the door and went back for Gerry, guiding him into the kitchen to the chair Garth usually claimed. "Now, Mr. Raycraft. Sit right here."

"This room hasn't changed a bit," he said. "Did you know that once I lived next door, but on the other side? I used to be friends with the girls who lived here. We were in and out of one another's houses all the time."

"Anna mentioned it," I said.

"Those were the good old days. Whoever thought the time would come when I'd be so old I'd have to be helped inside this house?"

"I don't think of you as an old man. If you're weak, I suspect it's because of the poisoning episode."

I filled the glass with cold water and added a few ice cubes.

"You're kind to say that, Katherine."

"Here, drink this and then I'll make you a cup of tea and drive you home. If you still feel ill after you take your pill, I'll call the doctor."

"You really are a nice young woman," he said. "I'm sure there's something else you'd rather be doing."

"Not really. Not today." I watched him take slow sips of the water. It seemed to me that some of his color was returning.

"Ah, that's better," he said.

"Now, for that tea. I'll make it weak."

He glanced at the teakettle on the stove and nodded. "If you don't mind, Katherine, very weak, please."

"I will." I turned on the burner, and measured half a teaspoon of Darjeeling into the teapot.

"It'll only take a few minutes."

"We never drank tea or coffee here in the old days. The girls liked soft drinks. For me, it was always beer or wine. I haven't had a glass of wine in years. Doctor's orders."

"I always thought wine was good for you."

"Not for someone in my condition."

I realized that I was thirsty too, but first I wanted to make sure that my guest was taken care of, whatever that entailed. Then I'd come back home and relax. For some reason I was beginning to feel stressed. That wasn't supposed to be the after effect of doing a good deed.

It seemed as if the water was taking forever to boil. I was relieved to hear the teakettle's whistle. "Do you take sugar or cream?" I asked.

"Just a little sugar. A quarter teaspoon."

I poured the tea, added the sugar, and set the cup in front of him. Then I sat down in the opposite chair and swirled the spoon through the sugar bowl absently.

"Thank you." He sipped the beverage slowly, as if it were too strong. "I think that sugar is going to give me the energy boost I needed."

"I'm glad I could help, Mr. Raycraft. It's a good thing I was home."

"I'll be forever grateful for that." He drank the last drop and set the cup carefully back on the saucer. "You have to understand something, Katherine. I truly like you. You're such a lovely woman and so compassionate and generous with your time. You remind me of a girl I loved a long time ago. She was a little like you."

I looked at him, wondering where he was going with these extravagant compliments and noting with growing alarm that his voice had grown perceptibly stronger. Certainly not from a quarter teaspoon of sugar.

"I'm not the kind of man to forget a kindness, but in this case..."

He paused and I waited. "In this case what, Mr. Raycraft?"

"Regrettably, in spite of your sterling qualities, I'm going to have to kill you," he said.

# THIRTY-ONE

GERRY RAYCRAFT DREW a handgun out of his jacket pocket and pointed it at me. His transformation from ailing tea drinker to armed enemy was so quick it took me a minute to realize what was happening.

Then I did, and I knew the full extent of my danger.

Rosalie, Cora, and I had threatened this man in different ways. I had allowed myself to be tricked into inviting him into my house, banishing my watchdog to the back porch, and waiting on him. His weak spell had been a ruse to appeal to my sympathies and gain access to the blue Victorian. In the past, he would have simply unlocked the door with a thirty-year-old key. The new locks had kept him out for a while.

*Until you let him in, Katherine. That was a deadly mistake.*

I couldn't imagine a greater dilemma. I only hoped I'd be able to find a way to save myself before he pulled the trigger.

*Think, stall, and keep him talking. That's what they do in mystery stories.*

"You're going to kill me, Mr. Raycraft? I don't understand."

"There's no need for you to know why," he said. "It's necessary."

How could I have failed to consider him a serious suspect in the murder? Because of his wealth and position in the community and the enchanting toys he set out on the grounds of his mansion? Or because he used a cane and subconsciously I'd dismissed him as frail? Certainly it wasn't because I'd liked him.

Willing myself to appear calm, I shifted in my seat and surveyed the kitchen in search of something I could use as a weapon. I couldn't see a thing except the cane, and that was only inches away from the gun.

"Sit still, Katherine," he said. "There's no way out for you."

I refused to believe that, but where could I turn for help? Vicky was on the porch barking her displeasure at being excluded from our company. No one was at home on either side of me, and Mrs. West was across the street, too far away to be of help. The street was usually deserted at this hour, as most of the families would be inside their houses having dinner.

I came back to Vicky whose barking had alerted Garth to my predicament when I was locked in Rosalie's old room. If she kept barking, someone might be annoyed enough to complain. If I were lucky, they'd call the police.

"You're the one who killed Cora Valentine," I said. "The one who poisoned the apples."

"Guilty as charged. I thought you'd already figured that out."

"But you were poisoned too."

"So I was. It was easy to manage and good insurance in case anybody suspects me."

I had readily believed that Gerry Raycraft was the second victim. The man was clever to have fooled the doctors. He must have taken just enough of a toxic substance to make himself ill and then lied about the contaminated pastry.

"But why a poisoned caramel apple?" I asked. "And how did you manage the logistics?"

"As to how, that's none of your concern. But why? Cora loved caramel apples. One time the girls and I whipped up a batch right here in this kitchen. It was the perfect lure. I thought my plan was brilliant, and it was a quick death. I regret killing Cora, but it was a murder of necessity. She was supposed to be my friend, but she turned on me."

"Didn't you stop to think about the other people who might die too? And suppose someone besides me had bought an apple from your poisoned tray? Suppose in the confusion of Cora's collapse, some kids had helped themselves to free caramel apples?"

"That didn't happen."

"No, but you couldn't know that."

"Please, Katherine. Additional deaths would have been unfortunate, but I simply couldn't come up with another way to implement my plan. It all came down to timing and Cora being at the Cider Mill booth at the right time. If other people bought apples, it would just be their bad luck."

Debating with this amoral man was pointless. Maybe a different approach would be more successful. "I'm no threat to you," I said. "I won't tell anyone what you just said. I don't believe it anyway. It's a delusion, probably some side effect of the poison."

"My dear, you've been nothing but a threat, ever since you started snooping around. You found something that should have stayed hidden."

I pretended not to understand. "Such as?"

"That cameo and God knows what else."

Of course. Gerry Raycraft had been at Nell's party when she told Alarice about my discovery. I realized that I had one small advantage. He didn't know that I'd also found Rosalie's bracelet. But how could that help me?

"You're the one who broke into my house and stole the cameo brooch," I said.

He didn't deny it. "That wasn't your property."

"I don't think it was yours either."

"Over the years, thirty-four people have lived in this house. You're the only one who had to dig up the backyard. That's why you have to die, and that's all I'm going to say." He raised the gun.

"So if you killed Cora, you must have killed Rosalie Grier too," I said.

I could tell by the flash of fear in his eyes that he hadn't expected that, but he was quick to answer. "That was a mistake. I never meant to hurt Rosalie. I loved her."

"But she's still dead."

"It happened. Then there was no way to undo it. I couldn't let a tragic accident ruin my life."

At my elbow, the telephone began its shrilling ring.
*Thank God.*

"Don't answer that phone," Gerry said.

"People know that I'm home, and—I'm expecting a call from my boyfriend, Dalton. That's Lieutenant Dalton Gray of the MCPD."

"A nice try, Katherine, but who do you think you're fooling?" He paused, frowning. "Answer it then." He pointed the gun at me. "Say the wrong thing, and you're dead."

I picked up the receiver. "Katherine Kale's residence. Hello?"

"Hi, Katherine. Are we still on for tomorrow?"

I had never been so happy to hear Garth's voice. How could I let him know that I was in grave danger without alerting Raycraft and hastening my death? I didn't want to drag Garth into the trap with me. At this point, a grand show of force from the police would be sufficient. To see this dapper woman killer encased in a straitjacket, struggling in vain, was the height of my present ambition.

Keeping my eye on the gun, I said, "I'm sorry. There's been a change in plans."

"Did something happen?"

"I'm going to be busy with Dalton. We're driving up to Port Huron for dinner. We're going to make a day of it."

"What are you talking about?" Garth demanded.

"So…" I searched my brain for inspiration. "Maybe we can go to the antique shop another time. I'll call you next week. Goodbye."

I hung up the phone, hoping that I'd fooled Raycraft and given Garth a substantial hint that I was in trouble.

If Vicky kept barking, if Garth had been calling from Sky and MacKay Title, and if I could distract Gerry Raycraft for a while, I might still have a chance to live. Where was the owner of the ghostly voice who had promised to be with me? I needed help now.

"I'm sure Rosalie would forgive you for killing her, since it was all a mistake," I said. "Where did you do it? In the attic?"

He gripped the handle of the gun tighter and cast a dark glance at the back porch. Vicky's barking was beginning to annoy even me. I hoped Raycraft wasn't thinking of shooting her.

"Why do you say that?" he asked.

"Because the attic is haunted. I've heard strange noises up there like…" I needed more inspiration. Quickly. "This is going to sound funny, but it sounds like someone is up there scratching at the lid of a coffin, trying to get out. Like in all those Edgar Allan Poe stories. I'm thinking of moving to a bedroom on the first floor so I can get some rest. Did you kill Rosalie up there?"

"She died in this very kitchen, not far from where you're sitting," he said. "We're through talking, Katherine. I have to get out of this house."

I couldn't believe that no one on Walnut would investigate non-stop barking or that Garth wasn't at my front door. The last minutes of my life were ticking away with the stove clock. Raycraft was ready to shoot me and run. In growing desperation, I pulled ideas from the air, not taking the time to test them for soundness:

*Think of this man as one of his own wooden toys coming unglued. Give him a few more graphic images, anything you can think of, and stand back while he melts down. Watch his eyes and his hand. Especially his hand. Before he pulls the trigger, duck under the table.*

*And then?*

*Think of something new.*

"I've heard Rosalie's voice too," I said. "Don't tell anybody, though. I wouldn't want them to think I was crazy."

"And what did this so-called voice tell you?" His voice stumbled over the words, contradicting the defiant tone.

"She wants her cameo bracelet back, the one everyone thought she left behind."

My inspiration was in full swing now. I noted with satisfaction that Raycraft's eyes had the frantic look of a trapped fox.

"That's one of the many things you forgot when you gathered up all her possessions after you killed her," I said.

Raycraft rose halfway in the chair and glared at me. "You're talking like you know her, like you were there."

"I've seen her. Rosalie is still in the house, waiting for you. She's up in the attic," I added.

"Rosalie is buried," he said. "Dead and buried. That's a fact."

"Her body may be in the ground, but her spirit is trapped here within these walls. She can't rest until you're punished."

With that, I'd exhausted my store of ideas, and I suspected that Raycraft's wouldn't listen to any more of my wild claims. I had nothing more to fight with. He had the gun.

"No one's going to punish me," Raycraft said. "Goodbye, Katherine. You're clever. A little too clever. That's an unbecoming trait for a female."

*Don't be afraid. I'll be with you,* the voice had said. I'd almost believed her. Now would be the perfect time for her to manifest herself, but she was silent. I was alone.

And then… I knew exactly what to say. "I was clever enough to slip a little poison in your tea."

"You didn't," he said. "You're bluffing." But he grabbed frantically for his throat with his left hand, and his grip on the gun slackened.

"I mixed a little poisoned powder into the sugar, hoping I'd have a chance to use it some day in just this way."

"You're lying."

I wasn't surprised at his reaction because my story had more holes than a colander, but I hoped he wouldn't question it too carefully. I needed to add a few details.

"Believe whatever you like," I said. "Wait a few minutes, about five."

He stared at the empty cup, reached for the glass of water, and apparently changed his mind.

"The poison isn't very fast, but it's effective and almost painless. I'm not a killer, but I did it to avenge Rosalie. That's what she wants. That's what brought me to this house."

He didn't answer me, but he looked at his watch. I had gained a five-minute reprieve.

"The police have been on to you from the start," I said. "All we needed was proof. How helpful of you to pretend to collapse so close to my door. It saved me the trouble of having to arrange an accidental meeting. I have your confession on tape," I added. "Go ahead and kill me. It won't do you any good. That was really Dalton on the phone. I gave him our secret signal. He should be here any minute now."

On cue someone began pounding on the door, a person with a large fist and incredible power behind it.

Raycraft fired the gun. I tried to shield my face with my hand, but I couldn't avoid the bullet. It tore into my right arm, above the elbow, scaring the material of my blouse and my flesh. I stared at the blood, not yet comprehending what had happened to me.

He fired again. In the seconds before the light disappeared, I heard the ear-splitting sound of shattering wood. Somewhere beyond the pain, a deep familiar voice called my name, and another one, as soft as a rose-scented summer breeze, whispered something to me.

*It's over, Katherine. You did well.*

# THIRTY-TWO

SOMETIMES ALL you have to do is move into a new house, set out your furniture and personal belongings, and the place is instantly and completely yours. For the privilege of owning the blue Victorian, I had to work hard and travel all the way to the border of the other world. But the journey was over now, and I had done well.

Dalton echoed the words of the Voice when he stopped by the next morning to collect the evidence. "Gerry Raycraft fooled everybody with his prominent citizen act and by making all those toys for charity," he said. "If Mr. MacKay here hadn't arrive when he did, he would have killed again."

"I'm glad Raycraft's aim wasn't better," I said. "And that cane. I wonder if he really needs it or if it's just a useful prop."

"He seems to be getting by without it now. How is your arm?"

I turned in the chair so that I could see my parlor lamp and the new bouquet of roses that Garth had brought me. They were ruby red, like the flowers on the globes, and their heady fragrance was a poignant reminder of the sunny November day outside that I was missing. "It still hurts, but other than that, I'm all right."

"You'll feel better soon. When you're up to it, I'd like you to come down to the police station. Raycraft confessed to both murders, but he still doesn't think he did anything wrong. He's sticking to his story. Rosalie Grier's death was an unfortunate accident, and he had to kill Cora to protect his reputation."

"He won't impress a jury with that defense."

"He claims that he's in no condition to stand trial for Cora's murder, and besides, no one missed Rosalie for all these years. Why should anyone care about her now?"

"That man is contemptible."

"The sad thing is that I think he really believes it. Take care, Katherine. I'll check on you later in the week." Dalton walked briskly to the door, taking the last of Rosalie's possessions with him.

"I'm glad that cop is gone," Garth said. From the sofa, he reached for my hand and squeezed it in his crushing grip. The band of his ring pressed against my palm, a comforting reminder of his strength and presence. "I was afraid I wouldn't reach you in time."

"I wasn't. I knew I could count on you."

"I don't see how you kept Raycraft from shooting you right away."

"By telling him ghost stories. I value honesty, but I found I'm pretty good at lying. I think Gerry Raycraft was almost convinced that Rosalie's spirit was waiting in the attic to wreak vengeance on him."

For a brief time, I'd almost believed it myself.

*You did, Katherine. You do.*

Garth moved the pitcher of roses closer to me. "I know the truth is important to you," he said.

"Secrets are dangerous. You look so serious, Garth. Is something else wrong?"

"I might have prevented this. If Raycraft had killed you, it would have been my fault."

"I'm sure you're exaggerating. Tell me."

"It's about Taryn and why she left town. She told me that Raycraft asked her to hand deliver a note to Cora at the Bell House. When I heard that Cora was planning to meet someone at the Fair, I thought that the killer had used Taryn to lure Cora into a trap."

"Why didn't you go to the police with this?"

"I take care of my own," he said. "Taryn did as Raycraft asked. I didn't know that she considered him a friend. Last summer she did light yard work for him, weeding flowerbeds, that sort of thing. She was afraid he had something to do with the murder."

"What did you do then?" I asked.

"I went over to Raycraft's house to talk to him. He claimed he'd only written a note asking Cora to reserve an armoire for him."

"I don't remember reading about a note."

"It wasn't in the paper. Only Taryn and Raycraft knew about it, and Cora."

"I'll bet it was an invitation to Cora to meet Anna at the Cider Mill booth for lunch, something like that. Only Anna didn't know anything about it.

"That sounds right."

"There's something else, and this is worse. Some time after I talked to Raycraft, Taryn told me that he talked her into leaving him alone at the booth while she went on a short break. She was only gone for a few minutes, but we figure that was when he must have substituted his poisoned apples for the good ones and put the tray in front of the others, so that Taryn would sell them first. With all the people milling around and the commotion, no one noticed him, and if they did, they'd think he belonged there."

"What an odd plan," I said. "It hinges entirely on timing and chance."

"But it worked. No one mentioned seeing Raycraft behind the stand."

So that was Garth's secret. I saw why he was reluctant to tell it even now. If he had gone to the police, Gerry Raycraft might have been caught sooner.

"Then you sent Taryn away."

"I didn't want her implicated in any way, shape or form. I took her out of school and put her on a plane for Tennessee to wait for this to blow over. I didn't know it would take so long."

"Oh, Garth, the police would have protected her."

"It turned out all right. Taryn likes the South, and now she can come home. I called her last night."

"Dalton will want to talk to her, but you were right. She didn't do anything wrong. Gerry Raycraft fooled women who were older and more experienced than your sister."

"I guess we'll take a trip to the police station, but I'm going to be with Taryn every step of the way," he said. "Can you ever forgive me for almost getting you killed, Katherine?"

"You didn't do that, Garth, and there's nothing to forgive; but you could have trusted me."

"It isn't easy for me to trust," he said. "If I'd known you were so chummy with Raycraft, I would have told you to stay away from him."

"We weren't chummy. I just saw him from time to time in the neighborhood. That's all you're keeping back?"

"That's it. Except I'll have to replace your side door again. It can't be fixed."

I laughed, and the tension in the room dissolved. All the goodwill rushed back, making me intensely aware of the sweet red roses, the sun shining on the painted flowers on the lamp, Vicky napping by the fireplace, and all the other good things the world had to offer.

"Yes you will, Garth. For the last time, I hope. You can't constantly be tearing my house apart."

He raised my hand to his lips and kissed it. "I'm never going to change what I believe, Katherine. I can't. It's part of me."

"I'm not asking you to."

"I'm going to stay in the Militia. Sometimes I'll break the law, and I'll never love the cops. And about what I did—I'm only sorry that it could have hurt you." He paused, but he still held my hand. "Can we still be friends?"

I smiled. "We're more than friends. Remember?"

"How could I forget?"

In the last few days, I'd missed his smile and the blue-green sparkle that made his eyes so bright.

"We never went on our drive to Port Huron," he said.

"We'll go next week."

"We can do it all now, Katherine."

I wondered what he meant by that. I started to ask him but then decided not to. It would be more fun to be surprised.

No SOONER HAD Garth left for Sky and MacKay Title than Nell and Anna were knocking on my door. Nell brought a plate of cookies, and Anna carried the morning edition of the *Tribune*.

"Two Murders Solved. Prominent Resident Arrested in Maple Creek," Anna said. "The story is on the front page with an old picture of Rosalie wearing her cameo."

I gazed at the cameo in the photograph for the last time. How lovely and undamaged it was, just like its owner.

She said, "I could have been Gerry's next victim. We planned to have dinner together tonight, and I was going to tell him about Stuart and Rosalie's bracelet."

"Good Lord, Anna, if you'd done that, you'd have been dead for sure," Nell said.

Anna's eyes were red, and a smudge of black mascara stained her cheek like a dark teardrop. She reached into her purse for a handful of tissue.

"I was beginning to think that Gerry and I could have a future together and neither one of us would have to be lonely. I've known him for so long, but it turned out that I didn't know him at all."

Nell said, "All this time Rosalie was buried in that acreage next to the mansion. He made those fancy toys, but he used to chase the kids away from his property. I always wondered about that. Now I know why."

I remembered how Vicky loved to run into the woods. Gerry Raycraft hadn't wanted dogs around either.

"Piecing together the news story and what I remember, I have a good idea what happened," Anna said. "Gerry killed Rosalie the night we went to Stratford. I think he took her personal belongings out of her room and hid everything in the attic until he could dispose of it."

"Even her body. I knew from the beginning there was something frightening about that attic," I said.

"I shudder to think that Cora and I slept through that night, not knowing Rosalie's body was in the house all the time."

"Then he waited until you and Cora were out of the house to move Rosalie's body and her possessions, a few at a time," I said. "He didn't realize he'd lost the diary and lipstick."

Anna said, "Somehow when he was clearing out the furniture, he missed the bracelet. No one knew it was in the chest until I donated it to the yard sale and Cora found it. That's what must have happened. She confronted him, but she wouldn't tell him where it was. I think he denied everything, but he knew he'd have to get rid of Cora. She wanted to discuss her suspicion with me, but she couldn't find me."

"Read the paper when you have a chance," Nell said. "You'll find a lot of answers. Mr. Raycraft claims that he never meant to hurt Rosalie. When she told him that she'd fallen for Stuart MacPhearson and wanted to break their engagement, he tried to convince her to change her mind. The next thing he knew, he was strangling her. He claims he doesn't remember doing it, but that if she died, she deserved it because she broke her vow to marry him. Then instead of dealing with what he did, he covered it up. His uncle helped him."

I continued the reconstruction. "Gerry typed the farewell letters and forged Rosalie's name in green ink. I wonder how he managed to send a letter from Savannah?"

"He or his uncle traveled there," Anna said. "I remember they went out of town frequently on business trips."

"What about the crushed cameo?" I asked. "Did he say how it came to be damaged or how it got in the ground?"

"Rosalie was wearing it that night. When Gerry moved her body out to his car, it must have fallen off. He thinks he crushed it under his tire. I don't know how, but it ended up at the back of the yard buried in the ground."

"Well, that could happen," I said. "Think of all those years of rain and squirrels and other wild creatures. Even little kids playing."

Nell picked up the narrative. "Then he heard that the cameo had turned up after thirty years. With modern DNA testing, he was afraid that his fingerprints would be on it. He knew that Rosalie's blood was there."

I flashed back to my dream in which Anna was wearing a cameo that dripped blood down on her white blouse but decided it was irrelevant and didn't mention it.

"I'm so sorry I talked about the cameo with Alarice at the party," Nell said. "I seem to remember saying that Katherine Kale was determined to learn its history."

"That must have convinced Raycraft that he had to steal it and get rid of me."

Nell said, "The police found the cameo in a small box in his bedroom, along with Rosalie's engagement ring, and here's something you won't find in the paper. Alarice told me that once, several years ago, she mentioned to Cora that Gerry Raycraft might have done something to Rosalie. Cora accused her of being jealous and vindictive. That led to hard feelings that lasted until Cora died."

"That reminds me, Anna. What did Myrold Barren want?" I asked.

"Something very ordinary. He'd like to furnish a model house in his Village with antiques from the Yard Sale as a tribute to Cora. As soon as I called him, he came over and selected several pieces. All very innocent, but I gave him a lecture about prowling around in the shrubbery, looking into other people's windows."

I said, "Well, I guess we tied up all the loose ends."

"I'm so glad you're going to be all right, Katherine," Anna said.

"Yes, all I have is a bullet wound and a slight sore throat. It's infinitely better than being dead."

"I'm going to see to it that Rosalie's remains are laid to rest in my family plot with a proper headstone, and I have one last comment," Anna said. "I think all those toys Gerry made for charity were separate from his act. He genuinely wanted to use his talent to help children."

I nodded. "Yes, maybe as an atonement."

"So that's the whole story as of now." Nell passed her plate of cookies around. "I baked two kinds, pineapple drop and pumpkin. Moving on to a more cheerful subject, did your Militiaman give you those gorgeous red roses, Katherine?"

"Yes he did. You two are going to be the first to know. Garth MacKay and I have decided to be more than friends."

Whatever that meant.

GARTH MADE A second visit to the blue Victorian after Sky and MacKay Title closed for the day. He brought dinner from the Blue Lion and Tac.

"I didn't think you'd want to eat alone tonight," he said. "This is the pre-Thanksgiving special, turkey with all the trimmings."

"That's wonderful, Garth, but would you mind if we ate on trays in the living room?"

"Not at all, and I'll build a fire."

"I keep remembering Gerry Raycraft sitting at my table, but I'll get over it. I'm going to give the kitchen a thorough cleaning as soon as my arm stops hurting."

Together we unpacked the white cartons and brought the trays into the living room, while Vicky and Tac watched us hungrily from the hall. Garth had brought them each a giant-sized biscuit, but they were more interested in the turkey.

After dinner, Garth and I sat close together on the sofa, watching the day turn to dusk through the bay window. His arm rested on my shoulder, and I held his hand and gazed at the lion's head ring with its black stones and diamonds shining in the light of the parlor lamp. This was a quiet, happy time, the kind that inspired intimacy and confidences.

"There's something I kept from you, Garth," I said. "I'd like to tell you now, but I want you to take me seriously."

"I will."

"I know you think those mysterious sounds in the attic were made by branches brushing against the house in the wind."

"That's the best explanation I can come up with."

"There could be another one. They might be a form of communication. I had a little help solving the mystery—from Rosalie, I think."

"How is that possible?"

"I'm not sure. Call it intuition, spirit intervention, a Voice of unknown origin…"

"In other words, your hallway ghosts," he said, and he pulled me closer.

"More like a spirit in the attic. I heard her voice in a dream. She warned me that something was going to happen soon, but that she would be with me."

"You're talking about a dream now, Katherine, aren't you, not a real voice?"

"Both in and out of the dream, it was a thought that wasn't mine." I sighed, wondering if I should have kept this particular secret to myself. How could I expect Garth to understand when I wasn't sure that I did? "I guess that doesn't make any sense."

"Sure it does, honey," he said. "I always suspected you were a little psychic. Now we know. I have an aunt who swears she can tell what's going to happen before it does. Have you heard this voice since they took Raycraft away?"

"No, and the house has a different atmosphere now. It's quiet except for the ordinary household noises like the refrigerator humming and the furnace blower coming on. There's no supernatural aura, only a sense of peace. Rosalie is gone, and the blue Victorian is finally my home."

"And you're my love, Katherine."

His eyes above me glowed blue-green with desire, and his arms tightened around me. His kisses burned like fire on my lips, demanding the response I was ready to give.

"And you're mine," I said.